ALSO BY TOMMY WALLACH

We All Looked Up
Thanks for the Trouble

The Anchor & Sophia
Strange Fire

TOMMY WALLACH
SLOW BURN

The Anchor & Sophia: Book Two

SIMON & SCHUSTER BFYR

New York   London   Toronto   Sydney   New Delhi

SIMON & SCHUSTER BFYR

An imprint of Simon & Schuster Children's Publishing Division
1230 Avenue of the Americas, New York, New York 10020

SIMON & SCHUSTER BFYR is a trademark of Simon & Schuster, Inc.
For information about special discounts for bulk purchases, please contact Simon & Schuster
Special Sales at 1-866-506-1949 or business@simonandschuster.com.
The Simon & Schuster Speakers Bureau can bring authors to your live event.
For more information or to book an event, contact the Simon & Schuster Speakers Bureau at
1-866-248-3049 or visit our website at www.simonspeakers.com.
Also available in a SIMON & SCHUSTER BFYR hardcover edition
Book design by Lucy Ruth Cummins
The text for this book was set in Adobe Jenson Pro.
Manufactured in the United States of America
First SIMON & SCHUSTER BFYR paperback edition November 2019
2 4 6 8 10 9 7 5 3 1
The Library of Congress has cataloged the hardcover edition as follows:
Names: Wallach, Tommy, author.
Title: Slow burn / Tommy Wallach.
Description: First edition. | New York : Simon & Schuster Books for Young Readers, [2018].
| Series: The Anchor & Sophia ; book 2 | Summary: "After their devastating journey from
the Anchor to Sophia, Clive and Clover Hamill, Gemma Poplin, and Paz Dedios . . . will be
compelled to question everything they thought they believed—and the conclusions they reach
could determine the fate of an entire civilization"— Provided by publisher.
Identifiers: LCCN 2018008930| ISBN 9781481468411 (hardback) |
ISBN 9781481468435 (eBook) | ISBN 9781481468428 (pbk)
Subjects: | CYAC: Faith—Fiction. | Clergy—Fiction. | Brothers—Fiction. | Technology—
Fiction. | Science fiction.
Classification: LCC PZ7.W158855 Slo 2018 | DDC [Fic]—dc23
LC record available at https://lccn.loc.gov/2018008930

To Christopher Schelling,
for braving the blackberry bushes

SLOW BURN

Prologue

EPISTEM HAL TURIN PACED BACK AND FORTH IN FRONT of the windows, enacting a manifold dialogue in his mind—an attempt to encompass the nearly endless potentialities inherent to a single conversation, the myriad futures that could be engendered by a single phrase. His cigarette had gone out some minutes before, but just holding it helped him to think more clearly. He stopped moving for a moment and gazed out over the city. It was a dark and drizzly day—the kind that made even the most rational man believe God must be feeling melancholy. Usually the sound of the rain soothed him, but today he found its relentlessness irritating, like a fly buzzing against a windowpane.

No escape.

The knock at the door came sharp and sudden; Turin dropped his half-smoked cigarette in surprise, kicked the stub toward the wall.

"Come in."

Attendant Rami Koury entered the office and closed the door behind him. He wore the standard uniform of his office—brown robes tied at the waist with braided white rope—yet somehow he still managed to look dashing. Standing just over six feet tall, his head freshly shaved and oiled, Koury carried himself with the unaffected arrogance of a mountain lion. Thankfully, his demeanor belied his bearing—warm and good-humored, almost impossible to hate. He'd started at the Library nearly seven years ago now, at the relatively advanced age of twenty-five.

Turin had been smitten with him immediately.

He'd probed the subject as subtly as possible over the course of that first year, and though he eventually decided that his advances would likely be welcomed, by then Koury had insinuated himself into the social and professional fabric of the Library. He was well regarded, and even worse, well liked. Turin was willing to risk his own career—he'd taken a handful of lovers over the years, knowing full well that every one of them had the power to expose his deviance—but he couldn't bring himself to put Koury's future in jeopardy.

He'd mourned the loss at the time (and it *had* felt like a loss, even if it was only the forfeiture of a fantasy), but he was glad for it now. That sort of intimacy would have made what he had to do today so much harder.

"Good afternoon, Epistem."

"Afternoon, Rami. How are the magic potions coming?"

Koury smiled. "Magic potions" was the term used within the Library to refer to medicines. "Well enough. Hulce thinks he may've found something in dandelions that alleviates stomach pain, but it needs more experimenting."

"Very good. Speaking of potions, would you like a drink?"

"It's a little early in the day, isn't it?"

Turin turned away, toward the cabinets built into the west wall,

TOMMY WALLACH

struck by a sudden fear that something in his eyes had already given him away. "Nonsense," he said.

"Well then, I suppose I'll join you in a nip."

Turin had prepared two bottles of wine for the occasion—that is, he'd readied two and prepared one. Both were more than forty years old, part of the collection left behind by Epistem Baraka: it didn't seem right to use anything of lesser quality today.

"Here you are," he said, offering the glass in his left hand.

"Thank you."

They sat down in the plush chairs Turin had arranged in front of the fireplace. "Now what shall we toast? Health? Happiness?"

"I've always liked the Wesah saying, 'May all your dreams be nightmares,'" Koury said.

"Yes. *Kahkiiyow pawatamihk kiishkwayhkwashi.*"

They tapped glasses. As Koury drank, his Adam's apple dipped and rose in his long neck, like a body twisting beneath a bedsheet. Turin had the urge to touch it.

"Delicious," Koury said, smacking his lips. "So tell me, when did you learn to speak Wesah?"

"Here and there, over the years, but I'm far from fluent. It's a beautiful language, the poetry in particular. It's a shame they've never bothered to write any of it down."

"I seem to remember one of ours attempting to transcribe a few verses, once upon a time."

"Attendant Chappuis. He planned to make a full rendering of the Wesah origin story, until he discovered that only a few tribeswomen are authorized to tell it. It would be as if only Honors were allowed to read the Filia."

"How strange."

Turin shrugged. "Every culture determines what knowledge is sacred and what profane. It's part of the fun."

"Gates must be built so there can be jobs for the gatekeepers."

"Exactly!" Turin said, laughing.

"Recite something for me," Koury said. "A beautiful Wesah poem, I mean." The attendant's eyes were sparkling, a combination of the liquor and a completely understandable misconception. Hadn't the Epistem called him in for a private meeting, only to offer him a drink in the middle of the day?

"I only know love poems."

With the same ease and confidence he brought to all his actions, Koury placed his hand atop Turin's. "And what's wrong with that?"

Had they ever touched before? Turin couldn't remember. He only knew that his heart was suddenly racing. He closed his eyes, as if that self-imposed darkness might slow the cruel onrush of time, hurtling heedlessly toward the cataract. The least he could do was give Koury this last moment of communion, of happiness. They both deserved that much.

"You believe in the mission of the Library, don't you, Rami?"

Koury was clearly confused by the abrupt change of subject. "I—of course I do."

"And you would do anything to further that mission?"

"You know I would."

"Good." Turin turned his hand over and interlaced his fingers with Koury's. "I've been watching you, you know, ever since you came to the Library. You're one of the brightest men I've ever met."

"That's kind of you to say."

"I imagine you must find the strictures of this place frustrating."

Koury raised an eyebrow. "Strictures?"

"You know—having to request books one by one, the waiting periods, all the talk of anathema."

"On the contrary, I enjoy constraints. They encourage creative thinking. Besides, if I had free rein, who knows the trouble I'd get into." Koury smiled flirtatiously, but Turin pressed on.

"And that sort of trouble doesn't appeal to you? Not in the slightest?"

"I don't know . . ." Koury trailed off, frowning as if at a joke he didn't quite understand. His left eye had begun to twitch. Did he sense what was happening? Turin had so little time to try to make himself understood, to justify his actions.

"You are about to undertake a grand task, Rami. More than that, you are about to be granted knowledge reserved only for the most blessed few."

"What . . . what are you saying?" Rami swallowed hard, and the first glint of fear appeared in his eyes.

"The Holy Order of the Damned was formed less than a hundred years after the founding of the Descendancy and has operated in secret ever since. There is no greater honor than to be inducted into this order. Nor is there a greater sacrifice the Church can ask of a man."

The panic was rising in Koury now. He clumsily tore his hand out of Turin's and tried to stand, but his balance was already compromised and he fell right back down into his chair. "Something is wrong," he said, his eyes moving wildly in their sockets, as if seeking escape. They alighted on Turin at last—accusing, betrayed. "What have you done to me?"

"Please, Rami, try and calm down. There's no use struggling."

But Koury was a fighter, and with a great effort, he managed once again to rise to his feet. Like a toddler taking his first steps, he plodded uncertainly in the direction of the door. But just as Turin was beginning to worry that he hadn't adjusted the recipe sufficiently to account for the attendant's size, Koury let out a terrible groan and went down on one knee.

"My poor giant," the Epistem murmured, running to Rami's side. The attendant looked up at him, and where Turin had expected to see rage or terror, there was only sadness—a desolation beyond words. That look would haunt the Epistem for the rest of his days, even after he'd consigned others to the same fate. It reminded him of a particularly cutting phrase from that odd, shambolic text the first generation of men had rated so highly: *My God, why hast thou forsaken me?*

Turin leaned forward and planted a soft kiss on Rami's trembling lips. "May the Daughter keep you, my son," he said.

A moment later, the attendant's eyes rolled back in his head, and the Epistem lowered him gently to the floor.

Koury woke in darkness to an excruciating hammering in his skull. His first thought was that he must be dead, only nowhere in the Filia did it say there would be pain in death, unless it was the unfathomable agony of hell itself. This was only a headache, though one of the worst he'd ever known: shinefog writ large. He spent the first few minutes of consciousness just trying to keep the waves of pain from overwhelming him. Slowly he became aware of the sound of breathing.

His throat ached, bile-burned, but he managed to speak. "Who's there?"

A torch flared to life, bright as the sun. Koury cried out and covered his eyes. When they'd at last adjusted, he squinted out through the lattice of his fingers.

"No," he said, as he began to discern the contours of the chamber, the nature of his sacrifice. "No, no, no . . ."

A hand landed on his shoulder and squeezed, sympathetic but firm, silencing his protestations.

Yes, it said.

Part I
STRANGERS

He who despairs of the human condition is a coward,
but he who has hope for it is a fool.
—*Albert Camus*

1. Gemma

THE MORNING AFTER HER ABDUCTION, GEMMA AWOKE to a rumbling in her belly, a hunger whetted by the succulent aroma and homey sizzle of roasting meat. For just a moment, she imagined she was back at her grandfather's house in the Anchor. Any second now, he'd call out—*breakfast!*—and then she and Flora would race downstairs to battle it out for the first helpings of scrambled eggs and bacon.

The fantasy dissipated when Gemma opened her eyes. She lay between two fur blankets in a small, conical tent supported by three smooth wooden poles. Her wrists were bound behind her back with leather straps, but her legs had been left unrestrained.

So it was all real: she'd been captured by the Wesah, who were taking her Daughter only knew where, and the odds were she'd never see her little sister or her grandfather ever again. She allowed herself to cry, but made sure to keep it quiet; she didn't want the Wesah to know she was hurting. More than that, she didn't want them to know she was awake. If they believed her to be asleep, she might have a chance at escaping.

After the tears stopped coming and Gemma awkwardly wiped her cheeks with her shoulders, she crept over to the tent flap and peeked her head through. The campsite was larger than she'd expected—at least thirty small tents and a couple of larger ones. Tribeswomen walked the snowy lanes between these tents, spitting and shouting, laughing their throaty, masculine laughter. Not a dozen yards from Gemma, two men silently tended to the meat roasting over a large fire. They could only be the "missives" she'd heard so much about; watching them made her think about those comedic plays whose plots revolved around cross-dressing princes and mistaken identities. Odd to see a man cooking for a group of women; odder still to consider just why it looked so odd.

But she was wasting time. Any moment now, someone would look in and realize they'd forgotten to truss the new prisoner's legs. Though there was no hope of getting through the campsite unseen, with luck she could lose her pursuers in the snowy woods. (*And then what? Don't worry about that now.*) She said a quick prayer, took a deep breath, and charged out of the tent, making for the sparse cover of the trees. The tribeswomen she passed watched her go with varying levels of amusement or contempt; no one made a grab for her, or bothered to give chase. Still, she ran as fast and as far as she could, sundering the silence of the morning with her ragged panting and muffled footfalls, leaving prints like a trail of bread crumbs in the snow behind her, until her muscles ached with the effort and the piercing cold had become a blessing. Only when her legs were on the verge of giving out did she press her back up against the trunk of a pine and begin rubbing the leather straps around her wrists against the rough bark.

"Come on," she whispered. "Come on."

She'd been at it for about ten minutes when she saw Athène

TOMMY WALLACH

approaching. The chieftain looked younger than Gemma remembered, shorn of the authority conferred on her by the rest of the *naasyoon*, and her expression was serene, almost beatific.

"Here," she said, approaching with her hands outstretched. Steam seeped from between her interlaced fingers, as if her soul were leaking out of her body, and the many copper bangles she wore on her arms slid down to her wrists; Gemma knew from Burns what they signified—a chronicle of death. The ruby ring on Athène's left middle finger glistered like freshly spilled blood in the brittle winter light. "Is food. You need eat."

"You can go to hell," Gemma said, still raking her restraints against the bark. Why did the leather have to be so wretchedly thick?

The chieftain frowned sympathetically. "Where you go, *chee*. No cities here. Only trees. You starve."

Gemma's arms felt like lead weights hanging off her shoulders. She twisted her fingers around to feel at the leather and found a barely palpable thinning in one spot; rubbing her way free would take hours. She slumped back against the tree, defeated. "Just kill me."

Athène smiled, as if at a joke. "I no kill you. You are only now alive. You are only now free."

"Free?" Gemma spun around to show off her bound hands. "You tied me up. You took me from my friends. If I'm so free, let me go back."

Athène shook her head. "You are even less free then. I show you."

Gemma couldn't help but laugh; it was all nonsense. "Like I said, you can go to hell." She tried to spit at the chieftain, but her mouth was so dry, she only managed a fleck.

Athène wiped it away, calm but disappointed. "You will let go this anger, then we talk like *nimish*." With that, she turned around and strode back toward the campsite.

Here was more false freedom: the chieftain was giving Gemma the opportunity to run, but both of them knew it would be certain death to strike out into that desolation alone and fettered. Still, Gemma was tempted. At least she would die on her own terms, unsullied by whatever the Wesah planned to do to her.

A breeze galvanized the leaves of a small, spindly oak that had survived half the winter with its coppery coat intact. Its crepitation seemed a kind of boast, a paean to its unlikely vegetal tenacity— *only survive*, it seemed to say.

Gemma sighed. Freezing to death just to spite her enemies held a certain melodramatic appeal, but she knew it was a selfish and vain fantasy. She wasn't alone in this world. How would Flora get by without her, or her grandfather, or even Clive and Clover, wherever they were now? Gemma had to do whatever she could to stay alive—for *their* sake, if not her own.

She would bide her time, play the compliant captive, so that when she eventually escaped, she could do it with all her limbs available for use, a bit of food in her belly, and a fast horse between her legs.

The only enjoyable part of her days now was how they ended.

When Gemma closed her eyes at night, she could go home again. She could walk the bowered paths of Portland Park with Flora at her side. She could plant herself outside Kahneman's Bakery in Armelle Plaza and inhale the yeasty sweetness of fresh bread. She could lower herself onto one of the plush kneelers of Notre Fille, swaddled in echoey silence, and gaze up at the great golden annulus floating like a hollow sun above the ambo. These dreams brought back all the quotidian details of her old life and, in the process, rendered them miracles.

Other nights, darker visions came. Gemma would find herself sitting cross-legged beneath the willow tree on the banks of the Ivan. Moonlight scythed silver through the gaps in the branches, bejeweling Irene's tearstained cheeks. The curtains parted; the play began. Shadows slipped into the bower, an infinite army of faceless Wesah warriors, while Irene simply faded away, as if she'd never been anything more than a phantom.

Gemma's heart still recoiled from the inescapable truth—that Irene must have played a part in the abduction that night. For the final few weeks of the journey to Sophia, Clive had been obsessed with the idea that Irene was a wolf in sheep's clothing, but Gemma had discounted his suspicions as sour grapes. Even now, there was so much about the betrayal that didn't make sense. Irene couldn't have been working for Athène's *naasyoon* from the beginning, so when did she turn? Had Clover known, or had she fooled him, too? And why would the Wesah go to such lengths to secure one unremarkable girl from the Anchor in the first place?

Unfortunately, the only way to get answers would be to remain with the Wesah, and that was the last thing Gemma wanted to do. After her pathetic first attempt at escape, she'd fashioned herself into a model prisoner—silent and docile, practically bovine. Neither Athène nor any other member of the *naasyoon* ever hurt her (other than to restrain her wrists and ankles at night), and almost in spite of herself, Gemma began to acclimate to her new lifestyle, even to understand a few words of the Wesah language.

Taanishi meant "hello."

Mafwe was a way to express surprise.

Chee acted as a signifier for a question.

The *naasyoon* usually woke before sunrise and rode for a few hours before stopping to eat. A small group of warriors would go off to hunt or forage, and only rarely did they return empty-handed. The preparation of meals fell to the two missives (or *nisklaav*, as they were known among the tribeswomen), Gornoy and Rugaru. Gornoy was short and burly, solid as a stone, while Rugaru was rangy and supple—he reminded Gemma of one of those slender, fragile-looking vines that turned out to be fibrous and impenetrable when you tried to cut it. Each man was rather handsome in his way, and Gemma doubted that was a coincidence. The Wesah didn't raise boys within the tribe, which meant missives had to be imported, either by invitation or abduction; physical beauty was almost certainly taken into account during this selection process.

Both missives were perfectly fluent in English—Gemma regularly overheard them telling bawdy jokes in a thick outerland patois—but they refused to speak it with her. Gornoy had only shrugged when she'd tried to engage him in conversation, while Rugaru had flicked a spoonful of boiling water her way and hissed like a snake. So much for solicitude from her fellow abductees.

In general, the tribeswomen treated Gemma more like a pet than a prisoner. The only exception was a sharp-featured woman called Noémie, who made a point of shouldering Gemma whenever they passed each other, muttering *dahor*—the Wesah word for "outsider"—under her breath. Noémie was Athène's favorite, often spending the night in the chieftain's tent, emerging bleary-eyed

TOMMY WALLACH

and messy-haired the next morning. It was common knowledge that the Wesah permitted and even encouraged such liaisons, but Gemma hadn't expected it to be so blatant. One night, the ruckus they made was so loud it caused quiet laughter among the others, and even kept Gemma from sleeping.

Nicimos, she eventually learned, was the Wesah word for "sweetheart."

On a clear morning a little more than two weeks after Gemma's abduction, the gray outline of the Ramshield Mountains appeared on the horizon, and over the next few days, the sierra grew more and more distinct, until Gemma could make out every snow-cut facet and cloud-wreathed peak. A steep path, scarcely wide enough for two horses to ride abreast, led up the side of one of these mountains. It took hours to reach the summit, and all the while, Gemma had the strange sensation that she was acting as a counterweight to the sun, rising as it fell. At the top, she found herself gazing down on a deep caldera filled with luminous turquoise water and set in a corona of rime. The lake was roughly the shape of an hourglass—two roundish bodies connected by a narrow opening, like a corseted waist. Neighboring lakes sparkled in the distance, each one contained within the stone chalice of a mountain crater.

Distracted by the view, Gemma didn't notice the *naasyoon's* preparations until the first drumbeats began reverberating around the caldera. She turned and saw the tribeswomen seated in a rough circle in the snow. Those with hand drums were already beating out a steady rhythm with small sticks wrapped in leather. After a time, an older tribeswoman donned a headdress of exquisitely beaded black feathers and began to sing. Her voice was strong and assured, if not particularly musical, and each phrase was echoed by the rest of the *naasyoon*. Gemma thought back to her days in the ministry and the call-and-response spirituals they would perform at gatherings. Not so different, really, from whatever this was. If she'd had her violin with her, she could've accompanied them; the song consisted of a single droning chord, so one could solo indefinitely on the same scale.

Gemma realized her eighteenth birthday must have come and gone sometime in the last few days. Strange that such a milestone could pass unremarked and uncelebrated. Did the Wesah care about birthdays? And why should they? Why should anyone, for that matter?

Flora's birthday was exactly three months after Gemma's. She'd be turning eleven this year—and who would be there to celebrate with her? Just their grandfather, unless Clive or Clover managed to make it home in time. Gemma stroked the necklace her sister had given her that last day in the Anchor: sweat-hardened and gritty, fibrous as hempen rope.

"You cry," Athène said, coming to sit beside Gemma.

"I miss my sister," Gemma replied, investing the words with accusation.

"This is from her?" The chieftain reached out to touch the annulus, and Gemma slapped her hand away. She expected some form of reprisal, perhaps even wanted it, but Athène only shook her head. "You still want run, *chee*."

"Of course I do! I'm a prisoner!"

Athène groaned with frustration, mumbling something to herself in Wesah. "You are not prisoner! You woman! You belong to you!" The chieftain pounded her chest, as if to drive the point home. "We make deal now, *chee*. You promise to walk with the *naasyoon* to the Villenaître. Then, you still want leave, I let you leave."

"Where is the Villenaître?"

"Not so close," Athène said, "also not so far." There was a playful glint in her eye, and Gemma hated how she couldn't help but find it slightly charming. She turned away from the chieftain, gazing across the caldera lake, its frosty corona glittering like millions of tiny diamonds. The chanting of the tribeswomen seemed to grow louder, and though Gemma didn't understand the words, she could tell that the song was a celebration of the majesty of this place. The Wesah tongue had never sounded so lovely, so full of meaning and mystery. The snowscape began to brighten, gleaming like a blown ember; Gemma closed her eyes against the dazzling white. In the darkness, time slowed, stumbled, stopped. Her senses began to merge. She saw the notes of the song, floating like rainbow motes against the black canvas of her eyelids. She heard the cascading melodies made by the day's last sunbeams as they burnished the bronze surface of the lake.

By the time she realized what was happening, the fit had already taken hold. She turned her gaze once again to Athène, who'd pushed back her fur hood and tilted her face up toward the sky. For the first time, the chieftain didn't look like an enemy. She looked pure, peaceful, radiant . . .

Gemma's last thought was of one more wonder, as unfathomable as any Wesah ritual, as compelling as any story told in the Filia.

A part of her no longer wanted to run.

2. Clive

SHE'S LOVELY, ISN'T SHE?"

Clive pulled sharply away from the guitar, as if he'd been caught doing something shameful. And maybe he had; his father used to say that playing music was the closest to the devil he ever wanted to get.

"Would you like to try her out?" Vernon asked. He was one of the trio of portly, hirsute brothers who ran Anderson's Music Shop.

"If you wouldn't mind."

"What do you think it's there for?"

Clive took the guitar down from the hook. He hadn't held one in so long, not since . . .

That telltale pressure behind the eyes, a whitewater of memory, a cresting wave of grief—he swallowed them all down. How many times had his father brought him and Clover here, to buy new strings, or have Gemma's bow rehaired, or simply admire the new merchandise? Old Man Anderson, dead these last three years, would have some sort of toy for the children—a shaker he'd made by filling a walnut shell with sand, or an impractically heavy terracotta bell. Once, he presented them with a six-tine linguaphone the size of a matchbox; Clover broke it the very next day when he tried to add an extra note.

The layout of the place hadn't changed in all those years: mandolins, fiddles, and guitars hung from pegs on the right wall, while the left wall was taken up by a couple of upright basses and various musical accessories. Through the doorway behind the counter, Clive could see into the workshop, where the other two Anderson brothers were at work on an upright piano; half-built, it looked like a dried-out animal carcass.

"Here," Vernon said, producing a tuning fork from the pocket of his overalls. "This'll be an A." He struck the fork against the counter.

A sharp shock of recognition—Clover used to have a tuning fork like that. They'd left it in the small wagon outside Amestown, along with the rest of their instruments. Clive remembered how his brother would tap it with his fingernail and hold it up to his ear, as if it were telling him a secret. The recollection twisted, Clover's smiling face contorting into a rictus of pain, as it had in those final moments outside Sophia—the black hole punched through his shoulder, blood staining his jacket and making perfect red circles in the snow. In the space of a day, Clive had abandoned the girl who might have been his wife and shot his own brother in the back. Nearly two months ago now, and yet the wound of wounding remained fresh in Clive's mind. Clover may've been a heretic and traitor, but Clive knew he'd never be able to forgive himself for what he'd done. He felt marked now, like Kayin before him; the guilt weighed heavy on his shoulders, every second of every day, like a mantle of stone.

"You all right?" Vernon said.

Clive mustered up the shadow of a smile. "Sorry. I'm just distracted this morning." He finished tuning, then strummed the open strings. The notes rang out clear and discrete, lingering like snow-flakes caught in an updraft.

"I'll take it," he said.

Vernon looked surprised. "You've hardly played it."

"I've heard what I need to."

"But, Clive"—and Vernon's expression went a little sheepish here, his voice dropping to an apologetic whisper—"I can't give you much of a deal on it. It's the rosewood, you see."

Like everyone else in the capital, Vernon knew what had befallen Daniel and Ellen Hamill, and he seemed to equate Clive's orphan-hood with destitution. But men of the cloth made a healthy living, and Honor Hamill had been thrifty. Clive's inheritance wouldn't make a man of leisure out of him, but he could certainly afford the occasional luxury. Or even the occasional *two* luxuries.

"I don't care about the price," Clive said. "Now, let's talk violins."

Snow had fallen heavy on the city last night, quilting the plazas in feathery white, glazing the roofs and balconies, laying narrow pipes of sweet icing along the balustrades and lintels. At the margins of the more well-traveled roads, it had already turned black with soot and hard as quartz.

Clive passed through Devon Square, where a lay preacher in tatty robes and sandals that exposed his chilblained toes was rant-ing about the dangerous path the Descendancy was walking. He coughed thickly, spat a virescent wad of phlegm. Clearly he was recovering from the weak strain of plague that had swept through the city's poorer quarters while Clive had been away, claiming a few dozen lives before a timely quarantine got it under control. In spite

TOMMY WALLACH

of his passion, no one appeared to be paying the poor man much mind. A month ago, he might've found a more sympathetic audience, but after the surviving members of the Protectorate contingent had returned to the Anchor, public opinion had shifted firmly and finally in the direction of war. Like any principle that has outlived its usefulness, the Descendant credo of nonviolence had been collectively shrugged off like a bulky coat, facilitating a certain moral flexibility, a wider range of motion. Doubts were swept aside, leaving only one word on the people's lips: *When?*

That word electrified the old men who spent their mornings talking politics in the city's squares and cafés. It precipitated fistfights between old friends after a few drinks in the local tavern. It inspired the soldiers of the Protectorate to spend long hours on the Bastion's training fields, readying themselves for glorious battle.

Other than a dicey moment on a couple of ice-glazed cobblestones, Clive made it across the city without incident. The Poplin house was almost completely free of snow—all of it borne to the ground by the steep V of the roof—but icicles hung from the gables in brilliant serried clusters, an inverted palisade of glass.

Clive had moved in almost three weeks ago, immediately after his return to the Anchor. His own home was entirely unlivable now—a bleak and silent memorial to everything and everyone he'd lost. Mitchell Poplin, Flora and Gemma's grandfather, was pushing sixty-five and said he'd be grateful to have another pair of hands around, not to mention someone to look after Flora. He helped to arrange the sale of Clive's old house and its furnishings to a family friend with children on the way. Going through the place one last time before the transfer, Clive had been surprised at how little he cared to keep: his father's papers, his mother's jewelry, some linens. Clover's things were all stuffed into a trunk, which now sat in a cobwebbed corner of the Poplins' basement.

Clive carried his new acquisitions upstairs and laid them out on the bed. It was technically *his* bed now, but he still couldn't help but think of it as Gemma's. He liked living in her space; it made him feel connected to her, as if he were keeping watch somehow. The room was so modest, so warm, so ineradicably *Gemma*. The only furniture other than the bed was the small vanity next to the window. On its surface lay the remnants of a life: a crystal vial of scent with a thin line of amber at the bottom; a tin vase full of wildflowers long since gone dry and crumbly; a silver bracelet, slightly tarnished, that she'd outgrown. A humble annulus of twigs was nailed just above the bed. Clive could remember the week he'd spent making it, and the light in Gemma's eyes when he'd given it to her, and suddenly he missed her with a keenness that took his breath away.

"Clive? Is that you?"

"Yeah."

Bare feet pattered along the hallway like raindrops. Flora peeked her head around the door. "Grampy wants to see you. He's down in the—" The words died on her lips as she noticed the violin. "Did you go to Anderson's?"

"I did," Clive replied.

"Why didn't you take me?"

"You weren't awake."

"You could've woken me up!"

"I tried. I poured a whole bucket of cold water on your head."

"Liar." Flora crossed the room to get a better look at the instrument. "It's sure something."

"I'm glad you think so, because it's yours."

Flora gasped; she knew what a good violin cost. "You mean it?"

"I do."

Reverent as a sinner entering the Dubium, Flora raised the instrument to her neck and plucked out a major scale. "I've lost all my calluses," she said.

"They come back quick."

She looked up at him, tears pooling in her eyes. "You didn't have to do this."

"Of course I did. Your birthday's coming up soon. And besides"—his voice caught like a wagon wheel hitting a divot, but he kept rolling on, hoping Flora hadn't noticed—"I know I let you down. I never should've let your sister come on the march."

"You couldn't have stopped her. Once she set her mind to something—"

"I should go see what your granddad wants," Clive said gruffly, turning away before Flora absorbed his grief. He had to be strong for her; he owed her that much, at least. "You get to know your new relation there."

"All right," she said, and Clive sensed the capitulation in her tone, as if it were her looking out for his emotions instead of the other way around. "Thanks again for the violin."

"It's my pleasure."

Mitchell Poplin would be down in the workshop, as he was every day at this time. A furniture maker by trade, he specialized in the profoundly unspecial: straight-backed chairs and sturdy footstools, square dining tables and unembellished cabinetry. These pieces fetched just enough money to pay for the food and materials required to get him through the next round of production.

Clive liked it in the workshop—the tang of freshly planed pine, the chug and whine of the treadle lathe, the sonorous back-and-forth of the saw blade. This morning Mitchell was finishing up an armoire that he'd already sold to a merchant a few doors down. The room smelled strongly of brass polish.

"That's coming along nicely," Clive said.

"I guess so. But these handles here refuse to look like brothers." The old man cocked his head and glanced toward the ceiling. The plangent strains of "Sister River" seeped down through the plaster; Clive could remember teaching it to Flora half a decade ago. "Do I hear a violin?"

"I bought it for Flora this morning. And a guitar for me."

Mitchell whistled. "Musta cost a pretty shekel."

"And an ugly one. And a few more besides. But I've got the money."

"Or you used to." Mitchell stepped back to survey his handiwork and harrumphed. "I think it's time I gave up on these things ever matching. Guess I'll have to say I planned it this way. Call it artistic license."

"So is this what you wanted to see me about?" Clive said. "Your handles?"

Mitchell blanched. "Daughter's love! I completely forgot. That marshal fella with all the scars came by while you were out."

"What for?"

"I didn't ask. No offense, but the man gives me the willies."

TOMMY WALLACH

Clive hadn't spoken to Burns since they'd returned to the Anchor. In fact, he hadn't spoken to *anyone* in the Protectorate, or so much as set foot inside the Bastion. "Dereliction of duty" was the official term, punishable by court-martial. But Clive didn't care; he'd earned the break. He only wished it could've lasted a little longer.

"Did he say if he was going to come back?"

"Come back?" Mitchell frowned, then his eyes lit up as he identified the misunderstanding. "He doesn't have to. He never left."

Burns stood on the back deck, gazing out over the small walled garden where Mitchell grew herbs and vegetables in the summer.

"I'm sorry, sir," Clive said. "I would've come sooner, but nobody told me you were here."

"Be sorry you showed up at all," Burns said. "I was enjoying the silence."

The marshal looked even more haggard and depleted than he had on the journey back from Sophia, as if only the starch in his uniform was keeping him upright. "And it's just us chickens here. No need to call me sir."

"Guess I got used to it somewhere along the way."

"Well, it makes me feel old. Everything does, these days." Burns grunted—his version of a sigh. "You know why I'm here?"

"I got an idea, but I hope it's wrong."

"It's not."

"So you want me to come right now?"

Burns shrugged. "Grand Marshal Chang's not gonna let you play hooky forever. Besides, she'll be the same girl in the same shit tomorrow. Why put it off?"

Because he didn't want to see her. Because he didn't want to think about the past. Because he wanted to pretend he'd never shot Clover, or abandoned Gemma, or lusted after the girl who'd betrayed him and everyone he loved. But it didn't matter what he wanted, did it?

He let out his own little grunt. "All right," he said. "Take me to the traitor."

3. Clover

H E OPENED HIS EYES TO BRIGHT WHITE LIGHT. SOME-
thing was holding him down, a weight strapped across
his chest. He tried to push it away, but the movement
sent a line of fire coursing across his shoulders and down
his back. His heart began to race, adrenaline pumping through his
veins. He was a prisoner. If he didn't escape, they'd kill him.

"Help!" he cried out.

But no one answered, and no one would. He was alone. Alone
in Sophia.

Clover forced himself to breathe deeply. If they'd wanted to kill
him, he'd already be dead. And now he realized the weight on his
chest was just the top sheet of a tightly made bed. He was in some
kind of infirmary, with six beds laid out three to a wall. Through
the window, he could see only an endless blankness of evening
sky. That meant he was high up, likely on the topmost floor of the
building.

He shifted position, and even that small movement reignited
the fire in his back. What had they done to him?

No. Not them—*him*. Clive had done this.

All at once, the horror of those last few minutes came rushing back: running uphill through the eerie yellow glow of Sophia's

electric lights, away from the gunfire and the screams; arriving at the academy panting and sweat-soaked beneath his winter clothes, awed by that massive gray cube of polished concrete; and Clive suddenly materializing between two snow-limned fir trees, his face and clothes caked with blood, holding the gun to Irene's temple. (Except Irene—the girl who'd kissed Clover in the Maple Garden, who'd said she loved him—was a fantasy. Only Paz the betrayer, destroyer of worlds, was real. And would he ever be able to reconcile the two? Was it possible to go on loving one while hating the other?) Even after their fight in the woods, even knowing that Clive was an armed Protectorate soldier facing the defection of a citizen with intimate knowledge of the inner workings of the Library, Clover would never have imagined his brother could shoot him. He'd thought the bond of blood went too deep for that.

He knew better now.

The memories were too painful, and the angel of oblivion was floating somewhere just out of sight, promising an end to thought. Clover closed his eyes, opened them to a fresh disposition of light, closed them again. At some point, he was spoon-fed a bitter liquid, and the sleep that followed was deep and dreamless, black as a freshly washed slate.

When he woke again, it was morning. At last he was strong enough to repel the tendrils beckoning him back toward unconsciousness and sit up.

A boy of about fourteen sat cross-legged atop the comforter on the bed directly across from Clover's, reading a book. His round head was surmounted by an immaculately pruned corona of kinky hair, and pale freckles dotted his nose and cheeks. Other than a

　　　　　　　　　　　　　　　　TOMMY WALLACH

pair of brass-rimmed spectacles, he was dressed all in gray: loose gray shirt, gray pants with a drawstring at the waist, and ill-fitting gray woolen socks that were bunched up at the ankles. His lips moved soundlessly as his eyes scanned the pages.

"Hello," Clover said. His voice came out scratchy and raw.

The boy started, fumbling the book. "Damn, kid! You scared me half to death." He took a moment to catch his breath, then jumped down from the bed and headed for the door. "I'll go get Sister Lila, tell her you're finally up."

"Who's Sister Lila?" Clover called out, but the boy was already gone. He returned a couple of minutes later, trailing a woman in her late thirties or early forties, dressed just like him. She carried a twine-bound notebook, which she immediately opened and began writing in, even as she spoke.

"Good morning. I'm Sister Lila Dawkins, head medical scholar here at Sophia. I've been looking after you since you arrived." Her manner reminded Clover of Bernstein's: perfectly poised between brisk and brusque. "First off, tell me your name, so I can stop calling you 'little guy.'"

Clover considered lying, but he was still fuzzy with sleep, and worried he'd forget his pseudonym. "Clover Hamill."

Lila repeated his name as she copied it into her notebook. "So, Clover, how's your shoulder feeling?"

Only now did he notice the linen sling supporting his right arm. "I thought I got shot in the back."

The boy, who'd returned to his spot on the bed opposite Clover's, piped up, "All the muscles are connected."

"Not quite all of them," Lila corrected, "but close enough. There was significant trauma to your trapezius, Clover, so it's best if you give the whole area some time to heal. Now, if you don't mind, I'm going to ask you to try a few things for me."

Clover did as he was told: shrugging, stretching, standing, sitting, and describing the accompanying sensations in detail. Lila scribbled furiously in her notebook all the while. The pain was intense but bearable; more upsetting was the odd delay he noticed when he tried to flex the fingers of his right hand, as if the message was getting lost on the way from his brain. When he mentioned it to Lila, she pursed her lips and nodded meaningfully.

"I was afraid of that," she said. "There must have been some damage to the nerve."

"What's a nerve?" Clover asked.

"What's a nerve?" the frizzy-haired boy repeated incredulously. "Don't you Anchorites know the first thing about anatomy?"

"Don't be rude, Lenny," Lila said. "It's not his fault where he was raised." Clover bridled at the condescension but tried to keep any sign of indignation off his face. "You see, Clover, the body has multiple systems—nervous, lymphatic, circulatory, et cetera. The nerves transmit sensation, so when they're damaged, there's always a chance that motor function will be impaired."

"Will it go back to normal?" Clover asked.

"It should improve over time."

"You're lucky she got to it so quick," Lenny said. "Last year, Tripp Belson smashed his hand in a thresher and didn't get up here for hours. Even after the bones healed, he said it felt like all five of his fingers ended right at the second knuckle, like he just had a bunch of nubs."

"Lenny!" Lila exclaimed. "There's no need to tell him about that."

"Sorry," Lenny replied. "I just thought he might be interested."

Lila shook her head. "Anyway, Director Zeno said she wanted to see you as soon as you came around. Think you're up for a walk?"

Do I have a choice? Clover wanted to say.

"Sure."

He slipped out from under the bedcovers only to discover he was wearing the exact same gray uniform as Lila and Lenny.

"Where are my clothes?"

"You mean the blood-soaked rags with the bullet hole in them?" Lenny said. "They're long gone, kid. I'll give you a moment to grieve."

Clover didn't like the idea that someone had undressed him in his sleep, but he had to admit, his new clothes *were* pretty comfortable. A pair of roomy, fur-lined moccasins were waiting for him just next to the bed. He slipped them on and followed Lila and Lenny out of the infirmary and into a long, narrow hallway, at least a hundred feet from end to end. Wide windows evenly spaced along the eastern wall looked out over a precipitous drop and the picturesque valley below.

At the juncture where the hallway turned right, they passed through a small round chamber; Clover imagined it would appear as a turret from outside. It was clearly designed for comfort: a thick white rug covered the floor, and soft-looking cushions were arranged around the edges. Two young women and a slightly older man, all of them dressed in gray, leaned back against these cushions; the women were both reading, while the man sketched some sort of diagram in a notebook.

"Morning, Sister Balewa," Lenny called out.

One of the women, who had blue-black skin and a smooth-shaven head, glanced up from her book. "Morning, Lenny." She noticed Clover. "Who's that?"

"New kid. Probably a spy."

This piqued the interest of the other two scholars, who looked inquisitively at Clover. He considered laughing at Lenny's "joke," or putting on a false attitude of outrage. Eventually, he settled on something in between: an awkward half smile. How was a spy supposed to act, anyway? Or more to the point, how was a spy *not* supposed to act?

Sister Balewa raised an eyebrow. "Well, that sounds very exciting. Have fun."

They took the turn and proceeded down another hallway. The windows here looked out on the snowy woods to the south. Clover knew the town of Sophia was down there somewhere, but all he could see of it was the corrugated iron wind vane atop the clock tower, spinning madly in the same breeze making beckoning fingers of the treetops. Lenny led the way down a set of stairs, then a second, then a third.

"Zeno should be in the foundry at the moment," Lila explained. "Half her lessons seem to be taught from the workshops these days. Ever since we started preparing for war, she's been obsessed with manufacture."

"You sound disappointed," Clover observed.

"I am! I recently managed to isolate and cultivate a particularly nasty strain of influenza, so that I could attempt to develop a cure. Instead I'm wasting half my time learning how to make my own scalpel. Science depends on specialization, but suddenly we're all expected to be generalists."

TOMMY WALLACH

Walking down yet another hallway, they passed a large archway framing a set of double doors. Lenny pulled on Lila's sleeve.

"We should show him the quad."

"The director said to bring him straightaway."

"It's faster if we cut through."

"What's the quad?" Clover asked.

"It's a quadrangle," Lenny said, as if that were obvious. Without getting formal authorization from Lila, he shouldered his way through the doors, which opened onto a small vestibule and yet another set of doors. The air was noticeably chillier here, though it was nothing compared to the icy blast that came when Lenny opened the farther set of doors. They stepped through, into a sunny forest swathed in snow.

Clover was momentarily disoriented. The windows in the hallway upstairs faced south, but they'd just exited the building in the opposite direction. How could there be "outside" on both sides?

"It's hollow," Lenny said, reading Clover's confusion. "Obviously."

Of course. The academy had been built around this enormous square of constructed wilderness. There were no clear sight lines across the quad; the topography must have been purposely designed in such a way as to maximize the sensation of spaciousness. Even at this time of year, when the plant life was at its barest, the canopy of spruce and pine felt lush. Clover could only imagine how dense and verdurous it would be after the warm turn.

Beyond the doorway, three paths diverged and meandered off through the foliage. Lenny chose the middle one, which appeared to offer the most direct route across the quad. After a few hundred feet, it crossed a small stream by way of a jangly wooden bridge. Though the surface of the water had frozen over, Clover could make out the current moving beneath the ice. He traced the hoary thread back to where it opened up into a large pond about fifty feet to his left. Cattails grew thickly along the bank, quivering like a horde of nervous suitors before a large weeping willow. There was movement between the reeds—two deer snuffling in the snow, seeking the secret grasses.

"How'd they get in?" Clover asked.

"We catch them and bring them here," Lenny replied, "so there's meat when we want it."

"And because they're pleasant to look at," Lila added. "Director Zeno believes there are cognitive benefits to be derived from regular contemplation of the natural world."

It took them a full five minutes to cross from one side of the quadrangle to the other—though only because the path curved and zagged and doubled back on itself. Another two sets of doors brought them back inside the academy proper, where they walked straight across the hallway and through yet *another* set of doors.

This time Clover was struck not by a blast of cold, but a staggering wave of heat and grit; at last they'd arrived at the foundry. It was an enormous chamber, stretching the full three stories upward and a good fifty feet from end to end. Against one wall, what was either a single incredibly complex machine or an assemblage of smaller ones gleamed dully through layers of grime. Clover didn't recognize every individual instrument, but the general workflow was clear enough: here was the gaping maw of the furnace; here the giant crucible and the labyrinth of troughs through which the molten metal would run; here the brick flues that ran the exhaust up through the ceiling and out into the open air.

TOMMY WALLACH

Three people were currently working the furnace, while another half dozen looked on, listening to a running commentary provided by a woman who could only be the famous Director Zeno. She was dressed in the same drab grays as everyone else, though with the addition of a bandanna to keep her unnaturally bright red hair out of her face.

"The flux removes the slag, as always," she was saying, "but unlike the blast of air used in a traditional converter, the open plan allows for a controlled introduction of oxygen. Though the process is slower, due to the need for periodic tests of the molten iron, it enables us to standardize our output, ensuring a consistent carbon content in every batch." She paused as she noticed the new arrivals. "Sister Aline will demonstrate that testing now. I'll return shortly."

Zeno left her students behind and crossed the room. She was older than Clover had expected, at least sixty. Specks of soot dotted her clothes, and a long stripe of black ran across her cheek. Clover felt himself begin to sweat, and he was glad for the excuse of the furnace. Everything hinged on her believing the lies he was about to tell.

"How's his wound?" she said, addressing Lila.

"No infection, but some neuropathy. I'll keep a close eye on it."

"Good. I'll be interested to see the results." With that, she continued walking toward the exit. "Come along, child. Sister Dawkins, you and Lenny can stay here for the rest of the lesson."

"Yes, Director."

Clover just caught Lila's eye roll before he turned and followed Zeno out of the foundry. Her stride was short but rapid; he had to half run to keep up.

"I'm going to ask you a series of questions," she said. "You'll answer them without hesitating. Who shot you?"

"My brother," Clover said.

"Who was the girl?"

"I don't know." Zeno looked at him askance. "I only mean she wasn't who she said she was. I knew her as Irene, from Eaton. But I guess she was someone else."

"Where are you from?"

"The Anchor."

"Were you in school?"

"I was an apprentice at the Library."

"Why are you here?"

Clover knew Zeno was trying to catch him out, to interrogate him so quickly he wouldn't have time to invent a story on the fly. But he'd had months to prepare for this moment, and in spite of everything he'd been through in the past few days, the answers were waiting for him when he needed them.

"To learn."

"You can learn at the Anchor."

"Not the things I want to learn."

"Which are?"

"Anything. Everything."

"Everything. A tall order." There was amusement in her tone, though not in her expression. "And what would your precious Daughter think of this defection?"

Clover had hoped she would ask that; it gave him the opportunity to play his trump card. "The Daughter was an asteroid. Asteroids don't think."

TOMMY WALLACH

"Neither do most people," Zeno said. If she was surprised he knew what the Daughter really was, she didn't show it. "What about your father? What would *he* think?"

"My father's dead. Your men killed him and my mother just north of Wilmington."

"Of course. You're the Honor's son. So why on earth would you pledge your allegiance to the people who murdered your parents?"

"I already told you that. I want to learn."

"You're begging the question, child. I know you want to learn. What I don't know is why."

"Isn't curiosity reason enough?"

"Not in these circumstances." Zeno stopped in front of an unmarked door. "Last question: Are you a spy or a traitor?"

His heart was pounding in his chest, so loudly he felt certain Zeno could hear it. "Do I have to be all one or all the other?"

"For now, yes."

"Then I guess I'm a traitor."

Zeno stared at him, probing, and he felt entirely exposed. "Maybe you are at that," she finally said, and pushed the door open.

The exact same furniture—a narrow bed with a single pillow, a small desk, an uncomfortable-looking chair—was arranged in the exact same way on either side of the room, like a mirror image. The only difference was that one side appeared to be occupied: there were books on the desk, and the bed had been quickly and inexpertly made. Clover stepped inside.

"We'll talk about all this again," Zeno said. Then, upon further consideration: "Unless we don't." She shut the door.

Clover was dizzy with anxiety; his knees almost buckled before he could make it to the bed on the unoccupied side of the room. He sat on the edge of the mattress and let his head drop down between his knees. He was still in that position, breath coming in ragged gasps, forehead beaded with sweat, when the door swung open again.

He glanced up, expecting to find himself facing Zeno's inscrutable countenance and the barrel of a gun.

Instead, he found Lenny.

"So you're my new roommate," the boy said with a scowl. "Lucky me."

4. Paz

A BRIGHT MOTE CAME SWIRLING UP FROM THE DARKness of her memory, like a flake of ash rising from a campfire.

"The first generation of men determined that time is relative. That means that my experience of time is different from yours, which is different from that of the boy or girl sitting next to you. So, in a way, it's as if time doesn't exist at all."

Some academy tutor on loan to the Sophian schoolhouse, her name and face abraded by time, had whispered this to the class as if revealing some grand secret. But Paz had been unimpressed. What child didn't know that time was relative? Oh, the evanescence of that miracle hour between supper and bedtime. Oh, the endlessness of a dull sermon on a hot Sunday morning, honeycomb sunlight spilling messily through the clerestory windows. Time was constantly dilating and contracting, slowing and quickening, eddying and running backward—what was this memory if not a retrograde manifestation of time, the past imposing itself on the present?

Since recognizing the folly of her childhood faith, Paz had spent many long hours ("long hours"—time's relativity coded into the language itself!) contemplating what drew men to religion. Certainly it was fear, but fear of what? Not pain, which faith did nothing to assuage. Not even death, which was only frightening insofar as it was a door opening onto the unknown. Paz had come to believe that the uniting human terror was of what came *after* death, specifically the collapse of chronology that dying might inaugurate, an eternal frozen sentience—paralyzed and sightless—prompting an everlasting appraisal of the self whose end result could only be madness.

Paz had tasted that madness now, after some unknowable number of days confined in the windowless dungeon beneath the Bastion. A single guttering lantern mounted at the end of the corridor illuminated the rusted iron bars of her cell, worn smooth by doomed hands, and the empty cell across the way. Her captors had taken her old clothes and left only a tattered and overlarge Protectorate uniform. Meals arrived at seemingly random intervals, and the soldiers who brought them refused to speak so much as a word. A mattress wrapped in porous gray ticking lurked in the corner of the cell; she would occasionally lie down on it, but though she closed her eyes, she couldn't tell anymore if she was asleep or awake. Now and then, she would hear one of the prisoners farther up the corridor crying or screaming, but they were all too far away for anything like a conversation.

In the absence of any outward stimulation, Paz's attention was bent inward, which was perhaps the worst part of her punishment. The events of the past six months played and replayed in her mind's eye: her coy seduction of Clover, offering him the love and attention he'd craved all his life so she could bleed him for information; her cowardly pragmatism when she'd been discovered by the Wesah, and how she'd stood by as that vicious chieftain threw

TOMMY WALLACH

Gemma over the back of a horse and rode away; her cruel pretense that last night with the contingent, when she'd pretended Clive had been attacking her and so turned brother against brother.

She'd never felt as if she had a choice in any of it. Every step on the road to perdition followed naturally from the last. But looking back from the sepulchral silence of the dungeon, she trembled at the portrait it painted, and she would weep for what felt like hours at a time. She wept for all the people she'd hurt: not just Gemma and Clive and Clover, but also their parents, and little Michael Poplin, and her own brothers, who would grow up without an older sister to guide them. And though she knew she didn't deserve pity, she wept for herself, for poor Paz Dedios, who'd traded away her soul for a chance at revenge. She wept for the torment of her circumstances, and for the fate that surely awaited her—to suffer, to break, to die unloved and unconsoled.

How did one prepare oneself for torture? She'd thought about it before, of course, but only as a sort of fantasy. She imagined how noble it would feel, to gaze steely-eyed and unrepentant into the face of her inquisitor, even as she was being subjected to the most terrible agonies the Descendancy could devise. But now that the moment was at hand, now that she faced the banal, corporeal reality, she found only fear in her heart—fear that grew worse with every passing hour.

In the end, though it was the restless and irrepressible meanders of her mind that nearly unhinged her during that first week in the dungeon, it was those same meanders that saved her.

She'd been thinking about her last conversation with Gemma, beneath the willow tree on the banks of the Ivan.

Do you think there's such a thing as a bad person?

No.

Not even whoever it was that killed your little brother?

Not even him.

Those three little words had shaken Paz to her core—she'd never been one to forgive a trespass—and in the intervening months, had taken on an almost incantatory power. She wished she could write them down, to stare at them, to draw some kind of nourishment from their purity and goodness, and then she realized—she could! The floor of her cell was dirt: nature's original canvas. By pulling pieces of straw out of the mattress and binding them together with a few strands of her long, brittle hair, she was able to fashion a rudimentary stylus.

She wrote those words down first, *not even him*, over and over again, as if in penance. Then, when she got bored, she wondered if she might fit them into some kind of larger composition. She'd never tried her hand at poetry before, but as she drafted the first line, then effaced it, then rewrote it, then adjusted a word or two, she felt the liquid swirl of time begin to harden, to take on a new objective reality. Hours and minutes were replaced with lines and verses, meter and metaphor, rhyme and rhythm and reason. One stanza. Two stanzas. Three stanzas. Four . . .

He arrived without fanfare or escort, a hulking man in a uniform aflutter with ribbons and jangling with medallions. She hid her stylus just in time, praying he wouldn't notice the almost invisible squiggles etched in the dirt.

He leaned back against the bars of the cell opposite hers. His was an unpleasant face, sallow and sour, jowly in the way of certain loose-skinned dogs. Paz sensed that his ugliness hadn't been inherited, but earned—purchased line by line and blotch by blotch with a lifetime of immoral acts and destructive decisions.

"What do you think of the accommodations?" he asked, his amusement just managing to lift the corners of his downturned lips to a straight line.

Paz found herself torn between defiance and obsequy. The former would be more satisfying, the latter more shrewd. "I'm glad to be alive," she replied, hedging.

"You should be. My name is Chang. Do you recognize it?"

Grand Marshal Chang: she'd heard him mentioned often enough on the long march to Sophia. "You're in charge of the Protectorate."

"That's right. And you know what that makes me to you?" He stepped forward, wrapping his hands around the bars of her cell. "It makes me a god." If she moved quickly, she could almost certainly get one of those fat fingers between her teeth. She wondered if she was strong enough to bite through the bone and take a knuckle. "Say it, girl. Say I'm a god."

Before Paz had marched with the Protectorate, she'd assumed that all of its soldiers were amoral, pugnacious thugs. It had surprised her, then, to discover that the contingent was primarily made up of principled and chivalrous men like Clive and Burns. She'd almost forgotten that the Descendancy must also have its share of men like Chang, whose lust for power had allowed them to accrue influence in spite of their clear deficiencies of intelligence and empathy. She made a visible show of fear, confident that Chang was the type who delighted in any fight where he had the upper hand.

"You're a god," she said quietly.

The Grand Marshal licked his bottom lip, as if just hearing those words satiated some deep-seated inner hunger. "They told me you were pretty," he said, pausing to look her over. "We'll see what we can do about that."

As he walked away, two guards took his place, and Paz retreated into the invincible palace of her mind. It was beginning.

Cell

There is no window in my cell,
No bright and polished square of glass
Through which I watch the people pass,
Or kiss hello, or bid farewell.

There is no window in my cell
That makes a whole of sundry panes,
Of colored glass and metal veins,
Recounting tales both fair and fell.

Yet there is a window in my cell
That looks not on the real or true;
It has no pane you can look through,
No parallax or parallel.

This secret window in my cell
Is but the way I choose to see;
So here is heaven given me
Though you would have me gaze on hell.

Almost disappointing, how closely the reality matched up to Paz's expectation. A straight-backed wooden chair and a length of

TOMMY WALLACH

rope. An order to undress down to her underclothes. A man wearing a black apron demanding answers in a dull monotone. When Paz failed to give him what he wanted, he flogged her with a leather strap. This went on until she passed out from the pain, and continued when she woke again.

She slept on her stomach that first night. The next night, after another interrogation, she slept on her side. By the third night, there was no part of her body not ribboned with welts. She took some comfort in the notion that future lashings could only reopen old wounds.

She gave it a week before appearing to break, hoping that was long enough to make her surrender look plausible.

"No more, please!" she shouted, suddenly tearful and wild-eyed. "I'll tell you anything you want. Anything!"

Her torturer put down the strap and took up the pen and paper. Paz lied with a facility she hoped made her sound honest, inventing facts as quickly as her torturer could write them down: Sophia was a town of only three hundred souls, and only thirty students were enrolled at the academy. Sophia did not possess the capability to make weapons more complicated than the ones the Protectorate had already seen. Sophia maintained only basic commercial relationships with a few small towns to the east, so would never be able to field an army.

Paz knew the ploy would likely be as obvious to her captors as it would have been to her, but she figured she didn't have anything to lose by trying.

That was her big mistake. It turned out you always had something left to lose.

The next morning found Paz taken to a new chamber in the dungeon, where she was tied down even more tightly than usual. She was left alone for a moment, and then a young pretty woman dressed in all purple—signaling her position as an employee of a bishop—entered the room. Her expression was grave, her eyes downcast.

"Good morning," she said. "I'm Diana."

"Good mor—"

Paz's voice died in her throat when she saw the razor blade in Diana's hand. Well, at least it would be quick. She closed her eyes and braced for the end.

The rasp of the metal scraping across her scalp took her by surprise, but some instinct told her not to struggle. Diana slowly shaved every speck of hair off Paz's head, finishing with the eyebrows. She left the room after that and returned a few minutes later with a small bowl full of blue-black liquid and a needle. At last Paz understood what was happening, and she began to tremble.

"The more you move, the more painful this will be," Diana said.

Until that moment, Paz had managed to hold on to the hope that she might beat them, that however much they might abuse her body, her spirit would remain invincible. But as the needle pierced the tender flesh just above her forehead, that hope began to drain out of her. She could feel the word as it took shape, as if it were being written in flame.

Heathen.

The tattoo took hours to complete. When it was done, Diana wiped Paz's head with a cloth that smelled of some strange medi-

TOMMY WALLACH

cine and drew fresh fire from the wounds, such that Paz couldn't help but moan.

"I'll be back tomorrow," Diana said. Then, more quietly, "Just give them what they want, girl. God wouldn't want you to suffer more than you have to."

"Save your pity," Paz snarled, her eyes widening in what was at once a performance and a manifestation of nascent lunacy. "Someday soon, I'll eat your heart."

She made as if to break free of her bindings, and Diana nearly fell over herself running out of the room.

"Fuck your pity!" Paz screamed out after her. "And fuck your god!"

A poem for every tattoo.

A tattoo for every poem.

Fire and blood.

Bruise and spit.

And still she didn't break.

How long had she been here? Days? Weeks? Centuries? Time was relative. Time was infinite. Time didn't exist. Reality began to shiver and split. She was no longer a person, just a repository of pain.

Only then, when all hope seemed lost, did he finally come. A respite. A caesura. An opportunity.

"Clive?"

5. Gemma

A SENSE OF DISLOCATION, OF SOMEHOW BEING IN TWO places at once: waves of heat against her face, cool air at her back. Something heavy and moist lay across her forehead. Gemma opened her eyes just as a snow-chilled breeze slipped beneath the hem of the tent and teased the nap of the fire, sending cinders flying toward the sun-bright hole overhead.

Athène, sitting cross-legged beside her, reached out and removed the weight from Gemma's forehead: a damp cloth. The chieftain dipped it into a clay basin of water and wrung it out, eliciting a plume of fragrant steam—sage, maybe, or thyme. Gemma felt an overwhelming sense of peace, followed by an equally potent sense of panic at the very thought of feeling peaceful. She knew she should refuse this comfort as a show of protest, only her head was pounding, as it always did after one of her fits, and the warm compress felt so good, and Athène's serene smile floating above her like a benediction . . .

A tribeswoman entered and handed the chieftain a bowl full of pemmican, a sort of granola made from dried buffalo meat pounded into tiny pieces and mixed with wild berries and melted fat. The *naasyoon* always kept a few parfleche bags of the stuff on hand and ate it whenever there was nothing better to be had.

"You need guard your strength," Athène said. "My mother, she is always hungry after a vision." The chieftain scooped up a few grains of the pemmican.

"I didn't have a—" Gemma began to say, but was interrupted by the unceremonious introduction of Athène's fingers into her mouth.

"You finish eat, then come to stream. Today we talk."

Gemma lay motionless for a while after Athène left, leaching the heat of the cloth and inhaling the sweet-smelling steam. But the crumbs of pemmican had piqued her hunger, and once the compress went cold, she sat up and began to eat. By the time she finished, the pounding in her head had lessened to a dull tap, and she felt strong enough to brave the outside world.

The *naasyoon* had set up camp on the lip of the caldera. Just outside Athène's tent, a few Wesah tended to the horses, feeding them the bark off cottonwood branches. The animals had grown skinny over the past two weeks; they wouldn't last much longer in these wintry climes, which likely explained why the *naasyoon* was traveling so quickly south. Another small group of tribeswomen sat with the missives around a fire halfway down the side of the crater. Two of them were visibly with child, which excused them from the *naasyoon*'s most physically demanding tasks.

Gemma heard the crackle of the fire behind her, back in Athène's tent. Clover had explained the origin of that sound to her once: moisture, held like a prisoner within the grain of the wood, turned to steam, growing ever hotter and more insistent, until it split the log asunder.

Wasn't she a little like that steam—trapped somewhere she

didn't belong, ready to burst free? So why didn't she take off running right now? Her arms and legs were unfettered; the *naasyoon* was scattered; no one seemed to be watching the horses that had already been fed. She'd be halfway down the mountain before anyone noticed she was gone.

Of course, she'd made a promise to Athène, that she would stay with the tribe until they reached the Villenaître (whatever that was), but a promise made by a captive to her captor wasn't a *real* promise. Prisoners said what they needed to say to survive.

So it was decided. She would run. This instant. All she had to do was untether a horse, jump on its back, and take off.

And yet . . .

She couldn't help but be a little curious about what Athène wanted to discuss with her. Not to mention the fact that her head still hurt, and her stomach was a little upset from how quickly she'd eaten. There would be plenty of time to make her getaway after she'd spoken to the chieftain.

She descended the caldera and approached Rugaru, the taller of the two missives.

"Did you see which way Athène went?" she asked.

He pointed toward a trailhead about a quarter mile around the curve of the ridge. "She brought spears," he said, smirking. "Maybe she plans to kill you."

The words rose to Gemma's lips unsummoned, natural as emotion. "Or maybe I plan to kill her." She smiled, and realized that something felt different this morning; *she* felt different. Maybe the fit had done it, or that crystallizing moment watching the sun set over the caldera while the *naasyoon* sang, or maybe it was simply the passage of time. Whatever the cause, her fear of the Wesah was gone; in its place, something not unlike fondness had taken root.

"This is dirty," Gemma said, handing the scowling missive her empty bowl. One of the pregnant warriors laughed loudly, and a couple of other tribeswomen chuckled. They didn't need to speak English to see that the new girl had just given her first order. And far from being offended by it, they approved. For the first time, Gemma wondered if the Wesah might not always see her as an outsider.

The thought preoccupied her as she climbed back up the side of the caldera, such that she didn't notice she was being pursued until someone grabbed hold of her arm and jerked it hard, forcing her to turn around.

It was Noémie, the woman who so often spent the night in Athène's tent. Gemma had never spoken to her before, but had long noticed the aura of menace she projected, even in spite of her stature: though she was scarcely more than five feet tall, her arms were rippled with muscle.

"*Moon*," she said, pressing a finger into her sternum. "*Moon*."

Gemma looked to the sky, but could see no sign of the moon. Perhaps it was a particular sort of greeting, meant to be met in kind. She pointed to her own chest. "*Moon*," she repeated.

Noémie's eyes went wide; her jaw tightened. Gemma understood she'd done something wrong half a second before Noémie slapped her across the face, so hard she went down on one knee.

"*Moon!*" Noémie barked at her. "*Moon!*" She spat loudly into the dirt and stalked off.

Gemma took a moment to blink the stars from her eyes. Then

she straightened up and continued on toward the trailhead, rubbing her sore cheek and trying to sort out what the hell had just happened.

The mountainside was riddled with waterways, snowmelt and Gravity performing an endless duet of trickles, splashes, and drips. As Gemma descended, these myriad rivulets would occasionally meet up and decide to travel onward together, like a metaphor for love, growing wider and deeper as they went. She followed the largest tributary, her feet crunching loudly through the crust of virgin snow, until a peal of laughter pulled her up short.

She'd passed within five feet of Athène without seeing her; the chieftain was crouched on the bank of the stream, her furs blending in perfectly with the mottled stones. "Good I'm not hunting yellow-hair girls from the Anchor. You never know what hit you."

Gemma sidled down the icy bank. Two spears were stuck into the dirt by the side of the stream; Athène extracted one and offered it up.

"Take."

"You'd give a weapon to your prisoner?"

Athène laughed again. "I see it here," she said, pointing first to her eyes, then to Gemma's. "No more anger. Now, you know how fish with spear, *chee*."

It took Gemma a moment to remember that *chee* signified a question. She shook her head.

"I teach you."

Athène stood up and shrugged off her fur coat, exposing her arms. Slim curls of black ink—reminiscent of how little children

TOMMY WALLACH

drew wind—ran down her neck and along her biceps, disappearing beneath the copper bands and reappearing at her elbow. They shifted prettily as she raised the spear overhead. At her feet, the silhouettes of fish flitted in and out of the shade cast by the trees, like silver shekels flipping—white to black, black to white. Athène watched with a preternatural focus, her eyes dancing from one shadow to another until she finally pounced. Her arm blurred. The spearhead hardly made a splash as it pierced the water.

Athène paused for a moment, then lifted the spear. Water dripped off the naked gray flint.

"First time is hard," she said, smiling sheepishly. She put her mantle of furs back on and sat down on the bank. "We must wait for the fish to forget us."

For a moment, Gemma stood above the chieftain, spear in hand. It would be so easy. A quick plunge, in and out—disfiguring the perfect filigree of tattoo, empurpling the snow, despoiling the crystal water . . .

"Why did you take me?" she asked. Athène looked up at her, and Gemma could tell the chieftain understood that her very life hinged on what she said next.

"Because you are special," Athène replied, without hedge or hesitation.

Gemma had expected some kind of mystical half answer—*Did we take you, or did you take yourself?*—or else an outright refusal to admit to the kidnapping; she wasn't prepared for a compliment.

"I'm not special," she said, thrusting the spearhead back into the mud.

"You know what is *otsapah, chee.*"

"*Otsapah?*" It wasn't a word Gemma recognized.

"*Otsapah* is also special. Spiritual leaders, like your Honors. They help to, they are helping to"—she fumbled with the words—"I forget how to say in English. *Ishiishchikaywin.* Like . . . like magic."

"A spell?"

Athène shook her head. "Not spell. *Ishiishchikaywin* is like . . . singing. Or dancing. Yesterday is *ishiishchikaywin*, because this mountain is sacred."

"Do you mean ritual?"

"Ritual," Athène said, testing out the word. In her charming mispronunciation, the word came out as a perfect rhyme of "vigil." Gemma smiled in spite of herself.

"It's something you do to celebrate, always the same way."

"Yes!" Athène said. "For us, ritual is *ishiishchikaywin.*"

"And you think I can help with the *ishi*—with the ritual? Because I'm this *otsapah* person?"

Athène looked amused. "No. *Otsapah* is born *otsapah.* She must be Wesah. But sometimes the spirit comes to an outsider, like you. When I see you dancing, I know it is the spirit speaking through you."

"Dancing?" Gemma said. She couldn't remember Athène ever seeing her dance, unless the chieftain was talking about . . .

The realization hit her with all the force of Noémie's slap: at last, after more than two weeks traveling with the Wesah, Gemma finally understood why she'd been abducted. The day the Protectorate contingent had been ambushed by Athène's *naasyoon*, Gemma had suffered one of her fits. But instead of recognizing it for the malady it was, Athène and her fellow tribeswomen must have believed it to be some kind of otherworldly communion. That was why they were treating Gemma differently this morning— because of the fit she'd had during the celebration last night.

The mystery was almost solved; only one question remained. "How did you make Irene bring me to you?"

Athène frowned. "Irene, *chee*."

"The girl who was with me that first night."

The chieftain's face lit up. "Ah! With me, she is calling herself Paz. *Mafwe!* I wish we take her, too. So beautiful. But we make deal."

"What kind of deal?"

"My scout find her spying. We say we plan to attack soldiers so we can take you, but your friend says, 'I bring you the girl so no one die.' Better for everyone." Athène glanced down at the water. "The fish are back."

Once again, the chieftain took up her spear and stood poised over the creek, but Gemma was still absorbing what she'd just learned. So Irene was actually called Paz, and though she hadn't been working with the Wesah, she'd made a deal with them to save her own skin. But who was she to need a false name in the first place?

Do you think there's such a thing as a bad person?

No.

Not even whoever it was that killed your little brother?

Not even him.

And what if it was me who did it?

In retrospect, it was as good as an admission of guilt. Gemma saw it all clearly now. Paz had been working for Sophia from the first. She'd been there at the pumphouse. She'd sabotaged their wagon and then gone to fetch her companions. She was the reason Gemma's father and little brother were dead.

Athène struck. This time, when she raised the spear from the water, a fish no bigger than a fist was impaled on the tip. It flapped helplessly a few times, like a bird trying and failing to get off the ground, then went still. Athène took a knife from the feathered sheath at her waist and used it to slice the fish open. She pulled out the guts and cleaned what was left in the river.

"You want some, *chee*," she asked.

"Raw? It'll make you sick."

"Never." Athène pounded her stomach with her left hand. "Iron belly."

She held the fish out under Gemma's nose; the cold creek water had rinsed away any smell.

"Just a taste," Athène said. "It make you strong."

It would be the height of foolishness to eat any; everyone knew uncooked freshwater fish carried disease. But strength was exactly what Gemma needed now. Paz would have to pay for what she'd done. All of Sophia would have to pay.

"Athène, can you teach me how to fight?"

"You want to fight? I thought you good Anchor girl. No believe in violence."

"Answer my question."

The chieftain grinned. "Yes, I can teach you how to fight. It is my pleasure."

"Good." Gemma leaned forward and stripped half the meat off the fish in one raking pass of her teeth. The flesh was sweet and tender, a lambent creamy white, like a bright winter moon.

Moon.

"What does *moon* mean in your language?" Gemma asked. "Is it like our moon?"

"No. Your moon *la leun*. I teach you words while I teach you fight. When we get to the sea, you will already speak like a Wesah."

"The sea? You said we were going to the Villenaître."

"Villenaître first. Then the *tooroon*."

Gemma remembered Burns mentioning the *tooroon*—it was some kind of big meeting for the whole Wesah nation. "I thought that wasn't until summer."

"End of summer. *Latonn*."

Gemma's eyes went wide. "That's months from now! I can't stay with you that long!"

"You want learn to fight, *chee*. You need time."

"But I have a little sister at home. She needs me."

Athène seemed unconcerned, as if the future were already written—and she'd read it. "I also have sisters that need me. Many thousands. They will be your sisters too." Athène threw what was left of the fish back into the water, where its bloodthirsty fellows immediately converged on it. "Come. I think it is time you know them."

They began walking back toward camp. After a couple of minutes, Gemma realized the chieftain still hadn't answered her original question.

"Athène, you never told me what *moon* means."

"I am thinking you already know. It is your people's favorite word." The chieftain laughed at what was obviously some sort of joke.

"Our favorite word?"

"It is how we say we own something." The chieftain pointed at her spear. "*Moon tahkahtchikun!*" She pointed toward the sky. "*Moon syel!*" She pointed toward the earth. "*Moon tayr!*" She pointed at Gemma. "My little dancer."

Gemma felt foolish for not figuring it sooner. *Moon* meant "mine." Of course.

She touched her fingers to her cheek, as if she could still feel the handprint burning there. *Mine*, Noémie had said. As in, *Athène is mine*. It had been a warning. A claim. A threat.

Perhaps Gemma didn't have quite as many sisters as Athène believed.

TOMMY WALLACH

6. Clive

H E WIPED HIS SWEATY PALMS ON HIS UNIFORM PANTS and took a few deep breaths. Two soldiers were stationed by the door—Jergens and Kassabian, the latter of whom waggled his eyebrows as Clive passed.

"Have fun down there," he said.

Clive began his descent. After he'd gone a few steps, the door slammed shut behind him, cutting out the light.

"Hey, I can't see!" he called out.

Jergens's muffled voice just managed to penetrate the thick wood: "It's the rules, Hamill. You'll live."

Muttering a curse under his breath, Clive continued downward, one hand on the wall to his right. He'd been here a couple of times before—dungeon duty was one of the more desirable tasks assigned to new recruits—but something was different today. Even before he reached the bottom of the steps, the noxious reek of captivity assaulted his nostrils—body odor and excrement, food scraps gone rancid. In Clive's experience, the dungeon had never housed more than two or three prisoners at a time; the severity of this stink spoke to a much larger population. Clearly the Grand Marshal was going out of his way to make his new authority felt.

The darkness took on a blush of torchlight at last; after one final corkscrew, the steps bottomed out. The dungeon was one exhaustively long corridor, the cells so far apart that no two prisoners could ever hope to communicate. Burns had warned Clive that Paz had been placed in the farthest cell in order to ensure the most extreme isolation. From here, the lantern at the end of the corridor was scarcely larger than a spark rising from a campfire.

Clive began to walk toward it—cells opening like wounds on either side, prisoners staring at him with naked hatred—and to steel himself for what was to come. He hadn't spoken to Paz since Sophia, not a single word during the whole trip back to the Anchor. He'd believed he was doing it to punish her, ensuring she would find no comfort or succor in their association. But now, as the moment of crisis loomed, as the spark grew to the size of a match flame, he wondered if he'd been fooling himself. His heart hammered, his palms perspired, the hairs on the back of his neck stood on end. This was fear, and perhaps it had been fear all along. Paz was a siren, a seductress, a succubus; her words were honeyed poison. Perhaps he'd avoided speaking to her so as not to risk being beguiled all over again.

At last Clive reached the end of the corridor. The match flame had transformed into a full-size lantern, casting a light so weak it failed to reach more than a couple of feet into Paz's cell.

"Clive?"

The voice was half an octave lower than he remembered and rough as sandpaper—the result of disuse, or screaming?

No pity, Clive reminded himself. *Don't forget what she did.*

"Paz," he said, the name still unfamiliar, an exotic confection in his mouth. "Come closer."

TOMMY WALLACH

A shadow separated itself from the greater darkness at the back of the cell. It moved hesitantly, fearfully, before at last emerging into the light. Clive had been warned that the sight of her might offend his sensibilities, but no warning could've prepared him for the reality.

Her head had been shaved clean as an egg and inscribed with three black annuli, like latitude lines on a globe—one running just above where her eyebrows used to be, one bisecting the bulb of her nose, and another completing the line made by her closed lips. But that wasn't the worst of it. A number of epithets had been written in large scripted letters across her bare scalp and partway down her neck: *traitor, animal, heathen, monster, demon, damned, deceiver, harlot*. Clive had seen disciplinary tattoos before—there were plenty of men walking around the Anchor with a word or two permanently inscribed in their flesh, *thief* or *debtor* or *inebriate*—but he'd never seen anything so radical. He suppressed the pangs of sympathy. Paz had reaped what she'd sown: no more, no less.

"Care to read them to me?" she asked, wrapping her hands around the bars. "I've forgotten what all of them say." Clive shook his head; he was still too shocked to speak. "Diana told me she has permission to cover my whole face if I don't talk. But it hardly matters now." Paz's tone was soft, almost wondering, as if she were speaking to an angel. Hunger had transformed her into a wraith, gaunt and thin-skinned, nearly unrecognizable. "I know why you're here, Clive."

"Do you?"

"They want information. They haven't been able to beat it out of me, so now they're hoping to use our friendship to get it."

Even beaten down and degraded like this, Paz hadn't lost any of her acuity. Clive felt the need to lash out, to humble her.

"We were never friends," he said.

The blow registered on her face as a pitiable crumpling. She nodded, recognizing that she'd earned that and more. "No, I suppose not."

"I told Burns you would see right through it, but he didn't believe me."

"So why come at all?"

"It was an order."

Paz smiled, momentarily embodying her former beauty. "You could've said no, given the circumstances. But you wanted to talk to me, didn't you? You've got questions."

Clive didn't respond. He hated that she was always a step ahead of him. He hated that he wanted anything from her.

"Would you like me to ask them for you?" Paz said. "I don't mind. I've gotten used to talking to myself." She deepened her voice a bit, taking on a preacherly cadence that Clive recognized as a parody of his own. "'Paz, did you love my brother, or were you just playing with him?'" She resumed her usual voice. "I came to like him, but I never felt any sincere romantic attachment. 'Irene—I mean, Paz, sorry—who was that boy you killed in the alley that night?' Well, Clive, that was someone from Coriander, the town I grew up in. He recognized me, and tried to blackmail me into fucking him, so I cut him open."

Clive had never heard Paz swear before—then again, he'd never really heard Paz say *anything* before. How deep had the character gone? Where did Irene end and Paz begin?

TOMMY WALLACH

"What else could you want to know?" she said, speaking more quickly. "Yes, I was there at the pumphouse, where your friend Gemma killed my father. Yes, I was the one who snapped the axle of your wagon and brought the men who shot your parents." Her voice was only getting louder and faster as she went on, as if she'd pulled a loose thread inside herself and was unraveling right in front of his eyes. "Yes, every single thing I did and every single word I spoke was a lie, and yes I wanted to see you and your family get what you deserve, and yes I want to see this whole rotten edifice come crashing down on your—"

"You kissed me," Clive said.

Paz went silent, casting her eyes to the ground. "You kissed me," she eventually said. "And it was easier to kiss you back than to say no."

Did she know how those words would affect him, that she might as well have reached between the bars and punched him in the gut? In spite of everything that had happened between them since that day, he'd maintained the belief that their kiss had been real, a speck of honest emotion sparkling in the rubble. But it had just been another part of the deception, and he was once again revealed to be a fool.

"I'll tell them I couldn't crack you," he said gruffly, turning away and beginning to walk back up the corridor.

"No!" Paz screamed.

It was as human a sound as he'd ever heard her make, a distillation of terror and grief so pure it stopped him in his tracks. A voice in the back of his head told him to keep walking, to take the stairs two at a time and then march right into Burns's office and announce that he'd sooner abandon the Descendancy than ever speak to Paz again.

"Clive, please," she said. "Please don't go. Oh God, please don't go."

He didn't flatter himself to think her desperation had anything to do with him personally. It was just that base animal need for stimulation, for connection. Even so, it slipped right through the cracks in Clive's resolve. Perhaps it was his father's legacy, the minister's drive to minister, or perhaps he still couldn't shake the belief that there had to be a good person somewhere inside of Paz. Whatever the reason, he couldn't leave her like this.

Still, he had to be sure it wasn't another layer of pretense, so he paced in place, letting his footsteps fall more and more quietly, until he stopped moving entirely.

"Clive?" she said. "Clive?"

He waited, silent and still, breath held. The first thing he heard was a long, drawn-out howl, pitched high and trembling, which trailed off into plangent, gasping sobs—dredged up from that deepest place in the soul, thick as Blood of the Father, as if she were drowning on dry land, coming faster and faster and faster, until finally they broke into a primal scream of unmitigated anguish.

Was it strength or weakness that allowed him to hear that anguish, to seek to soothe it? Was it strength or weakness that led him back to her cell, to gaze once again into those eyes that had somehow lost none of their potency, none of their penetration.

Paz went quiet, waiting to hear her sentence.

"You have one chance," he said.

"To do what?" she whispered.

"To tell the truth."

TOMMY WALLACH

The Grand Marshal's office was on the second floor of the Bastion, abutting the Anchor wall and overlooking the training fields. Even now, at twilight, more than a hundred soldiers were still hard at work: sprinting around the track wearing rucksacks full of rocks, perforating the archery targets, dueling with blunt-edged practice swords. Clive watched them with envy; what he would've given to be out there with them instead of in here.

"So what you're telling me is you have no new information," Chang said, stroking his thin black mustache.

"Not exactly," Clive replied.

Burns stood by the window, keeping an eye on the fields. "So what did you learn, Clive? Be specific."

What had he learned? That her name was Paz Dedios, and that she'd been born in Coriander, just a few hours north of the Anchor. That her older brother had died when he fell off the roof while trying to fly a kite, and that her mother had died of the plague a couple of years later, and that her father, José, blamed the Church for both of their deaths. That José's discontent eventually drew the family east, away from the Descendancy, toward the community of dissidents in Sophia. That she'd joined the Sophian town guard, which was how she'd ended up at the pumphouse that fateful night, watching her father's lifeblood seep out into the dirt. That all her subsequent crimes, from her seduction of Clover to her complicity in Gemma's kidnapping, were born of circumstance and instinct— not so much a plan as a heedless plummet.

"Do you regret it?" he'd asked.

"Every day," she'd answered.

And Clive had believed her.

He tried to relate all this to Burns and the Grand Marshal, but he could tell neither of them were particularly impressed.

"A bunch of shit about her childhood?" Chang shouted. "Why would I care about any of that? She was probably making it all up anyway."

"We can check," Burns said, in an attempt to mollify the Grand Marshal. "If she lived in Coriander, her family would've owned land. There'll be records."

"I don't give a rat's ass if it's true or not! I want to know about Sophia!"

"I just need more time," Clive said. "She'll tell me what we want to know eventually."

"Will she? What makes you so sure?"

Clive hadn't been planning to lie, but he couldn't see any way around it. Chang wanted information, and he wouldn't get it unless Clive was allowed to keep speaking with Paz. "Because she's in love with me. She's been in love with me all along."

Burns and Chang shared a look—skeptical but intrigued.

"How do you know?" Burns asked.

Clive considered telling them about the kiss, but figured it would raise as many doubts as it would quell. He shrugged. "I can just tell. You must know what that's like." He directed this comment toward the Grand Marshal, hoping to appeal to the man's towering vanity.

"Sure I do," Chang said, lips curling into a libidinous smile. "It's all in the way they look at you, like a dog waiting to be fed."

"Exactly," Clive replied. "And when a woman looks at you like that, she won't keep her secrets for long."

TOMMY WALLACH

"How long are we talking?"

"A few weeks, maybe? A month?" Clive braced himself; he knew he was already pushing his luck. "And you'll have to let her out of that cell when we talk."

Chang frowned. "Why the hell would I do that?"

"Because she's going crazy in there."

"So?"

"So if you break her mind open like an egg, you might lose the yolk."

"Daughter's love!" The Grand Marshal threw up his hands, grudgingly admitting defeat. His glower gave way to grim amusement as he leveled an accusatory finger at Burns. "This is your baby now, Marshal. If anything goes wrong, Diana will start working on *your* head."

"Understood," Burns said, glaring meaningfully in Clive's direction. "I'm sure the kid knows what he's doing."

"Of course I do," Clive replied, and hoped he sounded a lot more confident than he was.

7. Clover

THE LIBRARY AT SOPHIA WAS ONE LARGE, AIRY ROOM, THE polar opposite of the gloomy crypts and caverns of the Library at the Anchor. Tall windows on either end flooded it with light at all hours of the day, such that wide muslin curtains had to be pulled to dull the glare in the afternoons. On the western side—or slightly southwest, as Clover had determined that the building was set about thirty degrees off true north—one looked out over the quadrangle, still but for the occasional flash of a rabbit or a doe. On the eastern side, the ground fell away, granting an expansive view of the valley below. The Ivan River featured prominently, capering down the small cataract whose dam provided Sophia with electricity and meandering smooth and sinuous across the landscape, thinning to a silvery gleam in the distance.

Clover was attempting a comprehensive survey of every volume in the library, in order to determine Sophia's military capabilities as precisely as possible, but the task was difficult for a number of reasons. First, there was the sheer amount of information on display. Unlike the traditional leather-bound volumes Clover was used to, most of the books in the Sophian library were unadorned, no-nonsense repositories of knowledge and thought—a few dozen pages dense with barely legible text, interrupted by the occasional hasty sketch, and bound with a long piece of waxed twine strung through a couple of ragged holes. They'd clearly been written here at the academy; the author was always "Brother" Somebody or "Sister" Somebody Else. There were thousands upon thousands of these essays and treatises, covering every conceivable subject, and the only texts that Clover felt comfortable skipping over entirely were the few volumes devoted to the study of religion.

The second obstruction to his reconnaissance was Lenny—roommate, adviser, and perpetual thorn in the side. Lenny had been tasked with getting Clover up to speed on the practices and procedures of life in Sophia, and to that end, he always seemed to be underfoot. Clover had to assume the boy was also reporting to Zeno on the newcomer's doings around the academy, which meant caution and discretion had to be exercised at all times.

But the greatest impediment to Clover's intelligence gathering was simply all the *other* work he was expected to do, specifically a series of tasks the scholars referred to as "the primer" (and Lenny referred to as "that goddamn stupid primer"), which every new student had to complete before he or she could begin attending classes. In less than two weeks, Clover had taught himself to smelt a slug of iron and forge it into a horseshoe (receiving a check from Brother Geralt), to blow a rather unimpressive blister of black glass (receiving a check minus from Sister Dale), and to use a tap and a die to make screws and nuts (which had fit together so tightly Brother Alonzo said he wished there were a grade above check plus). He'd planed boards in the woodshop, mixed plaster in the chemistry laboratory, fired bricks in the kiln, and built a scale-model tower to demonstrate his grasp of basic architectural principles.

The only task remaining on the primer was to make his own paper, then write a short essay about the papermaking process *on* the paper in question, including a suggestion for a possible improvement to or variation on the standard technique. At the Anchor, papermaking was carried out by a small, devoted cabal of Library monks in a specialized mill on the Tiber. Clover wished he'd taken Bernstein up on the offer to visit; it would've made his work here a whole lot easier.

The papermaking room was low-ceilinged, pungent with pulp, set just off the woodshop on the academy's ground floor. Clover had left his scrap paper (which had taken a whole day to collect) in the soaking tub last night, and he'd hoped it would be ready for pressing by now. Unfortunately, the mixture was still chunky.

"What do you think I should do?" Clover said.

Lenny smiled his usual infuriating smile. "You know I'm not allowed to help you. That's the whole point."

"Fine. Be that way." Clover grabbed a large metal whisk from the rack and began mashing the paper scraps against the wall of the tub, as if stirring the lumps out of a pot of oatmeal. As there was nothing better to do while he stirred, he decided to see what personal information he could glean from Lenny, who was surprisingly adept at dodging questions about his past.

"Remind me, Lenny, how long have you been in Sophia?"

"Long enough for it to feel like home."

"How long is that?"

"You'd have to ask my ma. She's better with dates."

"Where'd you come from?"

"A town a little ways east of here."

"It have a name?"

Lenny's eyes narrowed slightly. "Sure does."

"Lot of people live there?"

"More than Sophia. Less than where you come from."

"I didn't think there were so many big towns outside the Descendancy."

"You Anchor folks are like Ptolemy. You think the whole world revolves around you."

"Who's Ptolemy?" Clover asked. "Is he a scholar here?"

Lenny made a show of dropping his jaw. "Ptolemy? The geocentric astronomical model? Copernicus? Nothing?"

Clover could only shrug. His brief time in Sophia had already revealed to him the depth of his ignorance; his understanding of the world was studded with lacunae, vast blank spaces labeled "anathema." Lenny was all too happy to fill them in, but never without a bit of pedantry and ersatz outrage—how could anyone not know *this*?

"Here's my question," Lenny said. "Wasn't it frustrating knowing there was so much the Descendancy wouldn't let you know?"

Clover was torn between telling the truth and trying to excuse the culture that raised him. Funny the way that worked; it reminded him of how he'd spent his whole life complaining about Clive, but would immediately rally to his brother's defense if anybody else dared to criticize him.

At the thought of Clive, Clover felt a twinge of pain in his shoulder, a heaviness in his heart. The soldiers who'd died in the assault on Sophia were buried in a mass grave outside the city. Every night Clover prayed that Clive wasn't among them, that he'd made it safely back to the Anchor. Whatever had transpired between them, he didn't want his brother to die thinking him a traitor.

"No answer, eh?" Lenny said. "I'll take that as a yes."

At last the texture of the pulp felt right, and Clover began pulling out great dripping handfuls and laying them to set in the deckle—a dense mesh frame about eight inches by ten. The resultant mixture looked a little like a storm cloud. After it congealed, Clover shook it out onto the table, expressed the excess moisture with a wood block, and introduced his innovation: a handful of black dust.

"What's that?" Lenny asked.

"Shavings of naturally magnetic lodestone. It should make the paper stick to anything ferrous."

"Why?"

Clover clipped the paper to a string that ran over the heater—a cast-iron contraption that was constantly pinging and hissing—and turned back to Lenny with a smile. "Why not?"

Another two weeks after his afternoon in the papermaking room, Clover decided to make his first foray into town—in spite of the potential risks. While the intellectual atmosphere cultivated at the academy rendered certain practical realities moot, in town the memory of last month's Protectorate attack would still be vivid. At least some of Sophia's citizens were likely to view Clover as an enemy. Which, of course, he was.

"Townsfolk and scholars don't mix too much," Lenny explained. "They're grateful for everything we do, of course, but they think some of us can be a little patronizing. Anyway, you'll be fine as long as you're with me. Everybody down here *loves* Lenny."

The day was clear and bitterly cold. Black ice had formed on the loose cobbles, making the walk treacherous. Clover hoped Lenny might open up a little more outside the academy proper—especially if he had a couple of mugs of beer in him.

"I still don't believe anybody's gonna serve you," Clover said. "Aren't you only fourteen?"

"I told you. We don't have dumb rules like that out here."

"If you say so. Where are we going again?"

"Well, there's two places in town: Ruben's is the inn, and the Wayward Pony's the public house. Personally, I like Ruben's better. The Pony's mostly for people who wanna get smashed at the end of the day. The general store's also got some food, but—"

"Damn," Clover said. He'd suddenly remembered that he didn't have any money on him . . . or at all, really. "Lenny, can you cover me today? I'll figure out some way to pay you back later. Maybe Lila kept my shekels somewhere."

"You wouldn't make many friends handing out Descendancy coinage," Lenny scoffed. "But you're in luck, kid. Scholars always eat for free."

"They do? Why?"

"Because the academy heats the shops and lights the streets and breeds the livestock and about a million other things. It's why we're going to win this war: because we all look out for each other."

They passed the clock tower, its door leaning against the stonework; Burns and his soldiers had torn it right off the hinges. An old woman, bent with age, emptied a tin bucket into a pigsty. When she noticed Clover and Lenny passing by, her expression soured, and she scuttled back into her house.

SLOW BURN

Clover was grateful when they ducked into Ruben's a few moments later. It looked like any old inn you'd find in a small town off the Tails: buck heads mounted on the wall, a roaring fireplace, a long bar where two silver-haired men quietly nursed their drinks. Lenny and Clover took a seat at a table by the hearth, and a moment later a young barmaid emerged from the kitchen. She was what Eddie Poplin used to call "country beautiful"—apple-cheeked and full-figured, with light brown hair down to her waist.

"Afternoon, boys," she said.

"Afternoon, Maya," Lenny replied. "This is my friend Clover. Clover, this is Maya."

The girl frowned briefly, as if trying to place the name. Then her face opened up into a smile. "You're the new boy, up at the academy."

"That's right," Clover said.

"Well, it's a pleasure to meet you. What can I get you boys?"

"Two meat pies and two beers," Lenny said. "Please and thank you."

"Make it four beers," Clover added. "We worked up quite a thirst on the walk."

Lenny laughed uncomfortably. "You sure about that? I'm not exactly looking to get drunk over lunch."

"Who gets drunk on two beers?" Clover's challenge was compounded by a provocative eyebrow raise from Maya.

"Fine!" Lenny said, throwing up his hands. "Four beers."

"Coming right up," Maya said.

Lenny watched her go with an expression of pained yearning. "She's something, isn't she? The girls at the academy—I mean, don't get me wrong, some of them are pretty enough—but none of them

TOMMY WALLACH

can hold a candle to Maya. Of course, she's already got a sweetheart. Some lunk a couple towns over. I saw the two of them necking at the Yuletide festival. He had his big dirty hands all over her—"

Maya reappeared with their beers. Lenny went quiet for just as long as it took her to cross the room, hand them their drinks, and return to the kitchen. Then he started right back up again.

"—and it was disgusting to look at, I'll tell you. You know that kind of kissing where you can see the tongues and everything? Enough to make you sick—"

"Cheers," Clover interrupted. Alcohol was metabolized fastest on an empty stomach, so it was best to get to drinking right away, before the meal arrived.

"Cheers."

Clover drank the whole first mug down in one go, and was pleased to see Lenny match him. He allowed the conversation to return to the subject of Maya's physical charms and agonizing inaccessibility, and by the time the barmaid returned with their food, all four mugs of beer were empty. Clover subtly ordered another round as they tucked into their pies.

"Not bad, eh?" Lenny said.

"Not bad at all."

The pies were indeed as delicious as advertised—flaky crust, perfectly spiced beef, onions and tomatoes cooked to a pleasing firmness—but Clover wouldn't be distracted from his mission. As the next round arrived, he realized he was already decisively inebriated. Lenny, who was more than two years younger and a good twenty pounds lighter, had to be feeling it too. That meant it was time to strike.

"So you really think Sophia will win the war?" Clover asked.

Lenny wiped a white slash of froth off his upper lip. "Obviously."

"But how? There are thousands of soldiers in the Protectorate. You couldn't match that if you conscripted everybody in town."

"We wouldn't need to. See, Sophia has done a lot of favors for a lot of people over the past fifty years. They'll come running when we need them. And besides, Zeno's got other tricks up her sleeve."

"Like what?"

Lenny put a finger over his lips. "I'm not supposed to say."

"Oh, come on. We're friends now, aren't we?"

"You wouldn't believe me anyway."

"Try me."

Lenny considered this, then broke into a smile. "Fine, fine, fine." He leaned over the table and whispered, "We can fly."

"Fly?"

"Yep. Like a bird! Woooo!"

Lenny made a little bird out of his right hand, his thumb and pinky acting as wings. It flapped around the table and came to rest on the lip of his empty mug, where it let out a single piercing squawk.

"I'm not interested in fairy tales, Lenny. I want the truth."

"Aha!" Lenny exclaimed, his bird transforming into a celebratory raised finger. "I told you you wouldn't believe me."

Clover chided himself for not taking things more slowly. Clearly Lenny was a good beer and a half beyond the point of no return; nothing he said now could be trusted.

When they were finished with their pies, Maya saw them to the door without any mention of recompense.

"You boys be careful out there," she said. "You're looking just a bit unsteady."

"And you're looking just a bit lovely," Lenny replied.

Maya smiled affectionately. "That's sweet of you to say, Lenny, even if you are half-blind from drinking. You come back soon now, all right?"

"You know I will."

Outside, the air was aglitter with tiny particles of snow, rendering the whole town picturesque and innocuous. Clover's earlier apprehension had been dissolved by Maya's kindness, the delicious meat pies, and the three mugs of beer.

"Lenny, before we go back, could you show me where the Dedios family lives?"

"I guess. But we don't have time to actually *go* there. It's a good ways out of town."

"That's okay. I just want to see it."

They followed the main road all the way down to the gate, then across the stone bridge over the Ivan. The snow-covered hills, which Clover knew would be golden with wheat and barley in the summer, reminded him of paper pulp drying in the deckle.

Lenny pointed toward a homestead in the middle distance—a bright red barn and a sprawling farmhouse.

"There it is. The three boys live there with Ms. Moses. She moved out from Amestown to take care of them after their da died and Paz left."

Blood on his lips the first time they'd kissed, her body a warm comma under the blankets. Lies upon lies upon lies.

"Did you know her?" Clover asked.

"I knew she was gorgeous. And smart as a whip, if what people said about her was true." Lenny belched. "You think she's dead now?"

Clover's voice caught—an unexpected upwelling of emotion. Stupid. If Paz was alive, she certainly wasn't sitting around worrying about *him*. He'd meant nothing to her. "Probably."

Clover noticed something in the sky to the west: a plume of smoke rising like a thin granite tower.

"What's that?"

Lenny squinted. "Probably just some Wesah."

"Zeno allows them that close to Sophia?"

"Why wouldn't she?"

Clover felt a flash of anger, remembering the night Gemma was taken. "Because they're savages who go around kidnapping innocent people. No *naasyoon* would ever make camp within sight of the Anchor. The Protectorate has a mandate to kill them."

"Well, I don't know what happens in the Anchor, but the Wesah here don't kidnap anyone." He was silent for a moment. Then, as if commenting on the weather, he added, "I was born Wesah."

Clover assumed Lenny had to be joking, or was back to his drunken fabrications. "No, you weren't."

"I was! But they don't ever keep baby boys, so they got rid of me. They left me just outside Geronimo, wrapped up in one of those pretty blankets they make. Some farmer found me and brought me to Huma, and she saw fit to raise me."

"Wow. I mean, I never would've guessed. Not by looking at you, anyway." Clover couldn't help but picture Lenny dressed as a Wesah warrior, and the image set him to laughing.

"Yeah," Lenny said. "I definitely wouldn't fit in. It's the willy, I think."

Then they were both laughing, and soon the alcohol dancing through their bloodstreams turned the laughter into something hysterical, breathless. Clover felt the tears leaking out of his eyes. He put a hand on Lenny's shoulder to steady himself, and Lenny did the same to him. He couldn't have said what was so funny, except that sometimes it seemed the better you got to know a person, the more bizarre they became.

"You two having a nice afternoon?"

Clover turned. Three boys stood at the other end of the bridge, blocking the way back to town. The one in the middle was the youngest—probably the same age as Lenny—while the others looked to be nineteen or twenty. The older two were definitely twins, only the symmetry had been destroyed by injury; one had a hook for a left hand, while the other was missing an ear.

"Speak of the devil," Lenny said. "Clover, that's Terry Dedios, Paz's little brother. And that's Eli and Leo Ferrell. They were part of the town guard that . . ." He trailed off as the palpable sense of menace at last penetrated his cocoon of intoxication.

"Are you the one who killed my da?" Terry Dedios said.

Clover was suddenly stone-cold sober. He considered trying to explain that it had technically been Gemma who wielded the knife that night, but what would be the point? He was every bit as guilty as she was, when it came down to it.

"We did what we had to do," he replied.

The boy missing an ear drew his gun. "Get out of here, Lenny," he said. "I wouldn't want you getting hurt."

"You aren't hurting anybody," Lenny said, stepping in front of Clover. Was it the alcohol making him reckless, or did he really care this much? Whatever the explanation, Clover was touched. "He's a scholar, Eli. Zeno made it official. You can't shoot him."

"Watch me." Eli cocked the gun and aimed it at Lenny's head. "On the count of three, I'm gonna shoot. It's up to you where you're standing."

"Get out of the way, Lenny," Clover said.

"I won't."

"One," Eli said.

There was nothing for it. Clover reached out and pulled Lenny backward so violently that the boy tumbled to the ground. Now he was staring straight down the barrel of Eli's gun.

"Two."

Clover felt surprisingly serene, almost relieved. Death had always been the most likely outcome of his inadvisable adventure in Sophia. And besides, he'd had a pretty good life. He'd traveled the country preaching the good word and singing songs with his family. He'd learned the secrets of the universe in the stacks beneath the Library. He'd known the ecstasy of love given and requited—even if it had turned out to be a lie.

Clover looked at Terry, into that face that was so much like hers. "I loved her," he said. "I just want you to know that."

He closed his eyes and waited for the end to come.

"Stop!"

A single word, shrieked from some great distance, too loud to ignore. Even before Clover opened his eyes and saw the shock of copper hair fluttering behind her like a standard, he knew it was Zeno. Eli grudgingly lowered the gun, though not before issuing one last threat.

TOMMY WALLACH

"Sooner or later, you're gonna pay for what you did."

Clover exhaled as Zeno reached the bridge. Red-faced with anger, she ordered everyone but Clover away: Terry back to the farm, Lenny to the academy, and the Ferrell brothers to the sheriff's office, "where we'll be having a nice long talk about your punishment."

When all of them were gone, she at last turned her rage on Clover.

"What the hell were you thinking, child?"

"I . . . we were just walking—"

"Hold on a moment." She stepped closer, sniffed Clover's breath. "Have you been drinking? Are you drunk?"

There was no point in lying. "Yes, ma'am. I'm sorry."

Zeno shook her head. Her voice dropped to a whisper, all the more terrifying for its softness. "I have agreed to let you stay at the academy only because I think you are intelligent. Your mind is your value. Do you understand me?"

Clover's gaze pawed the ground at Zeno's feet; even though she was his mortal enemy, he still felt guilty for having disappointed her. "Yes, ma'am."

"Good. Then get out of my sight before I have any more cause to doubt your intelligence."

8. Paz

TWO MEMBERS OF THE GRAND MARSHAL'S PERSONAL guard stood at the entrance to the Protectorate barracks, hands resting on the hilts of their swords, keeping a careful eye on Paz as she and Clive walked around the oval track that circumscribed the training fields. A jangling, panting pack of soldiers passed by every few minutes, hunched under the weight of their rucksacks, dripping with sweat even though it was still early April, only a week into the six-month season the Descendancy called summer. Paz never made eye contact; she despised them for the naked pleasure they took in seeing her physical degradation.

"How'd you sleep this week?" Clive asked.

"Better than before. But that's an extremely low bar."

"Did they bring you the pillow at least?"

"They did. For my sins."

Clive grinned. "Hard?"

"Granite."

"I'll see if I can get something else for you."

"Thanks."

The rules of the game were clear to them both: he would play the gentleman, attempting to earn her trust and through it, intelligence on Sophia. She would play the wounded bird, slowly nursed back to health by his care and attention. Except the fact that they both understood these rules changed them, created a game within the game.

Or was she overthinking it? Maybe the games existed only in her mind. Maybe Clive was telling the truth when he said that he'd given up on trying to get information from her, that he only wanted to provide her some comfort in this time of need. He was an Honor's son, after all; generosity and compassion were in his blood.

Paz wanted to believe him, but she was afraid to. There were dangerous currents of genuine feeling running beneath the frozen surface she presented to him, so when he'd asked her about the kiss they'd shared out on the old mining road, she'd had no choice but to lie. She wouldn't make herself so vulnerable as to admit that it had been as much Paz as Irene who had kissed him that day, or that her heart lifted whenever he came to see her, or that she wished they could start all over again from the beginning.

And what about the other thing—never to be mentioned, but all the more potent for remaining unspoken? Striding along beside her, long-limbed and clean-shaven, Clive cut an undeniably handsome figure. A part of her even responded to the uniform, its gleaming brass buttons and severe lines, like a well-made bed crying out to be disheveled. For weeks now, Paz had been without any human contact beyond Diana's savage ministrations. As she lay sleepless on the thin mattress in the hallucinatory darkness of her cell, it was impossible to keep her mind from wandering in Clive's direction. She was haunted by fantasies of what it might be like to run her fingers across his bare skin, to kiss his shoulder, his cheek, his lips. . . .

SLOW BURN   85

"I've been thinking a lot about Clover," Clive said.

Paz snapped back to reality. "What about him?"

"I don't know. Everything. Our childhood. How we stopped being friends."

"I thought that was my fault," Paz said, smiling just enough to thread the needle between joke and confession.

"It began a long time before you came along. We were so close when we were young, but then we turned out to be pretty different people—or turned *into* different people, anyway. I guess we couldn't figure out how to talk to each other once we realized that."

"Clover's not all that easy to talk to however you slice it. It takes work."

"You got through to him."

"Not me—Irene. He never knew the real me." Again, that strange duality—she believed what she'd just said, but she also wanted Clive to know that his brother had never understood her, never possessed her. She couldn't stop playing the game.

The soldiers passed by again, and Paz accidentally looked at one of them; immediately he hawked and spat, landing the glob on her unshod left foot. She managed to grab hold of Clive's arm just as he was turning to shout something.

"Don't," she said. "It's not worth the trouble."

"No touching!" one of Chang's guards yelled from across the training fields.

Paz let go of Clive and they continued walking. "I think about him too. Your brother, I mean. That look in his eyes when he realized who I really was—" She saw it even now, despite the intervening months and miles, and shook her head to clear it away. "I'll never forget it."

"Where do you think he is? I mean, assuming he's even alive."

A devious question, in its way—any answer would reveal *something* about Sophia. But was Clive inspired by genuine concern for Clover, or was he using his brother to guilt her into divulging Sophia's secrets? Even assuming the latter, Paz supposed she might as well tell the truth; she had to sacrifice a few scraps of information in every meeting with Clive, or else she risked losing the privilege of seeing him at all.

"Assuming your brother survived his injury, I can only imagine he's being treated well. He's the son of an Honor with knowledge of the inner workings of the Library. That makes him valuable."

"You don't think they tortured him?"

"I doubt they had to. After all, he went to them willingly."

Clive frowned. "I still don't understand why he did it. I mean, when did he start hating us?"

She was still considering how she might best deploy her trump card: the knowledge that Clover wasn't actually a traitor, but the Epistem's spy. The fact that Clive hadn't found out on his own by now could only mean that the Church was knowingly keeping the information from the Protectorate. And *that* meant there were schisms within the Descendancy—just when it most needed to be unified.

"I think I have an idea," Paz said. Here was the half-truth she'd decided to divulge today, hopefully buying herself another few minutes in the sun later on this week. "Do you know where Clover was the night of the plebiscite?"

"No, but I do remember him running off all of a sudden. Bishop Allen's innocent came to find him."

"That's right. But he didn't take Clover to Notre Fille. He took him to the Library, so he could visit the anathema stacks."

"That's ridiculous," Clive scoffed.

"I didn't understand it either, but it's the truth. And the things your brother learned that night, they changed him. He started saying the whole Descendancy was built on lies."

Clive narrowed his eyes. Obviously this was a lot for him to swallow, especially considering the source. "If that's true, then why didn't you tell him *you* were working for Sophia? You could've run off together."

"I knew he was upset. I never would've guessed he'd turn traitor. Besides"—and here she hesitated, suddenly afraid she might end up admitting to more than she wanted to—"I didn't want to run off with him."

They walked on in silence, and for a moment, Paz entertained the fancy that she and Clive were just a couple of sweethearts on a promenade through the park, content to say nothing, to simply be close to each other. She knew she'd never have someone like that, would never experience anything so blissfully ordinary. But her arm faintly burned with the desire to be laced through his, to bring her hip to his hip, her head to his shoulder. The backs of their hands were so close, she imagined she could feel the heat off his skin.

"No touching!" one of the guards shouted, and Clive quickly stepped away.

◆   ◆   ◆

TOMMY WALLACH

A few days later Paz awoke from a rare sweet dream to find a soldier she'd never seen before standing just outside her cell. He looked to be in his early twenties, with long black hair and an unruly beard. He held a gnarled birch broom in his right hand.

"Are you here to clean up?" she said groggily. "It's about time."

"One of the guards noticed that you've been writing poems," the soldier said.

She considered denying it, but what would be the point? Even in the flickering torchlight, the words were legible enough, if you knew where to look.

"Nothing seditious," she replied, trying her best to sound charming. "Just the idle musings of a girl. Mostly love poems. I could read you some if you like."

The soldier shoved the broom between the bars of her cell. "Sweep them up."

Her heart fell. The poems were all that kept her going in the days between visits from Clive. "Please let me keep them," she said. "I'll do anything." She reached out for him. "I used to be prettier than I am now, but maybe you—"

The soldier dropped the broom and drew his sword. "If you make me come in there to sweep it out myself, I'll take a piece of you back with me."

She recoiled, as much from her own behavior as his threat. Had she really fallen so far, that she would trade her body for the right to scribble doggerel in the dirt?

"Yes, sir," she said quietly, taking up the broom.

As she swept up the words, she tried to engrave them in her memory, like the tattoos engraved in her skin. But she knew it was a lost cause. In a good poem, every syllable was sacrosanct; to lose a piece was to lose the whole. She tried to preserve one of the smaller verses in the rearmost corner of her cell, but the guard noticed and made her stomp it out with her feet. She began to cry, silently, so he wouldn't have the pleasure of knowing he'd hurt her.

"If you ever write another word, we'll take your mattress," he said after she'd finished. Then he grabbed the broom and walked away.

When she was sure he was gone, she allowed herself a good cry, wringing the anguish out of herself like water from a wet towel. It was only after she'd finished wiping the blear from her eyes that she noticed it: a scrap of paper on the ground outside her cell. The soldier must've dropped it. Reaching her fingers through the bars, she was just able to pinch a corner—grease-stained wax paper, tightly folded. The message inside was written in a compact, elegant hand.

> *Brave Girl:*
> *Zeno has not forgotten you. Only survive. We are*
> *coming.*
> *—The Mindful*

9. Gemma

O N A MORNING SOMEWHERE NEAR THE BEGINNING OF March, Gemma woke to the sun rising like a curtain, spreading a layer of melted butter across the prairie. The rest of the *naasyoon* was still asleep; for a moment, the world belonged to her and her alone. Last night they'd made camp in a valley of stone, surrounded on all sides by towering cliffs, serried and serrated, banded with alternating strips of light and dark that reminded Gemma of the grooves that appeared on pots as they were thrown, how you needed only touch the surface of the spinning clay with your fingernail to carve a perfectly straight line all the way around. She took up her spear and set off through the tall grass, away from the encampment, in pursuit of nothing but distance. She felt like a child, momentarily free of the future, free of the past, reveling in the perfect present. Maybe that was why the garden of Aleph and Eva was referred to in the Filia as "Paradise." Not because of its beauty, or the temporary innocence of its ill-fated residents, but because of its existence outside of time.

Of course, a bit of beauty didn't hurt either.

Over the past week, the landscape through which the *naasyoon* traveled had grown ravishingly severe: vast plains divided by sheer rock walls that stretched for miles, castles of rust and umber, lone buttes looming like watchtowers. Just yesterday, they'd passed four impossibly enormous faces carved into a cliffside.

"Are they sacred?" Gemma asked, in her halting Wesah.

"No more than other stones," Athène replied.

After almost two months traveling with the *naasyoon*, Gemma's understanding of the Wesah religion—though "religion" was probably the wrong word for it—remained hazy. Growing up, she'd been taught that the Wesah worshipped everything—each passing cloud, each dead leaf skittering across the road, each creepy creeping beetle—and that this sort of indiscriminate devotion was equivalent to nonbelief. Their wild dances and protracted songs were judged as immodest and false, savage and strange.

But she knew better now. While it was true that the Wesah recognized the spiritual value in every plant and animal, this was only appreciation, not worship. Their dances and songs functioned as an expression of this appreciation, which made it far less obviously "religious" than the dancing and singing at a Descendancy gathering. And though the warrior women didn't believe in the God of the Filia, they had their own deities—and who was to say that the Almighty couldn't manifest to different people in different ways? Who was to say the Conflagration (known to the Wesah as *mooshkahun di feu*, or "the Flame Deluge") hadn't been brought to the world by the shape-shifting Fox, rather than God's Daughter? Did such distinctions even matter?

Gemma was at least a mile from the encampment by now—well out of sight. She hoisted her spear overhead and began running through some of the exercises that Athène had taught her: slip and spin, feint and thrust, switch hands and repeat. The weapon was

TOMMY WALLACH

five feet of solid ash, tipped with chert cooked over a fire and flaked to a vicious point. When she'd begun, Gemma could scarcely get through a single cycle; now she could go a dozen times before stopping to rest. She took pride in the fact that the other tribeswomen no longer laughed when they saw her practicing—but she still preferred to do it on her own.

Gemma groaned as she once again tossed the spear from one hand to the other. Her every muscle ached for respite.

Never stop until your body makes you stop, Athène liked to say. *Then go a little more.*

The rest of the *naasyoon* had woken by now. Their chortles and cries carried across the valley floor. A cloud of smoke billowed upward from the encampment, signaling that the *nisklaav* had begun preparing breakfast. Gemma scanned her surroundings for a target. She settled on a prickly pear cactus about sixty feet off and imagined the topmost pad was Paz's face. With her last ounce of strength, she sent the spear flying, whooping when it pierced the tough rind of the pad dead center.

Back in camp, Gemma took a seat at the fire and ate her breakfast. Though she wouldn't have said she felt "accepted" by the *naasyoon* just yet, no one seemed to actively resent her presence anymore. Well, no one except Noémie: the woman could've made a career out of giving dirty looks. Gemma did her best to ignore the waves of odium, focusing instead on the conversations going on around her. When Athène pulled her aside after the meal, Gemma predicted what the chieftain was going to say.

"You're going on a hunt," she said.

"Yes! Good listening, my little dancer!" Athène beamed at her student's progress. "Nearby, there is a place where the buffalo go for water. We're close to the Villenaître, and this will make for a good gift."

Gemma liked it when the *naasyoon* went hunting; it gave her time to wander, and to train. "Good luck," she said. "I hope you bring down some big ones."

"I hope so too," the chieftain replied. "That's why I want you to come."

Gemma assumed Athène's grasp of English must have failed her. Nothing was more sacred to the Wesah than the hunt. "Come where?"

"Where I go."

"But you're going hunting."

Athène groaned with frustration. "Yes! You come to the hunt. With me. With your sisters."

Gemma was nonplussed. "I—but I'm *aan dahor.*"

"No! You are sister. You are *nimish*. And you tell me you hunt many times before. You know how use bow on horse?"

Gemma failed to stifle a laugh. She'd been teaching the chieftain how to ask a question in English, by inflecting the final syllable upward. But when Athène did it, she often slid up a whole octave— *You know how use bow on HORSE?*

Athène couldn't help but notice Gemma's amusement. "I did it again, *chee.*"

"It's getting better every day," Gemma replied. "And yes, I know how to use a bow." She didn't mention that she'd been riding and shooting since she was six years old, or that she'd once won a prize for it at a county fair: five bronze shekels and a tin crown for hitting a scarecrow in the face while galloping past it at full tilt. Better to exceed low expectations than fail to fulfill high ones.

"Good. Then you come." The chieftain put on a playful scowl. "Soon you speak Wesah all the time. Then we won't need this stupid broken English."

The hunt always began with a ceremony. Over the beat of a single drum, a tribeswoman recited what was either a short story or a long poem. As far as Gemma could tell, the goal was to "summon" the animals the *naasyoon* was planning to hunt.

After the ceremony was over, the hunting party proceeded northwest, through a cleft in the cliffs and across a wide, dusty plain of yellow earth and sagebrush. Gemma rode alone, as usual; Athène was still the only person in the *naasyoon* she would call a friend, and at the moment, the chieftain was deep in conversation with Noémie. Watching them, Gemma felt gripped by something like jealousy, which she knew was silly. It wasn't as if she wanted what the other woman had—she only missed having someone to talk to. Overhead, a hawk made long, lazy loops—so seemingly serene, you'd never know it was a predator.

The hunting party traversed the plain and mounted a steep trail cut into the escarpment at the other end. The horses slowed, stepping gingerly among the crumbly, uneven rocks. Half an hour later, they gained the ridge. A surprisingly verdant prairie lay spread out beneath them. At the eastern edge, a few dozen buffalo were arranged around a sparkling sapphire of wind-flecked water. The *naasyoon* circled up and Athène briefly laid out the plan. The watering hole was bordered by high rock faces on two sides; if they approached from the right angle, they could corral the animals, leaving them nowhere to run.

On Athène's command, the warriors kicked their horses into a gallop. Their collective shriek echoed across the prairie; there was no need for quiet now, as the goal was to spook the buffalo into cornering themselves. Gemma took a deep breath, wanting so badly to join in, then exhaled without making a sound; she felt like an impostor, a little girl playing at being a Wesah warrior.

The buffalo began to react, and while the majority of them had the sense to run around the *naasyoon*, about a dozen fled backward, toward the cliffs. Daughter's love but they were big—fat brown clouds of fur and flesh. Gemma couldn't fathom how those skinny legs were able to support all that weight, or to move the animals so efficiently across the spongy ground around the watering hole.

Though the hunting party was still a couple of hundred feet away from the closest buffalo bull, Gemma heard the whistle of an arrow being loosed, followed by a harmonious chorus of whistles as the other warriors followed suit. She took her own bow off her shoulder and drew an arrow. The buffalo were a lot less stationary than the competition targets Gemma was used to shooting at, but they were also about ten times bigger. Here came one now, almost close enough to touch. Even before she fit the arrow to the bowstring, she knew she would find her mark.

Twang. Hiss. A cry of pain.

There was a chorus of celebratory shouts, which Gemma assumed had to be related to something else. Yet when she glanced around, the warriors nearby were staring right at her, nodding their approval.

Maybe she wasn't an impostor after all.

The buffalo she'd shot was still on its feet, moving fast; a single arrow was hardly more than a splinter to a beast so large. Gemma considered choosing a new target—there was a smaller bull splashing around the shallow end of the pond—but she didn't like the idea of hurting another animal unnecessarily, so took aim at the one she'd already hit instead. Even though its injury had spurred it to run even faster, to buck and weave unpredictably, she managed to land a second arrow, this one just below the hump. The beast bleated loudly, kicking out its back feet as if it might dislodge the bolt that way, but still showed no sign of stopping. A third arrow, placed just next to the second one, had a similarly imperceptible effect. The bull was nearing the open prairie and freedom; soon it would be out of range. Gemma nocked another arrow, knowing it was her last chance to take the animal down and fully earn the tribe's respect.

But before she could shoot, she was distracted by the high whine of an arrow rushing past her ear. She watched it go, a black minnow cleaving the air, momentarily doubled as it flew over the surface of the pond, then sliding smoothly into the buffalo's left eye socket. The beast took one or two more lumbering steps before crashing down onto its belly, dead.

Gemma turned her horse about and saw Noémie lowering her bow. Their eyes met. Noémie tapped her cheek and mouthed a single, unmistakable word—*Moon*—before riding off in search of her next kill.

Gemma mirrored the gesture. Her fingers came away smeared with blood from where Noémie's arrow had skimmed her skin.

SLOW BURN

It took the rest of the day to see to the buffalo—removing the hides, cutting away the sinew (which would be used to make bowstrings and rope), smashing the bones to reach the marrow. Afterward, the meat was laid out in thick marbled slabs, bloody and weirdly appetizing. The fat still had to be separated from the muscle, the former rendered and the latter broken into pieces, then all of it mixed with berries and reconstituted as pemmican. But that work would have to wait until tomorrow.

In the past, Gemma had kept away from the festivities that attended a successful hunt, refusing out of some sense of obligation to the religion she still liked to believe that she believed. But she'd been a member of the hunting party this time. More than that, it was her arrow that first found flesh. To fail to appear at tonight's celebration would be an unforgivable offense.

Besides, she didn't want Noémie to think she could be scared off.

Rugaru and Gornoy had spent the day gathering wood and arranging it in an elaborate pyre, and now they set the heap ablaze. A few chunks of buffalo meat were thrown into the fire—an offering to a minor deity called Wisakedjak. The drummers started up a dizzyingly complex rhythm, like the hoofbeats of a dozen horses galloping, and soon after, four of the tribeswomen donned capes festooned with feathers and began an elaborate choreographed dance, yelping and clapping, stomping and capering, sending clouds of dust up to shimmer in the firelight. After a while, the rest of the *naasyoon*—even the *nisklaav*—joined in the dance.

Gemma watched them for a few minutes, trying and failing to make sense of their movements. In the Anchor, there were really only two types of dancing: the slow, swaying kind, and the fast, frenetic kind, the first of which was reserved for couples, and the second for small groups. The Wesah's dances didn't involve any sort of partnering or grouping, or not by design at any rate, and Gemma couldn't discern any uniformity of gesture that she might mimic. An older warrior alternated between shaking her hands over her head and then folding in half and shaking them down at her ankles. Another tribeswoman, this one at least six months pregnant, strode purposefully around the fire as if she were stalking an animal. Others circled one another as if preparing to fight, making horrible faces and animal sounds all the while.

Gemma realized she was even more nervous now than she'd been out on the hunt. An arrow through the head seemed far preferable to humiliating herself just as she was beginning to win the *naasyoon*'s respect. But her stillness was conspicuous in its own right. She had no choice but to give in to the rhythm, bouncing around in her own particular way, and hope for the best. She kept her eyes closed, not wanting to know if people were looking at her, until she forgot about the very possibility of embarrassment.

An hour passed, then two; before long, Gemma lost track of time entirely. More wood was thrown on the fire. Clothes were shed, until the majority of the *naasyoon* was dressed only in leather skirts or loincloths. Gemma couldn't bring herself to join them in their half-nakedness, but she felt a strange joy in seeing all that flesh exposed, all those different sizes and shapes, shaking and shimmying and shining. Why was it that women in the Anchor were taught to be ashamed of their nipples when men were allowed to parade *theirs* around whenever they wanted? Men didn't even *use* the damn things!

Someone passed Gemma the pipe that she'd noticed circulating around the *naasyoon*. She put it to her lips and inhaled deeply—tobacco mixed with sage and sumac, filling her lungs with sweet fire.

"*Maarsi*," she said, handing it back again. She froze when she realized who it was that had given it to her. Noémie looked like a completely different person with her hair loosed from its braids and her skin sheened with perspiration.

"*Taanishi*, Gemma." She pronounced Gemma's name more like *Schemma*.

"*Taanishi*."

A pause. "I am sorry," Noémie said in heavily accented English. "Sorry for arrow." It was an apology in name only. The woman's clenched jaw could be seen through the skin of her cheek, and her eyes were hard as flint. She raised her hand, and Gemma flinched, afraid of being struck. Instead, Noémie drew her fingers down to Gemma's hip. "We go to sleep, *chee*."

Gemma frowned. "Now?"

"Yes. You and me. Sleep, *chee*." She stepped closer, snaking her arm around Gemma's back, sweat-wet and blood-hot. Her breath smelled of the pipe smoke, and twin fires danced in her black eyes.

Sleep didn't mean sleep; sleep meant the opposite of sleep.

Honor Hamill's face flared up in Gemma's memory, declaiming about lust and sin and eternal perdition. She pulled away, rejecting both Noémie's offer and the devilish curiosity she sensed in herself. "No!" she said loudly, as if chastising a wayward dog. "Get away!"

Noémie's false contrition melted away, revealing a terrifying rictus of pure hate—the sting of being spurned just another entry in

TOMMY WALLACH

her long list of grievances. She stalked off without another word, into the darkness beyond the bright circle of firelight.

Gemma considered calling out after her—but what would she say? Sorry? I just want to be friends? Her grasp of the Wesah language wasn't nearly strong enough to guide her through such an emotionally complex situation. Come to think of it, she probably couldn't have managed it in English either.

All at once, she realized how fooolish she'd been to think she might ever fit in here. Gemma was a stranger among strangers, *aan dahor*, the enemy. She ran back to her empty tent and leaned her forehead against the canvas, mind racing, body shaking with anxiety. Why would Noémie proposition her like that? What sort of trap had she been laying?

The tent flap opened. Gemma tensed, ready to pounce, ready for Noémie's next arrow. But it was only Athène, flushed from the heat of the fire and the dancing, eyes soft with concern.

"Why are you here?" she asked.

"I was tired," Gemma said.

The chieftain sat down beside her. Scent of salt and smoke, the distant tang of animal blood. "You did well today," she said in English. "You shoot like a Wesah."

"I was lucky."

"No. No luck."

Something cold pressed against Gemma's arm: one of Athène's copper bracelets. Gemma tapped it with her fingernail.

"Is it true that these help you keep count of the men you've killed?"

"Not just count. Also remember." Athène turned her hands over, showing off her many rings. "They have weight. Make hard to shoot the arrow. Hard to throw the spear. That is the cost. You understand, *chee?*"

Gemma nodded. She understood all too well. "I killed a man," she said.

The chieftain looked genuinely surprised. "You did?"

"He wanted to hurt me and my family. I didn't have a choice."

Gemma sank briefly into the memory. The briefest instant of resistance when the knife first found flesh. The sickening shudder as it slipped through the skin, so smoothly, as if it were only returning to the sheath. How easy it was, to take a life. And how hard.

She started when Athène took hold of her hand.

"Here," the chieftain said. She slid one of her bracelets down her arm and over both their wrists, fitting it snugly at Gemma's bicep. "You carry the weight now."

"Thank you," Gemma said. They sat there in silence for a moment, still hand in hand. "Noémie asked to go to bed with me, even though she hates me. Why?"

"I asked for this. To help you find friendship."

"That isn't how we find friendship where I come from."

Athène smiled mischievously. "I know. Your people like hide everything. Quiet, quiet. Pretend nobody makes the love. Pretend babies come from the sky." Gemma couldn't help but smile too. Funny how something that seemed so normal and necessary could be revealed as foolish when seen from a different perspective.

"Have you ever make love?" Athène asked.

"No," Gemma whispered, her heart beginning to pound. "I . . . I was never married. I was supposed to be, but it didn't work out. He didn't, or I didn't . . ."

She trailed off. There was a hand on the bare skin of her ankle. How odd. And even odder, the hand was gliding slowly up her leg, pushing her leather skirt aside, momentarily settling at the very top of her thigh. Gemma was watching herself from very far away now—a God's-eye view. (Iniquitous. Depraved.) The drumming and singing outside seemed to grow fainter, and all she could hear was her breath, shallow and ragged, as her legs parted involuntarily and Athène's fingers accepted the invitation, sliding ever upward, relentless, until the impossible moment . . .

She wouldn't let it go on for long. Any second now, she would slap Athène's hand away, feigning offense, feigning disgust, feigning horror. Any second now, she would once again become recognizable to herself.

Any second now . . .

10. Clive

CLIVE WATCHED FLORA SCRABBLE AT THE PAPER WITH her sharp little fingernails.

"You don't have to tear it," Mitchell Poplin said, to no avail.

Inside the package, a marionette lay like a little girl asleep, its tiny head pillowed by an aureole of corn-silk hair. Flora took hold of the cross bar and lifted the doll up, tittering at its queer almost-life—a reanimated corpse, dancing loose-limbed and joyless.

"You like it?" Mitchell said.

Flora glanced at Clive and gave him a little wink. She'd discovered the unfinished marionette in a workshop closet two weeks ago, so she'd known the gift was coming. Still, she did a decent job simulating surprise. "It's beautiful," she said, and threw her arms around her grandfather's neck, sending the doll flying over his shoulder.

"Careful! She's delicate."

"Sorry, Grampy." Flora leaned back in her chair and set the marionette to walking across the dining room table. "So where's *your* present, Clive?"

"Nice try, you little monster. I got you a violin."

"That wasn't a birthday present! That was just a . . . a *present* present."

"Oh, you want a *birthday* present," Clive said, as if he'd only just understood. "Well, aren't you lucky, I've got one right here. It's an ickle-tay."

"What's an ickle-tay?" Flora had already begun to laugh. "I don't want it!" she shouted.

"Too bad! Ickle-tay!"

He pounced, tickling Flora's belly until she fell off the chair and started writing around on the floor.

"Stop! Stop!" she cried out between giggles.

A flash of a memory, like something momentarily glimpsed through the trees—Clover laughing hysterically as Clive tickled him just like this. Had they been in the old house, or out on the road? Had their parents been there too, smiling to see their sons getting along so well?

Daughter's love, I shot him.

"What's wrong?" Flora asked. Clive hadn't even noticed he'd stopped tickling her.

"Nothing. I'm just tuckered out, I guess." He managed to dredge up a smile. "But I really do have another present for you."

"Is it another ickle-tay?"

"No." Clive glanced into the kitchen, where Mitchell was cleaning up the dishes. Lowering his voice, he said, "We're going to see Louise play."

Flora's eyes lit up. "You mean music?"

"Shh! And yeah, I mean music. Just don't say anything to your grandpa. Trust me, he wouldn't want us going where we're going."

Flora mimed sewing her lips shut, then sticking the needle in her eye. With lips tightly pursed and one eye squinted shut, she started humming a happy tune.

Clive had met Louise Delancey when they were both only eight years old, the two youngest members of the Notre Fille Children's Choir. They'd bonded over their love of the guitar, and though Louise's ability soon outpaced Clive's, they remained friends and collaborators, writing songs together and performing at numerous Church events. Louise even joined the Hamill ministry on a couple of short tours, where her virtuosic fingerpicking regularly stole the show. ("When she's around, nobody even bothers listening to the sermon," Clive's father had groused.) In the past few years, she'd managed to make a name for herself in the Anchor, and she and her band did regular tours around the Descendancy in a single large wagon that doubled as a stage. Clive hadn't seen her in years, but just last week, she'd reached out to invite him and Flora to tonight's performance.

I'm sorry we've been out of touch for so long, she'd written, *and I was real sorry to hear about what you all have been through. It would be a pleasure to catch up.*

Bennigan's Music Hall sat squat and unkempt in a dark corner of the Anchor's Second Quarter. The area was considered a slum by everyone except its residents—artists and musicians, pickpockets and prostitutes. Entering Bennigan's after so long away, Flora's hand held tightly in his own, Clive remembered the frisson of wicked excitement he'd always felt coming here with Louise. The place was exactly as he remembered it: grimy, clamorous, crammed to bursting. There were broken-down guitars nailed all over the walls; Bennigan, the owner, liked to call them his offerings to the god of music.

"Stay close to me," Clive said.

"As if I've got a choice," Flora replied. "I can't even feel my fingers."

Clive loosened his grip. "Sorry."

He found an open spot near the back of the room, which would allow them to make a quick exit if a fight broke out or the dancing got too rowdy, but Flora was having none of it.

"I can't see from here!" she moaned.

"You're two feet tall. The only way you'd be able to see is if we were in the front row."

"I'm four feet and three inches, thank you very much. And anyway, that just means we *should* be in the front row."

"It's already filled up."

"But it's my *birthday!*"

Clive groaned: he'd never been able to say no to Flora (or any of the Poplin children, really). He put his arms around her tiny waist and lifted her up, holding her in front of him like a squirmy human shield. Flora apologized as Clive shouldered his way toward the front of the room: "Excuse me. It's my birthday. Pardon me. Birthday girl coming through." The crowd grudgingly parted for this shameless exploitation of a winsome child, and soon enough, Clive and Flora found themselves pressed up against the stage.

The players were already in position, trying to tune over the din. Clive recognized the bassist, a flashy musician by the name of Roanoke, given to frequent and unnecessary slaps and spins, but the other members of the band were unknown to him. The fiddle player, he noticed, had disciplinary tattoos around each wrist.

Louise stood front and center, her ear bent to the sound hole of her guitar as she plucked the strings one by one. Though she'd never been traditionally beautiful, her confidence and skill as a performer made her attractive, and she'd grown into herself since Clive had seen her last. Her white dress, cut just above the knee, revealed at least twice as much skin as you could get away with showing off at a Church gathering.

She looked up from the guitar and smiled hugely.

"Clive!" she said, leaning down and offering her cheek for a kiss. "And little Flora. Only not so little anymore."

"It's my birthday!" Flora announced yet again.

"Is it? Well, happy birthday to you." She stood back up. "We'll talk after I play a couple of tunes, if that's all right by you."

The band got started a few minutes later. Louise had been an exceptional vocalist even at the age of ten, but her tone had only grown richer and more expressive with age. She growled and groaned. She whispered seductively. Then her voice would suddenly empty of affectation, turn limpid as a mountain stream. The set was half standards and half originals. Clive even recognized a variation of a song they'd written together during one of the ministry tours, though it took him a moment to realize why it sounded so different: Louise wasn't playing a normal guitar. This one had twice the usual number of pegs up top, making for twelve strings in all. This doubling changed the music in some fundamental way—the instrument shimmered where a six-string would only twang. Clive was sure the Andersons had never made a guitar like that; he'd have to ask her where she got it.

"This is a new number," Louise said, as the applause for the last song died away. "It's called 'We're Only Dancing.'"

She counted off a waltz tempo, and the fiddle double-stopped its way into the opening figure. Louise crooned a series of subtle innuendos—romance shading into raciness. When she reached the second verse, she turned her gaze down toward the front row. "*The clock's tick-tocking. Pick up the pace. The prey you're stalking is worth the chase. It's just a song. It's just a touch. We're only dancin'. Don't think so much.*"

It couldn't just be his imagination; she was looking right at him, out of the tops of her eyes. She'd always been an intense performer—Clive remembered seeing her cry once during a rendition of "What a Weight"—but he'd never had that intensity trained directly on him before. Was she flirting, or was it just part of the show? He looked away, suddenly nervous, then chided himself silently for it. What was there to be nervous about? They were two unattached young people. There was nothing stopping them from flirting, or kissing, or getting married if they wanted to.

So why did the very thought of touching her feel like some kind of betrayal?

It couldn't be because of Gemma; Clive had let go of his romantic feelings for her long before she'd been kidnapped. Which left only one explanation, as obvious as it was ridiculous: Paz.

He'd spent most of the past month either with her or thinking about being with her, and clearly it was starting to get to him. He dreamed about her almost every night. Some of these dreams were fanciful alterations of memories—the two of them lying together on that dusty mining road where they'd kissed, or admitting their love for each other after Clive caught her in the woods outside Sophia. Others were pure inventions, alternate realities in which Paz simply replaced Gemma whole cloth.

It was wrong, of course. Paz was a traitor. A monster. He

couldn't think of her that way. And here he was, not five feet from a charming, brilliant girl trying her damnedest to turn his head. What the hell was he thinking?

The next time she smiled at him, he made sure to smile right back.

"So?" Clive said after the set was finished. "What'd you think?"

Flora put on an ironically serious expression. "Pretty good. Not as good as *we* used to be, but still pretty good."

Clive caught sight of Louise pushing her way through a wall of adulation and inebriation to meet them at the foot of the stage.

"I'm so glad you made it!" she said, drawing Clive into a hug. She was damp with perspiration, and the smell of her reminded him of his childhood.

"You were great," he said. "Really great."

"Thanks."

"By the way, where did you get that guitar? I've never seen one like it."

"A luthier I met in the outerlands. He makes 'em for a hobby, if you can believe it."

Louise's fiddle player came up behind her. "These friends of yours?" he said.

"They are! Clive, Flora, this is Ralph."

"Good to meet you," Clive said, putting out a hand. As they shook, Clive was able to make out the word encircling Ralph's wrists: *violence*. It was one of the more common disciplinary tattoos, bestowed on the kind of men given to bar fights.

"So you want to give the twelve-string a whirl before you go?" Louise asked.

"Sure."

"Come on with me. It's in the dressing room."

They climbed up onto the stage and through the red curtains at the back. The dressing room was tiny and squalid, its furnishings a good decade past their prime: a chaise with stuffing leaking from holes in the upholstery, an old upright piano missing half the keys, and a bunch of thin, scabrous cushions. Louise took her guitar off a hook on the wall and handed it to Clive.

He attempted an arpeggio, but his fingers struggled to catch both strings at once.

"Here," Louise said, offering him a tortoiseshell plectrum. "Fingerpicking takes some practice."

"I can't believe you can do it at all," he replied. He took the plectrum and strummed a chord. The sound wasn't just louder than that made by a normal guitar, but thicker, sweeter—warm honey to a six-string's sugar water. He closed his eyes and began playing through the verse section of "In Her Name." It felt as if this one instrument were doing the work of a whole band. When he finished, he gave a little whistle.

"That's something, all right. I'd kill for one of . . ." He trailed off. He and Louise were alone. "Where's Flora?"

Louise looked around. "Ralph must've taken her to get a glass of water or something. I'm sure she'll be back. Let's sing something together, yeah? Like the old days?"

Clive set the guitar aside. "I really need to find Flora. Her grandfather will—"

"Clive! I never knew you to be the anxious type."

"I'm not anxious."

"No? You're practically shaking." She took a step closer, smiling the same way she had during the performance. "You know, I hadn't seen you in so long, I hardly recognized you. You've grown up to be quite a handsome man."

"Thank you."

She laughed. "This is the part where you tell me I'm beautiful, Clive."

"You are." Only why would Flora go off with a man she'd just met, and without saying anything? "But I need to go." He pushed Louise aside and stepped back through the curtains. From the stage, he could see out over the whole cramped venue, but there wasn't enough light to make out most of the faces.

The front door opened, and someone about Ralph's height and build hurried through.

"Hey!" Clive cried, but there was no hope of being heard over the cacophony. He jumped down from the stage and forced his way through the crowd. It seemed an eternity before he was able to make it outside.

The street was quiet. Light pooled in perfect circles under the gaslights, shrinking into the distance like an ellipsis. There was no sign of Ralph or Flora anywhere. Clive forcefully separated the couple canoodling just beside the door.

"Did you see a little blond girl pass by here a few seconds ago?"

The man, whose wispy mustache was smeared with lipstick, smiled snidely. "You into little girls, buddy?"

Clive grabbed him by the lapels and shoved him up against the wall. The woman he was with shrieked and ran back inside. "Did you see her or not?"

TOMMY WALLACH

"No, I fucking didn't! I wasn't exactly paying attention to the scenery, was I?"

Clive tossed the man aside and started running, down the narrow lane and out onto the Purple Road. A vagabond was slumped over like a black haystack in the doorway of a butcher shop. Two streetwalkers chatted with a potential john.

It was hopeless. One needed only a few seconds to disappear in this city. Clive turned at the patter of footsteps on the cobblestones behind him. It was Louise, wearing an expression of grim apology.

"I'm sorry, Clive. It was the only way."

His blood froze. So this was why Louise had invited him and Flora here in the first place; she and Ralph had been planning tonight's abduction for weeks. "Only way to do what?"

"To free Paz Dedios."

It was the last thing Clive had expected to hear, and rendered him momentarily nonplussed.

"I'm part of a group called the Mindful," Louise continued. "We're working with Director Zeno to help Sophia win the war."

"Why?" Clive whispered.

"Because the Church has purposely kept us in the dark for centuries! You have no idea what humanity is capable of when we're allowed to exercise our imaginations and our ingenuity. Do you know how much better our lives could be? I've seen the things Sophia has made. They're like magic!"

Clive had seen them too, of course. The telegraph machine, which had allowed Riley to summon the posse to the pumphouse. Those glowing glass bulbs that turned night into day. The guns that had blown the life out of so many people he'd loved.

"But why do you need Paz?"

"For what she represents. The citizens of the Descendancy don't trust the Protectorate yet. If the Grand Marshal loses his most important prisoner, the doubts will multiply."

"And what if I refuse to help you?"

Louise sighed. "Are you really going to make me say it?" Clive stayed silent: damn right he was going to make her say it. "I don't want to hurt her—"

"Then don't."

"—but I will. If a sweet little girl is killed in the middle of the Anchor by an anonymous group of Sophian sympathizers, the people will be terrified, and the Protectorate's reputation will suffer. We win either way."

Clive couldn't stand to look at Louise anymore; one more second of that fanatical brightness in her eyes and he'd smash her face in— which would be as good as signing Flora's death warrant. To agree to Louise's plan would almost certainly mean his life, whether he failed or succeeded. But what choice did he have? He'd already lost everyone else he cared about; he couldn't lose Flora, too.

Louise smiled sadly. "I know you think I'm the villain here, but I'm not. You're on the wrong side of history, Clive. Someday soon, you're gonna realize that, and then you'll forgive me for what I had to do tonight."

Clive didn't have any faith in his ability to predict the future; the last year had been one horrible surprise after another. But he felt confident that whatever happened in the months to come, he would never forgive Louise for putting Flora's life in danger.

"Enough of your goddamned sanctimony," he snarled. "Just tell me what you need me to do."

       TOMMY WALLACH

11. Clover

STEPPING OUT ONTO THE ACADEMY ROOF, CLOVER IMME-diately regretted leaving his sweater back in his room. The morning air still had an edge to it, whetted by the brisk breeze. He'd never been up here before; the roof doors had an ingenious mechanism built into the wood above the knob: brass buttons engraved with Greek characters that had to be pressed in a specific order to unlock. But last night, he'd returned from a long study session at the library to find a note on his pillow—*Come to the roof at sunrise*—along with the code for the door. He figured it was finally time for his inevitable dressing-down from Zeno; he hadn't seen hide nor hair of her in the two weeks since those twin boys had nearly killed him out on the bridge.

So here he was, stiff and bleary, eyelashes gritty with sleep. To the south, the town of Sophia lay perfectly still and silent, spread across the hillside like a toy model of a town. Everything was miniaturized by the distance, trivialized. The round white face of the clock tower appeared no bigger than a shekel, and the granite bridge over the Ivan was a stray strand of gray hair. He could almost pretend the tiny red dot of the Dedios farmhouse meant nothing to him.

He'd expected the roof to be more or less empty, and was sur-prised to find the whole thing covered in plant beds. They were built from a motley assortment of woods and in various sizes, such that each one looked unique. The warm turn was still six weeks off, so there was nothing to be seen in the beds but dark brown earth and a few snails. Little wooden stakes announced what plants would go where, and thanks to the training he'd undergone to prepare for his imaginary role as Library herbologist, Clover recognized many of them: vetiver and yarrow, kohlrabi and muskmelon. A set of eight raised beds were already trellised for wine grapes (or possibly tomatoes), though there would be no sign of the vines for a while yet.

The wind kicked up, raising goose pimples on Clover's skin and sparking the ache in his shoulder. He'd yet to recover full function in his left arm—it was as if there was a sort of delay every time he tried to use it—and Lila had grown cagier about his prospects. Would Clive feel guilty, knowing he'd lamed his brother for life? Or would he just be sorry he hadn't managed to finish the job? The customary combatants took to the battlefield: anger arrayed against guilt, vengefulness against grief. And the outcome was always the same—a draw, leaving Clover exactly as hurt and confused as he'd been at the start. Better not to think about it at all.

Across the quadrangle, on the opposite leg of the building, something flashed white above the peaked glass roof of a greenhouse—a pigeon on a leash?—then swooped out of sight again. Clover took his time getting there, making mental note of the plants he passed. *All information is good information*, the Epistem had told him.

The panes of the greenhouse were foggy with condensation, blurring the plants inside into a single verdurous cloud.

"This way, Clover!"

Zeno, her charcoal robe billowing in the breeze, stood at the northeastern edge of the roof, backlit by the roseate spectacle of dawn. In each hand she held a slim cord that connected to a bizarre contraption gyrating through the air overhead. It was made up of three cuboids fitted with bright white canvas on four of their six faces, making each one into a stubby, hollow tube. Two of the cuboids ran parallel, while the third floated a couple of feet behind the others. All three were linked by thin wooden dowels and stiff wire.

"It's called a box kite," Zeno said. "Marvelous, isn't it?"

Clover's mind reeled at the sight of it. He could think of no earthly reason this clunky travesty of a bird should fly, yet fly it did. An abrogation of God's most fundamental law. An abomination. A fascinating riddle.

"How does it work?" he asked.

Zeno pulled at the ropes, which caused the trailing edge of the parallel cuboids in front to twist in opposite directions and the whole thing to bank to the right; it was the most she was willing to offer by way of explanation. "One of José Dedios's boys died trying to fly a kite. Fell off the roof, because he didn't want anyone to know." Clover felt a slight sting: yet another of Paz's many secrets. "He must've been clever, to build a kite all on his own. And now he's gone. Nothing saddens me more than wasted potential." She offered Clover the two leashes. "Here."

"I don't know how."

"Keep the lines as tight as you can. If the kite rolls, pull with the opposite arm to level it again."

He took the cords and nearly lost his grip on them straightaway. The sudden upward force took him by surprise, as if the kite were an animal desperate to escape. His shoulder lit up with pain: a dark red crescent buried deep in the crease of the muscle.

"Tell me, Clover," Zeno said, "why do you believe in God?"

He couldn't help but laugh, which only made his shoulder hurt more. "That's what you want to talk to me about? I thought you were going to yell at me for what happened out at the bridge."

"Answer my question."

"I . . . I'm not sure."

"But you've thought about it."

"Of course." He took a moment to consider. "I suppose the more I learn about the world, the more intentional it seems. How could anything this complex come into being without a conscious designer?"

Zeno nodded. "I used to struggle with that same tension. But you know what helped? I began picturing God—the classic one, that is, with the long white beard and the flowing robes—pacing the crystal floors of his divine palace, agonizing over the question of who or what birthed *him*. Because if you think the world itself is complex, Clover, imagine how complex a deity would have to be to *build* such a world. And as this god broods over his genesis, he begins to picture a metagod pacing around his own timeless metapalace, riven with anxiety over who created *him*. On and on it goes, this infinite lineage of neurotic demiurges, until eventually it becomes so much more practical to do away with all of them, rather than keep one around simply to avoid admitting that the great crime of creation remains unsolved. Bank right!"

Distracted by Zeno's speech, Clover hadn't noticed the kite tilting toward the vertical. He wrenched the left rope just in time to keep the craft airborne.

"Do you know how many gods the people of Earth have worshipped since the dawn of recorded time?" Zeno asked.

He'd read a couple of books about the history of religion in the anathema stacks, but he hadn't bothered to count the gods. "A lot."

"Thousands. One for every sensibility. Clement gods and vengeful gods. Playful gods and humorless gods. Gods of wine, of love, of war, of *milestones*. All those gods, and yet your Descendancy recognizes only one! Don't you find that strange? Isn't it the slightest bit arrogant, to imagine that your civilization is the first and only one to have worshipped the true god?"

"I suppose so," Clover said. It was difficult to concentrate while managing the kite.

"Don't suppose—think! Think how both you and I have written off thousands of gods as mere superstition. The only difference between us is the one measly god you still believe in. And why? Why do you believe in your God and his Daughter, but not the great sky gods of the Wesah?"

"Because . . . because I don't."

Zeno gave a little high-pitched laugh, and for just a moment, Clover thought he could imagine her as a child—stalking imperiously around the schoolyard, browbeating her peers, unable to fathom how everyone around her was so obtuse.

"How quickly we arrive at the tautology, when reason lays down its sword and offers up its throat! No, I'll tell you the real reason you don't believe in the great sky gods of the Wesah, Clover—because nobody ever told you that you should. The blame lies entirely with those original gods, the only ones that all men and women worship: our parents, who shape the wet clay of our minds without our consent, and always toward a rough facsimile of their own. It's the most sinister sort of incarceration, a cage whose bars we fail to see because we are born behind them. That's what religion is, Clover: the art of convincing a free man to build a prison around his own mind."

Clover thought back to what the Epistem had said to him the night of the plebiscite. *With everything that's to come, you'll have to hold fast to your faith. Otherwise, you'll be lost.* Yet he could feel all his rationalizations and justifications dissolving in the face of Zeno's onslaught. Some part of him had always yearned to hear these words, to be told the Filia was nothing but a book of fairy tales, riven with contradiction and hypocrisy, and that he wasn't crazy or immoral for doubting.

"Director Zeno, why did you want to show me this kite? Is it some kind of symbol?"

"Symbols are for artists and priests," Zeno scoffed. "You and I are scientists. I brought you up here because, aside from the tenacious remnants of your faith, you're a rational being. And I assumed you'd want to understand the aerodynamic principles of flight before your life depended on them."

"Why would my life depend on them?"

Zeno put her hands on his uninjured shoulder. "Clover, how would you like to meet a god worthy of your idolatry?"

The path crisscrossed its way down the cliff face and alongside a small tributary of the Ivan. On the Sophia side, a small stucco building emitted a perpetual hum and clatter—the hydroelectric generator. Zeno strode right past it, across a wooden bridge and into the woods to the northeast.

TOMMY WALLACH

"We find ourselves in a misleading sort of lull at the moment," she said. "War is almost inevitable, but both sides are delaying, hoping to prepare themselves more fully for the conflict to come. The Anchor needs to drum up more popular support, while I need a bit more time to put the finishing touches on my arsenal."

"Why are you telling me this?" Clover said. "It wasn't so long ago you thought I might be a spy."

"I still think you're a spy. That's why you and Lenny were inebriated the day you nearly got yourself shot. You hoped the liquor would compel the boy to share Sophia's secrets." Clover tried to keep his face neutral; how had Zeno seen through him so easily? "Luckily for you, I've decided it doesn't matter. See, I've been monitoring your work here at Sophia, and whatever else you may have lied about, you are unquestionably a true student of science."

"I'm sorry, Director, but I'm not sure I understand your point."

"My point is that I'm making you a proposal. If I can convince you that the Descendancy cannot hope to win this war, you will help me to expedite its downfall, preferably with as little bloodshed as possible." Clover attempted to formulate a response, but Zeno cut him off. "I'm not asking for an answer right now. I just want you to keep it in mind."

They tramped onward through the woods, which were just beginning to return to life after the long winter. Intimations of green were everywhere, and the snow had regressed to only a few thin puddles of white here and there. There was no trail that Clover could see, but after another fifteen minutes, they left the forest and emerged onto a vast prairie of tall, swaying grasses. A dirt strip about ten feet wide and three hundred long had been cut into the middle of the field. Zeno walked briskly to the nearer end of this strip, where something hulked beneath a large piece of canvas.

"Help me with this," she said.

Together, they pulled the canvas away, and Clover's breath caught in his throat.

"We can fly," Lenny had said, after they'd knocked back a few beers in Ruben's. Clover had assumed it was just the alcohol talking, but now he knew better; this contraption was undoubtedly what the first generation of men referred to as an *airplane*.

When Clover had first read about them in the anathema stacks, he'd pictured a mechanical analogue to a particularly graceful bird—a starling maybe, or an eagle. The real thing turned out to be far less elegant, and the physics were utterly unfathomable. The body of the plane was roughly cylindrical, with two cavities in the top where people could sit. The wings—two curved tiers of planed wood bound with metal struts—were situated close to the front of the craft and extended about ten feet to either side.

"Her name is Kittyhawk," Zeno said. "We've been working on her for the better part of six years."

The director walked around to the front of the plane, where four twisted rods of steel were affixed to the pointed tip of what Clover remembered was called a "fuselage." She grabbed hold of one of these rods, lifted it up a few inches, then threw it violently toward the ground. A great explosion resolved into a shuddering hum, and suddenly the metal rods were spinning of their own accord, so fast they blurred into a circle of silver—like an annulus.

Zeno used a stepladder to climb into the front seat. "Come on!" she shouted over the racket.

TOMMY WALLACH

Clover clambered into the other seat.

"Put on your goggles!" Zeno gestured to the pair of fitted glasses she was already wearing. Clover found his own set hanging from a hook just in front of his knees. He fit the frames around his ears and cinched the strap down tight. Zeno pulled a lever, and the plane began rolling down the path—faster, and faster, and faster. Clover was gasping for breath, and his heart felt as if it were trying to beat its way out of his chest. He glanced over the side, watching the ground rush past. His last chance, to jump free of this infernal contrivance before . . .

But it was already happening. The wheels of the plane lifted off the ground, soundless and smooth, as if God himself had reached down and swept the veil of Gravity aside.

But this couldn't be God's doing, could it? According to the Filia, God would never allow something like this. Besides, the Sophians didn't even *believe* in God, yet their plane flew. Up and up it went, bouncing in the breeze like a kite, a testament to humanity's tenacity, a miracle of imagination.

Zeno was right. A civilization that could build something like this truly was unstoppable. And at the moment, Clover couldn't even think of a good reason it *should* be stopped.

And the name of that nectar was science, and its sweetness was the sweetness of death.

The world as Clover knew it fell away, and soon disappeared beneath the clouds.

That night he lay sleepless in his bed, adrenalized and anxious, both literally and figuratively unanchored. Every time he closed his eyes, he found himself up in the airplane again, gazing down on the patchwork world, ecstatic and unrepentant. Zeno's proposal seemed so logical, yet he knew that to accept would be to take the first step on the road to defection, to perdition. After everything Sophia had done to him and his family, could he really be turned so easily?

Something pulled at him, an ancient yearning. And because Clover knew there would be no sleep tonight anyway, he allowed himself to answer its call, slipping past a snoring Lenny and through the silent halls of the academy. The library was completely unoccupied, just as Clover had hoped. He went straight to the paltry collection of religious texts hidden away in an alcove on the second floor and began scanning the shelves. He'd visited the section only once before, to peruse a two-hundred-page treatise on the spiritual practices of the Wesah in the hopes of learning something about what might've happened to Gemma.

Tonight, however, Clover wasn't looking for information, only solace. All his life, whenever he'd been struggling, his father had encouraged him to seek answers in the Filia. And it was something like a miracle, how that book never failed to deliver some nugget of comfort or instruction. Was it too much to hope that it might also help him navigate his current predicament?

He scanned the row of texts, and his eyes alighted on a familiar red spine. It was a Filia, just like his father used to have.

No . . . not just *like.*

He reached for it slowly, as if any sudden movement might scare it away. The rasp of leather against paper as he pulled it free, smooth against his fingertips, almost warm. On the cover, the gold-leaf annulus he'd come to know so well over the years. How many times had he followed the sparkle of reflected candlelight around its circumference, half-hypnotized as his father recited a favorite passage after dinner? How many times had he watched from the nave as the august Honor Hamill opened to the page where he'd stuck that morning's sermon?

He cracked the cover. *Property of Honor Daniel Adams Hamill*, printed just on the other side, where the impress of the annulus had raised a nearly imperceptible ring. And on the blank page opposite ...

The book thudded onto the wooden floor. Clover stepped back, putting distance between himself and the impossible. Words! Words where there had never been words before, all written in the neat, tidy loops of his father's hand.

He knelt down and picked the Filia up again, afraid the message would have disappeared, a punishment for his doubt. But no, thank the Daughter, the words were still there, clear as day:

If and when I am killed, I ask that my captors see this Filia returned to my beloved sons, Clive and Clover Hamill. They can be found in the Anchor, capital city of the Descendancy, that one true nation blessed by the Lord, his Daughter, and holy Gravity. May it live on forever, as all true believers will. —DH

The text was rust red, the unmistakable hue of dried blood, darkening where Clover's tears fell upon the letters.

His father had survived that terrible night out on the mining road north of Wilmington. He'd made it back here to Sophia. And too much to hope: he might still be alive.

12. Paz

BOISTEROUS VOICES IN THE DISTANCE; WORDS ECHO-ing along the narrow corridor until they arrived at Paz's ears as blurry sonic hieroglyphics. Raucous laughter cut through the fetid air like a blade. A dream? A waking hallucination? As far as Paz could remember, she'd never heard anyone laugh down here before. The soldiers who delivered her food made a point of acting as aloof as possible, diligently denying her any scrap of fellowship or warmth, and the only audible evidence of the other prisoners was the occasional scream or the shuffle of faraway sobbing.

The voices grew louder. A bobbing torch splashed ever-brightening layers of red light against the wall opposite her cell. And though Paz knew it was foolish, she couldn't suppress the tiny flame of hope that burst to life inside her. More than a week had passed without any further communication from the Mindful, and she'd begun to wonder if the whole thing might have been some elaborate prank—dangling freedom in front of her only to snatch it away again. But what other explanation for this band of incongruously cheerful men making their way down the corridor? It couldn't just be a coincidence, could it?

She paced back and forth, unconsciously effacing a couple of fresh poems, straining to make out what the men were talking about. At last the words coalesced into something intelligible, and the little flame of hope inside her chest was extinguished.

"Of course I have," one of the men said. "Even with all that ink, she's still pretty enough for a tumble."

Paz recognized the voice—an older soldier named Loren. He came down into the dungeon sometimes just to look at her, licking his lips and fingering the hilt of his sword suggestively. In those moments, she was almost grateful to be in a cell.

"And the Grand Marshal really said we could all have a go?" That would be Christopher, the youngest of the guards. He was a shy boy, afraid even to look Paz in the eye when he came down to feed her, as if she were some kind of succubus.

"That's right. He figures this is all we've got left, short of killing her. The bitch still won't talk."

Paz's blood ran cold. That third man sounded exactly like Clive. But Clive wouldn't speak about killing her so lightly, nor would he ever involve himself in something this depraved.

And then he stepped up to the bars, smiling thinly. "Evening, Paz."

She nearly tripped backing away from him, her mind racing to find an explanation other than the obvious. Of all the degradations the Anchor had enacted upon her person, this was the one sacrilege not yet committed, and for Clive to be a party to it . . .

She felt as if someone had punched her in the stomach, hollowed out her center—an emptiness beyond hunger, beyond outrage. No sense in denying it any longer; she'd begun to feel something for him, or maybe those feelings had been there all along. And here was the cost of caring: betrayal. She could've laughed at the irony,

SLOW BURN

at the perfect symmetry of their disloyalty. But there was nothing funny about what these three had come here to do.

Christopher giggled nervously. "I never thought my first would be like this."

"Well, beggars can't be choosers, eh?" Loren said, and all of them laughed.

Their faces were ruddy in the torchlight: three ripe red blisters full of blood. Clive unlocked the door and Loren entered the cell, already slipping out of his uniform jacket. Paz jumped up onto the mattress and pressed her back against the wall.

"It's your lucky day," Loren said. He'd finished unbuttoning his shirt, freeing his tumid, sagging gut. "Three of the handsomest men in the Anchor all to yourself."

Paz hissed like an animal. Oh, but she'd make them fight for it. Though she hardly had any strength left in her, she'd make them fight. Loren came another step closer, reaching out with his hairy-knuckled hands.

Click.

Loren stopped, head cocked. They'd all heard it: a single, sonorous snap, like some huge mechanical insect calling out to its comrades. From her perch on the mattress, Paz could see over Loren to where Clive stood in the doorway of the cell, arms outstretched and steady, her salvation in his hands.

Loren turned to him and whistled at what he saw. "Is that one of those—" He snapped his fingers, trying to summon up the word.

Paz decided to help him out. "It's a gun."

"That's right. A gun! Where'd you get a—"

"Up against the wall," Clive said.

At last the older soldier understood what was happening, and his grin turned to a grimace. "What the fuck do you think you're doing, Hamill?"

Clive fired the gun into the wall just over Loren's head. The explosion, deafening in that small space, elicited a chorus of distant cries from the dungeon's other prisoners. A fragment of stone ricocheted off Paz's knee.

"Up against the wall and nobody gets hurt," Clive said.

Christopher practically sprinted to the back of the cell.

"Oh, someone's gonna get hurt," Loren growled, but he still obeyed the order.

"Your weapons," Clive said.

The two soldiers drew their swords and tossed them to the ground.

Clive cocked the gun again. "All of them."

Loren grudgingly pulled a dagger from his boot and added it to the pile.

It occurred to Paz that someone must've given the gun to Clive and taught him how to use it. Did that mean he'd had help in planning this escape? Could he be working with the Mindful?

"Paz, throw those outside the cell, would you?"

"My pleasure." She kept her eyes fixed on Loren as she knelt down to collect the weapons. Shorn of his blade, half-naked, he'd gone from menacing to ludicrous in an instant; his humiliation was delicious.

"Listen," Christopher said, "I'm real sorry about this. I wasn't thinking straight. I wouldn't have gone through with it. Really. I'm a good person."

Paz turned her attention to the younger soldier, and as she examined his sallow, sniveling countenance, a vast and irrepressible hatred bloomed inside her, stretching its tendrils out toward this soft-spoken, sweet-seeming grub of a boy, this moral nonentity, this sightless, wriggling larva who'd hoped to burst from the chrysalis of childhood by defiling her—his smile the baring of teeth, wolf in sheep's clothing, Chuck Barker running his hand up her thigh in the alleyway, and all the gluttonous, murderous men who took what they wanted by force. And what if none of this was real? What if she was still asleep in her cold, empty cell, dreaming of salvation, and baby Christopher would simply *pop* like a pimple and she'd wake once more into the silence and the darkness and Diana's needle digging beneath her skin, branding her forever—

"Paz, no!" Clive shouted.

Too late. The knife had already found the narrow slit between the boy's ribs and touched his black heart. Christopher dropped the torch, sputtered wordless pain. His palsied fingers scrabbled impotently at the hilt of the knife.

"Look at me," Paz said, her eyes inches from his, her voice gravel and fire. "I'm watching you die."

"Get off him!" Loren roared, at last finding the presence of mind to react. He put his hands around Paz's neck, lifted her up, and slammed her into the back wall of the cell, over and over, oblivious to her overgrown fingernails raking his cheek. His grip tightened, until there was no space for air to pass at all; the world began to blur and soften.

Another gunshot, indistinct this time, as if she were hearing it from deep underwater. Loren's head had sprung a leak, casting a

TOMMY WALLACH

livid constellation of blood and brain matter onto Paz's face and the stone behind her. He fell backward across the mattress.

"Daughter's love," Clive whispered, the gun clattering to the dirt floor. "What have we done?"

Though she was still faint from lack of oxygen, Paz scooped the weapon up—noting the serifed FP signaling it was a creation of Andre Portnoy, Sophia's premier gunsmith—and headed straight for the open door of the cell. "Come on," she said.

But Clive only shook his head. "What's the point?"

"The point is to get me out of here!"

"I didn't come here to save you. I came here to save Flora."

"Flora's in the dungeon?"

Clive's eyes flashed. "Of course not! Your people took her!"

"My people?"

"The Mindful. They said I could only get Flora back if I freed you."

At last Paz understood. Her frustration melted away, and all she felt was the familiar crush of guilt; even imprisoned, she was still managing to ruin lives. "Clive, I didn't know anything about this. You have to believe me. I would never have put Flora at risk to save my own skin. I promise."

Clive laughed darkly. "You promise, huh? And what good is that? Two men are dead."

"Two men who wanted to *rape me* are dead. You'll excuse me if I don't grieve."

"Paz, I . . ." Clive trailed off. "I know that. But two wrongs don't make a right. How am I supposed to live with what I've done here tonight?"

His expression was doleful, almost childlike, and Paz's heart filled with admiration for his impractical, self-flagellating virtue. "You'd be amazed what you can live with," she said, laying a soft hand against his cheek. "I'll teach you how to live with it. But right now, let's focus on the *living* part, okay?"

After a long pause, Clive nodded.

"Good." She knelt down and unknotted his left bootlace, tugged it free of the eyelets, then stood up and handed it to him. "Now tie me up."

A dull-eyed, oblivious girl sat at a desk in front of the Grand Marshal's office door, picking at her cuticles.

"Clive Hamill, here to see Grand Marshal Chang."

The girl remained intently focused on her fingers, holding them out at arm's length to get a more complete view. "He's busy for the rest of the day."

"He'll want to see me."

With a sigh meant to convey her irritation at being distracted from her self-grooming regimen, Chang's secretary finally looked up. When she saw Paz, she practically leaped out of her chair. "What is she doing here?"

"The prisoner has agreed to talk, but only to the Grand Marshal," Clive said.

This answer seemed to baffle the girl, who Paz guessed was very often baffled. "Shouldn't we call more guards or something?"

Clive frowned. "Are you implying the Grand Marshal couldn't defend himself from a woman with her hands bound behind her back?"

"Of course not," the girl replied. "It just seems dangerous to—"

"The prisoner has information that could save the entire Descendancy, and you want to talk about danger? For God's sake, announce us!"

"Yes, sir. Sorry."

The secretary slipped into Chang's office and reappeared a few seconds later. "The Grand Marshal will see you," she said.

"Damn right he will," Clive replied. "Come on, prisoner."

The girl kept her eyes glued to Paz, as if watching a poisonous snake who might strike at any moment. When they were right alongside each other, Paz indulged herself with a sudden snarl, and enjoyed the yelp it elicited.

Grand Marshal Chang's office was enormous, fifty times the size of Paz's most recent accommodations. Or maybe office wasn't the right word for it; though there was the usual desk piled high with papers, most of the room was given over to an array of gymnastics equipment: dumbbells and barbells, medicine balls of various sizes, and a number of more complex apparatuses whose specific purpose Paz couldn't divine. Chang stood near the back of the room, facing away from them, taking wild swings at a canvas sack hung from the ceiling. It had a woman's face on the front, *Zeno* written beneath it.

"So you finally broke her, eh, Hamill?" he said, giving the bag a couple of blows to the gut. "I'll admit it, I didn't think you would. I told Marshal Burns as much. We both know he's got some kind of stiffy for you, says you're officer material. But in my opinion, once a choirboy, always a—"

While the Grand Marshal had been talking, Paz had shaken off the loose knot around her wrists and drawn the gun. When Chang finally turned to address them, he found himself staring down the barrel.

"—choirboy," he finished.

"If you call for help, I'll kill you," Paz said.

Chang shook his head. "Oh, you foolish children. Why would you come here?"

"You know why," Clive said. "We can't exactly go out the front door, can we? And Burns told me a long time ago that you've got your own way of leaving the Bastion. So where is it?"

"Burns lied to you. You're trapped. You're gonna die in—"

Paz squeezed the trigger, blasting a hole through the forehead of the punching-bag Zeno. Dry rice spilled out from both the entrance and exit wounds, making two little pyramids on the floor. "We've killed two men already," she said. "If you don't tell me what I want to hear in the next ten seconds, you'll be the third."

"Sir? Is everything all right?"

It was the voice of the Grand Marshal's secretary. She'd heard the commotion but thankfully didn't have the initiative to open the door without express permission.

"Tell her to take a long lunch break, or else I shoot you both," Paz whispered.

"Leave us the hell alone, Kendra," Chang said, staring steely-eyed at Paz the whole time. "Go get some lunch. My treat."

A long pause. Paz imagined this sudden generosity from a man like Chang was every bit as suspicious as the gunshot had been. Luckily, the girl was nothing if not obedient. "Thank you, sir. I'll do that."

Paz waited until the sound of footsteps faded away before she spoke again. "We have nothing to lose if we can't escape. So either you show us the way out right now, or you die."

With a capitulatory sneer, Chang marched over to a grand mahogany bookcase in the corner of the room. There were no books on its shelves, only the accoutrements of the professional drinker: crystal decanters filled with amber and violet liqueurs, exquisitely etched glassware, and a silver bowl full of citrus fruits for garnish. When he pressed on the clamshell sconce just next to it, the entire bookcase swung away from the wall, revealing a narrow, lightless passageway. He turned back to them. "It won't matter. Within the hour, I'll have a poster of your faces on every lamppost in the Anchor. You'll be back here before sundown. And I promise I won't hesitate this time. Not for a second. I'll slit your goddamned throats myself. Honestly, I'm looking forward to—"

"Tie him up," Paz interrupted. "It'll give us more time." She held the gun steady as Clive used the bootlace to tie Chang's wrists together and then to bind him tightly to the rack of dumbbells.

When that was done, Paz quickly swept the room, looking for anything worth taking—a couple of curved knives in black lacquered sheaths, a small sack of silver shekels on the mantel . . .

She froze before a tall oval of polished brass, and the utter stranger she found within its circumference.

"No," she whispered.

The rings that ran around her face and the back of her head were freakish enough, but it was the density of the words that had transfixed her. They covered at least half the exposed flesh of her scalp and reached farther down her forehead than she'd expected.

Most of them would be obscured when her hair grew out, but the one that ran around her neck would never be completely concealed: *heretic*. The tattoos would be with her forever now, the first thing people would see when they looked at her. She felt dizzy with the horror of it, stumbling backward as if she might somehow escape herself that way.

Chang chuckled. "Don't like what you see, eh? Can't say I blame you."

Paz stalked up to the Grand Marshal and pressed the barrel of the gun against his forehead. She remembered that day he'd come to visit her in the dungeon. "You know what this gun makes me to you? A god. Say it. Say I'm a god."

"No," Chang replied, still smiling.

"Say I'm a god. Say it right now."

"Never."

A mantle of red fell across her eyes—blind, blistering rage. "Say it, you bastard! Say it or I blow your fucking head open!"

"Paz!" Clive shouted. She looked over at him. His face was kind, imploring. "There's been enough killing today."

Her index finger quivered. She couldn't think of many people who deserved death more than the Grand Marshal. But Clive was right. Or even if he wasn't, she owed him this small mercy—for everything he'd done for her, and for everything she'd done to him.

"Here," she said, handing him the gun. "I don't trust myself with it."

They crossed the room to stand in front of the hidden door. Paz couldn't see more than a few feet down the passageway, and that impenetrability felt like a symbol of something, or an omen.

TOMMY WALLACH

"Enjoy your little taste of freedom," the Grand Marshal said. "I'll be seeing you soon enough."

Paz turned back to him. A smile—sincere, serene—rose unexpectedly to her lips. "I can't wait," she replied, before plunging into the darkness after Clive.

Interlude

THREE MEN MET ON THE ROOF OF NOTRE FILLE TO DIS-
cuss the destiny of a civilization. Around them orbited
the great city, a vast annulus of stone and iron, flesh and
breath, not unlike a body: the thick skin of the Anchor
wall, gates opening and closing like four hungry mouths, the
sparkling blue spine of the Tiber, innumerable alleyways twisting like veins. Two of the men sat at a small wrought-iron table,
sipping mint tea. The third, the Grand Marshal Ruzo Chang,
soldierly even in his civvies, cut a brooding, hulking figure as he
leaned out over the railing, looking toward the Bastion: his home.
Though the other two men were not his enemies—were in fact
his most important allies—he knew they detested him. Or not
him, exactly. They hated their *need* of him. They hated their own
weakness.

They'd arrived before him, and at the sound of his heavy footsteps on the flagstones, went conspicuously quiet. He didn't bother
with the niceties, bowing and scraping like a subject, but walked
straight past them to the railing. Whatever they wanted to say to
him, they could just as well say it to his back.

It was Hal Turin, the Epistem, who finally broke the silence.
"How could this happen?"

Chang had always believed the best defense was a good offense. "How about you read the fucking report?"

"I'd like to hear it from you."

"Well, I'd like a harem of Wesah to tuck me into bed every night."

"Please," Archbishop Carmassi said. "There's no need for hostility, Ruzo. Just give us the broad strokes."

"Broad strokes? I lost her. I'll get her back."

"How?"

"I've put Marshal Burns in charge of the operation. He knows the Hamill boy better than anyone."

"So Clive Hamill was responsible for this?" Turin said. "You're certain?"

Chang finally turned around, discerning a suspicious disquiet in the Epistem's voice. "Why? You know him?"

"No. Just his younger brother."

"You mean the traitor you sent along with my contingent? The one who ended up handing himself over to Sophia?"

The Epistem hesitated. "Yes. The traitor."

"Like brother, like brother, I guess. Clive must've gotten caught up with the Mindful on one of those tours out east, because they're claiming responsibility for the breakout. Their people have plastered signs all over the goddamned city."

"What do you know about them?" the Archbishop asked.

"Not much. Taking the Sophian girl was their first real operation. Up until now, it's all been anti-Descendancy propaganda—pamphlets and graffiti and all that. But I've got men hunting for them now. We only have to catch one. We break him, he'll give us the others."

"You didn't break the girl," Turin muttered.

"Because you didn't give me free rein."

"Free rein? You tortured her for weeks!"

"We *questioned* her. She's still got all her fingers, doesn't she? She's still got her maidenhood, assuming she had it when she came in."

"Our civilization is founded on certain ethical principles, Grand Marshal. I'm sorry if you feel limited—"

"This is a fucking war, Hal! And you aren't even willing to give me guns!"

Both of them went silent as the Archbishop's innocent came out onto the balcony, bearing a tray of pastries and a fresh teapot. Chang threw up his hands and leaned back against the railing. Turin and Carmassi were fools. They thought a war was like a boxing match, where both sides would stand around throwing punches until somebody fell down. They'd never been in a real fight, where you made your first strike count because it might be the only strike you got—gouge the eyes, crush the windpipe, pierce the heart.

"All of that is beside the point," Carmassi said, once the innocent had toddled back inside. "I didn't ask you up here to eat crow."

"Oh no?" Chang said.

"Hal and I have been talking, and we think it's time to address the issue of our *other* war."

"What other war?"

"With the Wesah."

Chang felt his hackles rise. "The Wesah are the Protectorate's responsibility, not the Church's."

"Historically, yes," Turin said. "But my guess is that Zeno will soon seek to ally herself with them."

Chang laughed disdainfully. "You think those bitches give a rat's ass about our wars?"

"The *tooroon* isn't far off now. All of the Wesah will be gathered together, ripe for persuasion. We know the Sophians have brokered peace with their local *naasyoon*. If they were to extend this armistice into an official alliance with Andromède, the consequences for the Descendancy could be dire. On the other hand, if we were to beat Zeno to the punch, if we promised the Wesah that we would no longer attack tribeswomen found on Descendancy territory, we could ensure their neutrality, or even—"

"Don't say it," Chang growled.

"—or even convince them to side with us."

There was no defending against it now; Chang allowed the anger to burst its banks and sweep him away. He strode over to the table, picked up the teapot—an exquisite porcelain vessel glazed with a detailed depiction of the Conflagration—and smashed it against the flagstones.

"I'll die first! You hear me? I'll kill myself before I fight alongside those savages!" He could hear his voice shredding with emotion, shaming him, but it was no longer within his control.

Just a quick jaunt out west—the first time Chang's two daughters would see the ocean. They would visit his parents down in Horton, hike a few of the old trails through the great evergreen forests near the coast, sample the fresh seafood in Edgewise. But not a hundred miles out from the Anchor, Chang was awoken in the night by the cries of a Wesah *naasyoon* descending on the campsite, leaving him with an arrow through his leg and his wife and children gone, never to be seen again, never to be avenged, no matter how many tribeswomen he left broken and bloodied along the byways of the Descendancy.

A hand on his shoulder made him flinch. "I'm sorry for what happened to you, Ruzo," Turin said, "but we've made our decision."

"And what about *my* decision?" Chang replied. "I won the plebiscite. The people want change."

"The people are frightened. They aren't thinking clearly."

"You're the one who's frightened. You're scared shitless."

"Well, at least I didn't send seventy-five men to die on the streets of Sophia just to score political points."

"How fucking dare you!"

"Enough!" the Archbishop said, rising unsteadily to his feet. Daughter's love but he was old. Chang imagined lifting him up and breaking him on the flagstones, just like that teapot. "This infighting benefits no one but our enemies. Chang, all we want is your word that you will attempt to broker peace with the Wesah. And in exchange . . ." The Archbishop and the Epistem shared a glance, and Chang understood that all of this had been planned—right down to the tiny morsel of compromise they were about to offer him. "I will publish an encyclical officially loosening the strictures surrounding anathema research in times of war."

"So I'll get my guns?"

"You'll get the Library's sincere attempt to develop them. Do we have a deal?"

Chang considered the hand the Archbishop held out to him. He could go on arguing, but what would be the point? The time for talk was over; now was the time for action. He would go to the *tooroon*, but with his own agenda. He wouldn't see the men of

TOMMY WALLACH

the Protectorate—his family—forced to fight alongside a bunch of debaucherous barbarians, nor could he leave those barbarians to ally with Sophia.

"We've got a deal," Chang said, and shook the Archbishop's weak, palsied hand. He felt a twinge of conscience at making a promise he had no intention of keeping, but this was how wars were waged. More than that: this was how wars were *won*. And if the Epistem and the Archbishop couldn't understand that, then perhaps something would have to be done about them, too.

Part II
COLLABORATORS

We've been looking for the enemy for some time now.
We've finally found him. We're surrounded.
That simplifies things.

—*Lewis Burwell "Chesty" Puller*

1. Clover

HIS FATHER—ALIVE! HE HADN'T BEEN LEFT TO ROT ON the side of the mining road, hadn't been buried beneath the yucca tree with the others. And thinking back on it now, Clover remembered how small the body had looked, how the robes didn't seem to have decomposed as much as they should have. Someone from Sophia must have traveled all the way back to the site of the skirmish and arranged things to make it appear as if Honor Hamill had died there, and Clover could think of only one plausible explanation why: so his father could be secretly brought back to Sophia for questioning.

Questioning—a euphemism if ever there was one. What form would *questioning* take in a place like Sophia? Zeno would never stoop to outright torture—considering her impassioned denunciation of the moral bankruptcy and barbarism of the Descendancy, it would make her the worst sort of hypocrite—but that didn't mean Clover's father was alive. Most likely he'd been killed, quickly and cleanly, after giving up whatever information he had.

But what if the questioning wasn't over? What if Honor Hamill was still breathing in some lightless dungeon beneath the academy? Clover needed to know. He had to be able to tell the story of his father from the first moment to the last. Otherwise, he'd always wonder.

Clover rested his elbows on the table, gritty with sawdust, drawing as close as possible to his nemesis: a one-fiftieth scale model of Zeno's biplane, Kittyhawk, complete with a miniature engine (nonfunctional), propeller (functional), and ailerons (functional).

"The stress will be too much if there's more weight," Huma said, frowning in that odd pinching way of hers, as if her nose had suddenly developed a powerful gravitational field that drew the rest of her face in around it.

Lenny's adoptive mother was in her late thirties but looked a decade older, one of the few Sophians who seemed to wear the weight of the looming conflict on her face. She was in charge of developing a means of weaponizing Kittyhawk (which was how Lenny had known about the plane in the first place), and Clover had been added to her team just after Zeno returned him jelly-kneed and windswept to the landing strip three weeks ago.

Since then Clover felt as if the whole academy had relaxed around him, like a too-tight jacket loosened by time and use. Everyone knew that Director Zeno had chosen Clover to work on the biplane, which meant he must be trustworthy. It was the ideal situation for a double agent. Every day he was learning more about Sophia's military capabilities, insinuating himself more deeply into the hierarchy of the academy. Though it was slightly disconcerting to be aiding in the construction of a vehicle whose sole purpose was the annihilation of his countrymen, Clover comforted himself with the thought that the more intimately he was involved with the plane's development, the easier it would be for him to sabotage it in the future.

TOMMY WALLACH

"How much added weight will there be?" he asked, pressing down on the model's cambered wing.

"Whatever the payload is."

"It'll be fine," Lenny said, sanding away at their newest iteration of the full-size stabilizer, spangling the air with tiny particles of maple. "Clover showed you the math."

"I don't trust the math."

"If you can't trust math, what can you trust?"

"Experiment. Things you can see with your eyes."

"Like oxygen? Like gravity?"

Huma groaned. "Clover, would you sketch out a thicker strut and shut my son up?"

"Happily," Clover said, unable to keep the smile off his face. Though the three of them hadn't been working together for long, already Clover felt as if they made a sort of family. Not because Huma was particularly warm, or because Lenny had grown any less irritating (Clover had a newfound sympathy for Clive; in his more forgiving moments, he could almost understand how one might be inspired to put a bullet in one's little brother), but because of their shared sense of purpose. It was like being back on the ministry wagon, traveling from town to town, doing the Lord's work. Except in this case the Lord's work was figuring out how Kittyhawk could most efficiently murder Protectorate soldiers.

An hour passed in near silence—Clover sketching, Lenny sanding, Huma frowning at her notes. At some point, Lenny disappeared for a few minutes and returned with lunch from the academy refectory: trout cooked in butter and black pepper, freshly baked rolls, and some kind of sweet, milky drink that tasted of cinnamon.

"Reminds me of home," Huma said, savoring the first sip.

Clover didn't know much about Lenny's mother, other than that her parents had grown up in Sudamir and immigrated to the Anchor after hearing the good word from a Descendant missionary.

"Why did you come to Sophia?" he asked.

Huma glanced at Lenny, who shrugged. "Tell him if you want."

"Tell me what?"

"My father was homosexual," Huma said. "You know what that means?"

"Of course. Like the Wesah." *And the Epistem*, he might've added, though that was just a rumor. Clover remembered asking Bernstein about it once, but the attendant had waved the question aside with an "I don't know and I don't care."

"Technically, the Wesah are bisexual," Lenny corrected. "They make babies the same way as everyone else. Some of them even *prefer* men."

"My mother and father were forced to marry," Huma continued, "but there was no love between them. Not long after we all moved to the Anchor, my mother took her own life. My father grieved for her, of course, but I think some small part of him was relieved. He met a man who understood him, and they fell in love. But they were discovered, and my father and I had to flee the city. We traveled east until we found a place where he could live without being judged. That was Sophia."

"And Sophia doesn't care, I mean . . ." Clover struggled to express himself. "Nobody here minds if—"

"Two people with certain genetic similarities love each other?" Huma snapped. "No. We don't. We believe love is love, and no one should be persecuted for how they do it. Yet one more reason we have to win this war."

Clover didn't know how to respond to that. He hated these moments, when some aspect of Sophian ideology struck him as more logical or sane than its Descendant counterpart. It complicated things, made his job that much harder.

Huma sat back in her chair and closed her eyes. "How does it begin?" she said, as if to herself. The worry lines creasing her forehead disappeared. "'Before us great Death stands, our fate held close within his quiet hands. When with proud joy we lift Life's red wine to drink deep of the mystic shining cup, and ecstasy through all our being leaps—Death bows his head and weeps.'"

"Did you write that?" Clover asked.

Huma smiled. "No. A first-generation poet my father quite liked. He didn't even learn about poetry until we came to Sophia, and then he became obsessed with it. Once I was accepted as a scholar, I would lend him books from the library. By the time he passed away, I think he'd memorized every poem in the place."

Clover thought of his own father. In the weeks since he'd found the Filia, he'd explored every nook and cranny of the academy. But he'd found no sign of a dungeon or prison, and twice was obliged to improvise a justification for his presence in some suspicious location. The knowledge that Honor Hamill might be alive had created a new anxiety inside him, a clock perpetually ticking down to cataclysm. His father existed in some limbo state between life and death now, and Clover had come to the guilty realization that a part of him missed his former certainty. At least the dead could be mourned, remembered fondly, relinquished.

"As if anything we do could make death weep," Lenny scoffed, still thinking about the poem.

"And why not?" his mother replied.

Lenny picked up the model of Kittyhawk. "Because death always wins in the end." Simulating the whine of the engine, he mimed flying the plane into the table. "Kerbloom," he said.

Clover dreamed of Paz—Paz as distinct from Irene, Paz the girl behind the mask. They were walking through the Maple Garden, side by side, almost touching. He wanted to tell her that he understood her now, that his time in Sophia had taught him how it was possible to live halfway between spy and traitor, to come to love your enemy. He wanted to tell her that he knew she'd cared for him, just not as much as she'd hated what he represented. But just as he was about to say as much, he suddenly found himself standing in front of the Dedios farmhouse, incongruously relocated to the middle of Portland Park.

"Shall we?" Paz said, and then Clover awoke.

Lenny was breathing evenly, his light snore like an unrosined bow scraping across a low string, dead to the world. Clover slipped out of bed and got dressed.

The halls of the academy were quiet, though he knew if he went to the library or the workshops, he'd find a handful of scholars still working. As it was, his only interaction came when he passed the academy's front desk, where Sister Balaga looked up from her book just long enough to register who was leaving, so she could make a note of it in the log.

Zeno would likely give him hell for this, but he didn't care.

TOMMY WALLACH

The night air was bracing, and Clover stood for a moment breathing in the sappy smell of the pines. Had it been only two months since he'd first stood here? He remembered turning at the sound of his brother's voice, the despair in Paz's eyes, the bright bloom of pain in his shoulder as he tumbled across the threshold. He felt dissociated from his past self; how could that Clover and this one be the same person? They had different thoughts and beliefs, different likes and dislikes, different clothes and hair and fingernails. Every instant, he became something new again, a stranger. The only constant was change.

He walked downhill, glimpsing the glowing face of the clock tower through the trees: just past midnight. The electric lights along Sophia's main street were switched off at ten, but the night was clear, and a sliver of moon cast the whole town in lunar silver. Clover pulled his hood up around his face, just to be safe; he hadn't come to town since that ill-fated day with Lenny. The bridge gate was left open and unmanned at all times. Sophia was on good terms with the local *naasyoon*, and prospective bandits had long since learned what a well made gun could do. The river plashed and plunked down below, running fast with the fruits of winter's quietus. In the distance, some nocturnal creature's eyes briefly caught the light, spectral crescents of yellow and green.

The Dedios farm was farther away than it looked—the vividness of that red made it seem hardly a stone's throw from the bridge. After fifteen minutes, Clover was still only halfway there. The land around him had just begun to sprout with a cover of lentils, an effective rotation crop after the bounteous harvest of winter wheat, and a critical staple for a military campaign. More intelligence to be filed away and delivered when he returned to the Anchor—*if* he returned.

A funny thought: spies and traitors weren't so different, really. Both consorted with the enemy, lied whenever necessary, traded secrets to win confidence. The divergence came only in those ultimate moments: a spy became a traitor when he didn't give up his information.

The barn loomed, shadow-purple, limned with starlight. Clover unlatched the big door and went inside. The animals, catching his unfamiliar scent, snorted and shuffled with dismay. He could smell both horses and cows, but it was so dark that he could only make out the gloss on their coats.

He sat down on the dirt floor and imagined her here—all the hours spent mucking and baling, feeding and grooming, milking and dreaming. His heart swelled, or felt like it was swelling, squeezing the breath from his lungs. Daughter's love but he missed her, curled up next to him in his tent, speaking in that sultry way she had, teaching him the proper way to kiss. No one would ever really love him, he knew now, so in retrospect, her willingness even to pretend seemed a kind of gift.

The animals were further upset by the sound of his weeping, and the thick air in the barn was becoming suffocating. Clover ran outside and bent over, gasping for breath. When the tears finally stopped, he straightened up and saw a boy standing just a few feet away, watching him. Only seven or eight years old, but with the same tar-black hair and thick eyebrows, the same inquisitive expression: Paz in miniature.

"You're Carlos," he hazarded.

TOMMY WALLACH

"Uh-huh. Who are you?"

"I'm Clover. I knew your sister."

"What are you doing here?" It wasn't an accusation, but a genuine expression of curiosity.

Clover tried to choose between the many possible answers to that question, each one a version of the truth. He'd come because his father's trail had led him here. The twins who'd nearly killed him the day he came to town with Lenny were among the last people who'd seen Honor Hamill alive, and they clearly had some kind of relationship with the Dedios family. But he'd also come because he'd dreamed about Paz, and Paz used to live here. He'd thought by visiting her childhood home, he might learn something new about her, or even commune with her somehow.

"I wanted to meet you," Clover finally said.

Carlos looked skeptical. "Really?"

"Sure. Paz talked about you all the time. She said you were really smart."

"She did?" The cautious, fragile hope of the little brother: Clover knew it all too well.

"She did."

A triumphant grin crept across the boy's face. "Do you want to come inside? Ms. Moses made cake. It's why I came downstairs in the first place."

"Oh, it's pretty late. I should be sleeping. So should you, I imagine."

Carlos stepped forward and grabbed Clover's hand. "Just one slice," he said. "It's real good."

◆　　◆　　◆

A cool flavor, sweet but not sugary, sparkling on the tongue. Carlos said it was called vanilla, and that they'd traded for it with some traveling merchant up from the south.

"It's delicious," Clover said.

"You've never had it before? I figured the Anchor would have tons."

"The Descendancy's pretty specific about what it's willing to trade for. The Protectorate keeps track of everything that comes into the port at Edgewise."

Carlos talked with his mouth full of cake. "But doesn't stuff get through anyway?"

"Sometimes. But the penalties for trading unlicensed goods are pretty severe."

"You Descendancy folks sure have a lot of rules. I hate rules."

"There's nothing wrong with rules," Clover said, and remembered his mother saying those precise words to him once. "Without rules, there's just chaos."

"I like chaos."

Clover glanced around the room: a kitchen like any other, pots and pans and jars, a big wooden table with a checked tablecloth, two dozen straw hats hung on pegs around the walls as a kind of decoration.

How many breakfasts did she eat here? How many dinners? How many times did she laugh in that heedless way of hers, or say something cutting and brilliant, or tuck a lock of hair behind her ear?

"Do you miss your sister?" Clover asked.

Carlos shrugged. "Do you have brothers and sisters?"

"Just one brother."

TOMMY WALLACH

"Do you miss him?"

Clover smiled at the simplicity of the question, at the simplicity of his honest answer. "Sure I do."

"Yeah. Me too."

As Carlos shoveled another fist-size chunk of cake into his mouth, he dropped his fork, which clattered loudly against the tile floor.

"Uh-oh," he said.

There was the sound of footsteps upstairs, a door opening and closing. The steps grew louder, closer. Clover stood up just as an old woman burst into the room, her white hair wild, her expression severe.

"Carlos, what'd I tell you about the damn cake?" She noticed Clover on the other side of the table, tried to blink him away. "What the . . . ?" Her eyes widened. "Are you that boy from the Anchor?"

"Let me explain," Clover said. "I only wanted—now hold on a minute!"

The old woman took a long-barreled rifle down from its perch above the stove and pointed it straight at Clover's heart. "Get out this instant," she said.

"Yes, ma'am."

He tried to obey, but there were two other boys standing between him and the door now. He recognized one of them, from that day at the bridge.

"Hello again," he said.

A missile of flesh, a flash of arsenic white, and Clover was out cold.

2. Paz

PAZ WATCHED FROM A DOORWAY AS CLIVE NEGOTIATED with a portly Anchorite matriarch for her tatty red head-scarf.

"I'll give you four bronze shekels," he said.

The woman narrowed her eyes. "Why you want it so bad?"

My sister had one just like it when she was younger, Paz improvised in her head. But Clive had never been much for making up stories.

"That's my business. Take it or don't."

The woman shrugged, then undid the knot around her wobbly chin. "I never understand young people," she said, handing it over. Once she was out of sight, Clive brought the scarf back to Paz.

"Here."

She wrapped it loosely, draping the extra fabric over her fore-head; it would cover up most of the disciplinary tattoos, other than the rings around her face.

"Thank you, Clive."

"You're too conspicuous otherwise." He didn't look at her; in fact, she couldn't remember his meeting her eyes since they'd left the Grand Marshal's office.

"Clive, are you angry with me? I told you, I didn't know what the Mindful were planning—"

"I'm not mad about that," he interrupted. "I mean, of course I am, but that's not—" He ran his hands over his face, sighed. "Everything's ruined now, even if we manage to save Flora."

"Of course we'll save her."

Clive smiled sadly. "I thought you were supposed to be the smart one." Paz didn't know how to respond to that, so she was grateful that Clive didn't give her a chance to. "Come on," he said. "Somebody must've found Chang by now. They'll be looking for us."

According to Clive, the Mindful were waiting for them in a small warehouse by the Eastern Gate. It was late evening, and there were still plenty of people out and about, so the two of them stuck to the backstreets where they could. They passed just in front of the gate, close enough that Paz could make out the gleaming buttons on the uniforms of the soldiers standing guard, then ducked down an alley. Clive counted doors, stopping at the fifth. He knocked—three times, then twice, then once more. Immediately the door swung open, revealing two thickset men with guns drawn.

"Clive!" Flora shouted.

The girl was seated at a table with an attractive young woman and an unsavory-looking man in his thirties. She looked to be unhurt, if a little bedraggled.

"Not so loud, child," the seated woman reprimanded, then rose and offered her hand. "It's a pleasure to finally meet you, Paz. We've heard so much. I'm Louise, and this is Ralph." The unsavory-looking man nodded in greeting. He had disciplinary tattoos around his wrists, and his head was shaved almost to the skin. "Our friends at the door are Yuri and Lars."

Clive knelt down next to Flora and whispered something in her ear. Then the two of them stood up. "You all can take your time getting acquainted. We're leaving."

Paz made the mistake of catching Flora's gaze and felt herself momentarily transfixed. The girl had to know the truth by now—that Paz had betrayed her sister to the Wesah—but her expression was utterly inscrutable. It was something in the eyes, so many emotions mixed together in that ghostly blue brume: melancholy and pity, challenge and a detached sort of judgment. They reminded Paz of the Daughter's eyes in paintings, hard and soft at once.

"Not just yet, Clive," Louise said.

Louise flinched when Clive pulled out the gun, but he only tossed it onto the table. "I did my part. Now it's time for you to do yours. Let us go."

"I said Flora wouldn't be harmed, and I meant it. But if we let her go now, what's to stop her from running straight to the Protectorate and telling them where we are? We just need a little cushion—"

It happened in an instant. Clive's hands were around Louise's throat and he'd shoved her up against the back wall of the warehouse. Paz heard the click of guns being cocked, but Ralph put up a hand, warning Yuri and Lars not to fire. Likely he was more afraid of the guards at the Eastern Gate hearing the shots than solicitous on Clive's behalf.

"That is *your* problem," Clive growled.

"And yours," Louise managed to croak out. "You're a wanted man. You can't stay in the Anchor either."

Flora ran to Ralph and tugged at his shirt. "I won't tell anyone anything," she said. "Please let us leave."

But if the Protectorate got hold of her, they'd make her talk—Paz knew that better than anyone. "So what's your plan?" she asked. Clearly these Mindful people looked up to her; maybe she could use that to protect Clive and Flora.

"We leave the Anchor now," Ralph said. "A few days out, we drop these two somewhere off the beaten track. Then they can do whatever the fuck they want."

Somehow Paz doubted that was the real plan, but now wasn't the time to press the issue. Louise had begun to wheeze; her face was turning purple.

"Let her go, Clive," Paz pleaded. "You won't help anything that way."

He let Louise dangle for another couple of seconds before finally dropping her. She went down on her knees, coughing and spitting into the dust.

"We better get going," he said, "before somebody gets hurt."

They filed out of the warehouse and back into the alley. Ralph walked out in front with Flora, his veiny hand like a manacle around her pale wrist, while behind him, Clive was flanked by Yuri and Lars. Paz brought up the rear with Louise, who kept stealing brief glances at her, then looking away.

"What?" Paz finally snapped.

Louise's olive cheeks took on a tinge of red. "Sorry. It's just—they sure did a number on you, didn't they? Marked you up proper." There was a note of awe in her voice, almost jealousy. "Did you break? Nobody would judge you if you did. I can't think of anyone who could—"

"No," Paz said. "I didn't break."

Louise smiled. "I knew it. I knew it just looking at you."

Strange how even in the face of this young woman's admiration, Paz felt no sense of accomplishment or pride, only a bone-deep weariness that bordered on despair. What had she done that was so impressive? Merely survived? Allowed her body to be ravaged in the name of some distant city?

"Louise, why did you save me? Did Zeno order it?"

"Not exactly. She gave our cell another mission, a couple months ago, but it went wrong. We decided to break you out as a way to make amends. I still can't believe we pulled it off."

"You mean Clive pulled it off."

Louise laughed, one side of her mouth curling half an inch higher than the other. "Right."

"So what's next?"

"We'll circle back to the Anchor in a week or two, after things have calmed down, and keep working on our anti-Descendancy propaganda. Then, later on in the summer, we're gonna help out with a mission in Edgewise. There's a Mindful cell there, working out of an apothecary shop."

"No, I mean what are we going to do with them?" Paz nodded toward Clive and Flora.

"Oh. Another cell a day's ride south of the Anchor will take on the interrogation. I imagine they'll decide what to do with the prisoners after that."

"Interrogation?"

"Of course. Clive is a personal friend of a marshal. I'm sure he's got stories to tell." Louise cocked her head, examining him from afar. "He's handsome, isn't he? When I was little, I had such a crush on him. Ah well. So it goes."

They reached the end of the alley, where a covered wagon was already hitched up to four oxen. Yuri and Lars herded Paz, Flora, and Clive into the back, where they were each tucked into a claustrophobically tiny crevice between boxes and covered with a densely folded piece of canvas. After a minute or two, the wagon began to jounce over the cobblestones.

Paz was glad for the moment alone with her thoughts. She wasn't sure what had surprised her more, Louise's casual condemnation of Clive and Flora, or just how much the betrayal offended her. Considering everything she'd done in the past year— used love as a weapon, set brother against brother, collaborated in the killing of a ten-year-old boy—she knew she was no longer entitled to moral outrage. But Clive had sacrificed his entire future in order to save Flora's; he'd never be able to return to the Anchor again. And his reward was to be questioned and probably killed, and Flora along with him?

It wasn't right.

The wagon rocked to a stop. Muffled conversation bled through the canvas, and the floor dipped ever so slightly as one of the guards at the Eastern Gate stepped onto the back lip of the wagon to have a look inside. Paz held her breath.

"You're a musical group?" he said.

"That's right," Louise chirped in reply. "Louise Delancey, at your service."

"Any chance I can trouble you for a tune?"

Louise laughed girlishly. "We'll be back in town before too long. You can come by Bennigan's and see us play."

"I just might." The floor of the wagon rose back up. "Ride on."

A moment later they started moving again.

"We're clear," Ralph said. "You all can come out."

Paz tried to stand up, but the canvas was heavier than she expected, and she had to use both hands to shimmy it out of position. Finally free, she saw Flora struggling with her own canvas. Clive tried to go to her aid, but Yuri shoved him back. "She can do it herself."

Paz watched helplessly as Flora slid the canvas away in tiny increments, until at last she was able to pop her head out—gasping for air, tear tracks glistening on her cheeks like snail trails—and lift herself free of the hole. Yuri didn't stop her from clambering over the boxes and barrels and into Clive's arms.

At the sight, something deep inside of Paz crumbled, changed irrevocably. She couldn't allow this to happen. Too many people had suffered because of her, because of her mindless, dogmatic devotion to a cause. She wasn't sure how she felt about Zeno or Sophia, but she knew one thing for certain: Flora and Clive were not her enemies.

She summoned up all her courage and authority and directed it toward Louise and Ralph up in the driver's seat. "I can't do this anymore," she said.

Louise turned. "Can't do what?"

Paz gestured around her. "This. Any of this. I'm taking Clive and Flora and we're leaving."

"What are you talking about? Zeno would—"

"I don't care about Zeno. I just want to leave. Are you going to stop me?"

"Paz, after what you've been through, I'm sure you're not thinking . . ." She trailed off, squinted at something over Paz's shoulder. "Shit."

Paz turned. Backlit by a bright and fulsome moon, a posse of four horsemen were riding toward them from the direction of the Eastern Gate. They'd reach the wagon in less than a minute.

"You three, huddle up," Ralph said. "Hurry!"

Paz ran to Flora and Clive and knelt down beside them just in time for Lars to throw a single piece of canvas over all three of them. It was pitch dark underneath, hot with breath, stifling.

"Just make sure Flora gets out," Clive whispered.

"I'll do whatever I can," she said.

The wagon ground to a halt. There was the sound of men dismounting.

"Is there a problem, gentlemen?" Louise said.

"There's been an incident at the Bastion," a man said. "We can't let anybody leave the Anchor right now."

"Is there anything we can do to change your mind?" Ralph said, his voice folksy and friendly. "We've got a gig in Lundy later on tonight."

"Sorry, sir, but it's the Grand Marshal's orders. I really can't make an ex—"

He was cut off by a flurry of gunshots. Darkness exploded into light as Clive threw the canvas aside. Yuri and Lars were climbing out over the driver's seat. Through the cinched hole at the rear of the wagon, Paz could see two Protectorate soldiers lying in black pools of blood, their horses stamping uncomfortably beside them. Back the other way, Louise suddenly screamed, and there was another volley of gunshots.

Paz gestured toward the back of the wagon. "Quietly," she mouthed to Clive and Flora.

Just as the three of them reached the edge, Ralph poked his head around the canvas cover. His gun was drawn, but before he could aim it, Clive leaped from the wagon and tackled him. The gun flew free, skittering across the dusty road like a big black beetle. Though Clive had the element of surprise on his side, Paz doubted he'd retain the upper hand for long. She cast about for anything she could use as a weapon—and alighted on a canvas bag full of metal tent stakes.

Clive was dazed by a sharp elbow to the nose, and Ralph seized the opportunity to climb on top of him and take a couple of big swings. But Paz was behind them now, and with a shriek, she brought the bag of stakes careening into the side of Ralph's head.

"Thanks," Clive said, pushing the limp body aside.

"Don't mention it."

She stepped between the two dead soldiers and mounted one of their newly ownerless horses. Clive leaped onto the other and pulled Flora up after him. Then they were galloping as fast as they could away from the road, away from whoever remained standing of the Protectorate posse and Louise's Mindful cell, toward the protection of the trees to the south.

More gunshots sounded behind them, but Paz didn't look back.

3. Gemma

DELIRIUM.

That was the only word for it. She woke delirious, with the slow shifting of blankets and the rasp of legs sliding against one another, watching like some satiated grizzly as her lover rose naked and unashamed and prepared to meet the world. The way Athène plaited her hair, methodical and luxurious, as if she were moving underwater, made Gemma half-mad with impossible yearnings—oh, to be the hair under her hands, to be separated into strands and laid over herself, cinched down tight. Athène sensed the desire, and would hold Gemma's gaze with a playful seriousness as she slipped into her yellow hide dress and tied her sash, as she stretched her sweet anatomy toward the coin of morning light at the top of the tent. She would kneel down and find Gemma's foot under the blanket, lean over and bite the big toe, and Gemma would shiver—actually shiver.

Delirium.

She didn't dare speak the word "love." She was afraid Athène would laugh at her for even thinking it (and Athène was always laughing at her, as often for her innocence as for how eagerly she was embracing the loss of it). Besides, what was love, anyway? She'd loved Clive, or believed she had, and yet those feelings were so far removed from these feelings that they couldn't possibly go by the same name. She'd respected him, but never truly admired him. She'd enjoyed his touch, but never craved it. She'd been infatuated with him, but never consumed.

Sometimes Gemma would look at Athène and be unable to separate her wanting from her wanting to become. The chieftain's easy authority, her bawdy sense of humor (and the volume of her laughter—*loud enough to skin a bear*, as a Wesah saying had it), the reckless abandon of her dancing: all of it was as inspiring as it was alluring. And Gemma liked to think she *was* becoming, in her way. Her performance during the hunt had elevated her in the estimation of the *naasyoon*, and as her facility with the language improved, she discovered that most of the tribeswomen had never held any particular animus toward her, outside of their natural distrust of anyone from the Descendancy.

Yet it all felt so fragile. Gemma knew she'd displaced Noémie in the chieftain's affections, and that knowledge made it impossible not to imagine being displaced in turn—if not by someone older and more experienced or someone younger and fresher, than by Noémie herself, whose frosty formality toward Gemma was somehow even more disconcerting than her erstwhile hostility had been. Maybe she'd decided the best revenge wasn't *killing* the competition, but *winning* it.

All Gemma could do was take it day by day, hoping for the best. Every night that Athène welcomed her into her tent, into her arms, was a victory.

But the comfortable stasis of travel couldn't last forever. One afternoon, a few weeks after the first night Gemma and Athène

TOMMY WALLACH

spent together, the *naasyoon* found itself slogging across a vast wetland, a checkerboard of green grass and silver pools that periodically disgorged a raucous squall of birds.

"*Li Villenaître!*" someone shouted, and the cry was taken up by the rest of the *naasyoon*. Gemma glanced to Athène, who grinned.

As far as anyone in the Descendancy knew, the Wesah were an entirely nomadic people, so Gemma had been surprised to learn that the Villenaître was an actual town, built to serve as a safe haven for tribeswomen about to give birth. Over time, it had also become a sort of training ground for *otsapah*, and thus a pilgrimage site for any chieftain seeking a shaman for her *naasyoon*.

Gemma knew Athène wanted her to speak with the *otsapah*, to discuss her "visions." Once again, she was tempted to tell the chieftain the truth, that far from being the result of some preternatural spiritual capability, her "visions" were merely a banal side effect of illness, of deficiency. But she'd dug the hole too deep by now. There was nothing for it but to keep on digging. To lose Athène's devotion would be to lose the only important thing she had left.

"*Bootmaatch, chee,*" Gemma asked, as she made out the first signs of the Villenaître off in the distance. It was a term she'd learned only recently, describing something that was at once an end and a beginning.

"*Bootmaatch,*" Athène confirmed.

Athène led the *naasyoon* through an archway inscribed with the famous Wesah saying: MAY ALL YOUR DREAMS BE NIGHTMARES. On the other side, an open square was decorated with tall wooden carvings of grimacing animals and surrounded by several enormous log cabins. Though the town wasn't walled off like the Anchor, it was naturally protected by the rocky cliffs on its northern side, in which several dozen adobe huts were ensconced and mostly camouflaged, their domes curving like the papery bulbs of wasps' nests.

Wesah streamed out of the cabins and huts as the *naasyoon* arrived, filling the square with cries of recognition and long embraces. Even Rugaru and Gornoy had friends here: a quartet of chattering missives, each one with a baby in a leather sling strapped to his chest.

"I come back," Athène said as she slipped away into the throng.

Unsure of what to do or where to go, Gemma followed the crowd back into the largest of the log cabins. It was warm inside, fragrant with roasted meat and susurrant with quiet conversation. About twenty-five Wesah reposed in special chairs arranged against the walls, hands resting on their swollen bellies, rising and falling in the gentlest of swells. Everything seemed swaddled in serenity, familiarity, and affection—and all of it left Gemma feeling oddly melancholy. Life with the *naasyoon* had been too foreign and fraught to allow her much time for nostalgia. But the Villenaître reminded her of home, and all these joyful reunions only made her think of the reunions *she* ought to be having, with her sister and grandfather, with Clive and Clover, with her own people. All her progress with Athène's *naasyoon* suddenly counted for nothing; once again she was an oddity, an enemy, *aan dahor*. Gemma hated the way they all looked at her, and after a couple of minutes trying and failing not to smile at anyone (the Wesah saved their smiles for intimates, never strangers), she abandoned the cabin.

TOMMY WALLACH

But for the missives chattering away like gossipy Anchor wives, the square had emptied out; Athène's *naasyoon* had been absorbed by the Villenaître, effectively disbanded. Gemma walked south, into the sharp, briny tang carried on the wind. Athène said there was a large lake nearby—*Pchimayr*, or "Little Ocean"—whose waters were too salty to drink but considered sacred nonetheless. It seemed as worthwhile a destination as any. On the way, she passed a Wesah girl sweeping a cloud of dust out of her adobe hut. The particles were momentarily backlit by the faint red glow of a clay hearth, transformed into sparks. The girl, smooth-skinned and doe-eyed, just on the cusp of womanhood, stopped sweeping when she saw Gemma, stunned by this exotic apparition.

An odd thought—what would it be like making love to someone other than Athène? Gemma cast her eyes to the ground, irrationally fearful that the girl might have read the passing fancy somehow, and hurried on.

The narrow pathway, demarcated by smooth stones and the occasional wooden sculpture, wound its way between another clutch of huts and up a small, rocky hill. From the top of the ridge, Gemma got her first look at Little Ocean, and the sight took her breath away. She'd assumed the name was some kind of joke, but this really did look and feel like an ocean, and not just because of the saline tang in her nostrils. There was no sign of a far bank, only the gentle purple ridges of islands, like the smooth heads of sleeping sea serpents. The water was flat, an impossible bloodred shading to white where it met the white sky. The patchy grass on the downhill side of the ridge gave way to rocks, then pebbles, then pristine gray sand like fossilized snow.

But it wasn't the size or even the color of Little Ocean that most impressed; it was the great spiral somehow *inscribed* in the carmine surface of the water, as if God himself had taken a paintbrush, dipped it into the wet paint of the beach, and sketched himself a nautilus shell. Gemma jogged down to the strand to get a closer look. The spiral was even larger than it had seemed at first glance—wide enough for five or six people to walk abreast. It was made up of small rocks, glistening onyx on top but dyed to ivory below the waterline. Gemma scraped her nail across the white and sucked off the residue: saltshimmer on her tongue.

Choosing her steps carefully, stopping every dozen yards to marvel at the view, she took about twenty minutes to reach the inmost point of the spiral, where she sat down on a large rock, slipped out of her moccasins, and dipped her feet in the chill water. If only Flora could have been here, to share in this miracle. Gemma fingered the annulus around her neck, its threads hardened by sweat and time into something like gold, and imagined her sister sitting beside her. Her eyes would be wide with wonder, as her stubby little toes dug into the pebbly lake bed.

Time passed, the sun dropping steadily toward the horizon line. Gemma was distracted from her reverie by the sensation of someone watching her, and she looked toward the beach. A figure moved slowly across the sand, following its own lengthening shadow: a fair-haired child? No. An old woman, small and hunched, with a shock of unkempt silver hair.

Gemma retraced her steps around the spiral. When she was close to the beach again, the old woman began walking back toward the Villenaître, and Gemma followed after her. Somehow, she

TOMMY WALLACH

wasn't surprised when, fifteen minutes later, they ended up at the same hut where the pretty young woman had been sweeping up two hours earlier.

Inside the hut, an iron pot bubbled away over the fire. Vegetables were piled on a flat stone nearby. There was no sign of the girl.

"Are you the *otsapah?*" Gemma said in Wesah.

The old woman gestured toward the food, an unmistakable demand. Then she sat down in a wicker chair and closed her eyes. Gemma chopped the vegetables—a couple of wild carrots, some burdock, and a dirty potato she painstakingly peeled with a dull knife. All of it went into the pot, which smelled of chicken and salt. Little nosegays of herbs, cinched at the stems, hung from hooks over the stove. Gemma smelled each one—thyme, wild onion, some sort of mustard—and added the ones that seemed most likely to improve the stew. She stirred it with a wooden spoon, skimming the fat off the top whenever it congealed and taking little sips to test the flavor.

When the stew was ready, Gemma brought a bowl over to the *otsapah*, whom she woke with a gentle squeeze of the shoulder. The old woman took the bowl and spooned a bit of the stew into her mouth. She turned it over for a few moments before swallowing.

"Athène wants me to teach you," she said in Wesah, her voice warm and creaky. "All our songs. All our stories. She wants you to drink the dreamtea. She says you have visions. Do you?"

That was the question, wasn't it? But Gemma had yet to tell her *lover* the truth; she wasn't about to come clean to a complete stranger. "Yes."

The old woman smiled. "Big, beautiful visions?"

"Yes."

"You see the future? You see the past?"

"Yes."

The *otsapah's* smile suddenly disappeared. "I will teach you nothing," she snapped. "You will cook and clean for me until you leave for the *tooroon*, and then I will never see your face again." She took another sip of the stew, grimaced, and handed back the bowl. "You cook as well as you lie, *dahor*. More sage."

Gemma bristled at the epithet, but swallowed her anger. If she couldn't find some way to bring the old woman around, she could lose everything—Athène's love, the respect of the *naasyoon*, perhaps even her life.

"Sorry, *otsapah*," she said, and gently crumbled the rest of the sage leaves into the pot.

4. Clive

CLIVE REACHED DEEP INTO THE THICKET AND PINCHED the plump, bloody fruit between his fingers. He pulled it back out and admired it for a moment before popping it into his mouth. Farther along the briar patch, Flora was also picking berries—though her height made it difficult to get to the best ones—dropping them into a sling she'd made out of a gray woolen blanket. She looked up at Clive and displayed a gruesome-purple-black smile.

Paz was back at their campsite, staking the tent they'd found in one of the stolen horses' saddlebags and getting a fire going. Clive and Flora would bring back what food they could find, and while the girls invented a way to prepare it, Clive would scrounge around for enough wood to keep the fire going the rest of the night. Only three days out from the Anchor and already the formula was beginning to set. Ritual: that was how you transformed the extraordinary into the ordinary, the frightening into the banal. For hours at a time, Clive could forget that he was a criminal on the run, traveling with a girl he'd only recently stopped thinking of as his mortal enemy.

"Ow!" Flora exclaimed. She sucked on her finger, then took it out to examine the tiny wound. "Blackberries are stupid."

Clive laughed. "Does that mean I can have all of yours?"

"No." Flora pouted. "But why have these tasty berries if you're gonna put thorns all around them? Do you want me to eat you or not, berries?"

"That's a very good point."

"Thank you." Flora gave a little curtsy, staining thumbprints into the hem of her dress.

They carried their spoils back to the campsite. Paz knelt beside a ragged ring of stone, chapped lips pursed as she breathed life into the nascent fire. Watching her, Clive was struck by a strange thought: she was *his* blackberry plant. A tangle of thorns surrounding something you couldn't help but be drawn to—the promise of sweetness. He remembered the feel of her mouth on his, then forcefully banished the memory with another: the black blood cloud bursting from Michael's head. She might've helped him and Flora get away from the Mindful, but a single good turn could hardly outweigh a thousand bad ones.

"How'd you make out?" she asked, sitting back on her heels as the kindling caught.

"Just fine," Flora replied, laying out the blanket. "But blackberries are stupid."

"I know Clover would agree with you on that."

Flora frowned. "Why?"

"Well . . . it's a long story. I'll tell you some other time."

They feasted on berries spread over hardtack inherited from their late Protectorate benefactors, whose saddlebags had been swollen with clean shirts and underclothes (which a grateful Paz had used to replace her grimy prison garb), padded bags for sleeping, cutlery, bread and fruit, oats for the horses, and a small

TOMMY WALLACH

Filia whose pages hid a well-worn letter from a sweetheart, full of obscene promises.

Flora retired to the tent after dinner, leaving Clive and Paz alone at the fire. The logs slipped and settled, spraying sparks.

"Given any more thought to where the hell we're going?" Paz asked.

"Not really," Clive answered, which was the truth. He'd been taking them west, guessing the Protectorate would assume he and Paz would make straight for Sophia. But he didn't have much of a plan beyond that.

"Well, I've been thinking we might try Edgewise, since we're heading that way anyway."

"What's in Edgewise?" Clive asked, immediately suspicious.

"That Louise woman said the Mindful had some kind of group working out of an apothecary shop there. If we can figure out what they're up to and stop it, maybe we can get you back into the Protectorate's good graces."

"That's not very likely. And besides, if it worked, what would you do?"

"I can look after myself."

That was exactly what he was afraid of; Daughter only knew what kind of mischief Paz would get up to if left to her own devices again. Still, even if she did have some kind of ulterior motive, her idea was a decent one. Though Clive doubted anything he did now could ever make up for the dead bodies he'd left in the Bastion dungeon, Edgewise at least offered him and Flora a plausible chance of escape, on a ship bound for Sudamir. "All right," he said. "Let's go see the ocean."

Paz laughed. "Really? You're convinced that easy?"

"Why not? It beats wandering around and slowly starving to death."

"But what if I'm trying to fool you again?"

Clive shrugged. "I didn't say I trusted you, just that I'm going to Edgewise. I'm sure you'll do whatever's best for you."

The smile died on Paz's berry-stained lips. "I was only kidding, Clive."

"Sure."

"I mean it. Listen, I know I have a lot to make up for, but I'm trying my best. I really hope you and I can come to—"

"Let's get some sleep, yeah? I'm beat." Clive stood up and made for his bedroll. He wasn't ready for reconciliation—and doubted he ever would be.

"Okay. Good night, then."

He didn't look at her. "Good night."

Since they'd left the Anchor, Paz and Flora had shared the tent while Clive slept out under the stars, but that night he was woken in the wee hours by a light prickle of rain, hissing where it fell on the fire's lingering embers. He rose grudgingly and slipped into the tent. The girls were turned away from each other, taking up almost all the space beneath the canvas. Clive curled up like a dog at their feet but still ended up jostling Paz with his knee.

"Clive?" she said, voice heavy with sleep.

"Sorry."

"It's fine."

As if to drive home the point, she purposely stretched out, pressing her foot back into his knee. He couldn't pull away without

TOMMY WALLACH

rolling into the side of the tent, and if he argued, he'd just end up waking Flora. So he allowed her foot to rest there, a little flower of warmth, resenting the strange comfort it gave him.

The last time Clive had seen Edgewise, he'd been eleven years old, on a short ministry tour along the Oceanic Highway, and the gathering had been so famously riotous that Honor Hamill vowed never to bring his family there again. In Clive's memory, the place was bright and lively, replete with colorful characters and loud music.

Yet another reminder—as if he needed one—that memories were not to be trusted.

A gray cloud floated over and around Edgewise, visible from miles off, as if God himself were trying to hide the place. It turned out that the whole town existed on the narrow gradient between gray and black, the very air dense with morning mist and coal smoke, its inhabitants swaddled in ragged clothes the color of ashes, its clapboard buildings salt-stained and rotten from exposure to the sea air. The narrow dirt roads, cratered with potholes and sky-silvered puddles, served as byways for a perpetual scurry of fearless rats.

"We're really staying here?" Flora asked.

"For now," Clive answered.

It had been more than two weeks since they'd escaped from the Mindful. They would've made it to the coast in half the time if they hadn't felt compelled to leave the highway so often, but they couldn't afford to be seen. Even if word of their crimes hadn't reached this far just yet, the three of them made for a memorably conspicuous group: Paz's peach-fuzz coiffure and tattoo-ringed face, Clive's tattered Protectorate uniform, and the sheer incongruity of Flora's presence (any passerby would wonder what a pretty little blond girl was doing with such an eccentric pair—too young to be her guardians, too old to be her schoolmates, too dark-skinned and dark-haired to be close relations).

They made one exception, for a trader they ran into along a small farm road—a chatty and profane man in a straw hat and overalls who required an outrageous amount of haggling before his prices approached anything resembling reasonable. When the transaction was finished, Clive found himself the proud owner of half a dozen yards of black muslin, four spools of thread, and two glittering silver needles. Over the course of a few hours, Paz transformed these raw materials into three black robes with hoods deep enough to hide both her tattoos and Flora's extreme youth. When they reached Edgewise, Clive would play the part of a lay minister seeking passage to Sudamir, where he and his acolytes planned to spread the gospel of the Daughter far and wide.

Fitting, then, that the first recognizable landmark they passed was the local church—a squat toadstool of splotchy, moldering brick, its shingled dome missing half its terra-cotta panels, the underlayer flaking like sunburned skin. A sickly-looking man in the red robes of an Honor stood by the door, smoking a cheroot.

Beyond the church, the road angled downward to the ocean. Over the roofs of the waterside taverns and boardinghouses, Clive could make out the taller masts, waving back and forth with the tide like an insect's antennae. Most of the ships in the harbor would be smaller fishing vessels, the kind that went out every day in search of cod, hake, pollock, clams, oysters, and whatever else came up in

TOMMY WALLACH

the net or flapped at the end of the line, to be sold locally or carted to the Anchor (on ice in winter, smoked or brined in summer). The larger boats, on the other hand, would belong to traders up from Sudamir, and be packed with obscure and exotic foods, building supplies, and matériel for the war to come.

"This place smells," Flora said, crinkling up her nose.

"It's the fish," Clive said.

"You sure?" She nodded at a man coming toward them up the road. His face was one mass of silvery beard, and he carried what looked like a wet black rope over his shoulder. "I think it's that guy. And his eel."

"That's seaweed. They use it for seasoning. You can try it if you want."

"No, thank you."

Clive spotted a boardinghouse that looked slightly less derelict than the buildings around it. A sign out front advertised, FRANCIE'S: PAY BY THE ROOM, NOT BY THE GUEST! Inside, a portly middle-aged woman with rough red cheeks sat behind a desk, knitting a seemingly endless black scarf. She squinted at them as they approached.

"You checking in, or checking out?" she said. Then, seeing their confused expressions, she explained, "I can't remember faces. Everybody just blends together. You could be my own children, for all I know, except I don't have any." She barked out a laugh at her own joke.

"We'd like a room, ma'am."

"Just the one?"

"We're family."

"Sure you are," the woman said, in a tone that conveyed both skepticism and indifference.

Clive paid up for two nights and installed the girls upstairs.

"You have to go on your own?" Flora asked.

"He'll only be more suspicious with us along," Paz explained.

Clive nodded. "I'll be back before dark. Stay away from the windows."

The docks bustled with activity—sailors, stevedores, traders, merchants, and fishermen all shouting at once, trying to be heard over the others. An immense three-masted ship looked to have come into port recently; men trudged back and forth from the hold, carrying large canvas bags covered in unfamiliar markings, likely full of sugar or rice. About a dozen Protectorate soldiers patrolled the harbor, ensuring that nothing passed from ship to wagon without their knowledge. These men were stationed in Edgewise for years at a time, so there was little chance any of them would recognize Clive, but the sight of them still made him nervous.

He went looking for the customs office—the beating heart of Edgewise commerce—and found a short queue already assembled before the counter. It was nearly an hour before he reached the front of the line.

"Daughter's love be with you," he said, modulating his voice to sound like a zealous and slightly arrogant young preacher.

"What's your business?" the customs man said.

"To spread the good word of our Lord and his holy Daughter to those benighted souls in Sudamir."

The customs man rolled his eyes. "So you're looking to book passage on a ship?"

"That's right."

"Just for you?"

"No. Me and my . . . my ward."

"You need a cabin, or happy in a sling?"

"What can we get for fifteen silvers?"

The custom officer's eyes widened. "Whatever you want. When you wanna leave?"

"As soon as possible, good sir. The Lord's work brooks no delay."

"The *Whip-poor-will* leaves day after next. They've got plenty of room."

"Perfect."

"Where are you staying? I'll send word soon as I have confirmation from the captain."

Clive gave the name of the boardinghouse. "One last thing. Could you direct me to the local apothecary?"

The customs man snorted. "If you wanna call it that. Bitters for the barkeeps and pessaries for the whores, nothing much for anybody else."

"And where is it?"

"Back up the hill. Round the church."

"Thank you."

There were plenty of reasons not to look into it. Louise could've been lying about the Mindful cell in Edgewise, or Paz could've been lying about what *Louise* had said. And even if both of them had been telling the truth, that still left the question of exactly what

Clive was supposed to do about it. Say the Mindful really had set up shop here, and say he managed to single-handedly bring them down—even then, would the Protectorate ever consider pardoning his many crimes?

Of course not. But they might allow Flora to return to *her* normal life. And if there was a chance of that, however small, didn't Clive owe it to her to try?

A wooden cylinder beside the door, painted in angled stripes of red and white, spiraled hypnotically, powered by a fist-size windmill. A single four-paned window of poorly blown glass bulged and bubbled, making it impossible to see inside. Clive knocked on the door.

"Just a minute," someone said, amid a brief clatter. "All right. Come in."

The smell hit him first, or was it many smells?—herbs and spices, mushrooms and mosses, all of it mixed up into a sinus-clearing wall of sharp and sweet, acrid and fragrant. Behind the sales counter, hundreds of mysterious concoctions and reagents were arranged on the tables and shelves—flasks and beakers full of varicolored liquids, dried leaves and flowers, powders and oils. There was another doorway at the back of the shop, screened by a black curtain. Clive caught a snatch of whispered conversation before the curtain was pushed aside by an extremely small woman of forty or forty-five, granting him a momentary glimpse of the chamber beyond, where a bulky man with a thick beard was scribbling in a notebook.

"What is it?" the woman asked, as if Clive had interrupted her in the middle of something. Up close, he saw that her arms were pitted with tiny burn scars.

TOMMY WALLACH

"I . . . uh . . . I'm a preacher."

The apothecary pursed her lips. "There's nothing anathema here. Honor Olmstead oversees everything we do. Talk to him if you have a problem. If that's all—"

"I'm sorry. I think you've misunderstood me. I'm planning on traveling to Sudamir, and I was wondering if you have anything for the trip. I've always had a weak stomach, and I worry I'll spend half the trip bent over the railing, if you get my meaning."

"Ah, I see. Ginger should help. Here." She opened a small drawer in a whole wall of them and pulled out a bulbous beige root. "Peel it, cut it up into small pieces, and mash it into a glass of water."

"Thank you." The apothecary began to wrap the root in wax paper. Once the transaction was concluded, Clive would have no choice but to leave. If he was going to make a move, he needed to do it now. "I'm excited to go, I'll tell you," he said. "I've had just about enough of the Descendancy."

"Have you then?"

"Damn right. The Church has lost its way, in my opinion. We could use a fresh start."

"You shouldn't say things like that."

Clive raised an eyebrow. "Oh no? I was led to believe I'd find a sympathetic ear here."

The apothecary looked up at him, and there was an intelligence in her eyes that Clive recognized, the same questing, questioning penetration that had infected his whole childhood—Clover's eyes. "Then I'm afraid you were misled," the woman said. "That's two coppers."

"Sure." Clive left the coins on the counter and picked up the ginger. "Thank you for your time."

He turned, only to find the man he'd seen through the curtain blocking his way. A back door then, and a quick trot around to the front.

"Stay awhile, won't you?" the man said, drawing a gun from the waistband of his trousers.

"No need for that, brother," Clive said. He smiled broadly at this unfortunate misunderstanding. "Louise sent me. I'm afraid we have a lot to discuss."

5. Clover

HE OPENED UP THE COMPOST BIN AND INHALED DEEPLY—
interesting how quickly potato peelings and bread rinds
and apple cores lost their distinctive scents, fusing into
something rich and complex. This pile was only a couple
of weeks old, and already the earthworms had colonized it, glistening strands of pink sliding like plump sewing needles through the
scraps.

"It doesn't look like dirt," Carlos said, peeping his head over the
edge of the bin.

"And it won't for a long time yet," Clover replied. "Everything
worthwhile wants waiting. My ma used to say that." He plunged
the pitchfork into the pile and began turning over the compost.
"What I'm doing now is letting oxygen get in there, to help break
down the leavings. The heat will kill off all those earthworms, but
there's nothing to be done about that. They'll come back."

Carlos reached in and pulled out one wriggling ruby of a worm.
"I'm saving this one," he said, and gently laid it down in the puddle
that had formed around a brimming rain barrel.

After they'd finished with the compost, they went to the henhouse to collect the morning's eggs. Carlos pointed out a disturbance
in the dirt where a coyote had tried and failed to dig under the wall.

"I bet Bandito scared him off," Carlos said.

"Could be."

Bandito was the chirpy collie who had the run of the Dedios farm. He didn't strike Clover as particularly intimidating, but you never could tell. Every dog seemed sweet until you saw it hunting: shaking a rabbit back and forth to break its neck, tearing out gobbets of flesh, licking the blood off its snout.

They rinsed their hands at the well and went into the house, where Ms. Moses was laying out the table for breakfast. Frankie and Terry were already in their seats.

"Coyote tried to get in the henhouse," Clover said.

"Good luck with that," Terry replied. "Paz buried a metal fence a good foot down. A gopher couldn't get under it."

"Are you kidding?" Carlos said. "A gopher could get under it easy!"

"Could not."

"Could too. I reached my hand down a gopher hole once and my whole arm went in."

Terry groaned. "What a load."

"It's not! Clover, tell Terry he's wrong about gophers."

Clover could remember so many arguments with Clive just like this one, time and time again. But now, watching from the outside, he could see things he'd missed before—the older brother's fear of being surpassed, the younger brother's desperation for validation. It made him wish he'd gone easier on Clive, allowed him to win a few more battles. "Don't try to drag *me* into this. Besides, you should respect your older brother."

"That's right," Terry said, casting Clover a grateful wink.

The two of them had come a long way in the past few weeks, since Clover's eventful first visit to the Dedios house. It had been Ms. Moses who'd pulled Terry off him, who sat him down and dabbed the gash over his eye with a warm towel. But it was Carlos who smoothed the path to reconciliation, sitting there asking his million questions, eventually working his way round to the one thing they all had in common: Paz. Clover told the boys everything he could remember about his time with the girl he'd known as Irene—how completely she'd fooled him, how completely he'd fallen for her—and when the tale was finished, he could tell Terry was no longer looking at him the same way. He visited the house just about every other morning now, and always arrived to the same warm welcome.

"Coffee, Clover?" Ms. Moses asked.

"No, thank you, ma'am. Carlos and I should finish up in the garden."

"You don't have a lesson to get to?"

He did, actually, but he'd have to miss it: today was the day he'd chosen to put his plan into action. "Not till later," he said, grabbing a slice of toast with a fat pat of butter melting in the center like an egg yolk. "Come on, Carlos. Let's get this done."

An hour later, they were elbow-deep in piles of uprooted carpet blossom and cheatgrass. There was such a deep satisfaction to be found in ripping out the weeds constantly trying to undermine the useful plants. The pile of rubbish grew, tendrils of roots like so many fraying veins, bloody crumbles of soil: a vegetal charnel house. Carlos was talking a blue streak about snails, specifically the tiny one currently leaving a nacreous trail along the edge of the raised bed where the tomato plants were growing.

"How do they make those shells, do you think? With rocks?"

"They don't build them," Clover said. "They just develop, like your hair."

"But hair isn't hard."

"Fingernails are."

"That's true." Carlos examined his soil-blackened nail beds. "I want a shell like that. Then when Ms. Moses asked me to do something, I could just curl up inside it until she went away."

"But you'd have to carry it around with you all the time. It'd be pretty heavy."

"I guess."

Clover took hold of a stem of jimsonweed growing in the corner of the bed and tore it out. "These things grow five feet tall if you don't get to them early," he said. "They're in the same family as tomatoes."

"Can you eat 'em?"

"No. They're poisonous. Tomatoes are too, just not enough to hurt you."

Carlos gave a little whistle. "No wonder you got along so well with my sister—both of you know everything about everything."

Clover saw his opening. "Actually, I don't know everything—" He stopped. Terry and Frankie were passing by, carrying pails of milk into the house. They would transfer the milk into bottles and carry them up to town on their way to school. He waited until they were out of earshot to continue. "Carlos, there's something particular I'd really like to know. But I can't find it out on my own. I'll need your help."

The boy's face lit up with the joy of being chosen. "What is it?"

"It's about my father. I think he might've ended up here in Sophia a couple of months ago. But only the town guard would know for sure."

"You mean the Ferrell boys? I thought they tried to kill you."

"They did. That's why I can't ask them."

"So you want me to do it?"

Clover nodded. "But when you talk to them, you have to make sure they think *you're* the one who wants to know. You can't mention me at all. And you can't tell anyone else about this. Not your brothers, not Ms. Moses—no one. Can you promise me that?"

Carlos grinned: like all children, he loved secrets. "I promise," he said. "Cross my heart and hope to die."

Clover felt a twinge of guilt for taking advantage of the boy's naïveté, but he couldn't see any way around it. "Thanks, Carlos. You're a good friend."

The sun made a perfect halo atop Sophia's clock tower, no bigger than a pinky from this distance. Clover enjoyed the long walks to and from the Dedios farm; they gave him time to think.

Today, however, his contemplative mood was shattered when he saw four Wesah warriors cantering along the river toward the bridge. Though he knew the town had a peaceful relationship with the local *naasyoon*, he couldn't help the rush of fear and anger that just seeing the tribeswomen inspired in him. It was the Wesah who'd taken Gemma, after all, and who knew how many Descendant men and women over the years.

Clover had to remind himself that the Protectorate had killed off that many Wesah over the same period. History was a record of escalations, of violence inspiring greater violence inspiring greater violence. That was the cycle the Descendant Church had hoped to break with its idealistic renunciation of violence, its rejection of the demon called progress. And now that towering edifice of optimism was on the brink of collapse. Zeno would say the Descendancy had been doomed from the start, that war was a necessary outcome of human nature, engraved in the bloody folds of the brain at the dawn of time, but Clover wasn't convinced. He still believed in the central tenet of the Filia, that the solution to the cycle of violence was simultaneously man's ultimate salvation: forgiveness.

Clover picked up his pace and intercepted the tribeswomen just inside the town gate. The four of them were all riding bareback, and they turned at the sound of his cries.

"*Taanishi*," Clover said, one of the half dozen Wesah words he knew.

"*Taanishi*," answered the oldest warrior. Her face looked like cracked leather, warm and wrinkled.

"Do any of you speak English"—he remembered the strange way the Wesah asked questions—"*chee.*"

"English," said another warrior, this one wrapped in white fur and riding a beautiful piebald horse. "I know English."

Clover tried to keep any sign of enmity out of his voice. "Your people abducted a friend of mine. I want to find her."

The warrior spoke briefly to the others, then turned back to Clover. "You know who take your friend, *chee.*"

Clover pictured the hard but beautiful young woman who'd pressed her forehead up to the barrel of his gun. "Her name was

TOMMY WALLACH

Athène." The answer elicited a frisson of recognition from the group. "You know her, *chee*."

"She is a daughter of Andromède. The chief among chiefs."

"So you know where she is, *chee*."

Another brief discussion ensued before the English-speaking warrior delivered her verdict. "No. Her *naasyoon* travels far. But she will come to the *tooroon*."

Clover recognized the term: the biennial Wesah convocation out along the coast. If Gemma was still alive, she might very well be there.

"Thank you," Clover said, unable to remember the translation.

The warrior nodded. Then she and her fellows rode on up the hill, toward whatever business they had at the academy.

An electric light glowed behind the wavy glass of the greenhouse, and Clover moved toward it like a moth. Inside, the air sat still and heavy with moisture, almost claustrophobic. The space was divided up into three rows of tables, so dense with growth that he couldn't immediately tell if there was anyone here with him. Many of the plants were unfamiliar to him: a grape-size watermelon, a fern with huge furry leaves and tiny white buds, a cauliflower whose florets grew in swirling fractal patterns, spirals within spirals.

The note had been waiting in his room when he returned from his lessons a few hours ago: *Roof after dinner.*

"I hear you spoke to our Wesah guests this morning," Zeno said, appearing around the end of the row, "and accused them of kidnapping your friend."

"I only wanted to ask if they knew where she was."

"You offended them."

"Offended them? How?" Clover scoffed. "They *did* kidnap my friend. That's just a fact."

"Except they don't see themselves as kidnappers. They see themselves as liberators. And who's to say they aren't?"

He knew he shouldn't argue with her, but he couldn't help himself. "They steal women away from their families."

"From a society that views them as little more than walking wombs and slaves to the stove. Have you never considered why the hierarchies of your Church and Library are made up entirely of men? They pass power and privilege one to the next, down through the centuries—a codified squandering of slightly more than half of humanity's brainpower, as irrational as it is unjust. Stupidity! Monstrous stupidity!"

Zeno was fairly panting with emotion, and clearly embarrassed at the outburst. She reached out and stroked the soft needles of an exquisitely small juniper in a ceramic planter. Her voice softened to match it. "I wanted to work in the Library, you know."

"You grew up in the Anchor?"

"It was the time of Epistem Baraka, who presided over the Library before Turin. I met him once, at a gathering in Annunciation Square. I was scarcely older than you are now. I told him my dream of being an attendant, specializing in botany." Zeno noticed an irregularity in the smooth contour of the juniper's foliage and carefully pinched it off. "He laughed at me. Said he was sure I'd find a husband who'd let me keep a garden."

Clover thought about Gemma. While he'd been apprenticing with Bernstein and Clive trained for a life in the Church, what had

TOMMY WALLACH

she been doing? Waiting for Clive to propose—that was all she'd been allowed to hope for.

"I never thought about it that way," Clover said.

Zeno smiled sadly. "What a treat it must be, never to have to think about things."

"I'm sorry, Director Zeno."

"It's those tribeswomen who deserve an apology, particularly as they only came to me today to pass along information. Apparently, the Protectorate has officially stopped attacking Wesah found within Descendancy borders."

"Why?"

"Don't be lazy, child." Zeno picked up a pair of scissors and made a couple more quick trims around the miniature tree. "Use your mind."

It was a logic problem—simple enough, really. The Protectorate wouldn't have changed their policy so dramatically unless they wanted something from the Wesah. And as implausible as it seemed, there was only one thing they could want.

"They're hoping to convince the Wesah to ally with them against you. At the *tooroon*, probably."

"Very good," Zeno said, stepping back to admire her handiwork. "Which is why I'll be going too."

"You think you can convince them to side with Sophia instead?"

"I don't need their support, only a promise of neutrality. And I think it would help my case if you were to deliver your report to the Epistem before I arrive."

"My report?"

"I can only assume you've come to the correct conclusion by

now, that the Descendancy will lose this war. Am I wrong?"

Clover had seen some of the weapons the scholars were building in the academy workshop, each one a unique marvel of design—spewing a stream of liquid fire, or a cloud of poison gas, or bullets deviously fashioned to expand upon impact. He'd personally suggested improvements to the slow-burning oil Huma planned to drop from tanks mounted to Kittyhawk's fuselage. Daughter only knew what other machines and miracles remained half-built in the bowels of Sophia, or as yet unrealized in Zeno's boundless imagination.

"No," he said. "You're not wrong."

Zeno nodded. "Good. All I ask is that you tell your superiors exactly that. Hopefully they are still sane enough to spare themselves unnecessary bloodshed."

As she turned away from him, a smile played across the director's lips: the smile of a prophet who was seldom, if ever, unable to predict or mold the future. It put Clover in mind of an old proverb: *The eye sees not itself.* Arrogance was the most dangerous of character flaws because of the way it obscured its own existence; hubris recognized was no longer hubris.

So Zeno *did* have a weakness.

The next morning found Clover back at the Dedios farm, where he suffered through an interminable breakfast before he could get Carlos alone in the vegetable beds. He'd known from the moment he arrived that the boy had news to report; Carlos's eyes fairly sparkled with a secret to be shared.

"You talked with the Ferrell boys?"

Carlos nodded. "And I didn't even mention your name once."

TOMMY WALLACH

"So what'd they tell you?"

"They said they brought your da up to the academy, because he was hurt and the doctor needed to take care of him."

"And after that?"

Carlos shrugged. "All they knew was that he was up there for a really long time."

It wasn't much, but it was enough. Clover had spent some time in the infirmary himself, and he remembered how Lila had kept track of every detail of his recovery in her notebook; odds were she'd done the same thing for his father.

There was an expectant look on Carlos's face, an imploration. "Did I do good?" he finally asked.

"Well," Clover corrected, his mind already racing ahead to his next move. "And yes, Carlos, you did very well."

6. Paz

PAZ WATCHED FLORA STARE OUT THE SMALL, THICK-paned window of the boardinghouse bedroom, waiting for Clive with the sad earnestness of a dog abandoned by its master. He'd been gone only half an hour or so, but Paz felt anxious too. She lay back on the narrow bed and closed her eyes, less out of fatigue than a desire to escape her worries.

Some time later, she found herself standing at the center of a great plain. A distant wash of sound, like a wave crashing, grew steadily louder. And though she could see only empty fields and blank blue sky, she knew that something great and terrible was on its way, monstrous armies converging on this singular point, where she would be crushed between them. Someone grabbed hold of her shoulder. "Where's Clive?" echoed across the plain.

Paz sat up with a gasp, so abruptly that Flora jumped backward. While she'd been asleep, the light had changed its character, grown ruddy and illicit.

"Where's Clive?" Flora repeated, a note of rebuke in her voice.

Paz went to the window and looked out. Long shadows stretched like black taffy uphill. The sun was a luminous half eye sinking below the surface of the water. What if he'd been caught? What if he'd been killed? Or what if he hadn't even bothered to look for the Mindful cell? What if he'd decided to cut his losses and hop a ship out of the Descendancy, leaving all his obligations and all his demons behind?

"I don't know. Maybe he needed some time to himself."

Flora shook her head. "Something's wrong. I know it."

It had been a long time since Paz had thought of herself as a big sister, but anyone could tell that Flora was in need of comforting. A hug would've been the simplest opiate, but she doubted the girl would be receptive to her touch. Luckily, she had some experience with that sort of thing; around the time Terry turned ten, he decided he didn't like being hugged or kissed either. The whole family was forced to find other ways to show their care.

Paz leaned back against the windowsill. "Once, when I was little, I got lost playing in the woods. This is when we were still living in Coriander. At first I was real upset. I cried and cried. But that didn't get me anywhere, so I started planning. I found some berries, so I wouldn't starve, and a little creek so I'd have water. I collected some branches and made a little lean-to I could sleep under. And that's where my momma found me when it was time for dinner. She'd been watching me from the house the whole time. And I thought I was miles off."

Flora's eyes were vague, as if she'd barely been listening. "Are you saying I shouldn't worry?"

"I'm saying things are seldom as bad as they seem."

Flora almost divulged a smile but managed to suppress it. She sat up straight and folded her arms across her chest. "Why'd you do it?" she asked.

"You'll have to be more specific. I've done a lot of things."

"You gave my sister to the Wesah. Clive told me so."

"It was a little more complicated than that."

Flora set her jaw. "What's complicated? Either you did or you didn't."

"The Wesah caught me, okay? I wasn't careful enough and they caught me. But that chieftain, Athène, she was already planning on taking your sister. She said her tribe was gonna ride into camp and cut their way through to her. So I told them that if they let me go, I'd bring Gemma right to them."

"Why would they want her and not you?"

"Hand to God, Flora, I don't know. I've thought and I've thought and I still can't make sense of it. But I promise you this: they weren't planning on hurting her."

"How do you know?"

Paz remembered the intensity in Athène's voice, palpable in spite of her heavily accented English. "Just something in the way the chieftain talked about your sister, like she was something really special."

"She was," Flora said. "She is."

They were silent for a while, watching the sun disappear into the ocean, casting all of Edgewise into an expectant, ominous darkness. The sails of the ships in the harbor rose and fell, blocking out the nascent stars and revealing them again.

"Your sister killed my father, that night at the pumphouse," Paz said quietly. "I don't blame her for it anymore, because I know I would've done the same to protect my family. But the anger I felt—well, it changed something inside me. It turned me into Irene. But I'm not her anymore."

TOMMY WALLACH

"So who are you?"

The question could've been an accusation, but Flora's gaze was steady and earnest, and Paz heard it for the offer it was: an opportunity to become something solid again. How long could she go on drifting, her allegiances shifting out of expediency, out of contingency, out of chance? She resolved that whatever answer she gave Flora, it would be the truth, at least insofar as she could know it.

"I still think the world would be a better place without the Descendancy," she said, choosing each word with care, "but I'm finished sacrificing others for Sophia's sake. I'm done being a pawn. I promise I'll never hurt you again, Flora. I'll never hurt any of you. . . ."

Her voice caught as Flora grabbed hold of her hand. "It's okay," the girl said, with that purity of feeling of which only the very young are capable. Before she could think better of it, Paz pulled Flora to her chest, surreptitiously wiping the tears from her eyes. She felt foolish, unworthy of this sudden grace, but also liberated, cleansed.

"Can we go find Clive now?" Flora said into her shoulder.

At that moment, Paz would've agreed to anything the girl asked. "Of course."

The owner of the boardinghouse told them where to find the apothecary shop, but by the time they got there, the place looked to have closed up for the night.

"Let's check the docks," Paz said.

Flora got down from her tippy-toes, having failed to see anything through the shop windows. "Why there?"

Paz didn't want to infect the girl with her irrational fear that

Clive had decided to abandon them, so she told a different truth. "I've never seen the ocean before."

"Really?"

Paz nodded. "Never had reason to."

Hand in hand, they descended the main road to the waterfront, past dozens of wide-shouldered shadows trudging exhausted uphill, until their footsteps began to knock resonantly on the knotty planks of the docks. The salt smell of the sea was strong even up by the boardinghouse, but here it was augmented by a complex bouquet made up of equal parts freshly caught fish, mildewing oak, algal bloom, meat cooking in the quayside taverns, and unwashed sailor. In spite of the hour, the docks were still busy, clamorous with the obscenity-laden chatter of the stevedores and the polyphonic creaking of the ships.

"There it is," Flora said, leaning up against a stanchion. "What do you think?"

Paz squinted into the dark, but all she could make out was sparkling blackness, ridges of reflected moonlight dancing like will-o'-the-wisps. Somewhere beneath her, water lapped at the shore like a cat's tongue testing a bowl of milk. A sense of vastness, of ineluctable and interminable isolation, rendered her momentarily speechless.

A group of drunkards at a nearby public house exploded with laughter, interrupting Paz's morbid reverie, but before she could answer Flora's question, the girl was already tugging excitedly at her arm.

"Look over there!" she said, pointing at the revelers.

"What is it?"

"That's Clive!"

In the flickering light of torches arranged around the edge of the tavern's deck, Paz made out Clive seated at a table with three strangers. A fresh pitcher of golden ale was centered on the table, surrounded by an impressive collection of empty glasses.

"Come on!" Flora said, and took off toward the tavern.

Paz pulled her hood over her face and followed the girl into the public house—pungent with beer, sawdust damp and squalid underfoot, loud with conversation and the music performed by a scantily clad female fiddler and a burly accordionist dressed like a ship's captain—and out again, onto the back deck. Flora was already seated at the table, where Clive was making introductions.

"And here's the woman of the hour," he said as Paz approached.

The strangers stood up, and from the reverence in their eyes, Paz knew they had to be the Mindful cell that Louise had spoken of.

"I'm Devorah," said a small, white-haired woman on the opposite side of the table. "It's an honor to meet you, Paz."

Next came Erbe, a frail-looking fellow in his sixties, and then Ferguson, a big-boned and bushy-bearded man who took Paz's hand in both of his and held it there like an offering.

"So it's really you," he said. "You're really here."

Paz smiled uncomfortably. "Have we met?"

"I feel like we have. Clive's been telling us stories about you for the past couple of hours. Did you really trick his little brother into falling in love with you?"

"I—that is—"

"At least let the poor girl sit before you start interrogating her," Devorah said.

They pulled another chair up to the table. Erbe poured Paz

a glass of ale, the foam rising perfectly up to the lip. She'd need her wits about her to navigate this conversation, but it wouldn't look right to abstain. "Clive was just telling us about the breakout," Devorah said. "Is it true the whole cell is dead?"

"As far as I know," Paz said, putting on a tragic expression. "They gave their lives so I could escape."

"Fucking Protectorate pigs," Ferguson said. He raised his glass. "To our fallen friends: Ralph, Louise, Yuri, and Lars. They died as heroes."

They all drank. The ale was lukewarm but smooth; Paz hadn't realized just how much she needed it, and the glass was soon empty. Erbe refilled it from the pitcher.

"So," Clive said, "now that Paz is here, I know we'd both love to hear just what it is you're doing in Edgewise. Louise said you had some kind of mission, but we didn't get the chance to talk details."

Paz cringed inwardly. Clive might've convinced the Mindful that he was on their side, but it still wouldn't do to look overeager. She noticed the quick glance that passed between Devorah and Erbe: suspicion, or something less sinister? After a moment, Erbe gave a slight nod; a decision had been reached without words. Paz wondered if he and Devorah were lovers.

"Finish up your drinks and we'll head back to the shop," he said. "I think it'll be easiest just to show you."

"I miss electricity," Ferguson said, as he lit the first lantern and hung it from a hook in the ceiling.

They were in a chamber behind a curtained door in the apothecary shop. Paz guessed it was some kind of chemistry laboratory.

Ferguson lit another lantern as Devorah went to unlock a cupboard at the back of the room. Paz took the opportunity to sniff the tops of a few beakers, to get a sense of what the Mindful were working with: pine resin and ferrous sulfate, ether and linseed oil, the unmistakable powdery smell of ground soapstone and the bitter tang of opium.

"Obviously, scientific research is almost impossible within the boundaries of the Descendancy," Erbe explained. "A Library attendant is out here every couple of months, and he turns the place over looking for anathema. So we've had to be very careful. And mistakes have been made."

Devorah turned away from the cabinet, holding a stoppered vial of clear liquid. Paz noticed how Ferguson unconsciously stepped away from it.

"You may've heard about an outbreak of influenza in the Anchor earlier this year," Devorah said. "That was a member of Louise's cell, a chemistry scholar fresh from the academy. He had an accident in the Anchor laboratory, ruined the sample and exposed a bunch of folks to boot. Zeno was livid, so she entrusted the second sample to us." Devorah carefully positioned the vial in a metal clamp.

"What are you going to do with it?" Paz asked.

"When the war comes, we'll spread the virus throughout the Anchor. We don't expect the mortality to be greater than fifteen percent, but the effect on morale will be incalculable."

"There's enough there to infect the whole city?" Clive said.

Ferguson took down one of the lanterns and brought it closer to the cabinet. Behind a false back panel, a hole had been carved into the wall. Stepping closer to look inside, Paz saw row upon row of vials arrayed in wooden racks, like soldiers standing at attention.

"You're awful people!" Flora announced, storming through the curtain and back out into the apothecary shop.

"Hey!" Clive called out after her. He tried to play it off with a laugh. "Sorry about her. She's still coming around to the movement."

"Kids," Erbe said sympathetically.

Paz felt a presentiment of catastrophe, dozens of micro-observations joining together into something like a sixth sense. A moment later there was a scream from the other room. "Clive! The man's here! The bad man!"

Clive bolted back through the curtain. The three members of the Mindful followed, but Paz held herself in check. She'd already guessed who "the bad man" was, and what his presence here meant. Without pausing to consider, she grabbed one of the rags hanging on the wall, doused half of it in the ether she'd noticed earlier, and set it aflame with the candle inside one of the lanterns. As the voices in the other room grew increasingly agitated, Paz touched the flame to anything in the laboratory that might burn. A shelf of notebooks was the quickest to catch, and she distributed the papers around the room, making a special point of tossing a stack into the still-open hole where the influenza samples were kept. The rest of the flask of ether provoked the fire to even greater heights, and soon the whole cabinet was aflame.

Paz heard smashing sounds from the apothecary shop and ran to the curtain, only to see it part before her. She backed away, making room for Ralph to join her among the flames. He was in bad shape, supporting himself with a crutch and bleeding through the dirty bandages wrapped around his head. His blackened eyes coupled with his pale complexion made him look monstrous, half-dead.

"You're a traitor," he said wonderingly.

"No," Paz said, stepping forward. "This was an accident. If you'll just listen—"

As soon as she was close enough, she ripped the crutch out of Ralph's hand. He teetered for a second, then toppled over onto his side. Paz had kept hold of the crutch, and now she flipped it over and slammed the crosspiece down as hard as she could onto Ralph's face, over and over, until she was certain he'd never get up again.

Back in the apothecary shop, both Clive and Ferguson were laid out on the ground, visibly breathing but unconscious. Erbe had his gun out and pointed at Flora, who had knelt down next to Clive and was trying fruitlessly to shake him awake. Erbe and Devorah turned when Paz came in.

"What happened to Ralph?" Erbe asked.

His eyes widened as Paz threw the crutch like a javelin right into his forehead. He dropped the gun as he crumpled to the ground. Devorah lunged for it, but Paz was faster; she came up with the weapon and aimed it right between the older woman's eyes.

"Do it," she said. "I'll die a hero too."

The curtain at the back of the room had caught fire now; through the opening, Paz watched as the first couple of beakers exploded with the heat. Some of the liquid landed on Ralph and set his clothes alight. His skin puckered, blackened. The whole shop would go up soon.

"I leave with my friends, you leave with yours," Paz said.

SLOW BURN

She didn't wait to see if her offer would be accepted. Flora had already gotten her little body under one of Clive's shoulders, and now Paz hoisted the rest of him. Slowly they made their way to the door and back onto the streets of Edgewise.

Though she would've liked to head straight out of town, Paz knew they wouldn't get far without horses, so she and Flora made for the boardinghouse. They'd been walking for less than a minute when the first cries came—"Fire! Fire!"—and not long after, they passed a group of Protectorate soldiers sprinting uphill toward the apothecary shop. Luckily, Clive looked like any other blacked-out drunk, so the soldiers didn't pay him any mind.

At the boardinghouse, Paz left Clive and Flora downstairs and hastily collected their things from the room. Flora was waiting with the horses when she returned. Clive was just conscious enough to get a leg over the saddle. Paz mounted up and pulled him the rest of the way while Flora climbed onto the other horse.

"You know where we're going?" Flora asked.

"I sure do," Paz said. "The hell away from here."

7. Gemma

THE WATER FROM LITTLE OCEAN WAS TOO SALTY TO drink, so Gemma had to hike more than a mile to fetch fresh water from upriver. She carried it in two hide bags attached to a large stick balanced on her back. She was never thanked for her efforts on the *otsapah*'s behalf, no matter how arduous the chore she'd completed or how elaborate the meal she'd prepared. The woman the Wesah called Grandmother (a moniker Gemma had been expressly forbidden from using) never spoke to her except to order or demand, and never referred to her as anything other than *li dahor*.

Meanwhile, the education of Helene, the young Wesah woman Gemma had seen outside that first day, continued apace. When Gemma was in the hut with the two of them, she could absorb some of the lessons, but inevitably she'd be sent off on some tedious errand or another, and by the time she returned, the *otsapah* and her student would've moved on to another subject. Helene at least seemed bothered by the disparity in their treatment; she was always glancing guiltily at Gemma, then looking away as soon as they made eye contact.

One night Gemma was out behind the hut dressing and butchering a rabbit, listening to Grandmother's voice through the wall.

The *otsapah* was telling a piece of the great origin tale of the Wesah, a seemingly endless saga centering around Wolf and Fox, two deities at war over the souls of mankind. They were a little like God and the devil in the Filia, except Gemma couldn't tell whether Fox or Wolf was the more evil. Fox was a trickster; her playfulness often shaded into cruelty, fooling otherwise good women into iniquity. Wolf was less clever but more brutal, a god of carnage. In the tale Grandmother told that night, Fox had her followers murder a tribe of Wolf's adherents and dress in their pelts, so they could sneak into Wolf's camp and learn her secrets. Wolf recognized the interlopers too late, and one of them managed to steal away her great fangs, which were said to have the magical power to . . .

"*Dahor*, this is not for you!" Grandmother suddenly shouted. Even from inside the hut, she'd noticed the momentary lapse in chopping. Gemma had to swallow down a surprisingly intense burst of hatred; was there anything worse than hearing the beginning of a story only to be robbed of the ending?

"*Ni mihtatayn!*" she called out in response. *I'm sorry.*

However much it burned, she never showed anything but gratitude for every coarse insult and thankless task Grandmother threw her way. She *had* to win over the *otsapah* somehow; it was the only way she could ensure her continued acceptance by the Wesah, and more importantly, her place at Athène's side.

The chieftain had a large hut all to herself in the Villenaître, and inside that hut was an actual, honest-to-goodness bed, with a rough-weave mattress and a quilt prickly with goose feathers. The quilt's design—cross-stitched squares in various colors—didn't

TOMMY WALLACH

seem in keeping with the usual Wesah textiles, which meant it had probably come from some Descendancy trader; Gemma found its bland familiarity surprisingly reassuring.

She turned over, intertwining her legs with Athène's, feeling momentarily luxurious.

"Good morning," Athène said in English.

"Good morning," Gemma replied in Wesah.

They spoke in a hodgepodge of their two languages when they were alone, helping each other articulate more and more complex ideas.

Athène brought her face close, but Gemma shied away.

"No kiss?" Athène used English for that, preferring the word "kiss" to the undeniably less palatable Wesah analogue, *oochaym*.

"You don't want to. My breath—"

"Your breath is sweet," Athène countered, forcing the issue. Gemma allowed herself to be kissed, deeply and softly at once, pulling back only when she sensed that doorway inside her opening up again, the one that her pious upbringing had done its best to brick over. The Filia said carnal acts between an unmarried man and woman represented a venial sin, while those same acts carried out between two members of the same sex were a mortal one. But did love compound the wickedness, or diminish it? Before Athène, Gemma wouldn't have been able to say how two women might even attempt such wrongdoing; now she understood all too well. It was a little bit like making music—a communion made up of equal parts technical coordination and emotional harmony—only the payoff was, to put it simply, a hell of a lot more satisfying: exactly why Gemma now pushed Athène away, laughing at the sheer magnetic difficulty of it.

The light around the flap of the door was cobalt blue; sunrise loomed.

"I have to go," she said. "Grandmother will want me."

But Athène only squeezed Gemma's leg more tightly between her own. "Not just yet. Tell me a story."

Gemma marshaled her strength and pushed off the mattress, coming to perch atop Athène. "You know too much about me already. Your turn to tell."

"Tell what?"

"Anything. Everything. What happened between you and Noémie?"

Gemma hadn't seen hide nor hair of the woman who'd nearly murdered her since they reached the Villenaître, and she was glad for that. Still, Noémie was more unsettling as a cautionary tale than a physical threat; Athène's abandonment of her previous lover seemed to presage Gemma's inevitable fate.

"I have told you before, I'd stopped loving her long before you arrived," Athène said.

"It didn't look that way. She still slept in your tent."

"Lovemaking and love are not the same thing."

"I know. But what caused it? What did she do wrong?"

Athène shrugged. "Who can say? Love dies, like everything. It is no tragedy. This subject is boring."

"Fine. Then tell me something about your childhood."

"My childhood is boring too."

"Not to me."

Athène remained evasive about her history, preferring to hear about life in the Anchor, or to discuss the subtleties of hand-to-

TOMMY WALLACH

hand combat, or, whenever possible, to forgo conversation in lieu of more pleasurable pastimes. Gemma was surprised to discover that you could feel close to someone you knew next to nothing about, as if the hard facts of a person's life were merely ornaments, and the essence was to be found in the trivialities of her presence—how she walked, how she laughed, how she touched you.

"You know about my mother already," Athène said.

"Andromède," Gemma replied—the leader of the Wesah nation. She imagined it was a bit like being the daughter of the Archbishop and the Epistem and the Grand Marshal all at the same time. "You said you used to travel with her *naasyoon*. When was that?"

"Two years ago. I was not—what is word—respecting?"

"Respectful."

"Yes. I was not respectful enough to her. When I leave her *naasyoon* and make my own, there was anger between us."

"Why?"

"Some of the old ways, the rituals and the songs—I did not believe in them. I learn English very young. I meet people from your Descendancy, and they tell me the stories in your *Filia*. They are like our stories of Wolf and Fox, only different. Suddenly I am seeing how strange my own stories are, and I begin to wonder if they are true. After I leave my mother's *naasyoon*, she tell me, 'I hope you find belief.' But I did not think I would." Athène reached out to stroke Gemma's cheek. "Then I find you. My little dancer. You have made me believe again."

Gemma donned a smile, hoping it looked sincere. Grandmother still hadn't told Athène what she'd discovered that first day—that the *dahor* was an impostor. Maybe she didn't care enough to bother, or maybe she'd tried and the chieftain had refused to hear it. Whatever the explanation, somehow Athène maintained the foolish notion that Gemma was a genuine medium to the spirit world. But what would she do when the truth finally came out, that her lover had no magic inside her, just a sickness for which there was neither name nor cure?

"Are you all right?" Athène said.

"I'm just worried about the *otsapah*. I don't think she likes me very much. She hasn't taught me anything."

"The *tooroon* is still months away. There is all the time in the world. And I'm sure Grandmother has her reasons."

"Maybe. But I'm not about to give her another one." She rolled off the bed and began to dress, mentally girding herself for another day of drudgery and disdain.

"You'll come back tonight?" Athène said.

Gemma smiled sadly. "If it were up to me, I'd never leave your side at all."

It was one of those limpid, windless days where everything seemed stiller than usual, as if the world had crystallized. The sun spilled warmly down Gemma's left side—cheek to arm to the strip of bare midriff between her vest and skirt—and she noticed how her skin had darkened over the past few months, how her arms and legs rippled with new muscle. All her life, people had told her she was beautiful; yet only now, since she'd come to travel with the Wesah, did she *feel* beautiful. More than that, she felt competent, powerful, *embodied*.

The Church taught that every human being was first and foremost a soul, while school had emphasized the primacy of the mind.

Both believed the body to be a mere husk, a container for higher things. But Gemma knew now that the body was so much more than that. She'd learned from the instinctual hustle of the hunt, the wild abandon of the dance, the blissful exhaustion of her nights with Athène. Before the brain could think its first thought, before the soul knew to seek God's grace, the body was there. Alpha and omega. World without end. Amen.

The *otsapah*'s hut was empty but for a couple of chickens tapping away at a small pile of corn, clucking contentedly. Out back, Helene stirred a small cast-iron pot hanging over the fire. As Gemma watched her, she caught a whiff of what was brewing, and a fully formed plan suddenly manifested in her mind, begging to be executed. It was bold, patently stupid, but also oddly consonant with the stories she'd absorbed from the *otsapah*. Today she would be Fox, hustler and trickster, beholden to no one.

"Where's the *otsapah*?" she said.

Helene started, turned to face her. "Laure has begun her *kishiwaashiwin*," she said, using the odd Wesah word that meant both "insanity" and "childbirth." "Grandmother is there to bless the child when she comes, and to journey if it is a girl."

"And you're preparing the dreamtea now."

"Yes. Grandmother says the birth should be an easy one."

That was exactly what Gemma had been hoping for. She came to kneel beside the pot, leaning over the top and breathing in the steam. It had a deeply unpleasant smell—acrid, almost putrid.

"Careful," Helene said.

Gemma looked up at the younger girl and smiled mischievously. "Have you ever tried it?"

"Of course not. It's not allowed until I have been training for one turn of the seasons."

"Oh no? So this isn't allowed?"

In one smooth motion, Gemma picked up the wide-mouthed clay cup next to the pot and scooped it through the dreamtea. Helene was shocked into paralysis at the audacity of it; by the time she realized what was happening, Gemma had already danced away. The girl jumped to her feet, chittering incomprehensibly about "shame" and "danger," but Gemma was resolved. If the *otsapah* wouldn't teach her what she needed to know, then she would damn well teach herself.

"To your health," she said, raising the cup and throwing it back.

Daughter's love, but it tasted even worse than it smelled; she only barely managed to keep it down. Helene's shouting had died on her lips, and now she could only gape. The hard part was over; all that remained was to wait for the journey to begin. Gemma reached out a hand to Helene—"Come with me?"—and the girl took it. Fingers interlaced, they walked up over the ridge, gazing down on the spot where that elegant spiral of stones began unfurling through the rubicund water.

"Why do you call it Little Ocean?" she asked. "The ocean is hundreds of miles away."

"This lake connects to the ocean, through a tunnel dug by Mole," Helene replied. "The *tooroon* is held at the place the tunnel meets the sea."

Gemma imagined Clover would have had a few things to say about the likelihood of an underground tunnel stretching across the continent, but she only nodded.

TOMMY WALLACH

They sat down on the rocky hillside between stands of tall, spindly grasses. A fresh breeze skipped across the water like a stone, stippling the surface. Gemma began to sing something, a melody she knew by heart but couldn't name, and as the notes coalesced and dissipated in their perfect sequence, the currents of time began to slow. She looked to Helene, as if for confirmation of this distortion, but the girl was still focused on the water, and it seemed possible that hours might pass before she glanced over again. Gemma felt frightened at first, until the terror resolved into amusement. The dilation of time revealed a fundamental misunderstanding of the universe.

"We've been living in a dream," she whispered.

She remembered how they'd all laughed at Clover when he'd claimed to have read a book that said time didn't exist. But it was true! She'd stepped outside of time, was looking down on it, looking down on everything. She was seeing the spiral from the sky, a puppy curled up on itself, a nautilus shell, and bursting through the membrane that separated the centuries came a flock of great roaring beasts of rusted iron, articulated joints jumping and juddering, taking huge bites of sopping earth, keeling over backward to drop their load of rocks—*clattersplash*—into the water (not red, not yet red), and the pale-skinned man walking along the beach, equally time-less, envisioning one possible future and then discarding it, realizing he'd gotten it all wrong, would have to start again. Thousands of men and women walked the spiral, a blur of life, like running water, chanting a fragment of fossilized poetry Gemma had picked up somewhere: *I had not thought death had undone so many.*

This was a gravestone. And more: *all* monuments were gravestones. It was the first note of sourness in the vision, changing the key from major to minor. The sun slid untrammeled down toward the horizon, like a bead seeking the bottom of the necklace. It would not be stopped. The darkness would not be stopped.

Where was Helene? She had gone, all gone, *undone so many*. Gemma reached for the braided annulus that still rested against her chest. Flora, beautiful Flora: the very name was an invocation. Here she was, capering down the hillside, oblivious, hair glittering like sand at sunset. Gemma rose and ran to catch up, and together they skipped along the shore.

"Why did you go?" Flora asked, though her lips never moved. "When will you come back?"

"It wasn't my choice. I love you."

"Do you?"

Gemma froze, watching helplessly as her sister strode into the lake and was swallowed up.

"Flora!"

She wanted to follow, but she couldn't move. Looking down, she saw that the water around her feet had thickened, trapping her. Only it wasn't water; it was blood. Blood all along: a premonition. The sun flipped over, black on the back, so that the world was lit only by the falling crimson stars streaming down from the infernal heavens. The first one landed right in the middle of the lake— *clattersplashhiss*—and sent up a great plume of water and steam. Others slammed into the beach, the distant hilltops, the Villenaître, and Gemma knew in her soul that the whole world would suffer this same fate: a hailstorm of Daughters, a conflagration of

TOMMY WALLACH

conflagrations. She was the angel, the herald. She had to tell them!

Voices now, a tumult. Gemma looked up toward the ridge and saw Grandmother standing there, a thousand feet tall, lightning bolts shooting from her eyes, and Helene and Athène beside her.

"It's coming!" she shouted in Wesah. "Blood and fire! There's nowhere to hide. Everything is ruined! Everything is . . . is . . ."

She lost track of the words, lost control of her body. Time had stopped for good. This moment was forever, a perpetual cataclysm that could not be prevented because it had never started, had always been. She screamed, and the sound ramified, enveloped her, blinded her. She screamed again, and again, and

8. Clive

TO HIS LEFT, INNUMERABLE SHADES OF GREEN FLOWED past, from the glaucous, velvety underside of the alder leaves to the polished emerald of the hemlocks, darkening with density and distance to an ivy-colored snarl, rich and deep, green doing an impression of black—that fantastical verdure of high summer, before the Midas sun baked the world into its golden image. To his right lay the fog-wreathed strand, strewn with seaweed and driftwood in random patterns that begged for the explication of a tasseomancer or astrologer, sand shading away into the ocean, mysterious undersea worlds distant as the sun, distant as heaven.

Clive held on to Paz's waist as he drifted in and out of sleep, watching these divine borders unfurl. At some point, he noticed that Gemma was riding just alongside him, and they smiled at each other. He wanted to ask her how she'd gotten there, but he was distracted by an eagle soaring through the sky behind her, and in that instant he was looking elsewhere, she transformed back into Flora.

Eventually, he managed to remain conscious for long enough to wonder exactly how he'd come to be on the back of a horse cantering south along the shoreline, and began to piece together the events of the past few hours. He'd spoken to the Edgewise harbormaster. He'd visited the apothecary shop and been greeted with a gun. He'd gone out drinking with the Mindful, met up with Paz and Flora, then . . .

Jars full of poison. Flora screaming. Ralph in the doorway like some grim revenant. Hands grabbing, spinning, wrestling himself free, throwing wild punches, and somehow catching the mountainous Ferguson clean on the chin. Then a shock of pain as Erbe or Devorah slammed him in the back of the head with something. Darkness. He'd been completely helpless. It should've been the end. Yet here he was, alive and well, and all thanks to Paz. The thought suffused him with a deep sense of security, and for a moment, he felt as if he were back in the old ministry wagon, rattling over the Tails, surrounded by his family. Half-asleep between the warmth of Paz and the warmth of the horse, sun-heat flickering against his cheek, he felt an incongruous, irrepressible joy burbling out from somewhere deep inside.

And why? His impractical plan of sailing away to Sudamir was scotched, and if he were ever seen near the Anchor again, he'd be put to death. He was neither soldier nor preacher, brother nor son—just a leaf skittering along the road, prone to any passing gust of wind. What did he have to feel joyous about?

Nothing, and everything: the simple pleasure of resting his body against Paz's, lulled by the meaty clop of hooves on dirt and the restless cries of the littoral birds, watching the shadows cast by the trees dance across his eyelids. It seemed such an impossible miracle, just to be allowed to breathe and smell and feel—all the evidence of providence one should need.

They stopped late in the afternoon, tied the horses up a ways off the road, and walked down to the water. Neither Flora nor Paz had slept since their arrival in Edgewise the previous afternoon, and after they all shared a bit of bread and honey left over from the previous leg of their journey, the girls lay down in the shade of a massive rock and succumbed to exhaustion.

But Clive couldn't have slept for all the shekels in the world. He left the girls and wandered barefoot along the shore, marveling at the million little jewels the sea was constantly offering up for his delectation. Bits of shell, rough and white on one side, smooth and silvery purple on the other, reminiscent of the black opal that had once been the centerpiece of Clover's mineral collection (gone now, all gone). Fragments of wrack, opaque and glassine, slick to the touch, like the skin of some mysterious sea creature. Smooth stones built for skipping. The empty armature of a crab, paper-thin and sun-bleached, soul-departed.

On a spit of glossy black stone, he crouched over a tide pool and gave names to the creatures clutching the walls, like Aleph and Eva in the Garden. The Sickly Sunflower, with its big black mouth and waving petals. The Rough Star. The Purple Sea-Porcupine. His eyes slid past the pool to the ocean beyond, and it seemed the difference between the two was merely one of scale, rather than kind. Back the way he'd come, far across the pale speckled strand, two more mysterious creatures lay, serene as clouds, still but for their hair whirling in the gusting wind like a couple of tethered tumbleweeds—one raven, one flaxen. Clive felt paralyzed by the intensity of his feelings for them, for every living creature, for the whole world.

Alive. He was alive. To walk the beach. To stroke the gritty barnacles that clung tenaciously to the walls of the tide pool. To suffer

TOMMY WALLACH

this awful but exquisite ache in his bruised ribs. To gaze from afar on the people he . . .

Twice now she had saved him. First in the wagon, during the skirmish between the Mindful and the Protectorate, and again last night, when she'd masterminded their escape from Edgewise. And could it all be part of some more elaborate ploy to regain his trust, only to betray him again? Maybe. But if so, then he would allow himself to be betrayed. Life suddenly seemed too short, too precious, to squander in constant doubt. From this moment forward, he would choose faith. He would choose love.

He crossed the beach and sat down beside them, watching the waves eat away at the uncomplaining shore, brooding on the strange disparity between how important his life felt to him, and how obviously insignificant it was next to this ocean, that sky: one gleaming grain of sand on an infinite beach.

They rode a couple of hours more that day, using up the rest of the light, and made camp on a bluff overlooking the sea.

Within a week, they'd left the official boundaries of the Descendancy behind.

"I think it looks cute," Flora said.

Paz tutted. "Looks can be deceiving."

"That's true," Clive said. "You seemed so nice when we first met."

"Exactly my point."

They'd been traveling at a breakneck pace for the last week and a half, putting as much distance between themselves and Edgewise as possible. But there was such a thing as *too* much distance; habitations would grow sparser as they continued moving south, until civilization gave out completely. Though Clive had the know-how to build a cabin, and Paz was a skillful hunter, neither of them was interested in trying to survive on their own indefinitely. Flora, at the very least, deserved some semblance of a normal life.

Which was why they now found themselves at the top of a hill, gazing down on what had to be the sleepiest, quaintest fishing village Clive had ever seen. It looked more like an idealized watercolor than a real place—a loose conglomeration of simple, sturdy houses gilding the edge of a picturesque cove, columned with cozy plumes of translucent gray smoke. A few dozen small boats were spread out around the bay, and one large ship bobbed peacefully in the harbor, its wide sails inflamed with the red of sunset.

"Forty-five, forty-six, forty-seven," Flora said, finishing her count. "There's forty-seven houses. That's barely any."

"Could be good," Clive mused aloud. "Not likely that they've got any sort of ongoing relationship with the Descendancy."

"But in a bigger town, we might be able to blend in," Paz said. "We'll stick out like sore thumbs down there."

"No offense, but I think we're gonna be sore thumbs wherever we end up."

He'd been horrified the first time he saw Paz's tattoos, but he hardly noticed them anymore. Her hair had grown out about an inch—still short enough to draw stares, but not to merit concealment. As for all those terrible words Diana had printed on Paz's skin, only a few were still decipherable: *witch*, soon to be obscured by bangs; *heathen*, curling prettily around the top of her right ear; and *heretic*, running up her neck and severed by her hairline, leaving only the *here*. And though the rings around her face remained

TOMMY WALLACH

as conspicuous as ever, at least they weren't immediately recogniz-able as disciplinary tattoos; maybe she was so incredibly devout she'd volunteered to have annuli permanently inscribed in her flesh.

"We're nearly out of food anyway," Clive said. "This seems as good a place as any to stop. Besides, it gives me a good feeling. I like the smell of it."

Flora snorted. "I don't smell anything."

"Well, maybe you aren't smelling hard enough." He tweaked her nose. "Come on. Let's check it out."

They rode down the gently sloping seaward side of the hill, passing the first few salt-spackled clapboard houses. In almost every yard, strands of smoked fish hung from a driftwood rack; in one case, freshly laundered shirts had been set to dry just next to a dozen pink-brown salmon.

"You're looking good this morning, Henny. Did you make me a little present? Looks like you did."

An old man, bent with age and jowly as a bulldog, was talking to the chickens in their wire coop. Clive and the girls dismounted and tied their horses to a fence post.

"Excuse me, sir," Clive said. "What town is this?"

The man looked up. One of his eyes appeared to be perma-nently shut. "It's called Settle," he said. "Story goes it was just 'that settlement,' so they shortened it up to Settle. Now we say it's what you gotta do if you're gonna live here: settle." He laughed—a single rooster-like squawk that set his birds to flapping.

"That's a fine coincidence," Paz said, voice set to maximum charm, "because we're looking to do just that. Is there somebody here we could talk to about moving in?"

"Nobody official. But Greeny Collins sees after the docks, which is the only reason any of us are here in the first place."

"Thank you, sir."

As they walked on, the old man continued his one-way conversation with the chickens: "Sorry, ladies, where were we?"

They passed a few other Settlers on their way down to the water—each face lined and leathered by seawater and sun, seldom sporting a full set of teeth, but always with a gummy smile for the strangers.

A handful of men were working out on the docks. Clive asked after Greeny Collins and was directed toward a tiny canteen nearby. Other than a young, aproned barmaid, the only occupant was the stout woman sitting at a corner table, scribbling something in a ledger and puffing away at a pipe. Her graying hair was tied back with a red bandanna, and she wore a polished wooden T around her neck. Clive knew it to be the symbol of one of the pagan religions practiced outside the Descendancy.

"Greeny Collins?" Clive said.

The woman didn't glance up from her ledger. "That's right."

"We were told we should talk to you about finding some work."

Greeny snorted. "You must be pretty hard up if you had to come all the way down to Settle just to"—she hesitated, brought up short by her first look at Paz's face—"to get a job."

"Not just a job," Paz said. "Also a home."

"So you're seeking safe haven?"

"I didn't say that."

"You didn't have to. I know what those tattoos mean. We see them on sailors out of Edgewise often enough. But never quite so bad. What did you do to earn 'em, girl?"

TOMMY WALLACH

Clive wanted to spare Paz the evocation of those memories. "How she got them isn't important—"

"Are you a girl?" Greeny interrupted, eyes suddenly blazing. "Was I talking to you?" She turned to address Paz again. "You steal something?"

"No," Paz said.

"You kill anybody?"

"Yes."

"How many?"

"A few."

"Good folk or bad folk?"

Paz shook her head. "Folk who wished us ill. That's all I can speak to."

Greeny took a long, contemplative draw on her pipe. If she was surprised by Paz's unapologetic admission of murder, she didn't show it. "Last time we heard anything from the Descendancy was more than ten years back. They sent some preacher who tried to sell us on pledging allegiance and building a temple to God's daughter. We laughed him right out of town." Greeny smiled at the memory; Clive wondered if the preacher had been anyone he knew. "Let's get down to brass tacks. I know what you want from me. What are you offering?"

"I'm a trained soldier, if you need that kind of thing," Clive said.

"The only thing we fight here is fish."

"Then I'll fight fish," Clive said. "Both of us will."

"All three of us," Flora added.

Greeny finally acknowledged the third member of their party. "Aren't you a little young to be caught up in all this?"

"I'm eleven," Flora said, as if it were a badge of honor. "And I can work as hard as anyone."

"Can you? Then show me your hands. All of you: hands up."

Six palms were raised in Greeny's direction. As she scrutinized their palms, a memory flared to life in Clive's mind's eye. Back in the ministry days, after they'd stopped for the night, all the kids would splash their hands around in a bucket of water before dinner, fifty fingers fighting dirty beneath the surface, trying to get clean.

"Smooth as a baby's bottom," Greeny said of Flora's hands, somehow making the comment sound like an insult. Clive's hands merited slightly more investigation but earned an equally damning review: "You probably play a mean guitar, at least." Only Paz's hands turned out to be worthy of Greeny's respect. She pulled them into the circle of light cast by the smoky lamp on the table.

"You've worked the land," she said.

Paz nodded. "My family had a farm."

"Had?"

"Long story."

"Save it. I get bored easy." She dropped Paz's hands. "You're lucky," she said. "About a year ago, a couple here in town went missing out on the water. And because I'm an idiot, I ended up taking in their two kids. Let me tell you, they're a fucking handful. You two work the docks every day and see that dinner's on the table every night, you can set up camp in my attic. Deal?"

She offered a hand to shake.

"Almost," Clive said.

Greeny grimaced. "You heard that saying about beggars and choosers, son?"

"We need to know you're not going to turn us in the first time somebody asks after us. You gotta give us your word. Otherwise, we'll have to keep walking."

"My word was already implied, kid. But I'll warn you, the whole town's gonna know you're here by this time tomorrow, so you better be nice as hot apple pie to everyone you meet. We're a loyal bunch of bastards, but only to folks we think deserve it."

"Fair enough."

"Good. Now shake my damn hand already."

They did, and Settle suddenly had three new residents.

9. Clover

IT HAD TAKEN WEEKS FOR THE PERFECT CIRCUMSTANCES to align. Sister Lila's office could be accessed only through the infirmary, and as the academy's medical capabilities were well-known among not just the citizens of Sophia, but also those of a dozen neighboring villages (and even the local *naasyoon*), the infirmary was seldom empty. Even in the dead of night, at least one of its occupants was bound to be awake—kept up by pain or fear—not to mention the fact that Lila was prone to visit at odd hours to run a test, administer a fresh medicine or palliative, or simply check in on the course of an illness or treatment.

For the past few days, there had been only two patients in the infirmary, both academy scholars: Brother Marcus, who'd suffered a serious burn to his right forearm while smelting a replacement bolt for Kittyhawk, and Brother Alonzo, who'd slipped on the stairs and fractured his ankle. It would've been a golden opportunity to sneak in, but for the fact that Lila never seemed to leave her office. Night after night Clover had watched the infirmary from the cushioned study alcove at the end of the hallway; and night after night he'd given up when the hour grew too late for his continued presence there to read as anything other than suspicious. He'd been about to do the same tonight when the door at last swung open and Lila emerged, still scribbling in her notebook.

"Evening, Sister Lila," Clover said as she scurried past.

"Evening," she replied, though he doubted she'd even noticed who it was who'd greeted her.

When her footsteps had finally faded away, he dashed down the hall and cracked open the door to the infirmary. Both Brother Marcus and Brother Alonzo looked to be asleep; Clover made certain by snapping his fingers a few times. When there was no response, he stepped into the room and closed the door behind him. What seemed to be silence grew more complex over the course of the next few seconds, like a mouthful of wine taking on unexpected flavors. A blanket of thick, steady breaths was punctuated by the occasional rasp of a snore. A branch tapped imploringly against the windowpane. Floorboards creaked beneath Clover's feet as he crossed the room, and the rusty hinges of Lila's office door practically screamed as he pulled it open and shut again.

Finally.

He flipped the small metal switch on the wall and a lightbulb buzzed to life overhead. He still felt a sort of religious awe for that miraculous technology, even though he now understood its scientific underpinnings; in the end, the difference between "the Lord created light" and "photons create light" was more semantic than theological.

Sister Lila's office was scarcely larger than the bedroom that Clover and Lenny shared, though at least it had a window overlooking the shadowy tangle of the cliffside vegetation. A potted azalea on the sill needed watering—etymologically apt, as the Greek root *azaleos* meant "dry." (Clover could almost hear his brother's sarcastic riposte: "Another fascinating bit of trivia from our resident genius.") There were papers strewn about a simple walnut desk in the center of the room, but Clover had already located his quarry, mounted on a shelf next to the window—an enfilade of at least fifty identical notebooks, each one bound with one long strand of waxed brown twine.

He pulled out the one farthest to the right, but a quick skim revealed that it only covered the period between two and six weeks ago; no one could accuse Lila of being anything less than thorough. Another notebook over and Clover found the account of his own recovery, but nothing was recorded there that he didn't already know—*Total recovery of arm function unlikely*, Lila had written near the end of the report. And it was true that his shoulder still ached when he woke up in the morning, still went tight and sore whenever he tried to lift anything much heavier than a skipping stone.

Two more notebooks back and he found what he'd been looking for. Lila had left the patient nameless, but that only made it more obvious.

7/22: Patient arrived, feverish and likely septic, having suffered two gunshot wounds and approximately a dozen smaller lacerations. One bullet had lodged in the bone of his left hip and fragmented. This injury had been stitched up and was undoubtedly the source of the infection. The second bullet had passed through the patient's left bicep completely. After administering ether, I proceeded to reopen the wound at the hip and remove the shrapnel. Antibiotics were administered intravenously, but the patient's fever did not immediately improve. I estimate chance of survival at around 25 percent.

TOMMY WALLACH

Clover looked up from the notebook. There were sketches on the opposite page, graphic depictions of "the patient's" ragged wounds. It hurt his heart to see them, to imagine his father here all on his own in such pain. The account continued—page after page of cold, clinical descriptions, of detailed pictures and comprehensive charts, of unlikely therapies and unfamiliar medicines. It had been nearly a week before Lila pronounced her patient out of immediate danger, and around that same time, the tone of the report began to change. It became less formal and factual; clearly Lila was warming to Clover's father. *Patient in good spirits, expressing gratitude for the "fine accommodations"; at times, his forbearance makes it difficult to determine his physical condition.* The thought made Clover smile. His father had always had a way with people; it was why he'd become a minister in the first place.

Clover turned to the final entry, dated sixteen days after his father's arrival at Sophia.

Patient finally deemed strong enough for questioning. I carried out the initial excision (the distal phalange of the subdominant index finger), and found the patient's response—beseeching his "god" to forgive me my sin—unnerving. I fear the patient's misguided beliefs will compel him to suffer unduly in the days to come. After discussion, Director Zeno and I decided it would be best if Brother West continued the questioning in my stead.

"What are you doing in here?"

Lila wore a pair of large reading glasses that made her eyes look huge, almost bovine. Clover wiped the tears from his cheeks.

"You tortured him," he whispered.

"Tortured who?" Clover picked up the notebook and opened it to the gruesome drawing of his father's left hand: the truncated index finger, complete with suture. Recognition flooded Lila's face. "Of course. You wanted to find out what happened to your father. I should've seen this coming."

"You're supposed to be better than this. You're not supposed to be cruel."

Something like sadness clouded Lila's features. "Cruelty is subjective, Clover. We could have done much worse, if he—"

"Did you break him?" Clover asked, though he knew that no answer would assuage him. If yes, then his father lacked courage. If no, then Daughter only knew the torments he'd been through.

"As you must've read in my notes, I didn't carry out the questioning. My understanding is that your father gave up very little information before he was moved."

"Moved where?"

"Last I heard, he was in the custody of a Mindful cell out west."

"What's the Mindful?"

Lila sighed. "I think you should save the rest of your questions for Zeno. She's going to be very disappointed to hear you've been snooping around like this." Clover imagined "disappointment" wouldn't even begin to cover it. Even if Zeno didn't have him killed, she'd never let him see the Anchor again. "And I'll take that back, thank you very much," Lila said, gesturing for the notebook. Clover handed it over, and as Lila turned away to replace it on the shelf, he noticed a tray of glittering surgical instruments on her desk—including what might have been the very scalpel that had been used to carry out the despicable acts described in her notes.

It all came down to one question: Whose side was he really on? There was no point in pretending he was still the same person he'd been when he first came to Sophia. He'd learned so much over the past few months—not just about chemistry and manufacturing and history, but about himself. About what he could accomplish without the limits imposed on him by the Church. Unquestionably, his time at the academy had been the most intellectually satisfying, the most fulfilling, the plain *happiest* period of his whole life.

But how could he side with Zeno now that he knew she'd had his father tortured? Even if the Descendancy was wrong about nearly everything, even if they worshipped a false god and lived by a mistaken philosophy that demonized the very notion of progress, was their overprotectiveness really more pernicious than the despotic arrogance of Sophia and its scholars? Which was worse—the obliterating darkness cast by sanctimony and superstition, or the light that would see the whole world burned down in the name of truth? In the end, he had to choose the devil he knew over the devil he didn't.

He picked up the scalpel . . . but hesitated. How many times had he stood on this same precipice, paralyzed by thought, frozen in the face of what he had to do? What might be different now if he'd been able to act that night outside the pumphouse, or during the contingent's run-in with the Wesah? Maybe nothing—but maybe everything.

As Lila turned back around to face him, he lashed out, drawing the blade across her exposed throat.

"What did you—why?" Lila gasped. Her hands went to her

neck; blood poured out from between her fingers. Her eyes widened before rolling back into her head, then she crumpled up and fell meatily to the floorboards.

Patient arrived with serious laceration just below hyoid bone, appearing to sever the carotid artery. Chance of survival estimated at less than five percent.

Lila shivered a little, stilled. It was done. Clover tried to step outside of his own mind and survey his feelings objectively. Was there remorse? A little. But it was mixed up with so much else: frustration that he'd been driven to such a drastic measure; sorrow, at ending the life of someone he'd respected; and of course the fear of being caught and punished.

It was this last that jolted him out of his reflection. He had to do something about the body. Even if the patients in the infirmary were still asleep, he could hardly drag Lila through the halls of the academy, which left only one option. As quietly as possible, he slid the desk farther away from the wall and opened the window. His shoulder screamed with pain as he hauled the body up onto the sill. Blood pattered onto the leaves thirty feet below. With a groan, he heaved her over the edge. She fell silent as a stone, landing with a thud and sliding onward down the cliff and out of sight.

He found an old shirt in a drawer and used it to mop up the blood on the floor and around the window, then threw it and the scalpel down after the body.

He would remember the rest of the night only in fragments. Moving quickly across the infirmary floor, his footsteps as loud as gunshots in his mind. Exiting through the cliffside door, the stars like a spray of blood across the sky. Dragging Lila's body, sickeningly scrambled by the fall, deep into the undergrowth, as far as possible from the trail that led past the hydroelectric dam. The sparkling sickle arc of the scalpel as it flew through the moonlit air. The icy river water washing the dark stains from his hands. Empty hallways like some sort of illicit gift, the quiet creak of his bedroom door, the benediction of Lenny's even breathing.

He succumbed to exhaustion the moment his head hit the pillow. Later, he'd wonder what it said about him, that sleep came so easy.

A week passed, then two. Lila's disappearance was remarked upon, of course, but the central mystery seemed to be less what had happened to her and more what would make her flee Sophia so suddenly.

Still, when Zeno unexpectedly appeared at Clover's bedroom door one evening, his only thought was that he hoped she'd grant him a quick death.

"We're leaving," she said.

"Leaving?"

"Yes. Believe it or not, your brother has caused a problem with the Mindful cell working out of Edgewise."

Clover frowned, uncomprehending. "My brother?"

"We're quite sure it was him, along with the Dedios girl." It was too much information to take in at once. Clive and Paz were alive, and traveling together, and somehow making trouble for Sophia all the way out in Edgewise. Not only that, but they'd struck their blow against "the Mindful": the same organization that Lila claimed had taken custody of Honor Hamill. "At any rate," Zeno continued, "now I have to go there and salvage things. Afterward, I'll travel south for the *tooroon*, and you can make your report."

After Zeno had finished speaking, she went on standing in the doorway, as if she were still awaiting some kind of answer from Clover. It was a few seconds before he realized what was happening.

"Wait, do you mean we're leaving *right now?*"

"Obviously. Everyone else is ready and waiting. I left you for last because I hadn't decided if I wanted you to come. Now I have."

She tossed him an empty canvas bag and watched in silence as he packed up his meager belongings. Then he followed her out of the academy and down through the town. Just inside the gate, about a dozen people were milling around a large wagon, clearly waiting for Zeno to arrive. Enough horses were on hand to pull the wagon and provide mounts for the whole party. Clover recognized most of the faces—academy scholars and a few townspeople he knew by reputation, but when he spotted Lenny and Huma in the crowd, he assumed they must have come to see him off.

"Can you believe this?" Lenny said. "This'll be the first time I've been more than a few miles away from the city since I was a baby."

"What do you mean?"

Lenny punched Clover on the shoulder. "I mean we're coming with you, kid. Zeno said we should keep working on Kittyhawk as we go. I brought all our notebooks with me."

Clover plastered on a smile. He'd come to care about Lenny and Huma, which was why he would've preferred that they stay in Sophia. Though they didn't know it, they would be in danger every second they remained at his side. "That's great!"

"I know!"

Within an hour, the wagon was loaded and everyone had mounted up. As their procession made its way across the bridge, Clover realized he'd likely never be back to Sophia, and the thought filled him with sadness. Yes, he would get to see his home again. And yes, he'd managed to survive a mission he'd fully expected would claim his life. But in spite of everything, he would miss this place, and the noble fantasy it represented: the pursuit of knowledge purely for knowledge's sake.

As the cobblestones gave way to hard-packed earth, Clover turned his mind to the future. Clive had survived the journey back to the Anchor, could at this very moment be waiting for him somewhere in the city. And even more miraculous: their father might also be alive, though Clover had no idea where to begin trying to find him.

He couldn't have said anymore whether he was a spy working for the Anchor or a traitor working for Sophia. All he knew was that he loved his father, and his brother, too. And if he'd learned one thing in his time at Sophia, it was that he would do *anything* for the people he loved.

10. Paz

BOBBING GENTLY IN THE RICKETY FISHING BOAT, BUF-feted by the brisk wind blowing across the tide-ruffled waters of the cove, Paz at last knew peace. She turned her body toward the sun, letting the light spill over skin etiolated from its time in the Bastion dungeon. Her hair was about two inches long now, completely obscuring the slurs on her scalp. The other fishermen called her "pretty boy"—funny because of her boyishly short hair, funny because she was no longer pretty. They didn't mean it as an insult, but a term of endearment. Even disfigured, she hadn't lost her ability to charm, particularly now that her very life depended on it. She was confident the Settlers liked her—for her reticence, for her air of ruin, for her stoicism in the face of the backbreaking work they did day in and day out.

The boat was called the *Cutlass*—about twenty-five feet from end to end, bearing the flaking remains of what had once been a vibrant blue paint. The sail was currently down, bunched at the boom like a heifer's dewlap, and the anchor rested on the shallow floor of the cove. Paz stood on the foredeck, watching her fishing line where it pierced its reflection in the water. On the leeward side of the boat, two other fishermen were tending to the crab pots—large, ingeniously designed boxes that enticed crabs inside and trapped them there. Paz had just finished helping unload the pots, and now they would be reattached to the line and lowered back into the water. Everything stank of fish, an odor that sank into the pores, that even Greeny's abrasive black soap ("It doesn't so much clean your skin as scrape it off," she'd said, as if this were a point in its favor) couldn't eradicate.

They were only half a mile from shore, and if Paz squinted, she could just make out Clive, hauling a barrel out of the hold of a Sudamiran ship that had come to Settle that morning. Traffic through the port had increased significantly in the past week or so; likely the Anchor was stepping up its orders of raw materials in expectation of the coming war.

Clive had taken to the job as if born to it—another manifestation of his newfound optimism. At first Paz had been disturbed by his sudden change in temperament; now she was more concerned by how quickly it had rubbed off on *her*. A few days ago, when he'd asked her how long she wanted to stay in Settle, she'd replied, "Why not forever?" It had been intended as a joke, but once the words were out of her mouth, she realized some part of her had meant them. She was happy here. Or, if not quite happy, at least serene. The seemingly humdrum days fairly sparkled with tiny pleasures, just as the homeliest slab of sandstone could catch the light in such a way as to reveal the secret starscape embedded in its surface. To wake in the moon-chilled hour before dawn, to eat eggs scrambled with wild onion, to drink a mug of hot coffee with fresh cream and Sudamiran sugar, to walk with Clive and Greeny down to the docks, to sail out into the cove or out through the opening made when the isthmus was submerged by high tide, to spend her hours engaged in honest, unthinking labor in the sun and spray—after all the horrors she'd witnessed, not to mention all the horrors she'd inflicted, this reliably uneventful routine was more than she ever could have hoped for.

Of course she missed Sophia, missed Frankie and Terry and Carlos, missed those passions and ambitions that had once given meaning to her days. How far she'd come from the life of science and scholarship she'd once believed awaited her. And yet, for the first time since the siren sounded above Sheriff Okimoto's office, or maybe even since the morning she'd watched her beloved older brother Anton fall from the roof of the house in Coriander, she felt like something other than a force moving inexorably toward a goal. At long last, she felt like a human being again.

One day, after not quite three weeks in Settle, a pelting spring storm brought the *Cutlass* in from the water just before noon. Work on the docks had also been suspended, and Clive was waiting for Paz under the eaves of an A-frame storehouse when she returned. Together they trudged back through the mud, splashing from one puddle to another, arriving at Greeny's house soaked to the bone.

"Hello?" Paz called out.

"There's nobody here," Clive said, extricating himself from his boots. "Greeny told me she was gonna stick by the docks in case the rain let up, and the kids'll be at the schoolhouse until lunch."

The schoolhouse was just another name for the town church, where a plainspoken, easygoing man named Vernon Young served as both minister and teacher. The Settlers practiced an old religion called Christianity—a holdover from before the Conflagration— and though Paz had as little patience for one faith as another, even she had to admit that Young's sermons were easy enough to swallow: litanies of platitudes about the value of hard work and the inevitability of suffering. Flora probably wasn't learning much in Young's classroom, but at least it gave her something to do during the day. Though she'd already made admiring acolytes of Greeny's two young charges, Mariana and Paolo, she was having trouble adjusting to life in Settle and had recently grown taciturn and irritable. Probably the girl was coming to understand that their situation might not be temporary, and knew no better way to deal with her frustration than to act out. Paz could relate to that.

"It's so quiet," she said. "And cold."

"Why don't you get the fire going?" Clive said. "I'll rustle us up something to drink."

Paz lit a fire in the hearth and dragged over the patchwork pelt rug. The heat began to seep into her clothes and skin, chasing the chill away. After a while, Clive came back from the kitchen with two steaming mugs filled to the brim. Tiny black lumps floated near the top.

"I think the coffee needs a bit more straining, Clive."

He smiled roguishly. "It's not coffee. It's called cocoa. Mariana told me about it. Apparently Greeny only serves it on special occasions."

"And this is a special occasion?"

"Obviously."

"Why's that?"

"Because . . . the rain."

"Ah yes: rain. Extremely special." She raised the mug up to her nose: the liquid was slightly darker than coffee with cream, and the smell was sweeter, richer.

"Mariana said I just had to grind it up and mix it with hot milk and a little sugar. I don't know how much I was supposed to use, so I'm sorry in advance if it's awful."

"I'll consider forgiving you."

Beyond the dense glass of the window behind the dining table, the rain was coming down as hard as ever, blurring the world outside, like another set of walls beyond the stone, a double layer of protection. Paz blew across the top of the mug, making the steam billow and swirl, and took an exploratory sip. Too hot at first; then, as the liquid cooled, the flavor unfurled across her tongue. But was it one flavor, or many? Dry summer grass and oily nuts, dark fruits and the must of wet earth, something bitter but pleasant in its bitterness. She felt as if the universe had just let her in on one of its greatest secrets.

"What do you think?" Clive asked.

Paz let out a little groan of pleasure by way of an answer.

"That good?" He took a sip, then rolled his eyes as if swooning. "Daughter's love that's delicious."

They didn't speak much for the next few minutes. Paz sensed that something would be lost when the milk cooled, and she wanted to make the most of every drop. The flavor intensified as she went, until she reached the thin layer of brown coating the bottom. She scraped some off with her fingernail and tasted it.

"It isn't sweet," she said, surprised.

"No?"

Clive drank off the last of the liquid, frowned into the empty mug. "I don't have any. It must've melted."

"Here." She scooped up another glob from her mug and presented it to him; he slid his index finger across hers to get it.

"You're right," he said. "It's the sugar that makes it sweet."

There was a freckle of chocolate just below his bottom lip. "You've got something," she said, pointing at the same spot on her own face.

"Here?" he said, missing it by an inch.

"No, just—" She reached out, wiped the chocolate away. "There you go."

"Thanks."

Her voice dropped to a whisper, though she couldn't have said why. "Don't mention it."

A clattering at the door gave them just enough time to lean away from each other. Flora entered with Mariana and Paolo and another friend from school, all of them talking at once, oblivious to what they'd interrupted. Paz stood up, warm all the way through from the fire and the cocoa, from Clive's touch.

Could he?

Of course not. After everything she'd done to him and his brother, friendship was the most she could hope for.

Could she?

Of course not. They'd had their moment, that first day along the mining road. It was sheer delusion to think they could get back to that place after everything that had happened since.

And yet, as she went into the kitchen to make lunch for the children, she touched her tongue to the stain of chocolate on her finger, imagining what might've happened if Flora hadn't come home when she did.

Bittersweet.

One Saturday morning, Paz woke to find Settle's main street lined with unlit torches. Children ran about hanging daisy chains along the fence posts. Out on Greeny's porch, Flora lay draped across a two-seat rocking chair, idly tracking the progress of the preparations.

"Is it Midsummer's Eve already?" Paz asked.

"Guess so," Flora replied sullenly.

"Don't you wanna join in with your friends?"

"Those aren't my friends. None of my friends live here."

"What about Paolo and Mariana?"

"They're little kids."

Paz gestured for Flora to make room on the rocking chair and barely managed to perch on the three inches grudgingly granted her. "Listen, I know this hasn't been easy for you, and I'm sorry for that. But I promise you, it'll get better. You just have to give it time."

"I don't want to give it time," Flora said. "I want to go home." She stood up and went back into the house, ending the conversation.

By midafternoon, Settle's population had swollen to three times its usual size, augmented by the farmers who worked the lands to the south and the east, fishermen from up and down the coast, and arriving just after dark, a small contingent of Wesah warriors from a local *naasyoon*. By coincidence, a Sudamiran ship had been held up in the harbor for the past few days after sustaining significant damage during a storm, and the eighteen crewmen had become fixtures of the canteen in the evenings, where they entertained the locals with raucous songs and tales of adventure on the high seas. Their presence at the festival only added to the general merri-

TOMMY WALLACH

ment, and by the time the torches were lit and the band—made up entirely of Settlers with finicky homemade instruments—began to play, Paz almost felt as if she were back in a big town.

She was sitting on the stoop of the cooper's workshop, drinking a cup of dandelion wine and watching the wide spinning skirts of the women waltzing through the square, when Clive appeared out of the darkness. He was dressed in a homely version of formal wear: his old Protectorate jacket, mended and patched back to respectability and dyed black to obscure its provenance, topped off with a bright orange poppy in the topmost buttonhole.

"Care to dance?" he said.

Paz smiled wanly. "I shouldn't."

"Why not?"

She didn't want to tell him the truth, that she was hiding from all the strangers in town, whose inevitable gawking at her tattoos would make her feel like a freak all over again. "It's been a long time. I don't even remember how."

"All the more reason to do it."

The wine must've already gone to her head, because she took his hand and allowed herself to be led into the square. The song was unfamiliar, but Clive was confident in his movement, and it was easy enough to follow. A month of twelve-hour days working the docks had changed the shape of his body, turned it sinewy and tough. His hand in hers was ridged with calluses.

"I miss playing," he said, glancing up at the band.

"I forgot you were a musician."

He feigned offense. "Were? Being a musician is forever. When I got back to the Anchor, I bought a new guitar for me and a violin for Flora. We were putting together a little act, just for fun. Shame we had to leave the instruments behind."

"I'm sorry I never got to hear you."

"It's all right. Maybe someday you will."

"Mind if I cut in?"

It was Teddy Hudock, one of Paz's fellow fishermen on the *Cutlass*. He was a portly widower of forty, good-natured and paternal. After everything he'd done to make her feel welcome on the boat, she could forgive him for taking her away from Clive. But after a few minutes of being clumsily spun around the square, an idea suddenly popped into her head.

"Excuse me," she said, "but I'm feeling a little dizzy."

"I'm told dancing with me can have that effect on women," Teddy replied with a smile.

Free again, she went up to the stage and waited for the song to end. The bandleader, Judd, was a good friend of Greeny's, and a regular at the house. Paz called him over and whispered her request.

"Easy enough," Judd said. He went back to stand center stage and addressed the crowd. "Ladies and gentlemen, I've just learned we have a couple of *very* famous musicians with us tonight. Would the Hamill family band please come on up here and play us a tune?"

Paz watched Clive drag an extremely reluctant Flora across the square to a chorus of hoots and shouts. The musicians already onstage were all too happy to give up a guitar and a violin to the newcomers; it would give them a chance to drink.

"Just to be clear," Clive said, once the audience had quieted down, "we are not even a little bit famous. But we're still happy to play something for you tonight. Here's an old one you might know, 'Under the Linden Flowering.' Hope you enjoy it."

He looked to Flora, counting off, and the two of them began to play. It was one of those songs that sounded happy until you listened to the lyrics, which were about the end of a love affair. Clive and Flora sang it as a duet, their voices intertwining, crossing over each other when Clive's voice broke into a limpid falsetto. His eyes were closed, as if he were accessing some secret chamber inside himself. Paz had never seen this side of him—the soldierly bravado and son-of-a-minister piety cracked open, revealing something soft and soulful. Flora looked happy too, as happy as she'd been since they'd arrived in Settle. As she and Clive played the final figure, they smiled at each other, playful and conspiratorial, and Paz felt strangely envious of their connection. It made her miss her brothers, miss the deep-down *knowing* of family.

The applause was thunderous as Clive and Flora took their bows and descended from the stage. The town band started up again, and Paz pushed through the crowd to try to find Clive. Eventually she spotted him, off at the very edge of the square, heading down toward the water. She followed him, and found him again a few minutes later, standing at the edge of the pier, gazing out over the cove. Overhead, the moon had just emerged from behind the clouds—emboldened, luminous, white as bone.

"It was nice hearing you play," Paz said. "I mean, it was more than nice."

"Thanks."

There was a telltale gruffness to his tone. Close up, she could make out the thin tracks of silver running down his cheeks, and the very sight of it wrenched at her heart. "What's wrong?"

"Nothing."

"It's not nothing! And it's my damn fault! Like always!"

She never should've sprung that on him; music was a symbol of everything he used to have, everything he'd lost because of her. What had she been thinking? How was it that no matter what she did, she couldn't stop hurting him?

"It's not like that," Clive said. "I was glad to play. Honestly. It's just . . ." He sighed, struggling to find the words. "Every now and then, when I think about my old life—it just lands on me, all at once. And yeah, it hurts to remember, but that doesn't necessarily make it bad. It's just . . . how it is, you know?"

"I really do," she said. "I think about my father and my brothers, about the life I wanted for myself, and sometimes I can hardly breathe for how much it hurts. But I still go on thinking about it. About everything I've done—"

Her voice caught. Clive had taken hold of her hand. "We've both made mistakes," he said. "We've both lost things. But there's still so much we could have. The whole rest of our lives."

Our lives? Could he mean . . . ?

Paz looked into his eyes for any sign of irony or deception, but found only tenderness. She put her hand against his cheek, and to the distant music of the band and the gentle soughing of the waves, their lips met. They stepped into each other, pressing, then crushing. Paz really did feel dizzy now, drunk on wine and desire. She put her hands against Clive's chest and forced him down onto the uneven planks of the dock, where she would exorcize every demon of her past, where they would forge their contract with the future.

The modest moon hid once again behind the clouds, and they were cast in darkness.

TOMMY WALLACH

11. Gemma

GEMMA WOKE INTO THE SUSPENSEFUL DARKNESS OF early morning. A fire flickered in the clay oven. Someone was humming something slow and soothing nearby.

She sat up and nearly retched. She wasn't sure which hurt more, her belly or her head. It felt a little like shinefog, only ten times worse. The humming stopped. Grandmother came to stand over her, her lined face blank in the weak light. "You are awake," she said in Wesah.

"Yes."

Gemma considered apologizing for what she'd done, but couldn't see the point; the offense was simply too large for something as trite as an *I'm sorry.* She'd known the importance of the dream-tea to the *otsapah*, to the Wesah as a whole. She'd known what it meant for her, *aan dahor*, to taste it without permission, without an understanding of its historical context, or training in how to interpret the visions it elicited. Drinking the tea had been a rash and foolish act, and now she would have to face the consequences.

"So?" Grandmother said. "What did you see?"

"See?"

"You will forget. It goes away, just like dreams. You must tell it now, before the memory disappears."

A prelude to punishment, or might the right answer save her somehow? Gemma thought back on her "journey." Grandmother was right—the images were already fading, faint words written on wet paper, falling to pieces as she tried to grasp them. What could she remember for certain? Time had seemed to contract. She'd felt as if she were seeing the past, present, and future all at once. The rocky spiral had featured prominently, and bizarre creatures made of iron. She'd walked the strand with Flora and felt an almost unbearable upswell of love and guilt.

"It was good at first. I saw my sister, and I saw someone building the"—she didn't know the word for "spiral" in Wesah—"placing those stones out in the lake. But then it all went wrong. The sun turned black. Rocks fell from the sky and set everything on fire. The water turned to blood. The world was ending. I was . . ." Gemma trailed off. The Wesah didn't readily admit to fear, and she was embarrassed to do so now. "I was frightened."

The old woman nodded. "I also see these things. I also am frightened." She went to the oven and returned with a bowl full of water and crushed mint leaves. "This will help with the pain."

It was the first time the *otsapah* had ever given Gemma anything other than an order.

"Thank you, Grandmother."

The land around the Villenaître was especially peaceful this morning, populated only by a few birds and darting lizards. Gemma had come upriver to fetch water again, a task she now went back and forth fulfilling with Helene: as was often the case in life, sharing the load had instantaneously transformed an onerous burden into a

　　　　　　　　　　　　　TOMMY WALLACH

pleasant pastime. The long walk gave her a chance to be alone with a former version of herself, to think about things as Gemma of the Anchor, rather than Gemma of the Wesah. Today, as she traipsed through the tall reeds at the edge of the river, letting the soft heads of the cattails brush against her skin like so many fingers wrapped in velvet, she mused on everything that had changed since the night of her transgression with the dreamtea, when she'd proven to the *otsapah* that she was more than an ordinary *dahor*.

The very next day she'd been invited to begin her training alongside Helene. Together, Grandmother taught them how to carry out the rituals of the Wesah, to sing the songs and dance the dances, to tell the tale of the tribe's origins. Gemma went to the birthings now and was awed by the intensity of the ceremony, how all the tribeswomen panted and moaned along with the mother, how the *otsapah* ripped the umbilical cord away with her teeth, how the placenta was divided among the mother's closest friends and eaten. Whenever a girl was born, there was a great feast held in the mother's honor; if the child was male, Grandmother led the tribe in a dirge, wordless and droning, and the boy was quickly spirited away. Later, the *otsapah* explained to Gemma how the mother would travel from town to town until she found someone—usually a family without any sons—to take the newborn.

"This journey cleanses her, makes her ready to bear children again, should she so choose."

How to explain the strange pleasure it gave Gemma, that the Wesah believed a female child was more worthy of celebration than a male? In the Descendancy, daughters were seen as liabilities—reputations to be defended, dowries to be paid—whose only compensatory virtues revolved around the skillet and the sewing needle.

Having reached her favorite spot on the bank of the river, where a rocky outcropping cast a long oval of shade, Gemma set down the pole and buckets and slipped out of her moccasins. Her toes went numb as soon as they dipped below the surface of the water, but after a few cycles in and out of the river, they began to adjust. A wayward minnow nibbled at her big toe and dashed off after its school. If there was a heaven, Gemma doubted it could be any better than the real world at this moment—sun and breeze and shade and babbling water, a girl she loved and a new world opening up before her.

After a few luxurious minutes, she climbed back up the bank, dried her feet in the grass, and put her moccasins back on. She filled the buckets and hung them on either end of the pole, which she then lifted onto her shoulders. On her very first trip back from the river, she'd had to stop half a dozen times to rest, and still her whole body had been shaking with exhaustion by the time she'd made it to the *otsapah*'s hut. But more than two months had passed since then—two months of grueling chores, punishing combat drills, and an almost unsustainable regimen of lovemaking. These days, Gemma could make it all the way from the river to the Villenaître without stopping, and even with both buckets full to the brim, her muscles were hardly even sore at the end.

At the top of the riverbank, her foot caught on a rock and she stumbled, nearly upsetting the buckets. At the same time, a high whistle carried across the plain, ending in a thump. Gemma recov-

　　　　　　　　　　　　　　　　　　TOMMY WALLACH

ered her balance and looked around for the source of the strange sound, but saw nothing.

Odd.

An almost inaudible tapping intruded on her consciousness, corresponding to the trickle of cold seeping into her left moccasin: drip, drip, drip. She glanced over at the bucket.

An arrow was sunk deep into the wood. Water beaded at the shaft and dripped down from the fletching. Gemma's first instinct was to laugh, as if this were merely a bizarre coincidence; she realized her mistake just in time. Something moved in her periphery, a shadow slipping surreptitiously through the golden grass. Gemma threw the pole off her back and managed to duck the next arrow.

"In a fight, you must never stop moving," Athène had advised. "Learn to plan even while you run."

Gemma somersaulted through the reeds and slid back down the bank of the river. It bought her a moment's respite, but at a steep cost; there was no room to maneuver within the chute carved out by the water, nowhere to hide when her assailant inevitably found her again.

Her assailant—Gemma knew of a handful of warriors who resented her position within the tribe, but she could think of only one person who might want her dead.

"Noémie!" she called out. "Why are you doing this?"

But Noémie didn't reply, and Gemma immediately regretted speaking. Not only had she given away her location, but she already knew the answer: Gemma had taken Noémie's place not only in Athène's bed, but in her heart. And if the woman had consoled herself with the thought that an outsider could never hope to hold on to such a coveted position for long, the *otsapah*'s endorsement must've been the last straw. Clearly she'd decided to take matters into her own hands.

An arrow clattered against the rocks behind Gemma, then three more in quick succession. Noémie was firing blindly, hoping to freeze her prey in place until she could join her down by the river, where she'd have a clear shot. Gemma needed to generate some element of surprise or distraction, but how? She had no weapon, and no avenue for escape; if she tried to climb up the bank, the movement of the reeds would give her away.

But maybe weakness could be turned to strength. Maybe Noémie would lower her guard if she believed the fight was already won.

Gemma listened for the next twang of Noémie's bowstring, and a moment later masked the arrow's clattering impact with an anguished cry, as if she'd been hit. Then she clambered quickly up to the very top of the riverbank and waited. She could hear Noémie galumphing through the grass, scenting blood. At the first flicker of skin between the reeds, Gemma launched herself upward like a cat. Noémie had already nocked an arrow, but even she wasn't fast enough to pull back the string and release it before Gemma crashed into her. They fell to the ground together and rolled painfully across the rocky earth, grappling and scratching at each other, unconsciously producing all sorts of wordless animal noises: growls, hisses, howls. Gemma ended up on top of Noémie and heard the crack of her opponent's bow snapping. It was to be a short-lived victory, as just a moment later, the warrior woman lodged a foot in Gemma's belly and sent her flying, up and over, to land on her back with the wind decisively knocked out of her.

They stood up and faced each other. Gemma was panting with

effort, while an entirely unruffled Noémie bounced playfully on the balls of her feet, eager for the next round to begin. The tribeswoman reached down to her belt and withdrew a short dagger of black glass. Athène had given Gemma one just like it (though they never used it while sparring, as the blade's edge was sharp enough to shave bone), but it was currently sitting on a wooden stool in the *otsapah*'s hut. Gemma cursed herself for being so careless, for forgetting she was still among enemies. Was there anything she could say to mollify Noémie? Would it help to beg? To threaten? No. The woman's eyes were narrowed, fanatically wrathful; there were only two possible endings to this story.

They circled each other for a few moments, Noémie occasionally lunging forward with the knife, only to pull back from a definitive engagement again and again, laughing at Gemma's unconscious flinches. Finally, immediately after another seemingly false thrust, she double-stepped and charged. Foolishly, Gemma raised her arm in defense, as if it were a shield.

An unexpected clang accompanied the expected bite of pain— the blade had been deflected by Athène's bangle, and what should have been a debilitating injury was reduced to a flesh wound.

Gemma took advantage of the other woman's surprise to lash out, sending a wild punch swinging into Noémie's right temple. She allowed herself a second of internal celebration, which was exactly a second too long; the glass blade flashed, drawing a line of fire across her exposed stomach. It was only thanks to Athène's training that she had the presence of mind to grab hold of Noémie's wrist at the far end of its arc and slam down on the hilt of the knife, knocking it to the ground.

Gemma could feel blood pouring down her belly, imagined it was her innards spilling out onto the ground. She'd grown strong in her time with the Wesah, but Noémie had been born into the tribe, had been preparing for moments like this her whole life. Gemma put her hands up as she'd been taught, but Noémie batted them away like they were nothing. Then a well-placed foot, a shove: Gemma suddenly found herself on her back, Noémie straddling her hips. With something like wonder, she watched as the leather fringe of the warrior woman's skirt painted crazy lines of vivid red blood—Gemma's blood—across the shared canvas of their skin. Slowly, luxuriously even, Noémie leaned over and picked up the knife.

Gemma bucked her hips upward, screaming as the gash on her belly exploded with pain. Noémie hooked her feet under Gemma's legs, clamping down tightly. There was no real hope of unseating her now, but Gemma had to try. She bucked again, screamed again.

Noémie laughed. "You're only making this worse for yourself," she said.

But Gemma had noticed something. She thrust her hips up a third time and watched the arrows in the quiver on Noémie's back jump, sliding halfway out before falling back down into the sheath.

"Enough," Noémie said, and her amusement was gone now, replaced with a cold fury. "I should've done this the first day you joined the *naasyoon*, before you poisoned our chieftain's heart. But she'll forget you soon enough. We all will."

Noémie raised the glass blade overhead, but before she could bring it down again, Gemma summoned all her strength and bucked one final time, emitting an unearthly, agonizing roar from the very depths of her soul. As the arrows flew free of Noémie's quiver and tumbled over her shoulder, Gemma plucked one from the air, drew it back, and plunged it into her enemy's chest. In the same motion, she snapped the shaft off as close to the skin as possible.

Noémie dropped the knife, scrabbled at the little nub of wood sticking out of her left breast, her mouth working like that of a dying fish, soundless and terrible. Gemma pushed the woman off her and scrambled to her feet. Then she was running for all she was worth, every footfall inflaming the gash across her belly, as if she were coming apart at the seams, until she collapsed at Grandmother's door and went down on her knees—sobbing and spent, but alive.

Later that night, after her wounds had been stitched up, after a search party had been sent to check the site of the struggle and found no sign of a body, only the broken shaft of the arrow and dark patches of dried blood in the dirt, after Grandmother herself had overseen the ritual to excommunicate Noémie from the tribe, Gemma lay alone in Athène's bed with her eyes closed, exploring the dull burn of her injuries, of her brush with death. A part of her didn't believe she could've survived, was certain she must have died out there by the river. This here was just the last stuttering burst of consciousness before the final darkness descended.

At some point in the night, Athène came into the hut. She'd been out riding, searching for Noémie's trail—tracks or blood-stains, some spoor flavored with guilt and shame—but the look on her face made it clear she'd found nothing.

"Are you asleep?"

"I don't think I'll be sleeping at all tonight," Gemma replied. She spoke in Wesah; it just felt more natural. "I've never been able to fall asleep on my back, and it hurts too much to lie on my side or my front."

Athène knelt down next to the bed. "The pain is bad?"

"I shouldn't complain. I'm lucky even to be alive."

"No," Athène said. "You were taken by surprise, with no weapon, by a skilled warrior. It was an unfair fight, dishonorable. Yet you won."

"Sounds like luck to me."

"No!" Athène said again, impassioned now. "You were not lucky. You were fierce. You were the wonder I always knew you would be, from the moment I saw you dancing in the forest. And that is why . . ." She trailed off, taking hold of Gemma's hand and squeezing it between her own, forcefully, as if investing it with something, or else drawing some much-needed strength from it. Her gaze was soft but intense, and Gemma sensed the full quivering potentiality of the moment; she felt as if she were about to be proposed to. "That is why I love you," Athène finally said.

Love. Gemma hadn't realized how much she'd wanted to hear that word from Athène until this moment. Only the reasoning was all wrong; she didn't want to be loved because she'd won a fight. She shook off Athène's hand and reached over the edge of the bed to pick up the brass armlet. "Look," she said, pointing to the deep divot in the metal. "If not for this, I'd be dead now. That's luck."

"That is not luck. That is a block."

"But I wasn't trying to block! I didn't even remember I was wearing the bracelet. I was being stupid."

"Not stupid. A blade in the arm is a blade that isn't in the head."

Gemma sat up, frustrated at her inability to express herself more clearly, and winced with the pain. Suddenly it seemed incredibly important that she make herself understood—that she make herself known. The truth cascaded out of her, a river breaching its bank, blood streaming from a mortal wound. "I am not a fierce warrior, Athène! And I can't see the future, either. That thing you call 'dancing,' when I start shaking and seeing things—that's an *illness*. I have an illness!" The chieftain was shaking her head, smiling as if at the nonsensical gibberings of an infant; her good humor only made Gemma angrier. "Listen to me!" she shouted, harshly enough to wipe the smile off Athène's face. "It's not a joke. I'm not what you think I am. I *lied* to you. And what I saw when I took the dreamtea was just . . . just . . . dreams! I need you to believe that. I'm just a normal girl. Love me for that or don't love me at all."

Athène looked stern now, almost patronizing. "Why do you insist on calling yourself a girl? You are a woman. No girl could defeat Noémie."

"I told you, I was—"

"Do not say lucky. Luck is only the favor of the spirits. So when I say you are fierce, I only say you are favored. Just as what you call an illness, I also call favor. You see things that are not there. How do you know they are not visions of the future?" Gemma wasn't sure how to answer that. How could anyone say they hadn't seen the future? It was the future—it hadn't happened yet. "Grandmother says she has seen the same things as you on her journeys. How do you explain that? Are you both ill? Or are you both favored?"

"Maybe I heard her mention them to Helene."

"Maybe. Who can say? Not me. Not Grandmother. Not you."

Gemma actually groaned; all that was beside the point. "But what if I'm right? What if I'm just an ordinary person, who can't fight, or talk to the gods, or see the future? Would you still love me?"

Athène took Gemma's head in her hands. "You are asking me if I would love you if you were not you. I don't know. I don't know the you that isn't you. I can only say I love *this* you. I can only say I take this you for my partner, for my equal. And when we go to the *tooroon*, I will bring you to my mother, and I will tell her the same." She leaned forward and kissed Gemma's trembling lips. "Is that at last enough, my little dancer?"

The tears pooled in the corners of Gemma's eyes, broke free and streamed down her cheeks, running under Athène's strong fingers.

"Yes," she whispered, smiling with relief, with love. "Yes, that's enough."

12. Clive

HERE WERE A MULTITUDE OF LANGUAGES HIDDEN within a language, dialects that signaled a particular status or field of expertise. Clive had grown up steeped in the esoteric vocabulary of the Church. "Eschatology" was the study of death, judgment, and the fate of the soul. "Theodicy" described the attempt to reconcile God's immanent goodness with the existence of evil and suffering. "Hamartiology" was the branch of theology concerned with sin, while "soteriology" described that concerned with salvation. Within each of these categories there were subcategories, and subcategories within *those* subcategories: an encyclopedia of encyclicals, theories and treatises, point and counterpoint. Even though Clive had never formally begun his training at Notre Fille, his father had spent untold hours quizzing him on the subtle variations between the Gospels and demanding extempore recitations from the Filia.

He hadn't realized how fluent he'd become in this language until he joined the Protectorate, whose members spoke an entirely different dialect. The words were shorter, sharper; this was the parlance, of feint and parry, of flank and peel, of punch and counterpunch. As an ideology, it was diametrically opposed to the one Clive had learned at his father's knee. But as a language, it bore many similarities to religious vernacular. Both emphasized the importance of sacrifice, community, and suffering. Both correlated with rank, such that more and more of the lexicon was revealed as members rose up the pecking order.

And both were utterly irrelevant to what turned out to be the most important dialect of all: the one spoken between two people in love.

Clive was surprised to learn just how inarticulate he was when it came to the language of love, had always assumed that when the emotion finally struck him (as it never had with Gemma, he understood now), the ability to express it would follow naturally. Instead he found himself perpetually tongue-tied—clumsy and crude, embarrassed and embarrassing. He blamed his father, who'd always been more comfortable speaking of God's love than his own. Clive knew his father had cared deeply for him and Clover, but it was a care they'd had to infer from his actions; his words outside the ambo tended more toward the concrete, the admonitory, the pragmatic.

Clive wanted to be more emotionally forthright with Paz, but he worried the intensity of his feelings would frighten her; after all, they frightened *him*. The fragile, jittery joy of finally getting the thing you'd most wanted, and underneath that joy, a hardness like a cherry pit—the terror of losing it again. He was overwhelmed by a sensation of need that bordered on desperation—to see her, to talk to her, to touch her skin. In the language of the Church, it was lust and sin. In the language of the Protectorate, it was weakness. But in the only language that mattered to Clive now, it was love: pure and simple.

TOMMY WALLACH

With all these powerful emotions ricocheting around, it was only a matter of time before Flora began to suspect something. Even if she hadn't been unusually perceptive for her age, no one could've failed to notice the thousand tiny ways that Clive and Paz's interactions had changed—all the soft looks and unnecessary touches, the excuses to be alone together. One morning Clive was out working on the docks when Flora suddenly appeared and demanded to speak to him alone.

"Shouldn't you be at school?" he said, but she ignored the question. He'd still failed to establish any kind of parental authority over the girl; she'd thought of him as an older brother for too long.

"Are you and Paz boyfriend and girlfriend now?" she said, the childish locution belying the seriousness in her expression.

Clive sighed. "I guess we are."

He was ready for histrionics—for shouting and crying, maybe even a slap or two. But Flora's response was the exact opposite. The light in her pale eyes seemed to go out completely, and her face went blank.

"So you're really never marrying my sister," she stated in a monotone.

Clive was momentarily speechless. "Gemma . . . Gemma's gone," he sputtered out.

"You don't know that," Flora whispered, and ran away before he could say anything else.

She'd been moody and difficult for weeks by then, but after that day, she retreated into herself completely. Clive couldn't even get her to join them for meals. Though she kept going to school, Pastor

Young told Clive that she'd become listless and distracted during lessons and had stopped talking to the other children at lunch.

"She'll come out of it," he insisted. "Probably just something to do with a boy. It usually is."

Clive hoped the minister was at least half-right, that the despondency would lift given time. But he worried that in surrendering to his feelings for Paz, he'd broken faith with Flora somehow, and that she wouldn't forgive him until he found a way to make things right again.

"There's something I have to tell you," Paz said.

"That sounds ominous."

"It is, a little."

They were walking across the Lacey family's farm, a little ways northeast of Settle. It was the beginning of July, and the reaping had only just been finished. Now the hay was piled up in hundreds of head-high golden stacks spread across the field. In the distance, near the farmhouse, the Lacey boys and a few men from town were beginning to bale.

"Well, let's hear it."

Paz took a deep breath. "Clover didn't betray the Descendancy. He gave himself to Sophia because the Epistem asked him to."

"So he's a spy?"

"Something like that. I've wanted to tell you for months, but I guess I was afraid you'd be angry at me, or else at yourself, for what happened with your brother."

Paz's story fit too neatly not to be the truth. Clover's sudden defection at the gates of Sophia had never really added up; though he'd occasionally complained about the strictures imposed on his studies at the Library, it had always been in good humor, parroting the neurotic grumblings of that kook, Bernstein. And Clive bore some responsibility for the deception as well; by joining the Protectorate, the ideological enemy of the Library, he'd made it impossible for Clover to confide in him about the mission.

It meant he'd shot his brother—maybe even killed him—for no reason at all.

"Are you mad?" Paz said.

Clive shook his head. He understood why she hadn't told him before now, and the truth was, it wouldn't have changed anything. He could only hope Clover was all right, and that someday he'd get the chance to make amends.

Still, the admission was a reminder that however close he might get to Paz, he could never be certain of what was in her mind, or her heart.

"Do you feel like you've ever really known anybody?" he said.

Paz laughed. "I know lots of people."

"But how deep? Like, all the way down? I grew up thinking my parents understood each other about as well as any married couple could, but now I'm not so sure. They were pretty different people." He remembered them fighting outside the doctor's office in Wilmington, while Eddie was having his leg looked after. His mother had wanted to hide out in the basement of the church, but his father had insisted they make a run for it. You could drive yourself crazy, thinking about how things might have gone if you'd chosen a different path. "What were your parents like?"

Paz grabbed a blade of hay from a nearby stack and put it

between her teeth. "I know they loved each other," she said after a while, "but they were pretty different people too. My da was the sweetest man, just a big old softy. Momma was different. I think because *her* da was a real son of a bitch, and it made her sort of hard. I'm not sure. He was already dead by the time I was born, and she didn't much like to discuss it."

"See, that's exactly what I'm talking about," Clive said, connecting one point to the other. "Every little thing I learn about you, it turns you into a different person. That's what I'm trying to figure out. Can you ever know enough about somebody to see them clear?"

"Oh." Paz frowned, an expression that began as a pretense of thoughtfulness, then darkened. The blade of hay fell from her lips. "I guess not. I mean, I've never felt like anybody really knew who I was, so how I could ever know anybody else? There's too much going on in my head all the time. Too much history to tell."

Clive nodded; that was just what he'd been feeling. "The one nice thing about thinking I was going to end up marrying Gemma was that we'd grown up together. She already knew all the history. Or most of it, anyway."

"Do you miss her?" Paz asked, a hint of jealousy in her tone.

"As a friend. And I guess I miss the dream we made up together, of sharing a life. But I didn't ever love her. Not like I love you." It wasn't the first time he'd said those words to Paz, but it still gave him a little thrill, as if he were committing an act of rebellion.

She smiled. "Even though you don't know who the hell I am."

"Yeah. Even so."

They walked on through the fields, until they were far enough from the Laceys' farmhouse that there was no chance of anyone seeing them. Then they undressed and embraced in the shade of a haystack.

In the Filia, the act of love was referred to as "knowing"—Aleph knew Eva in the Garden, and again in the wasteland beyond the flaming sword, where she begat Kayin and Hevel. And Hevel would've known Aclima, his sister, if not for Kayin. This "knowing" was sinful only after one had eaten from the Tree of Knowledge—a mixed message if ever there was one. Did that mean it was good to know, or evil?

"Hey," Paz said, when they were finished and lying out in the afterglow, the breeze wicking the sweat from their skin. He liked how she just went on with their previous conversation, as if she'd been mulling it over the whole time. "Maybe we don't know each other, and maybe we never will. But I promise I want to know you as well as I can, and I want you to know me, too. I think that's the most anybody can offer."

He took her hand, because he believed her, and because he wanted to know her too. Again he felt that profound happiness; and again he felt the melancholy at its core. This moment was just a bead suspended on the thread of time, like a dewdrop on a spiderweb, infinitesimal compared to the twin eternities that bound it—that before they'd met, and that after which they would know each other no longer.

"Thank you," he said huskily, as together they drifted off to sleep.

That night Clive and Paz were sharing a drink at Settle's waterside canteen. A tradesman stopping in town for the night caused a small stir when he reported that he'd seen "half the damn Protectorate" riding out from the Anchor not two weeks earlier.

"Heading east?" Clive said. Burns had implied that the Protectorate wouldn't be ready to march on Sophia until the cold turn at the earliest.

"Southwest," the tradesman said. "Word is they're making for the *tooroon*."

"Why would they do that?"

"Beats me. But you Settlers should start stockpiling now. When those soldiers get here, they're like to be buying up whatever you've got on hand."

"Assuming they don't just take it," Greeny said darkly. She was sitting at her usual table in the corner, surrounded by two empty glasses and a couple of ship manifests. "All bets are off during wartime. Mark my words."

Clive's first thought was that the soldiers must be coming for him—only that was ridiculous. Assuming that the search was still on *and* that the Protectorate had somehow discovered where he and Paz were, it would hardly take an army to recapture them. No, Chang must have decided he had something to gain by meeting up with the Wesah . . . but what?

The Settlers kept interrogating the tradesman after that, but Clive had heard enough. He spoke under his breath to Paz.

"We can't stay here if the whole Protectorate's coming through. We'd be putting everyone in town at risk."

"I know," Paz said wistfully. Under the bar, she wrapped her legs around one of his. "Let's just enjoy the time we've got left."

He pulled her close, kissed that spot on her forehead where

you could still make out fragments of a word through her bangs. "Works for me."

But the days flickered past like starlings headed south for the winter, each one bolstering the illusion that things could remain as they were forever. Clive was paralyzed by his own contentment, fooled himself into thinking he had all the time in the world. He assumed there'd be word when the Protectorate was a day or two out, at which point he'd buy a small sailboat from one of the settlers and set out north with the girls, keeping well wide of the coastal roads and Edgewise. Greeny had told them about a fishing village called Hull, about four days' hard sailing past the northernmost boundary of the Descendancy.

"It's a lot like Settle, only twenty degrees colder," she'd said, chuckling darkly. "I know the mayor. I'll send you off with a letter of recommendation: 'Best damn fishermen I ever met.' He won't believe it, of course, but I bet he'll take you in anyway."

It was a decent plan, but one that would never come to fruition. Out on the docks one morning, not two weeks after he'd heard about the Protectorate's mobilization, Clive felt his gaze drawn to the very top of Settle's main street. A lone figure was walking slowly down toward the water. Clive couldn't make out a face, but he knew that uniform well enough: the good old red and gold. He fumbled the barrel he was carrying as his instincts told him to drop it and run—but of course that would be even more foolish than staying where he was.

He set the barrel down and started moving as nonchalantly as possible toward the canteen. "I've got to take a leak," he said to Oliver, one of his fellow longshoremen.

"The ocean's not good enough for you?" Oliver called out after him.

"I don't want you trying to get a look at my willy."

"I only want to see if it's as small as everybody says!"

As soon as it was safe, Clive cut to the right, heading uphill by way of narrow alleys and unkempt yards. By a stroke of luck, Paz had come down with a cold the previous day, so she'd slept in that morning. That meant all he had to do was pick up Flora from the church-cum-schoolhouse and then make for home. Allowing a few minutes to pack their modest belongings and a bit of food, they could be out on the water in under an hour.

It was a peculiar church: built like a barn and topped with a tapering four-sided spire that culminated in a bright brass cross. Inside, the pews had all been pushed over to the walls and the students sat cross-legged on the floor before a large blackboard; Vernon Young led a recitation of the words written thereon.

"Sacrifice," he intoned.

"Sacrifice," the class repeated.

"Suffering."

"Suffering."

"Salvation."

"Salvation."

Clive watched Flora for a moment. She'd positioned herself in the corner farthest from the blackboard, perhaps in the hope that Vernon wouldn't notice her refusal to recite along with the rest of the class. Her lips remained motionless, and her gaze was trained intently on the view outside the windows to her left. And was it Clive's imagination, or had a tear just slipped surreptitiously down her cheek?

TOMMY WALLACH

"Flora?" Vernon said.

Clive watched her return to herself, wipe at her eyes. "What is it?"

"It seems you have a visitor."

When Flora noticed Clive, she immediately jumped to her feet and ran into his arms. He carried her out into the narthex and set her down. Her whole body was shaking.

"What's wrong, darling?" he asked.

"I'm sorry, Clive. I'm so sorry."

"About what?"

"I was mad at you, so I did a bad thing."

Clive knelt down so his eyes were level with hers. "I'm sure it's not so bad as all that. Just tell me what happened."

She could hardly speak for emotion; the words struggled to compete with her sobs. "I saw him on the way to school, and I knew I should've run and told you right away, but I . . . I went and talked to him instead. And he asked about you, and I said you'd be coming to pick me up around lunchtime, so he said—"

"Who did? Who did you talk to?"

As if on cue, the double doors leading outside swung open. Clive just had time to put his body in front of Flora's before he found himself facing down two feet of sharpened steel—and two hundred pounds of angry marshal.

"Morning, Clive," Burns said. "I think it's high time you and me had a little talk."

Interlude

THE ARCHBISHOP LUIGI CARMASSI STOOD BEFORE HIS open armoire, gazing at himself in the glass. His gut sagged below the line of his underwear. He held out an arm and gently slapped the flesh that had once been a bicep. Stress, as it turned out, wasn't particularly slimming. At least he still had his hair. Though a man in his position had leave to wear it however he liked, he'd chosen to retain the traditional ecclesiastical style: grown shoulder-length and drawn back into a bun. He'd washed it last night and now it fairly shimmered in the morning light. Still, if you looked closely, you could see pink patches of scalp between the hedgerows of platinum. The damned skin—that was the most galling part of growing older. Watching as that once soft and supple canvas grew rough and papery, transformed from a wall into a window, laying the inner workings bare, the labyrinth of arteries and veins and capillaries—what the Archbishop's personal physician, Attendant Lentz, called "the plumbing of life."

Powell, in his ninth commentary on the Filia, compared a mortal life to a ship with a leaky hull. As a younger man, the Archbishop had found the metaphor rather contrived. But now, with his own boat listing and beginning to founder, he'd come to see the truth in it.

A breeze blew through the open window, bringing with it the distant strains of trumpets. Sixty-two years old today. A holiday. A holy day. He smiled at the thought of all the pomp and circumstance that attended his birthday. Shops would open late, if at all. Every church in the Descendancy would hold a special ceremony. Boys wouldn't leave the house until their mothers wrapped a thread of corn silk around their wrists, for fear of receiving a sharp punch to the shoulder: *no yellow, poor fellow.*

"All for me," the Archbishop said to himself. He took his gut in his hands and jiggled it. "All for this." He laughed again, turned to the back of the room. "Isn't that funny, Preston?"

Innocent Preston smiled crookedly, the only way he knew how. A simpleton, yet in many ways, one of the Archbishop's closest friends.

"You want dee now?" he said.

"Dee?" Carmassi replied. He'd grown used to Preston's speech impediment over the years, but that didn't mean he could always translate on the spot.

"Dee, for drink."

"Oh, tea! Yes. That would be lovely."

Preston slipped out of the room, and with a sigh, the Archbishop began to dress. First the black cassock that every member of the clergy wore beneath his vestments, followed by the golden robes of his office. Each day, he marveled at the weight of them. Here they were at the very peak of summer; it would be sheer torture to go out in all that velvet and brocade, but such was his burden to bear. (The smell of him at the end of the day was truly something to marvel at.) Last of all came the biretta, a small square hat with a soft felted ball on top. The Archbishop owned more than a dozen of them, and yet another sat in a box on the table by the door. It had arrived even before the Archbishop had awoken, a birthday gift from Grand Marshal Chang. Bright red, with a golden tuft: Protectorate colors. Wearing it would signal acceptance of the new order, a willingness to compromise.

He donned the white biretta instead.

Fully dressed, he opened the doors to the balcony. Most people assumed the Archbishop still lived on the bottommost floor of Notre Fille, in the rooms attached to his offices, but he'd given them up more than a decade ago, retaining a crack team of builders to transform the cathedral's dovecote into spacious living quarters and, wonder of wonders, his own private garden—three terraced levels, crisscrossed with raked gravel paths and shaded by wisteria-swathed pergolas. It had taken months to cart up the soil, years before the plants reached the density suggested in Attendant Gokhale's original drawings, but now the garden exploded with color every summer. His happiest moments were those he spent out here alone, meditating on the Filia, or praying, or simply being.

The path leading out of his apartment was lined with dwarf apple trees and steepled wooden trellises thick with fruiting tomato plants. At the center of the garden's second terrace was a sculpture of the Daughter holding a flaming sword over her head. Water burbled out of the tip of the blade, and over the years, it had untangled the elaborate knots of the deity's hair and smoothed her features into an angelic softness. The Archbishop lowered himself onto the ledge that ran around the fountain and gazed upon her countenance. He felt his mind settle.

Some time later, Preston reappeared, bearing a small tray with an iron kettle and a single porcelain cup. The innocent set the tray down and poured the tea.

"Thank you, Preston. Summon me when it's time."

The innocent nodded. "Heppy . . . heppy birthday, sir."

The Archbishop picked up the mug and held it up to his nostrils. It wouldn't be cool enough to drink for a while yet, but in truth, he'd always preferred the smell of tea to the taste. This blend was brewed especially for him in the kitchens of Notre Fille, with rare ingredients from Sudamir and a couple of generous scoops of sugar.

Funny, how little Carmassi knew about that civilization to the south (or was it *those* civilizations?), or of the vicious monarchy that had apparently taken root on the far eastern coast of his own continent. A privilege, not to know, and one that wouldn't last forever. The Archbishop sensed that the days of blissful isolationism would soon be over. Even after the wrinkle of Sophia had been smoothed, things could never go back to the way they were; cherubim guarded the gates of Eden now.

Turin said there were books in the Library that told the truth of the heavens, how each star in the firmament was itself a planet, just like Earth, and how there were billions of stars in the sky, most of them invisible to the naked eye. The Archbishop had been apprised of this reality when he received his purple bishop's robes, and sometimes he wished he could unlearn it. Such perspective made all his actions seem empty and futile, like pissing into the ocean.

He felt light-headed: too much worrying about things he couldn't control. He stood up to shake off the sensation, but his legs were watery, and why did his collar suddenly seem so tight? He fumbled at the topmost button—fruitlessly, as his hands had begun to shake.

"Preston!" he shouted. "Preston!"

The sound of feet crunching loudly across the gravel, then Preston's wide-eyed, fearful stare.

"I'm not feeling well," Carmassi said. His breath had become labored, and his vision was beginning to blur. "Did you prepare this tea?"

The innocent nodded vigorously.

"And everything was just as it always is?"

Preston began nodding again, then abruptly stopped. He frowned. "There a man."

"A man? What man?"

"He bring sugar. For birthday. Say it secret present. Is bad?"

"Get Attendant Lentz right away. Tell him it's—" Carmassi's stomach clenched; the pain made him cry out. There would be no time for Lentz; the ending to this story had already been written. The Archbishop had no serious regrets, though he would've liked to see this war through.

Sugar for tea: such a silly way to die.

He spoke through gritted teeth. "Whatever happens, you need to get a message to the Epistem."

"Message. Yes, sir."

Carmassi had no doubt that this was Chang's doing. The Grand Marshal was finally making his play, cleaning house in preparation for the conflict to come—for his *reign*. No doubt the poisoning would be blamed on the Mindful, exploited as one more incitement to war against Sophia, to the investiture of yet more power in the Protectorate and, by extension, Chang himself. But that was far too much to relate to poor Preston, whose mind was like a sieve.

"Tell him that Grand Marshal Chang poisoned me. Can you do that?"

"Chang. I tell. Chang is the one . . . the one who . . ."

Preston trailed off. He furrowed his brow inquisitively, as if listening to distant music, and began trying to clear his throat; the attempt quickly grew desperate, and his befuddled frown transformed into an agonized grimace.

"Preston?" Carmassi said. "Preston, my boy, what is it?" But the innocent could no longer speak. His body was racked with coughing, and his hands were at his throat, as if he might massage the airway open again. "Preston, did you try the sugar?"

The innocent looked up between convulsions, nodded guiltily.

Carmassi reached out and placed an absolutory hand on Preston's wide forehead. He tried to smile. "That's all right. I would've done the same."

No message would reach the Epistern now, but that was no great matter. Turin was clever; he'd figure out what had happened. Blood dripped from the corner of Preston's mouth. It wouldn't be long now—only one thing left to do.

"Father in the ground," Carmassi said, as the universe unspooled and blackened before him, "whose fist is the Daughter, whose love is Gravity, thank you for your gift." Preston's eyes rolled back in his head. The Archbishop felt a powerful urge to follow his innocent into oblivion, but he fought it off. "Leave us not in darkness, but hold us to your mantle, as you always have, and always will." He was floating now, away from his body, drawn inexorably toward the Lord and his Daughter. Oh, but it would be good to see them after all this time, to cast off the heavy cloak of humanity and enter at last into eternal grace. In these final moments, he felt no anger, no hunger for vengeance. There was only gratitude, only hope. "Forever and ever, world without end. Amen."

His breath caught, and he knew no more.

Part III
B U T C H E R S

If I'd known it was harmless, I'd have killed it myself.
—*Philip K. Dick*, A Scanner Darkly

It is forbidden to kill; therefore all murderers are punished
unless they kill in large numbers and to the sound of trumpets.
—*Voltaire*

1. Clive

THIS WAS LIFE. IT GAVE AN OUNCE OF HAPPINESS ONLY to take away a pound.

Clive had never worn chains before. They were surprisingly unwieldy, heavy as sin, and the manacles chafed his wrists. The steel links connecting him to Paz slithered along the ground, catching on roots and rocks, pulling them up short again and again. Burns rode about fifteen feet ahead of them, the end of the chain wrapped around the pommel of his saddle. He seldom bothered to look back. Clive had no idea why they were traveling south, away from the Anchor. The only conceivable destination in that direction was the *tooroon*, but what use would a couple of prisoners be there? And would they even make it in time? Three days after their capture, they'd covered only fifteen miles or so. Burns's frustration was evident—and the sole consolation to be found in the whole situation.

Clive spent much of his time worrying about Flora, whom they'd left back in Settle. Burns had come to some kind of arrangement with Greeny to look after the girl until he returned, but had made no promises about exactly when that would be. On the plus side, for the past few weeks, Flora had gotten along a whole lot better with the salty old woman than she had with Clive. Maybe she would be grateful for the separation.

"How much farther to the *tooroon*, do you think?" Paz murmured.

"I'm not sure," Clive replied. The trail they were taking had bent away from the coastline late the previous day, and after traversing a few miles of foggy bluffs carpeted with manzanita, they'd entered a sparse forest of pine and sycamore. Though they couldn't see the ocean anymore, the scent of it still sharpened the air. "Greeny said it was about a hundred miles, but she also said she could drink a gallon of beer without throwing up, and we both know how that went."

"So what does that give us? Another week? Two?"

"Hey." Clive reached out to take her hand. Their manacles clinked. "We're still here, all right? We're still together. We'll figure this out."

He planted his feet and kissed her, waiting for the inevitable tug of the chain and Burns's accompanying bark—only neither came.

The marshal had checked his horse and was sitting very still in the saddle, eyes narrowed, listening. And now Clive heard something too: the jangle of reins and the clip-clop of hooves. Men laughing. Soldiers.

"Shit on a stick," Burns said. He dismounted and walked his horse back toward Clive and Paz, speaking quickly under his breath. "I need you two to listen to me real close. Those men *cannot* find us."

"Why not?" Clive said. "Aren't you all on the same side?"

"Is that listening? Is talking listening now?" The marshal's whisper had gotten away from him, but he managed to catch it again. "Clive, you're just about the most hated goddamned man in the whole Protectorate right now. And as for you"—he looked at Paz and emitted a morbid little chuckle—"I'd say you have about as much chance at getting a nice quick death as I do of becoming Archbishop." The sound of the soldiers was getting louder. Burns tugged at his horse's lead. "Let's go."

"Wait," Paz said.

Burns turned. "Are you deaf, or just stupid? We need to get off the road now."

"Unchain us first."

If the situation weren't so deadly serious, Clive might've laughed at the way Burns's eyes looked about to pop right out of his head. "Tell me you're not trying to fucking *negotiate* with me. Or don't you care that those men want to kill you?"

"Honestly, I'm not seeing much difference between them and you at the moment." Paz squinted, as if reading something in Burns's expression. "And I get the feeling you're not in the mood for a parley either. So what's it gonna be?"

The marshal took a couple of steps toward them, and Clive braced himself. But after letting out a grunt of disgust, Burns reached into his pocket and produced a small iron key. He unlocked the clasp that fastened the chain to his horse. "Happy?"

"What about this one?" Paz said, lifting up the links between herself and Clive.

"Don't push your luck."

Clive could make out the voices of the men now, could see their red-and-gold uniforms flickering through the trees. "Come on," he said.

They hurried downhill, away from the trail. When the first soldier appeared at the top of the ridge, they stopped in their tracks.

The trees here weren't wide enough to hide behind; their only chance was to stay perfectly still and hope they weren't seen.

A veritable river of military might flowed past: at least two hundred soldiers, all on horseback. As far as Clive knew, the Protectorate had never mustered a mounted division before. This force must've been organized specifically to impress the Wesah, who believed a warrior without a horse was hardly a warrior at all. After what felt like an eternity, the last of the soldiers disappeared down the trail. Burns fell back against the nearest tree and exhaled loudly. "Thank the Daughter," he said.

Suddenly a silver vine exploded out of the leaves and pine needles at the marshal's feet and rose all the way up to the level of his neck. Before he could react, Burns found himself pinned tightly against the tree.

Clive looked to Paz and found her tugging on the chain that bound them with all her might, a vicious gleam in her eye. He resisted the pull on instinct, which was all the pressure needed to keep Burns restrained. It was ingenious, really; while the soldiers had been marching by, Paz had subtly encircled Burns, so all she'd need to do to trap him was raise her wrists over her head and lean back.

As always, Clive was astonished by her cunning.

Burns, however, was something other than impressed. He'd managed to get a few choice obscenities out before the chain slid up his chest and onto his throat. All his efforts now were bent on creating some space to breathe, but the physics of the situation were against him. Clive knew he need only add his weight to the equation and the marshal would be out of their lives for good. With

Burns gone, they'd be in the clear. Who else would be able to find them? Who else would even bother trying? They could go back to their lives in Settle, or run away to Sudamir. They could be happy.

And though Clive knew that future was never to be, that any moment now he would have to step forward and put a stop to Paz's assault, the fantasy was still dancing through his mind when the chain suddenly went limp in his hands. Burns fell forward onto the dirt, gasping for breath. Clive looked over to Paz, whose own gasps of exertion quickly turned to sobs. He went to her, took her in his arms.

"I can't," she said. "I'm sorry. I just can't."

Clive stroked her hair. "Don't be sorry. You did the right thing."

Burns coughed for their attention. He'd drawn his sword, the point of which now hovered about an inch from Paz's throat.

"What are you doing?" Clive said. "She just saved your life."

"That's a pretty rosy way of looking at it," Burns replied. "She nearly killed me first."

"I wouldn't have let her."

"I hope that's true. Either way, it doesn't change our situation."

"And just what *is* our situation?" Clive said, newly emboldened by what now felt like a joint decision to exercise mercy. (And would he have stopped it himself? Of course. He'd been just about to. Yet he knew he would wonder for the rest of his life, and never be certain.) "Why did you hide from those soldiers?"

"I'm not hiding. I don't—it's none of your goddamned business what I do."

Paz plopped down on the ground like a fractious child. "Then I guess we'll just sit here until you're ready to talk."

"I'll drag you behind the horse if I have to," Burns said.

Clive sat down next to Paz. "That's a lot of work for one horse. She'll tire out fast."

It had been a bad few minutes for Burns—taken by surprise on the road, nearly choked to death, now faced with mutiny (insofar as prisoners *could* mutiny). His anger was exhausted; all he could do was throw up his hands, grunt, and sit down alongside them.

He picked up a twig and started peeling it with his fingernail. "Shit's gone to hell in a handbasket since you two ran off. Chang's gone rogue and the Church doesn't have a clue what to do about it. I was supposed to find you and bring you back to the Anchor, but the truth is, I was never gonna do that."

"Why not?" Clive said.

"Because"—Burns swallowed, trying and failing to hide his emotion—"because I promised your father I'd keep you all safe. To turn you in now, after I already failed him and your momma . . . it just didn't sit right with me."

"You don't care about what we did in the Bastion?"

"Well, I looked into that before I left, and I think I got a handle on how it all went down. That Louise girl, the musician, she was working with the Mindful. They kidnapped Flora and said you'd only get her back if you brought them Paz. Right so far?"

Clive nodded.

"I'm guessing you got in there by offering the guards on duty a little alone time with the prisoner, and when they realized it was a sham, things got ugly. You did what you had to do, and then when Louise's crew ran into trouble on the way outta town, you and the ladies managed to slip away."

TOMMY WALLACH

"What happened to her?" Clive said. "Louise, I mean."

"Stone dead, you'll be glad to hear."

Except emotions didn't work that way. Clive had known Louise for more than half his life, and in spite of what she'd done, he felt sorry for her. She'd just gotten caught up in something she couldn't control—like everybody else in this sad story.

"Shame it had to go that way," Clive said quietly. "She wrote real good songs."

"Here's the thing"—Burns paused to pull a ready-made cigarillo from an inside pocket of his jacket, a box of matches from his trousers—"I'm sure a good half of the men I've killed in my life were decent folks, all around. Not saints, of course, but good enough. If you asked their children, their neighbors, they'd all say, 'Oh, him? He's a real nice fella. Family man. Always up to lend a hand.' Stuff like that." Burns struck the match, one sharp blow against the side of the box, and held it to the end of the cigarillo. "But a good man tries to kill you, you're gonna try and kill him back, end of story." The marshal breathed out a lungful of smoke, as if releasing a spirit. "All I'm saying is, don't beat yourself up."

"I didn't even *think* about beating myself up," Paz said.

Burns snorted. "Don't I know it, girl."

"I still don't understand," Clive said. "If you aren't gonna turn us in, why chain us up at all?"

"She's chained up because I need her for something. You're chained up because I know you won't like what I need *her* for."

"Which is?"

"A trade."

"What trade?"

"For Gemma," Paz said. As usual, she'd gotten the drift before Clive had.

Burns nodded in confirmation. "If she's alive, she'll be at the *tooroon*. We know the name of the chieftain who took her, so it shouldn't be too hard to track her down."

"If the Wesah wanted me more than Gemma, they would've taken me in the first place."

"Maybe. Maybe not. But I made the same promise to Eddie Poplin that I made to Honor Hamill. So if I can get Gemma back, I will."

Paz smiled grimly. "I suppose I can see where you're coming from, Marshal."

"I won't let this happen," Clive said.

Burns snorted. "Hence the chain."

"I mean it. I'll kill you first."

"No, you won't. You had your chance five minutes ago."

"I didn't know what you were planning then. And I swear to God, you'll never—"

"It's fine," Paz interrupted.

Clive turned to her, aghast. "It's fine? He wants to use you as a bargaining chip!"

"So what? I'll be safer with the Wesah than I would be back at the Anchor, or even at Sophia. And the truth is I owe Gemma, for what I did to her."

"What about you and me?"

"We'll figure it out. You can come along, or else I'll find a way to escape." She reached over Clive and offered her hand to Burns. "You've got a deal, Marshal. Take me to the Wesah."

"Smart girl," Burns said.

Clive, momentarily nonplussed, watched them shake on this most improbable of compacts. He was finally finding his composure again, and preparing to mount a newly impassioned argument, when the crack of a broken branch drew his attention back toward the trail.

Six Protectorate soldiers stood in a half circle just a few yards uphill. Three of them had already nocked arrows. An older man, RENNET embossed beneath the chevrons signifying his rank of sergeant, stepped forward.

"Just what in the Daughter's name is going on here?" he said.

Burns stood to meet him. "Sergeant Rennet, I'm Marshal Burns, and these are my prisoners." He looked to the bowmen. "Weapons down, men. That's an order."

"Weapons damn well up," Rennet countered.

Burns scowled. "This some kind of joke? I'm your superior."

"Are you now?" Rennet balled up his fist and sank it into Burns's belly: a sucker punch. The marshal dropped to one knee, wheezing. "You think I don't recognize that boy of yours, and the bitch he's with? And here you all are way out in the middle of nowhere, looking chummy."

"When we get back to Bastion, I'll see you hanged," Burns growled.

"Oh, I doubt that very much. The world's changed, Marshal. The Archbishop is dead. The old order's gone."

Clive couldn't help but interject. "What happened to the Archbishop?"

Rennet replied with a straight right to Clive's jaw that sent him sprawling. "I don't conversate with traitors."

"Chang did it, didn't he?" Burns asked. "He killed Carmassi?"

The sergeant shrugged. "Who cares?"

"*You* should. We're sworn to defend the Church. That's the whole fucking reason the Protectorate exists."

"Personally, I care more about defending my family from those butchers in Sophia. But if you're so concerned about what the Grand Marshal might've done, you can just ask him yourself."

Burns's expression changed, a crack of fear appearing in the wall of brute confidence. "Chang's here?"

"On his way." Rennet smiled broadly. "And something tells me he's gonna be real glad to see all of you."

2. Gemma

THÈNE'S *NAASYOON* LEFT FOR THE COAST AROUND the end of June, a couple of weeks before the rest of the Villenaître (other than Grandmother and those tribeswomen too close to delivery to travel) would follow suit. Gemma would miss much of it—her lessons, the easy camaraderie that had grown up between her and Helene, the plush bed she shared with Athène—but it had been more than three months since they'd arrived at the Villenaître, and she was ready to go.

She'd always been that way: happiest on the move. Back in the ministry days, after she'd returned from a tour and was once again safely ensconced in the cozy little room she shared with Flora, she would find herself tossing and turning in bed, her body rejecting the softness, the comfort, the stasis. Already, the road was calling her back. She missed seeing a different town every few days, meeting a new group of people, living off the land and the generosity of strangers. Some part of her must have known to savor that nomadic existence, because it wouldn't be long before she became a wife—homebound, forever fat with child, prisoned in corset and petticoat.

Riding at the front of Athène's *naasyoon* now, her lover at her side, Gemma shuddered to think how narrowly she'd escaped.

It made her furious to imagine herself accepting such a bland existence—more than that, welcoming it!—simply because no one had ever told her any others were available to her. It had taken all this—abduction, seduction, education—to bring home to her the vast injustice that the Descendancy enacted upon every woman within its borders every single day.

And what would become of Flora, if Gemma didn't intervene?

"A copper for your thoughts," Athène said. She took a particular delight in using the English idioms Gemma had taught her, though they now spoke almost exclusively in Wesah.

"I was thinking about my sister. About how the most important job anyone in the Anchor would think to entrust her with is making babies."

"Making babies isn't so bad. It's the only way to get more Gemmas in the world."

"If it's not so bad, then why haven't you done it?"

"I'm a chieftain. I must always be ready to fight." Athène smiled provocatively. "Besides, you keep me too busy for men, little dancer."

Gemma smiled back, but her disquiet lingered for the rest of the day. She hadn't forgotten her obligation to Flora, but now she'd begun to recognize a greater obligation—to all the women of the Anchor, who didn't know that something vital was being withheld from them. It made her think of that voice from the phonograph machine: Zeno, she'd called herself. How odd, that it was a woman giving the Descendancy all this trouble, threatening to bring the whole edifice crumbling to the ground. Gemma couldn't help but be tickled by the novelty of it, and inspired by her expanding view of just what a woman could be and do in the world.

TOMMY WALLACH

Over the next month, the *naasyoon* traveled along a gradient of increasing verdancy, the plains and plateaus of the Villenaître giving way to emerald valleys and temperate forests riddled with rivers. After a seeming eternity traversing a forest as vital and vibrant as any Gemma had ever seen, they'd at last broken through to the scraggly, stony landscape on the other side. The ocean couldn't be far off now, nor the day when they would meet up with Andromède, leader of the Wesah nation and Athène's mother. Though Gemma had learned much of the ways of the tribe—how to sing the songs and tell the stories, to brew the dreamtea and journey, to hunt and fight and even make love—the prospect of that meeting still terrified her. Even if Andromède didn't see straight through her, would she really allow her own daughter to ally herself so closely with an outsider?

One afternoon a few days later, the *naasyoon* found a road that snaked its way toward a picturesque village nestled among the distant foothills. Gemma knew that attitudes toward the Wesah could vary widely from town to town, but Athène insisted she recognized this village as a friendly place, welcoming to her people and generous in exchange.

Yet as they rode into town, Gemma immediately sensed something off about the place. It was an instinct she'd learned to trust during her time with Honor Hamill's ministry, especially when traveling the far reaches of the outerlands, where resentment of the Descendancy ran the deepest. You'd notice it first in the quality of the locals' attention, the way they stared after you like hungry dogs but refused ever to hold your gaze. Conversation would dry up when you popped your head into the local public house or general store. Streets would empty out before you. "Good old-fashioned hostility," Honor Hamill liked to call it.

"Something's wrong," Gemma said quietly. "They don't want us here."

Athène nodded. "We'll just march straight through. No stopping."

But that turned out to be easier said than done. As the *naasyoon* reached the town's central square, a cadre of Protectorate soldiers stepped out of a building with a yellow annulus painted above the door and formed a relaxed but unmistakable roadblock. There were about a dozen of them, all wearing the same red-and-gold uniform. Gemma could tell from their epaulettes that they were all first- or second-year recruits. She would've preferred to see an officer or two among them; inexperience meant incompetence, and incompetence meant danger.

"Evening, ladies," said a square-jawed, officious-seeming solider. "I'm afraid I have to ask what brings you to Pottersville tonight. Any of you speak English?"

"We are traveling to the *tooroon*," Athène replied. "We came through town to trade for food."

"I sure hope that's the case. You see, Pottersville has recently agreed to be incorporated into the Descendancy. That means me and my friends here are responsible for its protection—say, from anyone with a bad habit of kidnapping people."

Gemma wanted to ask what the Protectorate was doing incorporating new towns—historically, that work was the purview of the Church—but she figured it would be best to stay silent. Her

TOMMY WALLACH

lack of an accent would betray her as Descendancy-bred, and thus a Wesah abductee.

"We are only here to trade," the chieftain repeated.

A gaunt and pocky young soldier stepped forward. "Trade, huh? So how many of you could I get for this thing?" He grabbed his crotch and put on a lecherous expression.

Athène raised an eyebrow. "If you want me to remove it from you, I will gladly do so for free."

The other soldiers cracked up laughing at the riposte, and the only way the crude young man could think to recover his dignity was by drawing his sword. This provocation was swiftly met with a dozen nocked arrows, which then compelled the rest of the Protectorate detachment to produce their weapons as well. Up and down the street, windows were loudly shuttered in expectation of the imminent skirmish.

"Wait!" Gemma cried out. She'd grown up around soldiers like this—skittish boys who only seemed eager to fight because they were so afraid of getting hurt. She addressed the one who'd first drawn his sword. "What's your name, soldier?"

"What's yours?" he countered, spiky with fear.

"Gemma Poplin."

Chivalry compelled the young man to respond in kind. "I'm Luis. Luis Turner."

"Well, Luis, it's a pleasure to meet you. Now why don't we all just put our weapons down and keep chatting like the friendly folk we are?"

The boy pointed his sword in the direction of the *naasyoon.* "Them first."

"All right." Gemma turned to Athène and spoke in Wesah. "Tell them to put their bows away."

"You're sure?" Athène said.

"Nobody here wants a fight."

At a nod from their chieftain, the *naasyoon* lowered their weapons. The soldiers sheathed their swords immediately afterward.

"So why you speak English so good?" Luis asked.

"Because I grew up in the Descendancy, just like you."

"No kidding! Where?"

"The Anchor. My family still lives there, in the Seventh Quarter."

"So the Wesah musta kidnapped you, huh?"

Gemma hoped her laughter was convincing. "Of course not. I'm here because I want to be. And I promise you we aren't planning on raiding your town. We just hoped to rustle up enough food to get us to the coast."

Luis seemed befuddled that anyone might voluntarily travel with the Wesah. "Why'd you give up on the Anchor?"

Gemma considered which tale would be most likely to inspire the soldier's sympathy. "My engagement fell through," she said.

"What? You're saying some fella threw you over? He must be the dumbest man in the Descendancy."

"Careful there. He's still a good friend of mine. And he's a soldier too, name of Clive Hamill. Any of you know him?"

A decidedly unfriendly wind seemed to blow across the line of soldiers. Gemma felt her heart contract. Had something happened to Clive?

"Sure we know him," Luis said. "He's the one who broke the Sophian girl out of the Bastion."

The square-jawed soldier who'd first accosted them slapped his leg loudly. "Gemma Poplin—I knew I recognized that name! You and your brother were part of that ministry that got attacked. And you *did* get yourself kidnapped by these savages, during the march on Sophia. You're a prisoner!"

"You don't understand—" Gemma tried to say, but the soldier was talking over her now.

"By order of Grand Marshal Chang of the Descendancy Protectorate, we demand you all lay down your arms and surrender this citizen of the Anchor into our custody."

Athène smiled grimly, and Gemma knew something terrible was about to happen.

"Please," she said. "I can talk to them."

"You already talked."

"One more chance." Gemma approached the square-jawed soldier. "Listen to me. If you don't leave now, you're going to end up hurt. I don't want that on my conscience."

But the man only sneered. "So they've really turned you. Was it that one who did it?" He gestured toward Athène. "Did she make you her little plaything? Disgusting, every goddamn one of you. Now get the fuck over here." She backed away as he grabbed for her, and his fingers ended up snagged on the annulus around her neck. The lock of Flora's hair, already rendered flimsy by time and circumstance, came undone. Gemma watched the golden hairs float away on the breeze.

"Don't fight us, girl," Luis said, taking hold of her wrist and tugging her toward him.

A clean movement, drilled into her by a hundred sparring

sessions with Athène: the obsidian blade slid free of its sheath, and suddenly Luis's hand was hanging limply from the end of his arm, half-attached, blood spattering the dry earth. He screamed in expectation of an agony that never came; Gemma spun and brought the blade across his throat, silencing him forever. She landed splay-legged, dagger raised behind her, eyes flashing up at Athène. "Do what you have to," she said in Wesah.

"Yes, my love," the chieftain replied. Her smile was no longer grim.

The air filled with the twang of bowstrings, the whistle of arrows, and the cries of the dying.

That night, camped ten miles west of Pottersville, Gemma recited one of the stories she'd been taught by Grandmother in the Villenaître, about how Wolf once made himself so fearsome in appearance that half of Fox's army fled the battlefield at the very sight of him. It was a story to be told only after a great victory in battle.

Over the following week, they ran into other Wesah more and more often, all on their way to the *tooroon*. A small group of tribeswomen reported passing Andromède's *naasyoon* only a few days earlier, traveling west along an overgrown river road. After no small amount of deliberation, Athène decided it would be best to intercept her mother before the festival began, when Andromède would inevitably be pulled in a hundred different directions at once. The *naasyoon* turned east, moving quickly now, galvanized by the nearness of the *tooroon*, the nearness of their leader.

Gemma, on the other hand, only became more and more nervous with every passing hour.

"How I should I act around your mother?" Gemma asked.

"Act like yourself," Athène replied, advice as familiar as it was useless.

In retrospect, Gemma would be glad for how suddenly the great event was thrust upon her. A stretch of road no different from the thousand before it, a passing *naasyoon* like the three others they'd stopped to converse with that day alone. She'd expected some visible sign of royalty—special robes, an honor guard, perhaps even a palanquin—but all she got was a whispered "at last" from Athène. Then the whole *naasyoon* dismounted and Gemma found herself face-to-face with the wellspring of three months of low-burning anxiety.

"Mother," Athène said, and the two embraced. Except for a plain brass crown, Andromède looked like any other Wesah tribeswoman: thickly muscled, her elaborately braided jet-black hair shot with silver strands, a bow and a quiver on her back and a long knife at her waist. Athène motioned for Gemma to come closer. "Mother, this is Gemma. Gemma, this is Andromède."

"Good afternoon," the great chieftain said in flawless English. Something in her eyes made it clear she already knew what Gemma was to Athène. And on second thought, perhaps she *didn't* look like every other Wesah tribeswoman; there was something calm and heavy at the center of her, a potency that made Gemma think about the homilies Honor Hamill used to give on holy Gravity.

"*Taanishi*," she replied, stammering slightly.

It struck her as funny, that in spite of all the differences between Wesah and Descendant society, meeting your loved one's parents was every bit as intimidating here as there.

"You are from the Anchor," Andromède said, in Wesah now. "How long have you been with us?"

"Athène took me—that is, I joined the *naasyoon* in January. I was traveling east, with the Protectorate mission to Sophia." Gemma wasn't sure how much of this would make sense to Andromède, but she figured it was best to be as honest as possible. "Your daughter taught me your language, and I trained in the ways of the *otsapah* at the Villenaître."

Andromède's tone took on a note of accusation as she addressed Athène. "She's taken the dreamtea?"

"She has visions even without the tea," Athène countered. "She is special."

"So you believe in visions now?"

"I believe in her."

Gemma stood up as straight as she could and lifted her chin—hoping to look even a fraction as impressive as Athène had made her out to be. "I only want to do right by the tribe," she said.

Andromède considered this. Then she reached out to touch the three bangles around Gemma's right bicep. "Who?"

"A Sophian man, a Protectorate soldier—" She hesitated to finish the list.

"And a banished Wesah warrior," Athène said.

If Andromède was bothered by this revelation, she didn't show it. In fact, she didn't even seem to have noticed that her daughter had spoken. All her attention was focused on Gemma. "And you really wish to be Wesah?"

"Yes."

"Good." Andromède called out over her shoulder. "Nephra, Elodie, bind her. She travels with us."

From behind the great chieftain came two extremely large

TOMMY WALLACH

women holding a coiled length of rope between them. Gemma dropped her hands; there was nothing to be gained by fighting.

"What are you doing?" Athène demanded. When there was no answer, she planted herself in front of Gemma. "You can't have her."

"You heard your mother," one of the large women said, shoving Athène out of the way.

Gemma saw the murderous smolder in her lover's eyes; Athène's hand moved toward the hilt of her knife.

"No!" Gemma cried out. When the young chieftain looked her way, Gemma shook her head, sympathetic but firm.

Athène teetered on the precipice of the decision for another few moments, then finally gave in. "I'll come for you," she said.

In the end, Gemma departed from Athène's *naasyoon* the same way she'd come into it: as a prisoner, abducted for reasons she didn't understand, carried off toward an unknown destination. But she was a different person now—stronger, smarter, braver—and as the horse she'd been tied to turned about, granting her one last glimpse of the woman who'd changed her life, Gemma smiled to herself, secure in the knowledge that the separation wouldn't last for long.

3. Clover

SEVEN WEEKS ON THE ROAD FROM SOPHIA, PAST THE Anchor and on toward the coast, across a landscape once so familiar, now transformed by circumstance into something entirely foreign. Seven weeks performing a role he no longer understood—the repentant sinner, his faith transmuted by Zeno and Sophia into cold, hard rationality. Clover had hoped that returning to the Descendancy would feel like a homecoming, but he realized now that was naive. He had no home anymore, no country, no creed. The mission that had brought him to Sophia no longer provided clarity; Zeno wanted him to carry it out just as much as the Epistem did—so who did it really benefit? No one? Everyone? The circle of Clover's allegiances had shrunk until it circumscribed only those closest to him: Gemma and Flora, his father, and his brother. Everyone else might as well be a stranger.

The harsh regime of high summer levied its tax of sweat and energy; the roads grew dense with activity. A week's ride west of the Anchor, the stifling heat finally found its match in the cool breezes coming off the ocean, and not long after, a forest of ramshackle buildings tufted with the tips of spindly masts materialized in the distance: Edgewise, where Clive and Paz had reportedly struck their mysterious blow against Sophia, where Honor Hamill might even now be waiting for Clover to find him.

Zeno's party made camp about a mile outside Edgewise, and Clover and Lenny were tasked with carrying out a brief reconnaissance mission into town. Sophia's director hoped to determine just how much the locals knew about the Mindful cell that had been eradicated two months earlier, while Clover hoped to use the opportunity to learn anything that might help him locate his father. He and Lenny would pose as the two sons of an outerlands distiller, and to that end were saddled with about a dozen bottles of Sophia's most recent alcoholic innovation, transported all the way from the academy: a potent liqueur that smelled of pine resin, fennel, and sweetgrass.

They arrived at sundown, just when the shine would start flowing in earnest. Clover had expected the streets to be relatively quiet, but even after dark, Edgewise was as busy as Annunciation Square on a Saturday, its narrow dirt roads churning with rowdy local stevedores and even rowdier Sudamiran sailors, traders hawking their wares out of handcarts, crippled beggars rattling tin cups, tattily dressed harlots making coy eyes at every passing man, and a seemingly endless supply of Protectorate soldiers.

"What's with all the goons?" Lenny said.

"They're probably just passing through on the way to the *tooroon*."

"And you think Zeno's right, that Chang wants to ally himself with the Wesah?"

"I guess. But I don't know why you'd need this many soldiers just to parley."

The bottles in his backpack clanked as he adjusted the straps. Zeno said they'd probably pick up the best gossip down by the water, but Clover was eager to lighten his load a little, so he and Lenny ducked into the first public house they saw, a drearily lit, ill-smelling establishment whose weather-beaten sign advertised the EST ALE IN DGWIS.

The grizzled men at the bar glanced up, but before they could express anything like annoyance at the young outsiders invading their private dissipation, Lenny launched into a pitch that would've made any snake oil salesman proud.

"What are you drinking there? Shine? Ale?" He didn't wait for an answer. "Well, I'm sure it's just fine, but I'll tell you, you haven't lived until you've tasted the elixir my brother has in his bag right here. Bring it on out, Eli!" (For whatever reason, Lenny thought it would be funny if they went by the names Eli and Leo, the twin brothers who'd nearly killed Clover back in Sophia.) "This fine concoction has all the punch of shine without any of the bitterness, and it's only two silvers a bottle. Who wants a taste? You?" He seized on a couple of empty glasses, pouring an inch of the liqueur into each. "Go on. Try it."

The men weren't about to turn up their noses at free booze, whatever the source. "Not bad," one said after he'd finished. "How much for another try?"

Lenny filled the glass up about halfway. "Tonight, everything's on me. I'll be back tomorrow and we can talk about putting in an order."

"Gimme that," the bartender said, swiping the bottle and pouring himself a glass. He sipped, grimaced—"Too sweet."—but finished it anyway and poured another. "You boys gonna drink with us?"

Lenny shook his head. Zeno had made them swear on their lives that they wouldn't try so much as a single drop of the stuff, so they could keep their heads clear.

"A thimbleful of this and I can't remember my own name," Lenny said, "but you all knock yourselves out."

After another few minutes of idle conversation and enthusiastic drinking, Clover figured it was time to move in for the kill. "Say, we've only been in town for a couple hours," he said, as if the thought were just occurring to him, "but folks have been mentioning something crazy that happened a couple months ago. You know what I'm talking about?"

"Depends on your definition of crazy," one of the men at the bar said.

Another, much louder man attempted to take up the tale, but before he could get more than a few words out, the bartender slammed his fist down on the bar. "One more peep out of any of you and you're cut off for the rest of the week." He handed the bottle back to Clover. "I'll thank you to take your sugar water and your *questions* somewhere else."

They played things a little more slowly at the next establishment—an inn whose four sullen occupants polished off two bottles of the spirit in less than twenty minutes, thereby rendering themselves completely incoherent—but once again emerged without having learned anything useful. After that, they decided to take Zeno's advice and try their luck down at the docks, where half a dozen taverns competed for the silver of sailors and soldiers alike with live entertainment. At the first three, the musicians were playing too loudly for any sort of extended conversation (though another five bottles of the liqueur disappeared down the throats of several dozen grateful inebriates), but the fourth establishment had a different atmosphere entirely. The crowd was older and less boisterous, most of them enraptured by the gorgeous lutist performing a quiet ballad at the small stage in the back. The clutch of silver-haired stevedores at the bar seemed genuinely grateful for the attention of strangers, and they quickly pronounced the liqueur the best damn thing they'd ever tasted. After twenty minutes or so, when Clover finally got around to his question about strange happenings around town, the men were eager to answer.

"Sure I know what you mean," said a portly dockworker named Artie. "See, there was this old apothecary shop up the road. Run by the same guy for decades. Name of Indigo. But then these—"

"Inigo," said Reynolds, another of the stevedores. "His name was Inigo."

"That's what I said."

"No, you said 'Indigo.' Everybody heard it."

Artie rolled his eyes. "Anyway, these new folks came to town a couple of years back and bought the place off him."

"Not very friendly folks."

"That's right. And all sorts of strange smells coming outta the place at all hours." Artie paused to give his empty glass a sad little shake. "Say, you have any more of this stuff?"

"Sure do." Clover produced another bottle. There were only a couple left by now.

While Artie drank, Reynolds took up the tale. "So this past May, these kids show up in town and take a room over at Francie's."

"Kids?" Clover said.

"Well, everyone seems like a kid when you're our age. Two of them were probably about eighteen, but they had a little girl with them too."

A little girl? Did that mean Clive and Paz had brought Flora to Edgewise with them? Why would they do that?

Artie had already finished his drink, and now he forced his way back into the narrator's seat. "People saw them having drinks that very night with those folks from the apothecary shop."

"The unfriendly folks," Reynolds interjected.

"That's right. Next thing you know, the shop burns down. One body—a guy called Ferguson. No sign of anybody else. And apparently there was all kinds of weird stuff they'd been working on in the back."

"Bad stuff," Reynolds said. "Anathema."

"Honor Olmstead did a whole ceremony to clean it up. Spiritually, I mean."

Lenny refilled their glasses, along with those of a few other people who'd been listening in. "What sort of anathema?" he asked.

"Dunno," Artie said. "And I don't want to either."

"Amen to that, brother," Reynolds said, and both of them spat.

Clover figured he and Lenny had learned enough to please Zeno, who would be glad to hear that no one in town seemed to know the details of what the Mindful had been up to in that apothecary shop. Now if only these men had any information that might help him find his father.

"So the people who bought the shop, nobody in town knew them?" he asked.

A collective head shake from the stevedores. "Like I said, they weren't friendly," Reynolds reiterated.

"I might know something." A new voice: the lute player, who'd come down off the stage for a break between sets. Up close, she looked ten years older than she had from afar, and her skin bore the weight of too many long nights singing in seaside taverns. "And for one of those bottles of yours, I'd be happy to share it with you."

"Done," Clover said, relieving his satchel of half its remaining stock.

She took a long drink, smacked her lips. "Ah, that's not bad at all. So about nine months ago, a group of musicians from the Anchor came through town. They played here, and those apothecary folks showed up to listen. After the music was done, they all got a table and talked for hours. Things got pretty heated, too. I remember, because they were shouting through half my set."

"Who were the musicians?"

"The singer was called Louise . . . something or other. Young. Not so pretty, but she had a nice set of pipes." The lutist took another draught of the spirit, wiped her lips, and pushed back from the bar. "Duty calls. Thanks for the drink."

Louise—that could only be Louise Delancey! Clover hadn't seen her since the days they'd traveled together with the ministry, but he'd heard she'd made a name for herself on the Tails. Perhaps her travels had taken her out east, and she'd been won over to the Sophian cause along the way.

Lenny was oddly quiet on the walk back home, but Clover didn't care. He had a lead! Louise lived in the Anchor. If he could find her, he might be able to find the Mindful cell that had his father. He was tempted to take off for the Anchor as soon as he got back to camp, but it was already after midnight, and a few hours wouldn't make the difference one way or the other.

Most of Zeno's party had already gone to sleep by the time Clover and Lenny returned. The director herself was still up, however, sitting around the fire with Huma and Raff Park, a member of the Sophian town guard, who carried two fat pistols in his jacket's inside pockets.

"You're back early," Zeno said, something like anxiety in her tone. "I expected you'd be out till sunrise."

"We got lucky," Clover replied, setting his backpack down and taking a seat by the fire. "We met some pretty friendly drunks down by the water."

"It wasn't quite that easy," Lenny said. "We must've got fifty people sloshed before we found anyone willing to talk."

"Thank goodness for that," Zeno said, casting a meaningful glance toward Huma. "So what did they tell you?"

"That nobody in town knows what was going on in the apothecary shop," Clover said. "Other than something illegal, of course."

"And you don't think they were lying?"

"They weren't smart enough to lie that well."

Raff sighed. "Well, that's one less thing to worry about."

"Cheers," Lenny said. "To our success." He'd slipped the last remaining bottle of the spirit out of Clover's bag and had raised it halfway to his lips. Huma leaped up and knocked it away. It rolled across the dirt toward the fire, where a few drops sizzled in the ashes.

"Did you drink it?" she demanded. "You swore you wouldn't!"

"I didn't drink it!" Lenny said, hands up in apology. "But what's the big deal? I've had shine before. Maya, over at Ruben's—she serves me all the time!"

Huma glared at Zeno. "We should've told them."

"It's fine," Zeno replied. "You heard your son. They didn't drink it."

"Will one of you explain what's going on?" Lenny demanded.

But Clover had already begun to understand. "What's in it?" he whispered.

"A strain of influenza we've been developing for the past few years," Zeno said. "We'd originally planned to release it in the Anchor, but I was afraid the loss of life would be incompatible with keeping the city running after the transfer of power. Edgewise is a more strategically valuable site, as it turns out, because of the—"

"Oh God," Clover said, standing up and backing away from the fire.

Those chatty stevedores, eagerly finishing each other's sentences. The bartender serving the "est ale in dgwis." That lute player who'd sung so beautifully—all of them had tried the liqueur. All of them had been infected. And he'd been a part of it. More than a part—the perpetrator.

Zeno went on talking, cold and sharp as a scalpel. "The disease will spread quickly, and soon the Sudamiran traders will refuse to come to Edgewise. The Anchor will have lost its primary trading partner, significantly undermining its ability to wage war, and the loss of life will be much less than if we'd targeted the capital itself."

Clover's horror was quickly transforming into rage. He felt like that box kite, dancing madly in the wind—and Zeno was holding the lines. "I thought you were better than the people I grew up with," he said. "But you're not. You're . . . cruel."

TOMMY WALLACH

"We're making a better world, Clover. These are the growing pains."

A verse from the Filia came to mind, one of his mother's favorites. "'For what shall it profit a man, if he shall gain the whole world, and lose his own soul,'" he recited.

"Those are pretty words, only there's no proof the soul exists."

Clover smiled sadly. For the first time in his life, he saw how intelligence could be a kind of corruption, an insidious distancing from all the things that made a human human. "That isn't the point, Director. You've missed the whole point."

He turned to leave but was pulled up short by the sound of a gun being cocked. Raff Park had drawn one of his pistols and was pointing it right at Clover's heart.

"It's all right, Raff," Zeno said. "His part is done. He's more useful to us back in the Anchor, anyway. Good-bye, Clover. It's been a pleasure working with you."

Clover didn't return the valediction, didn't say anything at all. He just started walking, expecting at any moment to hear the gunshot, to feel once more the exquisite pain of a hot slug of metal piercing his flesh, but it never came. He mounted his horse and kicked her into a trot, but stopped at the sight of Lenny standing directly in the animal's path.

"Where were you that night?" he said, eyes burning.

Clover didn't understand. "What night?"

"The night Sister Lila went missing. I woke up and you weren't in the room. I never told anyone, because they would've thought you did something bad, and I didn't want that. But where were you?"

Clover turned the horse and skirted around Lenny. He didn't

want to answer the question, didn't want to talk about what had happened that night in Lila's office. But Lenny kept up, jogging alongside him. "I thought you were my friend, but you've been lying to me this whole time, haven't you?"

Clover urged the horse to move faster; Lenny began to fall behind.

"You're a liar! You're a murderer!" He'd started shouting now, loud enough that Zeno and the others must have been able to hear him. "You're back there judging everyone, but you're every bit as cruel!" Lenny tripped over something, tumbled to the ground. Still he kept on calling out, even as his voice grew increasingly faint and the warm night wind wicked the tears from Clover's cheeks: "Tell the truth for once, Clover! What did you do to Lila? What did you do? What did you do?!"

4. Paz

B Y NOW, PAZ HAD BECOME SOMETHING OF A CONNOIS-
seur of captivity. She knew all its flavors—from the dank
confinement of the Bastion dungeon, to the taut hours
she'd spent clamped to a chair in the tattooist's chamber,
to the relative tameness of the few days she and Clive had spent in
Burns's custody.

Her treatment at the hands of the Protectorate soldiers who'd
taken them prisoner fell somewhere in the middle ground—rough
but not violent, rude but not vulgar. While they were clearly eager
to beat Clive to a pulp, if not kill him outright, Burns had managed
to convince them to wait until Chang arrived. Of course, the Grand
Marshal wasn't likely to exercise any restraint himself, given how
Paz and Clive had left him the last time they met.

The soldiers stopped for the evening on a grassy bluff overlooking the ocean. Paz and Clive had been chained to a tree in full view
of the campsite—a loose agglomeration of about fifty tents, fifteen
campfires (complete with cooking smells that made Paz's empty
belly grumble: the closest the situation had yet come to outright
torture), and, at any given moment, a good dozen soldiers giving
them the evil eye. Burns was nowhere to be seen; Paz didn't even
know whether he was being treated like an enemy or an ally.

"All right, Clive Hamill," Paz said, "now that you've got some perspective, which side are you going to pick?"

"Pick?"

"That's right. Should Sophia win the war, or the Descendancy?"

Clive shook his head. "If the Archbishop is really dead, then I'm not sure there *is* a Descendancy. The Anchor's just another city now."

"So what's your answer?"

"I don't know. Neither, maybe. They both want to kill me."

Paz smiled. "If we get out of this, you wanna run away with me?"

"You know I do."

"Good." She kissed him. "Then I guess we'll have to get out of this."

They saw Chang approaching from miles off, traveling with a surprisingly modest retinue—three men dressed head to toe in black, walking alongside an elaborately paneled black wagon pulled by six horses. Paz remembered the first time she'd met the Grand Marshal—*Say it, girl. Say I'm a god.*—and felt her insides twist with anger. An enormous tent was erected in expectation of his arrival, and less than an hour later, Clive and Paz were escorted inside by the black-clad honor guard.

Chang was seated cross-legged on a red velvet cushion with golden tassels at the corners, arguing with Burns. The Grand Marshal wore only a white undershirt and maroon trousers. His socks and jacket were folded neatly beside him, and his shoes were in the process of being polished by a soldier at the back of the tent.

"Well, I suppose I can just ask them myself," Chang said with finality, gesturing for Burns to get out of his way. His eyes—black in the weak lantern light—found Paz's. "Paz Dedios," he said, savoring every syllable. "And Clive Hamill." He clapped once. "Knees!"

Paz felt her legs buckle—kicked out from under her by one of Chang's guards. Clive grunted as the same was done to him.

Chang smiled. "It's been far too long."

"Is it just me, or have you gotten uglier?" Clive said. Paz snickered—oh, but she did love him.

"Yes, we're all very impressed, young man. You're so brave, murdering your fellow soldiers in cold blood and fleeing the punishment you deserve."

"If you're gonna kill us, just kill us."

"I'm sure you'd like that. But you will be brought back to the Anchor, where you'll get a nice quick trial and then a very public execution, right in the middle of Annunciation Square. Everyone will see how we punish traitors and enemies of the state."

"If you've already decided everything, why are we even talking?" Paz said. "Just so you can gloat?"

"Well, I think I've earned a bit of gloating, to be honest, but no, I brought you in here to help me with something. Together, we're going to decide if the marshal here will be joining you on the scaffold."

"I did the job you asked me to do," Burns said. "I captured the fugitives."

"Then what are you doing south of where you started?"

"I already told you. I was taking them to the *tooroon* because I knew you'd be there."

"Except you were charged with returning them to the Anchor."

Burns groaned, as if with frustration; Paz was impressed by the performance. "Who cares? I got 'em, didn't I?"

"Sure you did. After you lost them in the first place."

"I didn't lose them!" Burns said, raising his voice now. "It was the Mindful who—"

But Chang wasn't about to be shouted down. "To hell with the Mindful! And to hell with your excuses! It was your idea to bring Hamill in to interrogate the girl. He's your protégé and he's a goddamned turncoat. You wouldn't believe what I've had to do to maintain the Protectorate's reputation in the face of all this."

"Did you kill the Archbishop?" Clive asked.

The question lowered the temperature of the room a good ten degrees. Chang took his time answering.

"Me?" he finally said, feigning innocence. "Why would I do that? Because the man didn't understand the first thing about waging a war? Because an old book was more important to him than his own fucking people? No. I didn't kill him. I was just the instrument. It was Sophia that killed him. It was that whore at your side."

Paz saw Burns bristle at the epithet, and in that bristling, born of the man's unique combination of permanent outrage and old-fashioned propriety, saw her opportunity. The truth was, she'd always liked the marshal. He reminded her of the men she'd grown up with in Sophia, gruff but practical, and surprisingly soft when you got to know them. That he'd never planned to bring her and Clive back to the Anchor, that he still hoped to do right by Gemma, was proof that he lived by his own moral compass, that he saw basic human decency as a higher calling than his obligations to the Protectorate.

Or she hoped so, anyway.

"I'm not a whore," Paz said.

"Your scalp begs to differ," Chang replied with a smirk.

"Doesn't make it true."

"Forgive me, whore, but I was led to believe you seduced this boy's brother in order to pump him for information. And from the look of things, whore, you've also succeeded in seducing this one. So what does that make you exactly?"

"Come on now," Burns said. "There's no need for that."

But just as Paz had expected, the warning only inflamed Chang further. He wouldn't be told what to do by anyone. "No need for what, Marshal? Calling her what she is?" Chang stood up, carried away by his fury. "How about I call her an animal, then? Or a lying, ugly, murdering heathen? Or a dirty bitch?"

Paz could see the outrage building inside of Burns—his jaw quivered with emotion, and he kept clenching and unclenching his fists.

Do it, she willed. *Go on and do it.*

Chang got right up in her face, breath stinking of garlic and tobacco. "Are those better, *whore*? I wouldn't want to offend your friend's delicate ears, *whore*. So please, *whore*, tell me what you'd—"

The Grand Marshal was interrupted by a sharp right jab to his nose, which immediately started gushing blood. Burns stepped back, hands up like a child caught rifling the larder for cookies, but it was too late. Chang's guards rushed forward, swords drawn, creating something of a pileup as they tried to decide who should attack first. Burns dodged the first swinging blade, which lodged in the central post holding up the tent, and threw himself bodily at the other two. Clive took advantage of the distraction and charged at Chang, tackling him to the ground.

Paz knew she didn't have long to act; Burns was trying to fight three men at once, and Clive's hands were tied. She could think of only one possible solution, and though it was a long shot, she didn't hesitate. The guard who'd lost his sword to the tent pole had given up on recovering it, and now Paz grabbed hold with both hands—still bound at the wrists—and pulled with all her strength, putting a foot on the upright to get more leverage. As she struggled, she watched Chang flip Clive over and pin his arms to the ground; time was running out. With a last great heave, she pulled the sword loose. As soon as she recovered her balance, she whipped it right back into the same cleft—once, twice, three times.

"Don't kill him!" Chang shouted to his guards. Clive lay dazed and bloodied against the wall of the tent, and Burns wasn't faring much better. Two of the guards had gotten hold of his arms, which allowed the third to deliver blow after blow to his ribs.

It was now or never. Paz retreated a couple of steps, took a deep breath, and leaped at the post, kicking out with both feet. The wood snapped and the top of the tent immediately fell in. The canvas was heavier than she'd expected, impeding her movements, suffocating her. The sounds of struggle started up again, half a dozen men fighting blind beneath the burdensome fabric. Paz crawled on all fours toward the edge of the tent, getting down on her belly to shimmy under the hem.

Outside, the night was serendipitously moonless. She took off through the tall grass, staying low, listening intently for the thunder of hoofbeats or the whistle of arrows. But the soldiers closest to the tent must have been preoccupied with helping the Grand Marshal, and it would be a while yet before they realized one of the prisoners was missing. After a few minutes, when she'd put enough distance between herself and the camp to feel momentarily safe, she stopped to look back.

A great bonfire blazed in the distance, flames dancing madly in the spirited sea breeze. One of the torches must've come loose when the tent collapsed; the canvas wouldn't have taken long to catch.

"Clive," Paz whispered. The last she'd seen of him, he'd been incapacitated. What if he hadn't made it out of the tent? She should go back, she *had* to . . .

Or . . . she could keep running. Just pick a direction and take off, not stopping until she reached Sophia, or the rough-and-tumble lands north of the Descendancy, or hell, why not Sudamir? That way she wouldn't end up swinging from a gibbet in Annunciation Square, or traded away to the Wesah like a sack of coffee.

She sighed. There was a time when she might've done something like that, back when she went by Irene, back when the only people she cared about lived in Sophia—but that was a long time ago now.

Chang wouldn't have let Clive and Burns die in that fire. He wanted his public execution, and that meant he had to keep his prisoners safe until they could be brought back to the Anchor. All Paz had to do was stay close and wait for her opportunity.

She watched through the night, hidden in the boughs of a tree, as the tent finished burning, as the ashes lost their glow, as the search parties came and went below her. She was still watching as the soldiers packed up the encampment and continued their journey south, toward the *tooroon*. When they were out of sight, she clambered down from the tree, stretched out her aching muscles, and followed after them—making sure always to keep the two ragged prisoners at the back of the formation in view.

5. Clive

WORSE? HOW COULD IT BE WORSE?"

Burns shrugged. "In my experience, it can always be worse. Unless you're dead, of course. But we ain't dead."

"Not yet."

"Exactly."

The soldier holding Clive's leash jerked on the rope. "No talking!"

Clive dropped to one knee but regained his footing before he could be kicked over—one of said soldier's favorite pastimes. He and Burns had a dedicated escort now; the Grand Marshal wasn't about to lose *another* prisoner. Clive had watched with smug satisfaction (if through one eye swollen shut and the other blackened) as Chang ran around camp like a headless chicken, screaming at each scout who returned without having found Paz. By now she'd be well on her way back home: to that farmhouse on the outskirts of Sophia and her many long-suffering brothers—the life she'd thought was gone forever.

Or that was what Clive hoped, anyway. There was also the chance that Paz hadn't gone anywhere, was at this very moment waiting somewhere just out of sight, planning something stupid and heroic. Which was why he couldn't stop scanning the woods to the east for some sign of movement.

The detachment was marching along a trail cut high into the side of the cliffs—a remnant of some ancient road built by the first generation of men. Tissue-thin strata of clouds scudded across the azure sky, white and pellucid, like the foam left by the surf on the rocks below. Clive and Burns walked near the back of the formation, their view forward obstructed by the black lacquered wagon Chang had brought from the Anchor. It had no windows and, as far as Clive could see, no doors, either.

"What do you think it is?" he whispered.

"Some fancy gift for the Wesah," Burns said. "A fishing boat, or a big ol' pile of shekels. Or maybe it's a sculpture of an elk or something. They go in for that sort of crap."

"I thought Chang hated the Wesah."

"He does. But right now he needs 'em more than he hates 'em."

"So why'd he bring the whole Protectorate along?"

"It's a show of strength, with a side of threat. 'Do what we say, or you'll find yourself on the pointy end of all these swords.' That kind of thing. Of course, I've never known the Wesah to respond too well to threats."

"But they wouldn't want open war with the Descendancy—"

Clive's voice caught in his throat as the cliffside trail rounded a bend and the view opened up over the beach below. All his life, he'd been told that the Wesah exaggerated their numbers to make themselves sound more powerful. Those few Anchorites who'd been to a *tooroon* and come home spinning tales about "a vast ocean of warriors" were quickly laughed out of the tavern, accused of sampling the famous dreamtea or falling prey to the charms of a pretty tribeswoman. But there were at least fifteen thousand

Wesah milling about the sands down below (and who could say how many hadn't yet arrived, or had chosen to forgo this year's *too-roon*). More than a gathering, more even than a garrison, it looked like a makeshift city, stretching as far as the eye could see: a good ten miles of beach, bluff, and wood.

Clive didn't doubt that this many warriors announcing for one side or the other might very well determine the outcome of the war to come; so whatever gift Chang had in that wagon better be damned good.

The trail began to snake down the side of the cliff, from which vantage Clive could look down on the northernmost end of the beach, where the Protectorate had made camp, miles away from the closest Wesah tents. Their section of the strand was densely populated with soldiers and noisy with laughter, barked commands, and the clash of steel on steel—simultaneous practice and performance. Clive kept his head down as the detachment reached the ridge that ran just beside the beach. Though Chang had zealously enjoined his honor guard to keep Clive and Burns safe, they'd hardly be able to stand up to a mob of Protectorate soldiers bent on revenge.

When the detachment reached the southern edge of the Protectorate camp, Clive and Burns were shoved into a small, lightless tent erected around a huge piece of driftwood shaped like a seal. The ropes that bound their wrists were hitched to a thicker rope, which was strung through a knothole in the driftwood and tied off on the other side.

"Don't go anywhere," one of the guards said with a chuckle, just before leaving them on their own.

Burns sat down and took off his shoes and socks. He rubbed at the sole of his right foot, letting out a contented little groan. Clive paced at the limit of his leash, trying to see out through the intermittent crack in the tent flap made by the breeze off the ocean. Waves lapped at the glittering shore. Soldiers went about their duties. Chang's glossy black wagon finally trundled to a stop.

"Relax," Burns said. "There's nothing we can do about any of this now."

"I guess not."

A brief silence as Burns switched to massaging his other foot. Then: "So . . . how was she?"

"What?" Clive didn't understand until the grin had spread halfway across Burns's face. "Seriously? We're facing down execution and you want to ask me about *that*?"

"Why not?"

"Because I'm not the kiss-and-tell type."

"Oh come off it, ya damn preacher's son. I saw the way you looked at that girl from day one, like you'd never even *heard* of the Filia. And after all the crazy shit that's happened since, the two of you finally get together, and you think that's not a story worth telling?"

"But it's not the story that you asked me about."

"Sure it is. It's just the, uh, *climax*."

Clive tried to suppress a smile. "That's private."

"We're not exactly in Annunciation Square, are we? Come on. I mean, hell, if I'd known my last roll in the hay was gonna be my *last* roll in the hay, I would've made it, well, last! It would've been a tale for the ages, and you'd be sitting there for the next hour listening to me describe every little detail. So just give me something, all right? One word. Give me one good word."

Clive grunted—acquiescence in the Burnsian mode. At least it would shut the marshal up, and besides, there was something intriguing about the challenge. How to describe his time with Paz in just one word? "Good" was too vague, "amazing" too extreme. "Religious" would be accurate but, ironically, profane. Clive just didn't have it in him to be graphic, or obscene, or even ecstatic. He *was* a preacher's son, after all.

Then a word occurred to him that perfectly captured his feelings on the matter—both the moment itself and the impossibility of adequately describing it. "Damn," he said quietly.

Burns frowned, then understanding dawned. "'Damn?' That's your one word?" He let out a bark of a laugh, slapped the sand. "'Damn,' he says. Damn!" Clive started laughing too, because who the hell cared what he said anymore, and he kept on laughing until his cheeks ached and he could barely breathe.

"You're all right, Hamill," Burns said, wiping tears from his eyes. "I never would've expected it, but you turned out all right."

Slowly the line of light visible through the tent flap faded to black. Clive slept and dreamed of the night the contingent had marched on Sophia, when he'd chased Paz through the woods with his brother's blood on his hands. In the dream, she appeared as a white hart always dancing just at the edge of his vision, as if mocking him for trusting her again and again.

He woke into a silence that didn't make sense—there were too many soldiers in camp for such stillness. By the quality of

Burns's breathing, he could tell the marshal was awake as well.

"Shit," Burns said.

The space between the bottom of the tent and the ground flushed, flickered. Whispers were shushed, and there was a collective intake of breath, as if in preparation for something. A moment later, a mass of silhouettes burst into the tent, backlit by a single torch. Clive managed to bark out a syllable of surprise before someone shoved a gag into his mouth. The rope securing him to the driftwood was unknotted; then both he and Burns were dragged out of the tent and up the beach, away from the ocean and the rest of the encampment.

Clive's stomach dropped as he realized this wasn't Chang's doing. Word must've leaked around camp that Clive Hamill— murderer of his fellow soldiers, Sophian collaborator—had been taken prisoner, and justice could be meted out at last. That they could take down Marshal Burns at the same time would only be the icing on the proverbial cake.

The torch had been extinguished (no doubt to make the company less conspicuous; Chang's directive that the captives be kept alive was still in effect), but a crescent moon shone bright as the electric lights of Sophia, limning the sweating faces of the soldiers and the fat lobes of the carpetweed underfoot. Clive didn't recognize anyone he knew, but it was possible he'd bunked with some of them in the Bastion, or traveled alongside them on the mission to Sophia. Maybe he could prey on their sympathies, their shared history as Protectorate soldiers.

He tried to make himself understood in spite of the gag. "Brothers, you've got the wrong idea about—"

A ringing backhanded slap set his head spinning. "Shut your mouth, traitor."

Well, it had been worth a try.

They marched east, past the place where the scrubby coastal vegetation gave way to quaking aspens and peeling birches, leaves already glistening with the coming morning's dew. In the distance, a lavishly limbed monster hulked at the center of a wide, grassy field, brooding on its solitude: a wolf tree. Clive had learned the term from Clover, could still hear his brother's voice waxing poetic on the subject.

"They're the trees left standing when land gets clear-cut to make pastures, so the animals have a place to get away from the sun. They look different because they don't have to compete with anything. Trees in forests try to grow tall, so they can steal light from their neighbors. But wolf trees have all the sunlight they could ever want, so they can afford to grow laterally."

"Makes me wish I were an only child," Clive had joked.

As always, Clover had been ready with a clever reply: "Only if you'd rather be wide than tall."

Clive still held out hope that his brother was alive, but now he wondered what would happen if the two of them were reunited in heaven. Even there, would Clover be able to forgive him for what he'd done? And what made Clive so sure he'd even merit heaven?

The company of soldiers stopped at the base of the wolf tree, where the massive trunk roiled like whitewater, knotted and whorled, stippled with what moonlight filtered down through the leaves.

"This'll do," one of the soldiers said. Another produced two lengths of rope, both of which had already been noosed; the loops were fitted around Clive's and Burns's necks and the remainder thrown over a thick, sinuous branch about eight feet off the ground. A low wall built out of loose stones ran around the edge of the pasture; the soldiers lugged two over to serve as pedestals. Clive and Burns were ordered to step up onto them, and then the ropes were pulled taut. Clive's chin was forced upward, as if he were smugly looking down on the proceedings. Someone untied his bindings and removed the gag.

"Any last words?" one of the soldiers asked.

"Go fuck yourself," Burns replied.

The meaty thunk of a punch, Burns's answering wheeze.

"What about you, traitor? Anything to say?"

Clive was considering seconding Burns's reply when his attention was arrested by something strange—a shadow creeping up to the far side of the tree and beginning to climb.

"Figures," the soldier said. "There's nothing you could say that would absolve you of what you've done. Therefore, as a representative of the Protectorate, defender of the Descendant faith, I hereby sentence you—"

"I do have something to say, actually," Clive interjected. "It was my father's favorite passage from the Filia, and I'd ask to be allowed to recite it before you . . . before the end."

A sigh: Who would deny the dying man's request to speak the word of God? "Fine. Just be quick."

"Of course," Clive said, though he planned to be anything but; he took ten seconds just to clear his throat. "The sky went dark. The world grew cold. Those blessed few chosen to carry on the mission of humanity could be forgiven for doubting the mercy of the Lord. But after many years, the last fire finally died out. Noach emerged from his stronghold within the earth and gazed upon the wreckage." Clive could feel it now, light vibrations around his neck; someone hidden among the branches overhead was sawing through the noose. He raised his voice to drown out the sound. "Noach's heart sank at the sight of such devastation, and he wept for his lost brothers and sisters, and for the sacrifice the Daughter had made. And the Lord did speak to Noach, and bade him rise and go out to the fields, and see where the first green shoots were breaking from the black ash. He said, 'Behold, the world returns to its former glory,' and Noach saw those shoots rise before his very—"

Clive was interrupted by a sharp yelp of pain. One of the soldiers fell to his knees.

"Something cut me!" he shouted. "Oh God! I'm hurt bad!"

There was a second shadow out there in the darkness. Clive watched as it darted behind another soldier, who dropped instantaneously with a wordless scream of agony.

"We're under attack!" one of the uninjured soldiers said. "Draw your weapons!"

Swords slipped out of scabbards as the soldiers cast about for their mysterious adversary. Clive was every bit as bewildered as they were. He couldn't think of anyone other than Paz who would bother trying to rescue him, but she would certainly be traveling alone. . . .

His train of thought was broken when the stone pedestal was abruptly knocked out from under his feet. He dropped a few inches

TOMMY WALLACH

and caught; the pain was instantaneous, excruciating. No matter how hard he tried, air wouldn't come through his constricted throat. He found himself kicking against the empty space beneath him, as if he were underwater and could fight his way to the surface. Burns gasped and choked beside him. The sawing up above grew louder, more emphatic; he could hear the rope giving way.

"It's a fucking girl!" one of the soldiers cried.

"So what?" another answered.

"So what do I do with her?"

"The same you'd do with a fucking boy! Kill her!"

A snap as the rope frayed, another as it gave way—but somehow the pressure on Clive's windpipe didn't abate. He understood when Burns dropped to the ground and immediately pounced on the nearest soldier. Whoever was up on that branch had chosen to cut the marshal free first—the logical choice, given Burns's skills as a fighter, but one that did nothing to help Clive's current predicament. He could feel the blood building in his forehead. The grunts and shouts of battle coalesced into a hum, growing louder and deeper as the seconds ticked away, like a bowed note on a standing bass. Sparkling lights appeared in the corners of his vision, and he sincerely wondered if they were angels.

Then, a miracle: his dangling feet found purchase again. He had to stand on tiptoe, but it was enough to make some space in his windpipe.

"Sorry! I dropped the knife and I couldn't unpick the dumb knot. Anyway, I put the stone back, so you should be okay for now."

"Flora?" Clive managed to croak out.

But she was already gone, running off to help Burns and Paz, heedless of the danger. Clive could only continue half hanging there, squinting into the dark, listening to the sounds of the people he loved fighting for their lives.

"You think you're smart, don't you?" The soldier appeared from around the back of the wolf tree. He was limping—one of the men Paz had hobbled in her initial attack. "But I'll be damned if you're getting through this night alive, traitor."

He raised his sword and drew back in preparation for the killing blow. Clive swung his leg out at just the right time, taking the cut across his thigh instead of through his belly.

The soldier laughed. "You've still got some fight in you. Good. That's gonna make this even more satisfying."

Clive landed back on his tiptoes again—and suddenly realized he wasn't quite as defenseless as he'd thought. If his assailant had simply run him through from behind, Clive couldn't have done anything to stop it. But the soldier had wanted to look his victim in the eyes, and that sadistic urge would be his undoing. Clive took a deep breath and stepped off the stone, pinching it between his dangling feet. His head was torqued upward again, making it difficult to aim; he'd have to make up for it with sheer momentum. Summoning every scrap of strength he had left, he hoisted the stone up with his legs and released it. There was a satisfying crunch as it caught the soldier square in the chin.

"My teef! You broke my gonnamned teef!"

Clive would've laughed, only he didn't have the air for it. The world was spinning, swirling; his consciousness began to slip away. The last thing he saw was the soldier coming toward him again, black blood pouring from his mouth, and a pretty sparkle of moonlit steel swinging through the air.

TOMMY WALLACH

6. Gemma

GEMMA WATCHED FROM THE CLIFFS AS THE FIRST LONG-boat carved a glistening runnel through the wet sand. The Wesah pushing the craft jumped in just as it began to float, and then they were off, spearheads glittering in the light of sunrise, paddles turning in perfect synchrony. Another boat took to the water, and another after that—eight in all, each one holding more than a dozen tribeswomen.

The boats had been waiting on the beach when Andromède's *naasyoon* arrived, and their launching signaled the official start of the *tooroon*. The majority of the Wesah nation was gathered at the shoreline to celebrate; Gemma could hear the drums and flutes, recognized the melodies that had once seemed so foreign as to scarcely be melodies at all. She would've liked to be down there, dancing with Athène, singing with her sisters, but had been ordered to remain on the southern cliffs, where Andromède's *naasyoon* was encamped.

At least she had a nice view; from this height, she could see out over the whole beach. Immediately below the cliffs were the longhouses that had been constructed specifically for the *tooroon*, and beyond that, the inverted starscape of the Wesah's tents. Between the two, hundreds of missives tended to a dozen coal beds throwing up great gray pillars of smoke. And though they weren't visible from here, Gemma knew there were vast fields up in the hills to the east where the tribe's horses had been set to graze for the duration of the festival.

The Protectorate encampment, blurred by distance and the morning mist, looked downright pitiful in comparison to the Wesah's—perhaps a tenth as populous, but congregated in a hundredth of the space, creating a dense and seemingly motionless knot of red and gold. Gemma didn't understand what need there could be for so many soldiers at a parley, but of the many things she didn't understand at the moment, that was probably the least important.

It had been almost two days since she'd been taken, and she still didn't have any idea why. Was Andromède angry that her daughter had become attached to a *dahor*? Could it have something to do with what had happened to Noémie, or Gemma's brazen first experiment with the dreamtea? Andromède's *naasyoon* treated their prisoner exactly as Athène's had in those early days: warily, and with an unmistakable air of condescension. Gemma's facility with the language impressed exactly no one; clearly they'd been warned off speaking to her. And though she could've tried to escape, something told her to exercise patience. She didn't feel any sort of imminent threat, and besides, Athène would have an easier time finding her if she stayed put.

After the boats had been out on the water for an hour or so, the celebrations began to die down, and it wasn't long before Andromède came hiking back up the cliff with her retinue. A few minutes later, Nephra, the chieftain's second-in-command, appeared at the opening of Gemma's tent.

TOMMY WALLACH

"Come," she said in English.

The two of them passed through camp—Gemma drawing her usual stares—and found Andromède sitting on a boulder at the top of the trail that led down to the beach. The chieftain shrugged off a thick robe of beaded furs—some sort of ceremonial garb she'd felt compelled to keep on even for the long climb—and let it fall to the ground.

"How are you feeling?" Nephra asked, picking up the robe.

"So many soldiers," Andromède replied. "They made the *otsapah* nervous."

"And you."

"And me." With a groan, Andromède lowered herself from the boulder. In profile, her resemblance to Athène was uncanny—the same wide nose and long neck, the same air of easy and unquestionable confidence. "The girl and I are going to go for a little walk. See to the preparations for tomorrow, and keep an eye out for my daughter. She's been making a nuisance of herself."

"What's new?" Nephra said, then turned back toward camp, leaving Gemma alone with Andromède.

"Athène's been looking for me?" Gemma said.

She'd spoken in Wesah, but Andromède responded in English. "Please, may we speak in your language? I am needing the practice."

"Of course," Gemma said, switching to her mother tongue and finding it strangely unwieldy after all this time.

Andromède began walking along the cliff top, and Gemma followed. "Athène confronted me during the ceremony this morning. I've never seen her so angry." The great chieftain smiled, and it was her daughter's smile in every line. "I'm sure she is planning some bold abduction even as we speak."

"I still don't understand why you took me in the first place."

"Because I need your help."

Gemma laughed ironically. "You could've asked for it."

"Maybe. But I don't have much time. I wanted to get to know you away from my daughter's influence."

"Influence?"

"She loves you. That is the most powerful influence of all."

They'd reached a little promontory that jutted out over the ocean. The morning fog had burned away, and now the sunlight poured down the bluffs and across the beach. Gemma noticed something glinting at the southern edge of the Protectorate encampment. A huge box of some kind? No, a wagon, lacquered black as tar.

"I am already hearing about you, from my people in the Villenaître," Andromède said. "I know you have learned something of the ways of the *otsapah*. I know you have journeyed with the dreamtea and learned the stories of our ancestors. This makes you—how you say?—divided. You are half Wesah, half *dahor*. It can only be fate, that you arrive here just when I need you."

"Need me for what?"

"Your people have not been friends to the Wesah, and now they ask us to help fight their war. Their enemy, who is no enemy of ours, asks only that we do nothing."

"You mean Sophia?" Gemma looked out over the beach for some sign of a third party. "I didn't know they were here."

"That is because *they* did not come with an army. Tell me, why have your people brought all these soldiers?"

"I don't know." She would've left it at that, but something in Andromède's phrasing had rankled her. "I spent the first sixteen years of my life traveling with a Descendant minister who believed all violence was sinful. If he'd had his way, the Protectorate wouldn't even exist. And I feel about the same these days."

"Why do you tell me this?"

"Because I want you to know that those soldiers aren't *my people*."

"Even so, you must understand them better than I do. Please, Gemma." The chieftain mispronounced it just as Athène and her *naasyoon* used to—*Chemma*. "In my visions, I see bloodshed in our future. It is there no matter what path I choose."

"I've seen it too," Gemma said, which was the truth, even if she still didn't believe it to have been anything more than a hallucination.

"Tomorrow I am to meet with the leaders of both parties. I would ask that you accompany me, to help translate."

"Your English is better than my Wesah."

"I need more than words translated. I need the thinking behind the words. I need your whole society interpreted, and Sophia's as well. Will you help me?"

Gemma was flattered, though it was still strange to think that Andromède had gone to all the trouble of kidnapping her merely to request a favor. But then again, hadn't Athène done the same thing, once upon a time?

"All right," Gemma said. "But on one condition."

"What?"

"I want Athène there as well. And I want her here with me now."

Andromède laughed. "I doubt I could keep you apart for much longer even if I wanted to."

The four of them—Andromède, Nephra, Gemma, and Athène—sat around the fire, waiting. Only Andromède had something like a chair, a block of cedar carved into Fox's grinning face. The rest of them sat on furs on the sand. Earlier that day, Andromède had sent a message to both Grand Marshal Chang and Director Zeno, inviting them to a parley. The message explained that political meetings during a *tooroon* always took place in the central longhouse, which was purposely situated so as to flood twice a day, when the tides came in. This time of year, low tide arrived in the early afternoon and the wee hours of the morning, and the parley had been scheduled for the latter.

"Wesah are used to riding through the night," Andromède had explained. "We'll be alert, and the *dahor* will be tired. That should make them easier to read."

Except Gemma and Athène were pretty tired too; they hadn't gotten much sleep last night, and not because they'd been discussing tonight's meeting. There'd been something different about their lovemaking, something desperate, as if both of them sensed a moment of crisis coming. All Gemma's muscles ached exquisitely, and her heart felt as full as a well-fed belly. Waiting in silence for the parley to begin, she smiled at Athène, and the grin she received in return confirmed that they were both reflecting on last night's recreation.

Zeno arrived first, accompanied by half a dozen men and women all armed with pistols. She walked briskly up to Andromède and bowed.

"*Taanishi, kaniikaniit. Kahkiiyow pawatamihk kiishkwayhkwashi.*"

Her accent was abominable, and she'd mistakenly used a valediction as a greeting, but at least she'd bothered to learn a bit of Wesah.

"Greetings, Zeno of Sophia," Andromède said. "Your people may wait outside."

If Zeno was bothered by this tacit command, she didn't show it. With a gesture, she sent her escort away. The room went silent again but for the crackle of the fire and the distant soughing of the waves. Gemma scrutinized Zeno across the flames. The woman was at least sixty, raising the question of just how she maintained her hair's vivid red hue. There was something cold and calculating behind her blank expression, a ruthlessness that reminded Gemma of Noémie.

The quietude was broken as the canvas flap covering the doorway of the longhouse opened again and Grand Marshal Chang stepped through. He wore an elaborate uniform bedizened with medals and ribbons, which made a stark contrast with Zeno's simple gray robes. Gemma had seen him up close only once before, at Honor Hamill's memorial service; there was no chance he would recognize her, yet she didn't like the way his eyes lingered on her as he approached, and she made a point of looking away. Just as Zeno had done before him, Chang approached Andromède and bowed.

"Greetings, Chief Andromède," he said.

"Greetings, Chang of the Anchor. Please, make yourself comfortable."

After the six of them were seated and Nephra spoke a short prayer, Andromède commenced the parley.

"Director, Grand Marshal, I formally welcome you to the *too-roon*. I also introduce my adviser, Nephra, my daughter, Athène, and my interpreter, Gemma." Gemma nodded, briefly making eye contact with both Chang and Zeno. "Though I have spoken to each of you privately, I would ask you to make your case again, here in front of everyone. Grand Marshal Chang, the floor is yours."

Was she stroking his vanity by allowing him to go first, or was it a slight, as the person who spoke last was often the one best heard?

Chang stood up and launched into his speech without hesitation. "As everyone here knows, Sophia has already engaged in acts of war against the Descendancy. Unprovoked, they have killed not only our soldiers, but also women, children, and men of the cloth. More than this, they have created weapons of death and destruction not seen on this planet since the great Confla"—the Grand Marshal remembered his audience just in time—"that is, since the Flame Deluge. If left unchecked, they will undoubtedly bring about another cataclysm. It will be not just the end of the Descendancy and the Wesah, but of all humanity."

Zeno let out a brief burst of breath, as if it was taking everything in her power not to immediately rebut these wild accusations. Chang threw her a sharp look, then plowed on.

"I know that there has been conflict between the Descendancy and the Wesah, but those days are behind us. As you know, we have changed our official policy toward your people. We hope the alliance we make today will serve us even after this war is long past, and Sophia is nothing but a distant memory."

"Who this 'we' you say?" Nephra asked in an unwieldy, thickly accented English. "Why is you here and not the Archbishop?"

Chang's jaw tightened. "In wartime, the Grand Marshal speaks for the Descendancy."

Was that true? Gemma couldn't remember ever hearing anything to that effect before; then again, she'd never heard of the

Descendancy going to war at all. "So why'd you bring all those soldiers?" she asked. Everyone looked a little surprised that she'd dared to inject herself into the conversation.

"To make it clear who is going to win this war," Chang replied. "I have thousands of men at my command. Sophia has a handful of toys."

"And what's in the wagon?"

Chang smiled graciously. "A gift, to cement our alliance."

"A gift is no gift if it comes with conditions," Andromède said.

"Which is why you'll get it either way."

Gemma had a few dozen more questions, but she figured she'd already interrupted enough. The truth was, she just didn't trust Chang, so it didn't really matter what he said.

Andromède turned her attention to Zeno. "Director, it is now your time to speak."

"Thank you." Zeno stood up and stepped closer to the fire, showing her back to Chang. "Wise Andromède, your people and mine have never had any quarrel. In fact, Sophia has been trading partners with a local *naasyoon* for over fifty years. While I don't agree with the Grand Marshal's interpretation of the circumstances surrounding our conflict, I won't bore you with a petty argument. All I ask is that, should war come, you remain neutral. Sophia will eventually emerge victorious, and the peace that has existed between my people and the Wesah will continue as it always has. Great chieftain, this decision is an easy one. Chang wants you to risk your people's lives to fight beside the men who've persecuted you for centuries. I want you to risk nothing, and gain everything."

Chang shot back up to his feet. "That's a load of horseshit!"

Immediately Nephra had her daggers drawn and poised to strike. Chang put on a pained smile and raised his hands contritely. "I'm sorry. I didn't mean to raise my voice. It's just hard for me to sit back and hear lies."

"Then the parley is over," Andromède said, rising from her makeshift throne.

"Already?" Chang said, clearly anxious. "We've hardly been here five minutes."

"I have heard what I need to hear. We will meet again tomorrow, and I will tell you my decision."

After Chang and Zeno left, Andromède asked for Gemma's interpretation of practically every word the two leaders had spoken. What was true? What was false? Was Zeno right to be so confident? Was Chang? The parley *about* the parley went on for hours, until well past sunrise. And who could say how long the Wesah scout had been standing in the doorway of the longhouse before Andromède finally noticed her.

"What is it?" the chieftain said.

"I'm sorry to interrupt," the scout replied, "but you have another guest."

"Tell her to come back in an hour."

"It's a he, and he's rather insistent."

"I only need a minute," a man said, in a rough but serviceable Wesah. He pushed his way past the scout and traversed the damp sand floor of the longhouse. Once again, Nephra drew her daggers.

"Stay back," she hissed.

But the man wouldn't be deterred. And now he was close enough

TOMMY WALLACH

that Gemma could make out his face in the firelight: a ghost, his eyes widening when he saw a ghost of his own.

"Gemma?" he said. "Is it really you?"

She stood up and nearly fell over again, woozy with fatigue and wonder. "Daughter's love," she said, the rusty phrase just coming out of her, summoned by the sight of this impossible revenant. "Burns?"

7. Clover

THE SUN WAS JUST RISING OVER THE TIPS OF THE TEETH as Clover caught his first glimpse of the Anchor since he'd left with the Protectorate contingent a lifetime ago. Warm light spilled across the valley and sloshed up against the Anchor wall. He hadn't expected to see his hometown again, but had assumed that if and when he did, the reunion would be a happy one. Disappointing, then, that all he felt now was fear: fear that what he'd done in Edgewise would follow him here somehow, fear of how Epistem Turin would receive his report, fear that his father was long since dead and he was chasing a phantom.

People came and went through the Western Gate, so many that Clover decided to enter through the less traveled Southern Gate instead. From afar, it appeared as a kohl-rimmed eye; only close up did the dark outline reveal itself to be black crepe, pinned all the way around the edge of the portal. Clover passed beneath it and turned left onto the Ring Road, where he found the same fabric fluttering from the windows of every house, store, and workshop in sight. It had to be a sign of mourning, but for what? The contagion out west could hardly have claimed so many lives already.

Clover addressed the question to an aproned shopkeeper

sweeping a cloud of dust off his stoop. "Excuse me, sir, can you tell me what all the black's about?"

The man stopped to lean on his broom and direct a potent scowl at Clover. "You been living under a rock or something?"

"I've been visiting family up in Coriander. Got back just now."

"Then you picked a hell of a time. The Archbishop passed on a few days ago. He was poisoned right in the middle of Notre Fille."

"Poisoned by whom? The Mindful?"

The man laughed darkly as he returned to his sweeping; Clover had to step out of the way to avoid being dusted. "The Epistem tried to make it *look* that way, sure, but it was him that did it. Guess he was tired of sharing power. He admitted it just before he offed himself."

Clover's stomach turned over. Not just the Archbishop, but the Epistem, too? The two people who'd masterminded Clover's mission were dead. Yet that wasn't the reason he suddenly felt sick; though they'd met only twice, Clover had come to think of the Epistem as a kindred spirit, even a friend. And he'd had so few of those in his life—fewer every day, it seemed.

"Honestly, I wasn't surprised," the shopkeep went on to say. "I never trusted anybody at that Library. Bunch of know-it-alls and heretics. Hey, where you going?" Clover was walking swiftly away up the Ring Road, the backs of his eyes stinging. "You're welcome, by the way!" the man called out after him.

It couldn't be true. The Epistem would never have murdered the Archbishop. He had no motive. Clover's mission to Sophia had been carried out on behalf of the Church and the Library both, a play against the political posturing of Grand Marshal Chang.

Beyond that, Turin had been impeccably devout, had even cautioned Clover against losing his faith. Daughter's love, the two of them had *prayed* together after Clover's night in the anathema stacks.

No, it simply didn't add up. Whatever the official story, the Mindful must have been behind the killing somehow—which meant Clover now had *two* reasons to find them.

He reached the outskirts of Portland Park and angled away from the Ring Road. Morning mist still crowned the tops of the evergreens, and the chirruping of the newly awoken sparrows made a complex counterpoint to Clover's brisk and even step. Once upon a time, he'd walked these paths hand in hand with a girl called Irene and had been something like happy. Was it wrong that a part of him missed those days, missed his own blissful ignorance?

Clover's relationship with Denver Suchland had never been particularly warm, but even so, he'd been looking forward to seeing a familiar face at the Library gatehouse. Instead he found two strangers watching from behind the painted iron grating—stone-faced men in red and gold.

"What's your business?" one of them said as Clover approached.

"I'm here to see Grand Attendant Bernstein. Where's Denver?"

"I don't know who that is. Or who you are, for that matter."

"Sorry. I'm Cl—" He stopped himself just in time. If it was true that his brother had become infamous for breaking Paz out of the Bastion, the Hamill name probably wasn't the sort of thing one should throw around casually. "Andy Leibowitz," he said. Where the infamous Epistem Duncan Leibowitz had left the Anchor for Sophia, Clover had just left Sophia for the Anchor. And "Andy" was close enough to "anti" that Bernstein couldn't fail to get the joke.

At least the duration of the wait was familiar; nearly an hour passed before the soldiers invited Clover back to the window.

"Grand Attendant Bernstein is too busy to see you at the moment, but he said he'd meet you for a drink after vespers at the usual place."

Clover tried to mask his puzzlement; he and Bernstein had never gone for a drink before. "The usual place? That's all he said?"

"Yep."

The other soldier smacked his forehead, as if suddenly remembering something important. "Wait! There was one other thing. I can't believe we almost forgot."

"What?" Clover asked.

"He said you should wear your prettiest dress tonight, so he can show you off."

Clover walked away as the two soldiers broke up laughing.

The Second Quarter was home to the majority of the Anchor's craftspeople: clockmakers and coopers, jewelers and tailors, cobblers and ironsmiths. They worked out of covered stands spread across a dozen open-air squares and the cramped, vermiform alleyways that connected them. Clover used to come here all the time on errands for Bernstein, to pick up the raw materials the attendant would use in his inventions and experiments. The place looked much the same as it always had, except for the swatches of black crepe pinned conspicuously in every shop and stall.

Louise Delancey came from a family of wainwrights who

operated out of a spacious warehouse off the quarter's largest plaza. Clover walked right through the open doors and into four generations of Delanceys working side by side, hammering and sawing and planing away, each one with a sweaty stein of ale or a thimble of shine in easy reach. Clover didn't expect to be recognized; he hadn't seen Louise in more than five years, and their families had never been particularly close.

"Can I help you?"

It was a girl of perhaps fourteen who'd asked. She resembled Louise in color and build, though she was a little stouter and a little prettier—a cousin, maybe.

"I'm looking for a relation of yours, goes by Louise."

The friendly expression that had welcomed him as a prospective customer immediately fled the scene. "She ain't here."

"You know where she is?"

"Only God and his Daughter know that now, I imagine."

"I . . . I'm sorry." It was yet another terrible revelation in a morning full of them. Had anyone managed to survive the last six months? Clover thought of Lila, falling silent as a hailstone and landing in a clatter of fractured bone and split skin. "How did it happen?"

"As if you don't know."

Clover frowned. "What?"

"You want me to say it for you? Fine. She was a traitor and she died a traitor's death. Happy?"

"No. I'm only trying—"

"I know exactly what you're trying. But we're a good, patriotic family, and you—"

"I'm not what you think I am!" Clover said forcefully. "I was Louise's friend. She used to travel with my father's ministry."

Now it was the girl's turn to be taken aback. "Hold on just a minute. Are you Clive Hamill's little brother?"

"That's right."

"Who you talking to there, Kita?" Their conversation had drawn the attention of an elderly member of the Delancey clan, his face pinched to a raisin by decades of hard living (and probably even harder drinking).

The girl—Kita—donned an easy smile. "Just a friend from school, Grampa. He's looking to borrow a cup of sugar."

"Well, go on and fetch it and get back to work."

"Yes, sir."

"Come on," she said, gesturing for Clover to follow. At the far end of the warehouse, a staircase without a banister led up to a small landing with a rusty woodstove and a stained and cratered dining table. Kita put a kettle on the hob.

"I can only offer you tea. Da says we gotta ration coffee, now that deliveries from Sudamir are suspended because of the outbreak."

"Tea's fine. So how do you know who I am?"

"Everybody knows who you are. You and your brother are the most famous turncoats in the whole history of the Anchor, probably. Even more than Louise."

"I'm not a turncoat!" Clover said, suddenly fiery. He'd promised the Epistem he'd keep his mission a secret, but the Epistem was dead now. "I was *spying* on Sophia for the Library."

Kita rolled her eyes. "Sure you were. Anyway, you shouldn't have come back. Just about everybody in the city wants your head."

"I had to come back, to look for my father."

"I thought he got killed. There was that big memorial and everything."

"Sophia faked his death so the Anchor wouldn't know he'd been taken prisoner and interrogated."

"And he's still alive?"

"I don't know. But I do know that the Mindful took custody of him, and that Louise worked for the Mindful. So if I can find out where Louise spent her time, I might be able to find my father."

Kita looked at him for so long he thought she might be playing some kind of staring game. Her eyes were hazel—green and blue and brown depending on the moment. "You're not lying, are you?" she finally said.

"No, I'm not. So if there's anyone in your family you think might know something—"

"Louise and me were practically sisters," Kita said. "She told me everything."

"So you know where the Mindful are?"

"I might. There was this place her band liked to rehearse, over in the First Quarter. The sign outside said it was a luthier's, but I never saw any instruments, and there were always a whole lot of people coming and going out the back door. Too many people, if you get my meaning."

"And you never told anybody about it? Not even the Protectorate?"

"'Course not! The Protectorate's the ones who killed Louise."

"True enough."

The kettle whistled. Kita took it off the hob and poured two cups of tea. "So you want me to take you sometime? It's not far from here."

"I'll go alone. It wouldn't be safe for you."

"Are you kidding? If anything, *I* should go alone."

"Why?"

"Because *you're* the famous traitor."

"I'm not a traitor!"

"Sure you're not," Kita said, picking up her teacup. "Listen, I gotta get back to work. I'll meet you out in the square at sundown. Oh, and remember to take a cup of sugar when you go, so I don't look like a big ol' liar."

And then she was gone, running back down the steps before Clover could lodge any further reservation, prohibition, or doubt.

"So you're saying you helped 'em?"

Kita had spent the entirety of their walk asking Clover every conceivable question she could muster about his time in Sophia. Though he'd succeeded in convincing her that he really had been a spy working for the Library, he almost regretted telling her the truth, as it vastly expanded the scope of her interrogation.

"I didn't help them, per se. I just—"

"Well, why didn't you help them 'persay' if you were already helping them with everything else?"

"What? No, 'per se' isn't a verb, and it doesn't mean—"

"What you should've done is *pretend* to work on their weapons and such, but actually sabotage everything as you went along."

"They would've seen through that."

"Not if you did it right."

Clover groaned. "That's easy for you to say, but you weren't—"

"Shh!" Kita pulled him down behind a waste bin. "We're here."

Clover peeked around the side of the bin. Across the way was a two-story brick building with a sign hanging from the lintel: MINSTREL MANUFACTORY, PURVEYORS OF FINE INSTRUMENTS. Lights shone in the windows, and a stream of smoke trickled merrily from the chimney. "I know it looks quiet, but there's always lots of people inside. Should I go knock on the door?"

"No," Clover said. "We're not going to be able to storm the place alone."

"So what do you want to do?"

"Nothing for now. I just wanted to see it."

"You just wanted to *see it?*" Kita exclaimed. "I thought we were going on an adventure!"

"Even if I had a plan, which I don't, I'm busy tonight."

"Doing what?"

"Having a drink with a friend, not that it's any of your business."

"Where?"

"At the . . ." Clover trailed off. He'd forgotten he still didn't know where he was supposed to meet Bernstein. "I don't actually know."

"How can you have a drink with someone if you don't know where you're drinking?"

"He said to meet him at the usual place, as if I would know what that meant. But we've never gone out before."

Kita smiled knowingly, and for just a second, she reminded Clover of Lenny. "I know where you're going," she said.

"Where?"

"Follow me."

TOMMY WALLACH

Clover grabbed hold of her arm before she could skip away. "You're not invited, Kita."

"I won't come inside," she said, grinning even more widely. "I just want to *see it*."

Apparently, the Usual Place was a well-known watering hole just north of Notre Fille in the Eighth Quarter. Clover arrived late, as he'd spent fifteen minutes outside explaining to Kita why she had to go home. She gave way only after he promised to fetch her as soon as he decided what to do about the Minstrel Manufactory. It was a promise he had exactly no intention of keeping.

Clover had never felt comfortable in taverns: too many people, too much noise. But that was probably for the best tonight, given the sensitive nature of what he and Bernstein had to discuss. Clover scanned the bar and the tables around it, eventually making his way to the corner farthest from the entrance. The sawdust laid down to absorb spilled beer and tobacco juice was thinnest back here, revealing large patches of the mildewing wood underneath, and the smell from the privies out back was eye-watering. He didn't recognize Bernstein at first glance. His old friend had aged ten years in almost as many months: fresh fault lines had emerged across the man's forehead and around his mouth; his salt-and-pepper hair had turned entirely to salt; despairing hollows ringed his heavy-lidded eyes. The attendant was dressed casually, in a linen shirt and dark trousers— the first time Clover had seen him in anything other than his robes.

"You're back," he said, as Clover took a seat across the table. At least his manner remained unchanged: nobody understated like Bernstein.

"I'm back."

The attendant had already ordered for the both of them, and now they raised their glasses in a toast. It was far from Clover's first pint of ale, but he couldn't remember ever enjoying a drink quite so much. Either the Usual Place excelled at the art of brewing, or Clover was at last developing a taste for the stuff, as his father had warned him he would.

"So? How did it go?" Bernstein asked.

"That's . . . difficult to say." Clover realized he'd never thought about his mission to Sophia in such simplistic terms. "I learned what I was supposed to learn, but I'm not sure any of it matters anymore. How are things here?"

"Awful, obviously."

"Is it all true? Did Turin really kill the Archbishop?"

"Of course not," Bernstein scoffed. "Chang did it, one way or another."

"The Grand Marshal? Why?"

"Because now he alone speaks for the Descendancy."

Clover's mind reeled at the implications. "But won't there be a new Epistem appointed, and a new Archbishop?"

"Eventually, but not in time to save us from a military dictatorship. The system is slow. And besides, people trust Chang in a way they never trusted the Church. They can relate to a man who wants to kill his enemies, instead of seeking to understand or forgive them."

That was the hard truth that had carved those furrows into Bernstein's face, that had defined Honor Hamill's whole life. What good was being good in a world that didn't value goodness?

"And he still thinks the Descendancy can win this war?"

"Don't you?"

"Not anymore. They have an airplane, Bernstein. It really flies."

The attendant's tired eyes lit up. "Did you go up in it?" Clover nodded. "And?"

He thought back to the moment when the plane's wheels first lost contact with the ground, the whole apparatus rising hesitantly, like a baby taking its first steps, then with increasing confidence, faster and faster, until it burst through the cloud cover into the clear, cold air beyond.

"It was incredible," Clover said, then remembered himself. "Even if it was a sin."

"Sin, in my opinion, is a lot more complicated than the Church likes to admit."

"What do you mean?"

Bernstein glanced around, as if only now were they discussing sensitive material. "I think Chang found something in the Library, when he came for the Epistem."

"Something? Like what?"

"I don't know exactly. But there have always been rumors—"

Before Bernstein could finish, Kita appeared next to their table.

"They're here," she whispered urgently.

"Kita," Clover said. "I told you to go home."

"I know, but I didn't, and it's a good thing, because—"

Over her shoulder, Clover saw a half-dozen Protectorate soldiers stream in through the front door of the Usual Place. One of them spotted him almost immediately.

"You! Stay where you are!"

Clover realized too late how foolish it had been to show his face at the Library; someone must have recognized him, and then Bernstein's message had led them straight here. Now, as the soldiers began to shoulder their way toward the back of the tavern, he could think of only one way out of this whole mess. On the plus side, he might kill two birds with one stone. On the minus side, he might end up killed himself. There wasn't time to worry about which outcome was the more likely.

"I'm sorry about this, Bernstein. They're gonna want to know what we talked about."

The attendant smiled wryly. "I promise my inventions will bore them to tears."

Clover looked to Kita. "You can still get out of this. I'm the one they want."

But the girl shook her head. "They've already seen us together. Besides, those bastards killed Louise. I say to hell with them."

There wasn't time to argue; the soldiers were literally within spitting distance. "Stay close," Clover said. Then he stood up and shouted—"You'll never take me alive!" Grabbing hold of Kita's hand, he bolted for the kitchen, and what he could only hope was a back door.

8. Paz

IN THE DISTANCE, BROWN TICKS DRAGGED A LIFELESS black beetle across the beach: Chang's wagon. Its shell glittered in the light, nacreous and slick. There was something inexorable in its movement, almost fatalistic, as if nothing in the world could stop or delay it.

"I don't like just sitting up here," Paz said. "Makes me feel helpless."

Clive pulled her close. "Enjoy it while you can."

The two of them were perched atop a makeshift wooden fence enclosing a good five square miles of sparse ground cover, thickboughed oaks and spindly sycamores, and the majority of the Wesah nation's mounts. Missives patrolled the borders of the pasture, eyes peeled for potential horse thieves. Flora stood a few hundred feet off, ripping grass out of the ground and hand-feeding a chestnut mare with a vibrant pink scar along her flank.

Apparently, she'd stayed in Settle for less than half a day before stealing Greeny's horse and heading south. She'd run into a Protectorate detachment early on, and they'd accompanied her all the way to the site of the *tooroon*. Paz, watching from the bluffs above the beach, had noticed the girl pacing around the tent where Clive and Burns were being held, and managed to swoop in and collect her without being recognized. The two of them were still devising a breakout plan when the lynch mob descended on the prisoners.

Flora leaned over to whisper some secret in the horse's ear. If one looked only so far, the scene was an unalloyed idyll: contented horses in a verdant field, a seraphic girl communing with nature, a young couple in love. Yet Paz could feel the impending pandemonium like the shadow of a storm cloud overhead. It filled her belly with butterflies, starch-stiffened her muscles, set her heart to fluttering.

"We could still run," Clive said, as if reading her mind.

"We could." Paz sighed. "What's the point of a life anyway, if not to try to do something worthwhile with it?"

"Can't it just be to live it?"

Paz kissed him gently on the cheek. "No. I don't think it can."

Flora looked over at them, giggled at the rubbery jowls of the horse slobbering on her palm. "He likes me!" she shouted.

Paz wondered if she and Clive would ever have a child. Did she even want one? It seemed such an unreasonable presumption, to force a human being to live whatever life you had it in your power to give, one destined to be filled with so much pain and loss.

"So you still want to go through with this?" Clive asked. "Giving yourself up for Gemma?"

"I'll make a good warrior, don't you think? My tattoos will be the talk of the *naasyoon*."

"I'm being serious. I don't want to lose you again."

"Then come with me. I'm sure they'd take you on as a missive."

She saw Clive bridle at the very thought. "That's not exactly the life I want for us," he said.

"I know. You want *me* doing the cooking and cleaning up and

TOMMY WALLACH

you doing all the fighting." She was mostly joking, but there was a kernel of truth there too.

"It's not like that. I'd be happy never to fight again, and I'll have you know I bake a mean apple pie. It's just . . . well . . . scary, I guess."

"It's scary to me, too. But a lot less so if you're there with me. Besides, where else would you rather be? We can't go back to the Anchor or Sophia, and if what Burns says is true, Sudamir won't be accepting emigrants until the outbreak is contained. Honestly, I can't think of a safer place to wait out the war than with the Wesah. And if we're not happy after a few months, we'll just leave."

Clive smiled, though whether in agreement or out of a desire to end the conversation, Paz couldn't tell. She was about to ask when both of them were distracted by a movement in the woods between the pasture and the bluffs that led down to the beach. Burns emerged from behind the trees, and beside him were two young women.

"Daughter's love," Clive said, leaping off the fence. The horses scattered before him, and even Flora was momentarily frightened by the sudden charge. Then she, too, saw who the marshal had brought back with him.

"Gemma!" she screamed, wiping her wet hands on her skirt and taking off after Clive.

Paz felt a momentary sting of jealousy. Though she knew Clive loved her, it was still unsettling to see him run so ecstatically toward the girl he'd almost married—a reminder that Paz wasn't a part of the family, and might never be. She lowered herself to the ground and walked unhurriedly toward the others. When she got there, the reunited Poplin sisters were still locked in a tight embrace.

SLOW BURN

"I never lost hope," Gemma said, wiping the tears from her eyes. "I knew I'd make it back to you."

"Me too," Flora said.

The other girl who'd arrived with Gemma—a lithe and serious-faced Wesah tribeswoman sporting a sleeve of copper bangles—coughed obtrusively, signaling her presence. It was a moment before Paz recognized her.

"Athène?" she said.

They'd met twice before—first in the outerlands, the day Honor Gordon ended up shot through the neck, and again when Paz was caught skulking around the young chieftain's *naasyoon*. It was Athène who had planned Gemma's abduction and set into motion the chain of events that had ended in Paz's capture in the woods outside Sophia. So what the hell was she doing here now?

"Hello again," Athène replied. "I am very glad to see you. I owe to you all my happiness."

At first Paz didn't understand. Then Athène reached out to Gemma. Their hands met . . . and clasped. Such a small gesture, such an enormous implication. Paz could've laughed at the absurdity of it all; was this really why she'd been sent back into the dragon's jaws of the Protectorate encampment—to play matchmaker for a girl with a crush?

For reasons she didn't entirely understand, she found herself leaning into Clive and taking his hand between her own. Gemma must've noticed, but she played it off as if it meant nothing to her. And was it Paz's imagination, or was Clive's erstwhile fiancée purposely refusing to meet her gaze?

"So here we all are," Burns said, clearly uncomfortable with just

TOMMY WALLACH

about every aspect of the situation. "I had myself a nice jaw with Andromède, and she agreed to let her daughter here escort Gemma out to see you. However, as for the, uh, exchange we discussed, it's a nonstarter. They don't wanna let Gemma go, and I guess Gemma doesn't want to leave, either."

"What if we volunteer ourselves?" Paz asked.

"Who's 'we'?"

"Me and her," Clive replied. "We're not welcome anywhere else at the moment."

Burns grunted. "I don't see why it would be a problem. Bring it up with Andromède after the parley."

"When's that?"

"Pretty late, I'd imagine. Tonight's some kind of finale for the whole *tooroon*. That right, Athène?"

"Yes. We call it the night of . . . how do you say? Apology? No."

Athène turned to Gemma and said something quickly in Wesah. Gemma responded fluently, then finished the chieftain's thought in English. "The Night of Reconciliation. It's a celebration of when Fox and Wolf came together here and spread water across the world, to put out the Flame Deluge."

"Why are you holding hands?" Flora suddenly interjected. Gemma and Athène shared a glance, but neither took the lead on answering.

"Because they're friends, obviously," Clive said. "Anyway, we've only got a few hours before that reconciliation thing. Maybe we should scrounge up something to eat."

"You are all welcome in my mother's camp," Athène announced. "As long as you don't mind a long prayer before you eat."

"You kidding?" Burns said. "It'll be just like old times."

The walk to Andromède's encampment passed in near-total silence. Paz figured everybody was upset at someone about something (except maybe Burns, who wasn't given to talking much anyway, and Athène, who spoke only quietly, and in Wesah, to Gemma). Andromède greeted them cordially when they arrived, and encouraged them to take seats around a large hempen rug set up just at the cliff's edge. After a woman called Nephra delivered the long and incomprehensible prayer they'd been warned about, the missives began delivering bowl after bowl of steaming meat and vegetables.

Down on the beach, preparations for the Night of Reconciliation were well underway. Torches blazed in neat lines across the sand, inflaming the black wagon that had at last made its way up to the doorstep of the central longhouse.

The conversation was stilted, dense with long, uncomfortable silences. Any question was likely to lead to an answer nobody wanted to hear, whether it was about the nature of Gemma and Athène's relationship, how Clive and Paz had managed to escape the Anchor, or simply what the future might bring. Flora was the most obviously upset—like most children, she'd yet to learn to hide her emotions—while Burns had retreated into his traditional tortoiseshell of total detachment.

Given her past actions, Paz felt a certain responsibility to try to mitigate the tension, to get them all back to a place of basic civility, if not yet warmth.

"So, Gemma," she said, "it sounds like you're completely fluent in Wesah now. Was that hard?"

"Not really," Gemma replied brusquely.

"Do you think you could teach me?"

"Why would I do that?"

"I . . . I don't know."

"Hey now," Clive said, lightly chiding. "Paz was just trying to make conversation. You don't have to be rude."

But Gemma's expression only hardened. "I can't believe you saved her life after everything she did."

"You're one to talk," Paz said, answering on Clive's behalf. "Or are you forgetting how your sweetheart there abducted you in the middle of the night?"

Gemma jumped to her feet. "Athène never tried to hurt my family! She never seduced an innocent boy!"

"There's no such thing as innocent!"

"That is enough!" Andromède said, firmly but not angrily. "Tonight is the Night of Reconciliation. So we are going to reconcile." The great chieftain's English was nearly flawless, and there was a profound empathy in her eyes as they landed on Paz. "You are angry. Why?"

"Why am I angry? Because . . . because . . ." The answer that occurred to her was irrational, but she could think of no other. She pointed at Gemma. "I'm angry because *she's* angry."

Andromède nodded, as if this response made perfect sense, and turned to Gemma. "And why are you angry?"

When Gemma spoke, it was with a coldness that Paz felt in the very marrow of her bones. She'd changed in her time with the Wesah: the mouse had become a cougar. "Because she's the reason my father and my little brother are dead."

SLOW BURN

"And she's the reason *my* father is dead," Paz replied.

"Your father was about to do the same damn thing—"

But Andromède didn't let Gemma finish. "You were enemies. You did what enemies do. Now I ask: Are you still enemies?"

Paz thought back to the day she'd saved Clive and Flora from the Mindful, the vow she'd made to never knowingly hurt the people she cared about again. And she'd cared about Gemma once, hadn't she? Didn't she still?

"I'm sorry," she said. "About everything. I was only doing what I thought was right."

"I'm sorry too," Gemma mumbled, though she kept her gaze firmly directed at the ground.

"Good," Andromède said. "Now finish your food. We leave soon."

A few minutes later the drums started up down on the beach, audible even over the sonorous crashing of the surf. Paz had been so distracted by her altercation with Gemma, she'd almost forgotten about the momentous event about to occur. Andromède would announce her decision tonight—a decision that could very well determine the outcome of the war. How would Zeno react if the Wesah decided to side with the Descendancy? And what would the Grand Marshal do if things went the *other* way?

The reunited friends—insofar as they could be called that—followed Andromède and her *naasyoon* down the side of the cliff, mirroring the sun as it sank into the ocean like something drowning. For a moment, Chang's wagon reflected the vivid purple of the sky, as if bleeding from between its lacquered slats.

As soon as they arrived at the beach, Athène went off to see to some aspect of the festival, leaving Gemma momentarily on her own. Paz went to stand beside her. "I really do hope we can be friends again," she said.

Gemma turned to face her and donned the sweetest smile ever smiled. "You know what I hope? That I'm the one who gets to make you pay for what you did to my family." She walked away before Paz could say anything in response, calling back over her shoulder, "Enjoy the party, *Irene*."

9. Clive

H E WATCHED FROM THE DRY DUNES JUST BEHIND THE flooded longhouses as the revelries began in earnest. Paz had disappeared into the scrum of whirling Wesah ("If we're going to be living with them, I better get comfortable dancing with them"), and though Clive had promised to join her there shortly, he was grateful for the moment to himself. He felt like he'd lived a whole lifetime in the past twenty-four hours. First off, he'd nearly died up there on the hill; if Paz and Flora hadn't shown up when they did, or if Burns weren't as good in a fight as he was, Clive knew he'd be swinging from an oak branch right now. Then, just a short few hours later, he'd been reunited with Gemma, only to discover that the soft and sweet-natured girl he'd grown up with was nowhere to be found. And after their tense and rancorous repast, where every available accusation was leveled and met with a suite of recriminations, they'd all come here to the beach, to witness the Wesah and the Protectorate attempt this unprecedented shared celebration.

Moments like these, Clive thought, made you wonder whether you had any control over your life at all.

He watched Gemma, standing down at the shoreline with half a dozen members of Andromède's *naasyoon*, including Athène. The rose-colored sky made an aureole around her yellow hair, and Clive remembered how it felt against his fingers as he brushed it back behind her ear, how she'd whispered to him that day behind the wagon—*Then we can do whatever we want.* And though he didn't love her the way that he used to, the thought of the life they might have had together still inspired in him a feeling close enough to grief as to be indistinguishable from it.

She met his gaze and, a moment later, crossed the beach in his direction. He made sure no sign of sadness was left on his face by the time she got there.

"Where's your lady love?" she asked with a hint of irony.

"Dancing with your sisters."

"Why aren't you with her?"

"It's not worth the risk. There are too many soldiers here who might recognize me."

"Aren't you a soldier too?" Gemma feigned epiphany. "Oh, that's right. They think you're a traitor. I wonder why that is?"

Clive wasn't used to this sort of subtle aggression from Gemma, and his first impulse was to write it off as some kind of misunderstanding. But there could be no mistaking the severity in her expression, the acid in her voice. He felt a distant pulsing of his old anger, but it subsided quickly enough: Gemma wasn't the only one who'd changed over the past year.

"You've got every right to feel the way you do," he said. "All I can say is sorry. I'll say it as many times as you need to hear it, until you can forgive me."

"Forgive you for what, Clive?"

She'd asked the question casually, as if she really didn't know what he had to apologize for.

"Where to begin? For putting your sister in danger. For falling in love with Paz. For—"

"You mean Irene?" Gemma interjected.

Clive ignored the gibe. "For not being a better friend to you after we got back to the Anchor, when we'd"—his voice caught, emotion getting the better of him—"when we needed each other most. For letting them take you that night and not doing everything I could to get you back."

"I'm happy with the Wesah, Clive. Happier than I ever knew I could be."

"You don't have to lie to me."

"I'm not lying. And the fact that you don't believe me is exactly my point."

"What does that mean?"

"You wouldn't understand."

"Then help me to!"

"I don't know how! It's just . . ." She closed her eyes and took a deep breath. When she opened them again, there was finally a bit of gentleness there—a glimmer of the old Gemma. "My momma loved pretty dresses. Do you remember?"

Clive nodded. "Of course."

"Michael could've wrapped himself head to toe in sackcloth for all she cared, but Flora and I had to have the best fabric that money could buy. The dress I wore for my coming-out party took her three months to sew, and when it was done, all she did was complain about how the lacework wasn't up to her standards."

"You looked beautiful in it."

"But that's just the thing, Clive. I didn't care. I *never* cared about that stuff. And honestly, I never cared that much about landing a husband or making babies, either. It was just so important to Momma, and I wanted to make her happy, so I pretended. I pretended so hard, I almost ended up marrying you." She shook her head—grateful wonder at her narrow escape from disaster. "Can you imagine how unhappy we would've been together?"

"You don't know that."

"I do, though. Because I would've been miserable, and that would've made *you* miserable, because . . . because you're a good man." It felt as if this simple admission changed something between them, warmed the very air. "I don't know what's gonna happen to any of us, Clive. But I do know I was lucky that Athène found me. She showed me there was another way to live than the one I was brought up with. A better way. That's a gift I'll never know how to repay."

Down at the shoreline, Athène had become a slim silhouette in the failing light, sparring playfully with another, smaller silhouette: Flora, armed with a piece of driftwood. How quickly the young adapted to new circumstances, however peculiar. Sisters-in-law.

"You love her?" Clive asked.

"I do. So much it scares me sometimes."

Clive knew he'd never entirely understand the choices Gemma had made, but maybe he didn't need to; maybe he just had to accept them without judgment. "Then I'm happy for you."

She looked up at him, smiled her old crooked smile. "It's dark now. I doubt anyone will be able to make you out in the crowd. I think it's time you got to dancing."

"Sure."

As he watched Gemma skip across the beach toward Athène and Flora, he realized she'd failed to offer him the same courtesy he'd offered her: the acceptance of his forbidden love. The oversight stuck in the back of his mind, like the first twinge that warned of a toothache to come. He did his best to ignore it as the moon wheeled through the firmament and across the glossy flank of Chang's night-black wagon, as the tide drew back in sedimentary lines along the sand, as the music grew louder and louder still.

He found Paz in the crowd, and without a word, they joined in the heedless abandon of the dance, kissed each other with a passion he never imagined he could summon up with other people around. It was as if their bodies knew something their minds did not, that they needed to seize this moment and squeeze every drop of joy out of it that they could, because who could say how many moments like it they had left.

The drums, which had sounded unceasingly for the last four hours, at last began to fade, their complex polyrhythms disintegrating into random sound, leaving a vast and eerie silence behind them. Andromède stood on a small dais in front of the central longhouse, its supports still glistening with seawater. This makeshift stage was lit with four large torches, such that the great chieftain appeared fire-touched and regal. Clive, Paz, and Flora made their way to the front of the crowd that was gathering before her, packed in as dense as wet sand beneath a heavy boot. The Protectorate soldiery had arrayed itself uphill of the Wesah, rather than farther down the beach, so they could more easily hear the announcement.

Andromède surveyed the crowd for a moment. Then, with a

TOMMY WALLACH

gesture, she was joined on the dais by Grand Marshal Chang and a woman who could only be the famous Director Zeno. Clive could remember the sound of her voice as it emerged from the brass blossom of the phonograph machine, afloat on a ghostly susurrus of hum and crackle. He'd expected a giant, or an enchantress, and was surprised to find her a perfectly ordinary-looking older woman—aside from the mane of bright red hair and the silver gun at her waist.

"*Taanishi*, Grand Marshal Chang of the Anchor," Andromède said in a sonorous half shout. "*Taanishi*, Zeno of Sophia." After these greetings, the rest of the chieftain's speech was delivered in her native tongue. She stopped at the end of every sentence so the words could be repeated by criers peppered throughout the crowd, first in Wesah, then again in English. Clive was grateful to have Gemma standing close by, translating exclusively for Flora, Paz, and him.

"She's still welcoming everyone," Gemma whispered. "Now she's telling the story of Wolf and Fox on the first Night of Reconciliation."

"Who are they?" Flora asked.

"I'll tell you later." The criers repeated the previous phrase as Andromède turned toward Grand Marshal Chang. "Now she's saying how difficult this decision has been. She has always respected the Descendancy's dedication to nonviolence, though she wishes they'd made fewer exceptions when it came to her people." Clive saw the great chieftain address Director Zeno. "The Wesah's relationship with Sophia has been a more peaceful one, but she shares the Anchor's fear that the world Zeno envisions is the same one that led to the Flame Deluge."

"The Flame Deluge?" Flora said.

"That's what they call the Conflagration," Clive explained.

Having spoken directly to her two petitioners, Andromède stepped up to the lip of the dais and addressed her people.

"In my vision, I have seen the war to come," Gemma translated. "While I do not know its outcome, I do know it will be a terrible thing to behold. More than this, I know it is not our war." Mumbles could be heard now, rippling through the crowd. "I ask the Wesah nation to join me in traveling north, where we will wait out this conflict, praying we return to a better world than the one we left."

The mumbling had risen to a din, the majority of which was coming from the Protectorate soldiers. Chang took the opportunity to step into the spot Andromède had just vacated.

"What's he doing?" Paz said.

"Friends!" Chang shouted over the clamor, which diminished slightly. "I want you all to know that I respect this great chieftain's decision. Though I wish she'd chosen differently, she has to do what's best for her people." He gestured toward the black wagon. "I also promised that whatever choice she made, I would leave this gift for her, as a sign of my esteem."

A cadre of Protectorate soldiers had arranged themselves around the wagon, and now, through some mechanism invisible from Clive's perspective, they made all the walls of the vehicle fall away at once. On what was now just a wooden platform, a large and bewildering device was arranged like a great black finger pointing out over the beach. Two men were already seated within its esoteric machinery.

Clive didn't understand; what sort of gift was this? He looked back to the dais for some kind of sign. Andromède's eyes betrayed only confusion, while Chang was beaming with pleasure, as if *he* were the one who'd received a present.

It was Zeno's expression, an incredulous gape of grief and horror, that finally provided the answer to the riddle.

"Run!" Clive shouted.

But there wasn't time to move before the enormous gun that had been hidden inside the wagon began to fire.

10. Gemma

THEY WERE STANDING LESS THAN FIFTEEN FEET AWAY from the device, and the noise it made shattered the senses, liquefied courage. Gemma ducked down and put her head between her knees, staying that way until the first screams infiltrated her perception, layering atop the stuttering fusillade, and some sense of duty to bear witness to the horror compelled her to look up. Light strobed at the tip of the barrel, and spent casings cascaded down onto the wooden floor of what had once been a wagon, like sparks off the blacksmith's hammer. Two men operated the machine: one feeding a long metal chain of bullets into its belly, the other aiming the barrel. Wherever it pointed, the weapon carved a line through the crowd, Wesah warriors slumping over like trees snapping in a hurricane.

Gemma had some experience with guns (though the speed at which this particular model fired, and the raw power implied by those deafening eruptions, made the Sophians' weapons seem like peashooters in comparison), but most of the Wesah had never seen one before. This explained why so many of them were standing in place, neither fleeing nor fighting: they couldn't reconcile one ugly metal contraption with the scale of the carnage being visited upon them. Though there was a small cadre of Protectorate soldiers around the gun, if just a couple of dozen tribeswomen had rushed it at once, they could've taken it. But the Wesah had been caught at their most vulnerable—exhausted from three days of feasting and dancing, almost entirely unarmed, their horses miles away—and all they could think to do was run. Chang had clearly anticipated this response and positioned the bulk of the Protectorate soldiers along the eastern edge of the beach, forcing the tribeswomen and their missives to flee north, where they would still be vulnerable to the gun. Within a minute of the walls of the wagon falling away, the Wesah had been routed, and the beach had become a roiling river of blood and terror.

Gemma looked to the dais. There was no sign of Andromède, which meant the chieftain must have escaped, but also no sign of Chang, which meant Gemma couldn't yet stick a blade through his black heart. She could see no better outlet for her fury than the skirmish developing around the gun, but as she drew her daggers—both the old glass one and a brand new steel blade courtesy of Andromède, to thank her for her help during the parley—and made for the emplacement, someone pulled her up short.

"What are you doing?" Clive shouted over the cacophony.

She tried to wrest her arm free. "Let go of me."

"No!" He dragged her close enough that he could whisper into her ear. "Your sister needs you."

A wave of guilt passed over her; she'd completely forgotten about Flora, who stood on the other side of Clive, paralyzed by the abomination she was witnessing. Gemma felt overwhelmed by obligations, all of them overlapping and contradicting: her sister; her homeland; the God of the Filia and the gods of the Wesah; the people who'd raised her and the people who'd taught her a new way to live; the boy she'd thought she loved grown into a man she didn't even understand; the woman who'd taught her what love really was. . . .

Athène—where was she? Gemma cast about for some sign of the young chieftain, but it was impossible to differentiate one face from another in the chaos. Athène might have escaped with her mother, or perhaps she was among those trying to overwhelm the soldiers around the gun, or those fighting fruitlessly in the bluffs.

Or maybe she was dead.

Gemma tore her arm out of Clive's grip and sprinted toward the emplacement. She caught the first soldier by surprise, plunging both daggers between the bottommost buttons of his uniform jacket. His companions to either side rushed to his aid; only the timely intervention of a nearby tribeswoman saved Gemma from one blow even as she prepared to parry another. Steel met steel; eyes locked. Gemma had caught her opponent's sword between her daggers, and now she slowly gave way beneath his superior strength, sliding down into a full split. With a shriek, she drew her blades diagonally downward, slicing both the soldier's shins open as the point of his sword found the sand between her legs. He went down on his knees, screaming; Gemma stepped onto his shoulder and used it to launch herself up onto the platform. The gun was within arm's reach, but as she lunged for it, she felt a hand clamp around her ankle and pull. She landed hard on her chin, dazed, and turned over. The soldier she thought she'd disabled had managed to find his feet. Grimacing, he lifted his sword up over his head. Gemma raised her daggers and braced herself, but before the sol-

TOMMY WALLACH

dier could strike, something slammed into the side of his head and he went down—for good this time.

She sat up. Clive stood before her, holding a gore-stained rock in one hand and Flora's lily-white fingers in the other. Paz was there too, and even had the gall to stroke Flora's hair soothingly, as if *they* were sisters.

"We have to go," Clive said. "There won't be another chance."

Behind him, Protectorate soldiers were streaming down from the bluffs, their buttons and medals glittering in the starlight. Having successfully funneled the Wesah down the beach, they were coming to ensure the gun kept firing for as long as possible. Gemma knew there was no hope of stopping it now.

They retreated behind the longhouse and followed the trail back up the cliffs. Below them, the sound of gunfire paused for a few seconds, only to return with fresh furor. The Wesah could be seen moving in a black swarm up the beach, leaving thousands of dark particles in their wake, all of them still or approaching stillness. Looking down upon the slaughter, Gemma recalled her visions of a world on fire, and her eyes began to burn with tears. The Protectorate couldn't be allowed to get away with this; they had to be punished. Yet what did that mean except the annihilation of the Anchor and the victory of Sophia, which was really no better?

Gemma had hoped Athène would be waiting for her when they reached the top of the cliff, but the encampment had emptied out. The only sign of life was the campfire, still smoldering.

"Why did they do that?" Flora asked. "Why did they kill all those people?"

Clive sighed. "I don't know, Flora."

"I do," Paz said. "It was a show of strength."

Gemma hated how certain the girl was about everything, how endlessly arrogant. Why was she even here, anyway? Clive and Flora were family, but Paz wasn't even a *friend*.

"What do you know about it?" Gemma demanded.

"It's basic strategy. Now Sophia knows the Anchor has weapons of its own. And I'm guessing Chang wanted to scare the Wesah, too."

"Scare them? He butchered them!"

"Same thing, really."

"How can you say that?"

"I'm just telling you what Chang is thinking."

"And what *you're* thinking too."

"That's not fair and you know—"

"Stop it, both of you!" Clive interjected. "We don't have time for this. We need to keep moving."

Gemma shook her head. "I'm not going anywhere. Those are my sisters being slaughtered down there."

"If you stay, you'll end up just like them."

"And if I leave, I might never see Athène again."

Clive raised his voice. "So you'd rather never see Flora again?"

"I..."

Gemma made the mistake of looking at her sister; the hurt in Flora's eyes was too much to take. "I need a minute," she said, storming away from the fire, ignoring Paz's censorious whisper—"We can't afford to wait. She's putting all of us at risk." She made for the woods east of the encampment, stopping only to glance briefly over the cliff's edge. The scene down on the beach was gruesome.

TOMMY WALLACH

White sand was streaked and speckled with black, as if it had rained blood. Waves crashed against bodies curled up like pill bugs, and curious seabirds wheeled overhead, awaiting the feast that morning would bring. Gemma's eyes filled again, but only after she reached the umbral privacy of the trees did she give herself over to her grief. Racking sobs squeezed the air from her lungs; tears streamed down her face. So much death. So much misery. The world was a cruel and indifferent place. Gemma wished the Daughter would come again that very moment and burn everything back down to the ground.

A crackle of leaves behind her, unmistakable footsteps. "Leave me alone," Gemma said. "I told you I need a minute."

The steps accelerated; instinct took over just in time. Gemma hopped backward, felt the ripple of disturbed air as the blade came within a hair's breath of her cheek. She drew a dagger and warded off one blow, then another, then another—backing away all the time, trying to make out the face of her assailant in the gloom.

Giving ground in order to deflect yet another strike, Gemma's back foot found air. She landed on her tailbone and kept rolling, down the stony escarpment that separated the woods from the bluffs above the beach. She felt bits of her exposed skin chafe and tear, and both her daggers were jogged loose along the way. Finally she slowed down enough to flip back up to her feet and turn to face her opponent.

She wished she'd had the presence of mind to conceal her naked admiration.

"I killed you," she whispered in Wesah.

Noémie smiled, touched a hand to the puckered scar above her left breast. "Come see how dead I am," she sneered.

The banished tribeswoman appeared to be fully recovered from their fight outside the Villenaître and was arrayed in full battle regalia: cured leather girded at the seams with gleaming bands of iron. She must've come to the *tooroon* for the express purpose of revenging herself on the girl who'd taken everything from her. Gemma was now completely unarmed, facing down two long black blades and the wild-eyed warrior behind them. There was no hope of screaming loud enough to summon Clive and the others, nor of remounting the steep incline back to the encampment. She was on her own.

A piece of advice from Athène's combat training came to mind: an armed warrior always moves more slowly than an unarmed one. Gemma would have to depend on that. She took off east, toward the pasture and the promise of a fast horse. Noémie's footsteps sounded loud as thunder in her ears—but were they getting closer with every passing second, or farther away? She didn't dare look back, as it would slow her pace, but she could hear Noémie's breathing grow increasingly ragged as they went; perhaps it was all that armor, or her time away from the regular sparring of the *naasyoon*. Gemma allowed herself a flicker of hope. She wasn't even tired yet. She was younger and stronger and swollen with a love that made her want to live forever.

It began to rain, a light pattering on the rocks and leaves, as if the whole world were coming to life. Gemma glanced up and saw something sparkling inside the clouds; it looked a little like captured lightning, growing more and more restless with every passing second. Was this the second conflagration she'd been wishing for just a few minutes ago? The sparkle was everywhere now—in the

TOMMY WALLACH

shivering boughs of the birches and the tangled thatch of the chaparral, atop the rain-slick wooden fence that bounded the pasture, even in the lustrous silhouettes of the horses.

Gemma gritted her teeth against what she knew was coming: a fit, and a bad one at that—the kind that could lay her low for hours, that she woke up from with blood in her mouth and boulders in her skull.

Except she'd never wake up from this one. The pasture was so close, scarcely a hundred paces away, but Gemma could feel herself slowing. Noémie's breathing grew louder again, closer, more certain. It was a beautiful sort of symmetry, really. The same condition that had bought Gemma a new life with the Wesah would now put an end to that life. Oh, but what she would have given for just a little more time with Athène. A last night. A last kiss. The chance to say good-bye, and thank you, and I love you.

Gemma smiled at her ingratitude, her greed. She didn't want to die full of regret, mourning what might have been. At least she'd gotten a *taste* of happiness. Some people went their whole lives without even that. Her gait grew unsteady. The world was only sparkle, only light. She looked up and saw Fox and Wolf capering across the glimmering, beckoning sky.

"I'm sorry, Flora," she whispered, and then the light at last went out.

11. Clover

DARTING THROUGH THE SQUALID KITCHEN OF THE Usual Place, where a sickly-looking cook in a stained apron was coughing over a greasy skillet, Clover was glad he hadn't ordered anything to eat. He and Kita burst through the back door into an alleyway pungent with rotting food scraps, hurtling past a couple engaged in a carnal act whose exact nature couldn't be determined in the gloom.

He stopped at the place where the alleyway met a larger road.

"What are you doing?" Kita asked.

"We have to let them catch up," Clover said.

Kita's eyes widened. "Why would we want them to—?"

"Quiet," Clover interrupted. "I need to think for a second."

He summoned up the Anchor map in his mind and began to visualize all the paths from point A to point B. The pool could be narrowed down by introducing conditions: no big roads, where the soldiers could recruit passing citizens to aid in the chase; no straight roads, as bends and zigzags favored the agile over the strong; most importantly, the route needed to be direct enough that their pursuers wouldn't have the opportunity to split up and head them off. Clover's plan depended on leading the soldiers all the way to the Minstrel Manufactory.

It also depended on Kita's hunch being right.

The back door of the tavern crashed open again, disgorging a jangling cadre of Protectorate soldiers. There was no more time for consideration, no point in entertaining doubts.

"Move," Clover said.

It had rained while they'd been inside the tavern, turning the paving stones into treacherous jewels. Clover's thin-soled shoes had little in the way of traction, and every corner he rounded was another roll of the dice. Speed made blurs of the people they passed: couples out strolling in the cool night air, children playing a last game of tag before supper, and, as they proceeded clockwise from the Eighth Quarter to the First, an increasing number of drunks, dandies, and all-around degenerates out for a good time. In Blackgarten Lane, where it was said one could acquire anything for the right price, a group of men dressed in fanciful, feminine clothing stood outside a nameless establishment, smoking cigarillos in long ebony holders. They exclaimed at the two young people roiling their private fog, then again at the Protectorate soldiers. Clover couldn't remember the name of the small colonnade just beyond, but he recognized the public fountain that the young lovers of the Anchor had turned into a landmark, festooning the stonework with an encyclopedic collection of initials joined in hearts. Somewhere in there was *C.H. + I.P.*—the memorial to a young boy's infatuation with a fiction.

The alleys twisted and turned. Spurred on by the threatening flutter of leather boots, Clover felt as if he were sliding down a chute, unable to slow or stop, a passive victim of circumstance. Hand in hand, he and Kita passed under a stone arch in which a clock face had been purposely mounted slightly off center—the Leaning Clock, people called it. Just around the next corner, the Minstrel Manufactory hove into view. A CLOSED sign hung from the door now, but there was a lantern flickering behind the curtained window.

"I get it!" Kita said. "You brought them here on purpose."

Clover nodded. "Just follow my lead, okay?" He took the three steps up to the building's porch in a single leap and began pounding on the door. "Hurry! They're after us! Let us in!" Kita joined in with relish, slamming wildly with both hands and screaming for help.

They were at it about ten seconds before the soldiers caught up with them. One jerked Clover's hands behind his back and shoved him up against the porch banister. His name was stitched above the pocket of his uniform jacket: MARSHAL ERTMANN. He had a thick red beard and mean blue eyes.

"Clover Hamill?" he said.

Clover frowned. "Never heard of him."

The backhanded slap took him by surprise and set his ears to ringing.

"It's him," one of the other soldiers said. He held both of Kita's skinny wrists in one hand. "I knew his traitor brother. Two of a kind, I guess."

Clover felt his heart lift. "You mean Clive? Do you know where he is?"

"Nobody answer that," Ertmann barked to his men. Then, to Clover: "That was pretty stupid of you, showing up at the Library today. What did you want with the attendant?"

TOMMY WALLACH

"Nothing. He's an old friend."

"Then I imagine you wouldn't want him to get hurt."

Clover swallowed. "Did you hurt him?"

"Not yet. But that could change. It all depends on how help-ful you are. Same goes for your little friend over here. Who is she, anyway?"

"I'm his wife," Kita replied tartly. "We just got married. We've got three kids already and a fourth on the way."

Ertmann slapped Clover a second time. "Try again, girl. Next time he gets the hilt of my sword."

"Fine! I'm Kita Delancey."

"And how do you know Hamill?"

"Our families go way back. That's all."

Clover spat blood, taking the opportunity to throw a conspicu-ous glance at the door of the Minstrel Manufactory, as if in expec-tation of something. He quickly averted his gaze when Ertmann noticed his interest.

"What's in there?" the marshal demanded.

"Nothing."

"Nothing, but you came straight here?"

"I don't know. I panicked."

"Panicked. Sure." Chuckling, Ertmann turned to the four sol-diers standing idly at the bottom of the porch steps. "Go on. See what's what." Clover did his best to look upset at this turn of events, straining against Ertmann's ironclad grip. The soldiers stepped up to the door and one of them knocked. "This is Marshal Ertmann of the Descendancy Protectorate! Open up or we'll have to force our way in!"

The announcement was met with silence. Somewhere, out in the darkness, a cat mewled forlornly. Clover felt the first tendrils of despair curl around his heart; what had he been thinking, taking Kita at her word? The Minstrel Manufactory was probably nothing more than what it purported to be—a luthier's—yet Clover had staked everything on its being some kind of Mindful headquarters.

"You really want us to break it down?" said the largest of the soldiers, whose belt, Clover noticed, had been notched all the way out to the very tip.

Ertmann considered, then shook his head. "They're probably asleep for the night and forgot to turn out the lamp. We'll come back tomorrow."

Clover startled at the thunk of a deadbolt disengaging. The door swung open to reveal a pretty young woman with a baby strapped to her chest. Her expression was poised somewhere between confusion and fear.

"Evening, ma'am," Ertmann said.

"Evening. What's this about?"

The marshal shoved Clover forward. "Do you know this boy?"

The woman leaned forward, squinting. "I don't think so. Should I?"

"Not necessarily. Does anybody else live here?"

"My husband. But he's out drinking."

"I see. Would you mind terribly if we had a quick look around the premises?"

"What for?" She sounded defensive, but Clover figured anyone would be disturbed by an unexpected late-night visit from the Pro-

TOMMY WALLACH

tectorate. "I was just about to put Liam here down for the night."

"I promise we'll be quick."

"All right, I guess."

The woman stepped aside to let them pass. There was nothing remarkable about the house at first glance—a small foyer opening onto a hearth-lit kitchen, a narrow flight of stairs up to the second floor, a couple of paintings on the walls. Marshal Ertmann and the soldier holding Kita stayed in the entrance, while the other men split up to search the house.

Ertmann looked around with an appraiser's eye. "This is supposed to be a workshop, Mrs. . . . . ?"

"Imida," the woman said. "Justine Imida. And the workshop's out back."

Baby Liam began to cry, and Justine placated him with a little walnut shell full of sand that the child immediately brought to his mouth.

"Business good?" Ertmann asked.

"Could be better. Wartime and all."

"And where did you say your husband was?"

"I didn't say, because I don't know."

Ertmann laughed. "I wish my wife were more like you. She's on me like a hawk from dawn to dusk."

Justine smiled weakly. "Good for her."

An uncomfortable silence followed, punctuated only by the eerie scraping of branches against the window above the kitchen sink. After another few minutes, the soldiers reconvened in the kitchen and reported that they'd found nothing of interest.

"Are you satisfied?" Justine asked.

"Almost," the marshal replied. "We'll just need to poke our heads into that workshop real quick, and then we'll leave you alone for good."

A flicker of hesitation. "Of course. Follow me."

Justine led them to a screen door at the back of the kitchen. "It's just through here." Clover noticed her reach into Liam's swaddling clothes; a moment later, the baby started bawling. "Excuse me, gentlemen, but I gotta put this monster to bed. You all can just head on out yourselves. Holler if you need me." She scurried back through the kitchen, and a few seconds later, Clover heard her footsteps on the stairs.

Behind the house, a wide dirt yard was bounded by rabbit hutches on one side and chicken coops on the other, their wire frames partitioning the blackness with borrowed light. A rangy hound lay asleep beside the hutches, but when it caught the scent of the soldiers, it jumped up and ran barking to the limit of its chain. One of the soldiers startled at the sound of it, then laughed at his cowardice. "Fucking mutt," he said. About fifty feet away, a large wood-frame building stood silhouetted against the billowing, moonlit clouds.

Clover felt his heart begin to race—not out of fear this time, but hope.

The building's double doors were secured with a massive wooden crossbeam; two soldiers groaned under the weight as they lifted it off its brackets. One of the men had borrowed the lamp from inside the house, and as the doors swung open, he raised it up like an amulet.

Marshal Ertmann cursed. The light reached only a few feet into the room, but that was more than enough: just inside the door, a partially bored gun barrel was held in a rusty clamp affixed to a tabletop. The air thrummed with an odor so acrid as to seem almost hostile: "Blood of the Father" to the benighted Anchorites, but what Clover now knew to be petroleum—organic matter subjected to intense pressure and heat over the course of millennia.

"Anathema," one of the soldiers breathed, with a horror bordering on reverence. His voice nearly obscured the distant click of a hammer.

"Now!" someone shouted.

Two shadows separated themselves from the brush beside the main house's back door and immediately opened fire. One of the Protectorate soldiers crumpled noiselessly to the ground, and the others scattered in search of cover. The prisoners, no longer a priority, were turned loose. So this *was* a Mindful hideout; Kita had been right all along. Clover grabbed her hand and dived into the protective blackness of the workshop. A bullet sparked against some metallic surface close by, caroming off and punching a milky, moon-filled hole in the ceiling. Clover moved as quickly as possible away from the fracas; his eyes had yet to adjust, and he banged his shins about a dozen times along the way.

"What are we looking for?" Kita asked.

"I'm not sure."

Finally, they reached the back of the room—a bunch of shelves and cabinets, a whole barrel full of what smelled like gunpowder, but nothing that could contain a human being.

"I'll admit it," Kita said. "I'm starting to regret coming along with you."

The sound of gunfire ceased. One side or the other must have triumphed, and whichever it was, Clover knew he would soon find himself surrounded by enemies. Was that really how this would end? Had he killed Lila and risked Bernstein and Kita's lives for absolutely nothing?

In the silence, something clanked.

"What was that?" Clover said.

"I think I stepped on it."

"Move!"

Clover dropped to his knees and felt at the floor around Kita's feet: a smooth slab of iron, flawless but for the crack running down the center. He fit his fingertips into the split and opened a perfect black square in the ground, like a portal into another world.

"Careful," Kita said, but he'd already swung his legs over the edge, half expecting to find nothing there, just endless empty space. He was relieved when his questing feet landed on a wooden step, and then another—twelve altogether, delivering him into a narrow basement passage, dank and lightless.

"It's too dark," Kita cried out from somewhere behind him—distant, irrelevant. He kept his hands on the dirt walls to either side as he advanced. Ten feet. Fifteen feet. On his right, the packed earth, stubbled with stone and root, abruptly gave way to something harder. A smooth cylinder of metal, empty space, another cylinder, another space: the bars of a cell.

He stopped, held his breath, listened.

Inhale. Exhale. Inhale. Exhale.

"Hello?" said a voice. "Who's there?"

Clover tried to speak, but his throat was already thick with emotion; he stifled a sob. "It's me," he managed to whisper. "I'm here."

TOMMY WALLACH

"Son?"

Clover reached between the bars and found the hand waiting for his. Their palms met for a moment—a kind of prayer. Then Clover grabbed hold of his father's fingers and crushed them to his tear-stained cheek.

12. Paz

THEY SAT AROUND THE CORPSE OF THE CAMPFIRE, watching as the embers cooled and died, turning the same dull black as the lowering sky. No one spoke, but in the silence, Paz imagined she could still hear the stutter of gunfire and the screams of the wounded. She closed her eyes, but even that didn't offer relief. The images were imprinted on the backs of her eyelids, on her very conscience, indelible as tattoos: holes appearing in bodies as if by some infernal magic, fragile old women blown off their feet; blood pooling on the wet sand and brushed into shadowy, swirling patterns by the tidal current.

Flora wept, quietly but unceasingly. Clive was stoic, almost blank, but Paz had learned to read the gradations of emotion in the twitching of his jaw muscles and the distance in his gaze.

"You never would've been a part of that," she said.

Clive shook his head. "I was a soldier. Soldiers do what they're told."

"Not you. You do what's right. I wouldn't still be alive otherwise." She reached out for him, but he pulled away.

"You can't know that," he said, accusing himself by accusing her. "I was set on being a preacher because my father was. I marched on Sophia because the Protectorate ordered me to. Chang asked me to question you and I did it."

"You freed me."

"Because the Mindful took Flora! I didn't have a choice! I didn't *make* a choice!"

"Yes, you did. Even if it didn't feel like—"

"Where's Gemma?" Flora interrupted. "Why isn't she back yet?"

"She just needs a little space," Clive said. "Give her a few more minutes."

Flora stood up, her anxiety fixed now. "It's not safe here. I have to go find her."

"The last thing we need is *both* of you wandering around out there," Paz said. "Stay with Clive. I'll get your sister."

"You sure?" Clive said. "Gemma's still pretty angry at you."

"I know. That's why I should be the one to go. She and I are gonna have it out once and for all. Things can't go on like they are."

Clive looked grim. "Fine. Just be careful, okay? And quick."

Paz leaned down to kiss him on the cheek. "You'll barely even notice I'm gone," she said, and set off toward the bosky hills east of the encampment.

She wasn't exactly looking forward to a fresh confrontation with Gemma, but the tension between them had to be resolved. Paz regretted her earlier belligerence; she'd been taken aback by the intensity of Gemma's animosity and had defaulted to defensiveness on instinct. This time, she would simply apologize, without reservation or recrimination, and hope the admission of guilt would set the two of them back on the path toward friendship. Even if Gemma didn't accept the apology in the moment, Paz would persevere; no one could hold a grudge forever, especially not in the face of genuine remorse.

She reached the dirt trail that ran along the top of the bluff, from which vantage she'd hoped to spot Gemma. But all that moved in the darkness were the leaves of the birches. Down by the water, the black beetle had been reconstituted; Chang's wagon rolled slow as grief across the moon-silvered sand. Paz was about to head back to the encampment when something caught her eye at the base of a nearby clump of sedge: a gleaming, cruciform shadow in the dirt. She sidestepped down the declivity—fresh footprints, unmistakable—and knelt beside it.

Two daggers had fallen haphazardly across each other, like crossbones. Paz recognized them as Gemma's and immediately knew something terrible must have happened.

She screamed as loudly as she could, hoping it would be enough to summon Clive and Flora, then scooped up the daggers and began following the trail of footprints and disturbed earth uphill, toward the pasture where the Wesah had grazed their horses (so many without masters now). She stopped only once, when the sudden crepitation of raindrops triggered the memory of cannonade and she threw herself to the ground in fear. She rose a moment later, heart slamming in her chest, ashamed of her cowardice, and forced herself to run faster, scrambling on all fours when she slipped but always moving forward. At last the pasture came into view. A Wesah warrior stood just in front of the fence, declaiming something in a rapid, fanatical voice. She held a glass dagger overhead, poised to strike the figure lying facedown in the grass before her—Gemma.

There was no time to hesitate; Paz charged. Her approach was masked by the racket of the rain and whatever the Wesah woman was shouting. When she was within striking distance, she drew back one of Gemma's daggers, aiming to pierce the warrior's heart through her back. But at the last moment, the Wesah woman turned—sensing the attack—and Paz ended up plunging the blade into her adversary's bicep instead. The warrior shrieked but somehow found the presence of mind to whip her other elbow around with such force that Paz was knocked off her feet. Her mouth filled with blood, and her vision warped. Still dazed, she raised the other dagger over her head just in time to ward off a vicious downward strike; if the warrior had still had the use of her dominant hand, the blow likely would've cloven Paz's head in two.

She needed to find a way to level the playing field. Stretching out her legs, she trapped one of the Wesah woman's ankles between both of hers, then flipped her hips over in an attempt to bring her opponent to the ground. But maybe she'd telegraphed her intentions too clearly, or maybe she just wasn't strong enough. The warrior bent her knees, lowering her center of gravity, and managed to keep her feet. Now Paz was lying belly down on the ground, helpless. She felt something like a punch to her back; it was a few seconds before she realized she'd been stabbed.

Far from incapacitating her, the pain was galvanizing—like a catalyst in a chemical reaction. She rolled to the side and heard the thunk of a blade lodging in wet earth. The wound in her back sparked exquisitely as she planted her hands and kicked out with both legs, catching the warrior full in the belly and landing in a crouch.

At last Paz had the opportunity to size up her adversary. The tribeswoman was scarcely more than five feet tall, yet she appeared to be built entirely of muscle and rage. A vibrant purple scar could be clearly seen just above the neckline of her leather breastplate, which didn't look to be of Wesah make. Her face was strong-boned and starkly beautiful, but twisted up with a hatred so wild and pure it set Paz's skin to prickling.

"This is personal, isn't it?" she said wonderingly. "Your people have just been slaughtered like animals, but you're doing this for yourself."

The Wesah woman cocked her head, uncomprehending, and then performed a small flourish with her daggers: a reply somehow more eloquent than any words could've been.

The rain had begun to fall more heavily now, turning the world into a wash of moonlit motion. When the warrior finally charged, there was a luxuriousness to it, even a kind of ferocious beauty. Paz remained crouching—*Never give an enemy an easy angle*, her father used to say—and prepared to fend off the assault. She deflected the first couple of strikes easily enough, but she hadn't been prepared for a flurry. The warrior's blades found their mark three times in as many seconds—shallow cuts all, but they would add up. Clearly the woman was enjoying herself, had decided to eschew the quick kill in favor of the slow burn. Paz's only chance would be to bring things to a head as quickly as possible, before she grew too weak to fight.

The next time the tribeswoman made to strike, Paz summoned up all her willpower and did the unthinkable: she allowed the blade through unimpeded. The pain was excruciating, but the ploy worked; the warrior had expected a block, and so had left herself open to counterattack. Paz dropped to her knees and plunged one of her daggers deep into her opponent's calf—and then ripped it out again. The warrior screamed, but instead of backing away, she slammed the wooden hilt of her dagger down onto the top of Paz's head.

An explosion of stars, intimation of apocalypse. Paz blinked the blood from her eyes and tried to stand, but the dizziness was over-

TOMMY WALLACH

whelming, and she vomited instead. When she looked up again, the warrior had become three warriors, all moving away from her, back toward Gemma's prone form.

"No!" Paz shouted. She lunged forward unsteadily, nearly slipping on her own sick, and threw her body over Gemma's. "I won't let you have her! You'll have to kill me first!"

She held her face to Gemma's sopping hair, awaiting the killing blow. But the seconds passed and nothing came. Finally she glanced back over her shoulder.

The warrior stood just where she'd been, silent and still in the pelting rain, but something was different now; the fire had gone out of her eyes. She said something in Wesah, her tone grave, almost contrite. Then she turned and vaulted over the pasture fence, disappearing into the gray verticality of the storm.

Paz slid off Gemma and pulled the girl over onto her back, already knowing what she would find.

"No," she said, simply, as if reality could be rejected like an unwanted gift. She dropped one of Gemma's daggers and pressed her palm over the worst of the wounds, but it was no use; there were so many of them, each one deep and black as a well. The girl's face had gone cloud-pale, and her eyes were wide open, blue as untroubled sky. Tendrils of rain-drenched hair lay glossy and golden across her forehead. Paz felt the tears coming, but she refused to allow them expression. There had to be something she could do: to grieve was to surrender.

"Stay with me, Gemma," Paz whispered. "Please stay."

Figures materialized out of the rain like ghosts: Clive, Flora, and between them, Athène. So she'd come back after all, come back to the woman she loved.

"Paz!" Clive said. "Thank God we found you! I heard you scream and I thought . . ." He stopped in his tracks, rigid with horror. When he spoke again, his voice was ice. "Daughter's love, what have you done?"

It took her a moment to realize what he meant, to see what the three of them were seeing. She stood up and backed away from Gemma, as if distance itself might exculpate her. "This isn't how it looks," she said. "Someone else was here."

But it was pointless to try to convince them. They'd all been there at Andromède's dinner, had seen the two girls arguing, each accusing the other of murder. And now here Paz was, holding a blood-drenched dagger over Gemma's body, with no other potential culprit in sight. And how many times had she fooled them before? How many times had she betrayed them? Of course they didn't believe her. They would never believe her.

Flora dropped to her knees, already sobbing uncontrollably, while Athène ran to Gemma and knelt down beside her. The chieftain pressed her ear to her lover's chest, listened for a moment, and then emitted a bloodcurdling scream.

Paz looked to Clive—the man she loved, the man who claimed to love her back—for some sign of understanding, but his eyes were dead now. She recognized that expression, the same one he'd worn the day he'd chased her through the woods around Sophia, before he brought her bruised and bleeding back to the Anchor, where she'd been thrown into darkness for weeks—tortured, tattooed, nearly driven mad.

Never again.

"I'm sorry," she whispered, and took off running.

TOMMY WALLACH

Epilogue

Six Weeks Before the Black Wagon Massacre

THE DOORS WERE A GOOD TEN FEET TALL AND PAINTED a vivid red, with decorative brass studs around the edge.

"Fancy," Chang said, running his fingers over the fine-grained wood.

"You want me to knock it down?" said Marshal Yuval.

Chang tried the knob: it turned. He looked to Yuval, grinning his astonishment. "Can you believe that? Unlocked! The balls on this one!"

"Grand Marshal, I still think it would be a mistake to go in there alone. If he's armed—"

Yuval's voice was cut off as Chang closed the door behind him. He'd never been inside the Epistem's personal chambers, and they were grander than he'd expected: two walls of floor-to-ceiling windows and two walls of floor-to-ceiling bookshelves, a spiral staircase caged in black wrought iron, dozens of mysterious contraptions built out of brass and bronze. Chang made a beeline for the wide desk opposite the door and picked up a few papers at random. Dense lines of hieroglyphs made pretty, incomprehensible patterns—another language, possibly, or a code.

"Chang." Turin stood at the balustrade on the room's second floor. His initial dismay gave way to a dubious smile. "What a pleasant surprise."

"Nobody told you I was on my way up? Guess your security needs some seeing to."

"I thought *you* were my security. *Quis custodiet ipsos custodes?*"

"That Wesah or something?"

"Or something," Turin replied with a condescending smirk. "So, what brings you barging into my chambers this morning? Or did you just miss the sound of my voice?"

Chang set the papers down and walked leisurely over to the bottom of the staircase. "I had a question for you."

"It must be important."

"Maybe. Maybe not." He began climbing the stairs, which shivered loudly with every step. The gaps in the wrought iron made a sort of zoetrope, Turin's trepidation increasing frame by frame. Chang reached the second floor and took a quick stroll around the Epistem's living quarters: a washroom with a claw-foot tub, a mussed bed with a massive mahogany frame, another few dozen stacks of books and papers. He didn't imagine it would take more than a couple of days to restyle the place to fit his personal tastes.

"The suspense is killing me," Turin said.

"Don't be melodramatic, Hal. Suspense never killed anyone. But I won't keep you waiting any longer." Chang fixed his gaze on Turin's pupils. "Where is hell?"

At the word "hell," Turin glanced briefly down toward the ground floor of his chambers, where a detailed relief of the Tree of Knowledge was carved into the paneling. When his eyes met Chang's again, both of them knew everything they needed to know.

The Epistem was halfway down the stairs before Chang realized what was happening, and the very suddenness of it made him laugh.

TOMMY WALLACH

He'd expected a little more conversation before things devolved into a chase. After all, months of effort had gone into securing the intelligence that had prompted this meeting—months of monitoring every single member of the Gloria, day in and day out, waiting for a misstep. Finally one of Chang's spies had caught a soused and satiated Bishop Allen coming out of a Second Quarter brothel. The old degenerate had cracked after less than twenty-four hours in the Bastion dungeon, surrendering a lifetime of secrets in one pathetic, blubbering cascade. The whole thing had been so easy that Chang worried the information might turn out to be spurious. Yet here was all the evidence of its authenticity he needed: the unflappable Epistem, sprinting as fast as his fifty-odd years would allow.

"Where's the little chicken running to?" Chang shouted, menacing and playful at once. He took off after the Epistem, but tripped at the bottom of the narrow stairway, landing painfully on his tailbone and cursing aloud. By the time he found his feet again, Turin was gone. A breeze blew through an opening in the wall: the secret door that had once been the carving of the Tree of Knowledge. On the other side, a covered stone parapet ran along the top of the Anchor wall, high enough so as to be entirely invisible from the ground.

"It's not just me," Bishop Allen had told them that night in the Bastion, his fat, bejeweled fingers worrying at his collar. "They're all a bunch of hypocrites. The whole institution is built on lies."

"Like what?" Chang asked.

"'And the name of that nectar was science, and its sweetness was the sweetness of death.'"

"If I wanted a sermon, I'd have come to see you on a Sunday morning."

The bishop smiled, his teeth still limned with red—they'd had to knock him around a bit, to drive home the seriousness of his situation. "So they've been drinking the goddamned nectar all along. And the place they do it is called 'hell.'"

The parapet became a hallway as it angled downward into the stony flesh of the Anchor wall. The light grew dim, so that when Chang saw the first thin shadow in front of him, he assumed it was a cobweb and tried to brush it away. His reward was a bright line of pain across the back of his hand.

"What in God's name . . . ?"

He reached out gingerly and palpated the skin of the vine—so many soft bristles colluding to create roughness, so many keen spines thirsty for blood. As his eyes adjusted, the tenebrous snarl before him differentiated into thousands upon thousands of creepers curling up through gaps in the stone. Had the Epistem really gone this way, or might he have escaped through some other passage?

Chang drew his sword and tried hacking at the vines, but the plants were healthy and fibrous, and the blade wasn't nearly sharp enough to cut them cleanly. There was nothing for it but to pull his hands into the sleeves of his uniform jacket, take a deep breath, and dive in. The prickles tore at his face and the sensitive skin beneath his thinning hair. New cuts made a crosshatching with old cuts, until the pain could no longer be discerned locally, but burned everywhere, like a fever.

"You think this'll stop me?" he bellowed, but more as an outlet for the agony than an attempt to intimidate Turin. The hallway had now descended so far into the wall that the creepers overhead blocked out the light completely. Chang moved as if blind—step

TOMMY WALLACH

after step, slice after slice. His uniform tore in a hundred places, the prickles finding their way between the very threads. Time dilated, perhaps stopped altogether, and Chang felt the first fluttering of fear. What if this went on for miles? What if it went on forever? What if the Daughter had seen his secret heart and was punishing him now for what he hoped to do at the *tooroon*?

And then it was over—miracle of miracles, God's grace made manifest. Chang emerged into a large chamber with a peaked-glass roof and almost tumbled into a small pool of clear water. Scarcely a hundred feet away, the Epistem stopped to catch his breath, leaning against the bookcase that ran the length of the room.

"So these are the anathema stacks, eh?" Chang said. "This is where all your power comes from." He snickered. "Sad."

Turin didn't respond except to push off the bookcase and take off running again. Chang slipped out of his tattered uniform jacket and let it fall to the floor. He took a moment to admire his arms: a ravaged landscape of crimson fissures, burbling blood. He'd never felt more alive. With a roar of pleasure, he returned to the hunt. It was only a matter of time now; he gained a step or two for every dozen Turin took. Even more to the point, as the chamber curved to the right, following the outline of the Anchor wall, Chang made out where it dead-ended in a wall of gray stone bricks.

"Nowhere left to run, Hal!"

But he'd spoken too soon. The Epistem produced a large metal key from somewhere within the folds of his robes and plunged it straight into the wall. A moment later, a section of the stone swung open—yet another secret door. Turin darted through the gap and emerged again only a moment later.

SLOW BURN

Chang froze. There could be no mistaking the object in Turin's hands—a gun, inlaid with gold and silver and polished to a flawless luster.

"Bishop Allen was right," Chang said. "You *are* a bunch of hypocrites."

"This place was only meant to be used as a last resort."

"And we're about to go to war!"

Turin shook his head. "Not necessarily. This conflict can still be avoided. If we convince the Wesah to side with us, Sophia will come to the table. They can't fight both of us at once."

Something pallid rose to the surface of the darkness behind the Epistem and then retreated again. This was hell, after all; of course there would be demons.

"You're a fool if you think the Wesah will fight alongside the Protectorate."

"Perhaps. And if we fail at the *tooroon*, we will consider other options. Either way, it isn't your choice to make. You and I both serve at the Archbishop's pleasure. He'll decide whether—"

"Carmassi is dead," Chang said. "Only a few minutes ago. Poisoned, I'm afraid."

"You're lying."

"You didn't leave me any choice, Hal. I have a responsibility toward the people of the Anchor. I swore an oath to protect them. Not just from the enemies in Sophia, but the ones right here at home."

There were tears in Turin's eyes; his emotion deafened him to the scuffling sounds coming from beyond the portal to hell. "You arrogant, shortsighted bastard. Don't you see that a military

TOMMY WALLACH

victory is meaningless if you've destroyed our whole way of life to achieve it?"

"We'll build a new way of life."

Turin cocked the gun. "I didn't want to have to do this. Honestly." His finger twitched, but he didn't shoot; his face was a pitiable muddle of futile grief and nascent remorse.

In Chang's opinion, a man who found it this difficult to kill had no business being a leader.

"You want freedom, don't you?" he said.

Turin frowned. "What are you talking about?"

"This man would keep you in the dark forever. But not me. I'll make sure everyone knows about your sacrifice. You'll be heroes. And together, we'll save the Descendancy from men like him. All you have to do is take your vengeance."

Turin blanched as understanding dawned. He turned around just as the first murderous spirit came rushing out of the shadows.

"Rami?" Turin whispered. "Is that—"

And then they were upon him, a dozen ashen wraiths pulling and tearing, vicious as blackberry bushes, unforgiving as death. Chang watched from a safe distance, wondering at the glorious savagery of their retribution.

When they were finished, he would follow these poor, light-starved soldiers of God into their dominion—the blasphemous workshop known as "hell"—and see the fruits of their centuries of labor. Maybe there'd be something powerful enough to solve the vexing question of the Wesah. Or why not dream a little bigger? Maybe there'd be something powerful enough to win him the whole goddamned war.

It seemed an eternity before the Epistem stopped screaming. Chang was sympathetic, but didn't dare to intervene. He wouldn't want to draw the fury of those fiendish revenants to himself, and besides, after everything they'd been through, hadn't they earned a bit of fun?

Turn the page for a sneak peek at

Scorched Earth,

The Anchor & Sophia: Book Three.

Athène

FOOTSTEPS THUDDING ON WET GRASS. SUSURRUS OF rainfall and the rumble of its thunderous birthplace. Distant surf crash. Her heart, jolting wild and arrhythmic as a wounded deer. So many distractions, muddying the senses, confusing the hunter's sense.

Should she have stayed? Kneeling beside Gemma in those first terrible moments, she'd felt paralyzed. She wanted to remain at her lover's side; though Gemma's spirit had already left her body, there were still prayers to be spoken, valedictions to be made. Yet the woman responsible for creating this tear in the very fabric of Athène's reality was on the brink of escape, already obscured behind a thousand translucent curtains of rain. The opportunity for vengeance might never come again, and the fury was lightning inside Athène's belly, crackling, demanding a target.

"*Miina kawapamitin, moon amoor,*" she said—*Good-bye, my love*—and took off running. Clive called out after her, but she ignored him. The hunt was on.

What did she know of her prey? The girl's name was Paz Dedios. She hailed from Sophia but no longer considered herself a member of any particular nation. That meant she knew no loyalty, no higher calling than self-interest, which made her the most depraved sort of creature, a sister to the jackal and the vulture. The Wesah viewed banishment as the ultimate punishment, yet Paz had chosen to banish *herself*—and not only once! First she'd abandoned her family in Sophia, and now she'd murdered Gemma, betraying those precious few souls who'd come to trust her. And why? Petty jealousy? What man's love had *ever* been worth the life of a good woman?

All these questions mattered, but only insofar as they informed the central riddle: Where would she run to now, this twice-exiled enigma, this beast without a country?

The pasture was large, dense with horses still blissfully unaware that they would never see their masters again. Athène couldn't yet think about that other tragedy, the massacre that had taken place down on the beach. It was too large to comprehend, like the depth of the ocean or the number of the stars. Easier to focus on one death—one terrible, avengeable death—then to try and make sense of carnage on such a scale.

She stopped. The silvery footprints she'd been following through the grass had disappeared. Perhaps they'd been disturbed by the horses' desultory grazing, or effaced by the torrential rain. Athène closed her eyes and extended her awareness, imagining it spreading out around her like a cloud. Something eddied at the feathered edge, a wayward stitch in the nap of the night. This acoustic anomaly seemed to grow louder and clearer as she focused on it, as if she were shaking the dust from some long-buried artifact.

She realized her foolishness just in time, opening her eyes to find a majestic palomino galloping straight at her, Paz clinging to its neck like a barnacle. Their eyes met. Athène was surprised to find no trace of satisfaction in her enemy's gaze—only rank fear. She sidestepped the horse and lashed out with her nails bared, scoring Paz's bare calf.

"*Baytaa!*" she shouted, chastising herself. If she'd grabbed the girl's ankle instead, she might have pulled her off. The horse was already twenty feet away. Athène took the bow from her back and drew an arrow. Her arms shook with cold and adrenaline, and the rain made everything slippery and vague. As she pulled the bowstring taut, she whispered a supplication to Fox, master of the hunt.

The bolt flew true as a hound racing to its master's side; there was a distant shriek. Athène watched for Paz's body to slip off the horse's back, but the girl stayed upright even as her horse jumped the fence surrounding the pasture. A moment later, she was gone from sight. Athène cast about for a horse she might use to give chase, but all the closest animals had spooked at Paz's sudden appearance. It was over. There would be no catching up now.

"No!" she screamed, falling to her knees, sobbing along with the sobbing sky. The possibility of revenge had momentarily anesthetized her grief; now feeling returned to the wound. Gemma, her lover, her love, her little dancer—never to dance again. Never to sing or cry or laugh or smile or curse or fight or kiss. And the very same night, Athène's people had been cut down by the thousands, a whole *naasyoon* annihilated in an instant, and the Wesah nation scattered to the four winds.

Gemma and Grandmother had seen all of this in their visions. There was no avoiding fate. It had been foolish to try.

Athène could see no reason to go on living. She drew her glass knife and brought the point to her chest. One quick thrust and she and Gemma would be together again. She tensed her muscles and sucked in a breath, praying her ancestors would forgive her this final crime.

Something touched her shoulder.

An impossible hope, momentarily buoyed by the vision that greeted her when she turned around: Gemma, miraculously reanimated by the spirits that had always favored her, returning younger and softer somehow, as if every minute in the land of the dead had returned a year of life to her. Athène blinked the tears from her eyes. Something was wrong. The spirits had erred. They'd made a false copy, a travesty of nature. Or else . . .

"Flora." The name was still foreign on her tongue, though Gemma had spoken it often enough.

The girl didn't respond. Her eyes were lifeless, broken.

"She got away," Athène said, answering the unasked question. "I am sorry." Flora's expression didn't change. Did she demand more of an apology than that? "The Sophian girl had a horse. I could not follow." Still nothing: just that blank face like a sheer stone wall. "Say something!" Athène shouted.

"Flora? Flora?"

Men's voices, carrying across the field like bats flitting through lightless caverns. Clive and the soldier Burns, calling out for their lost lamb. Athéne had no desire to speak to either one of them ever again. Both of them had trusted Paz, which meant both of them were responsible for what had happened to Gemma.

"I have to go," she whispered to Flora. "I have seen my mother escape the killing, up into the hills. I must find her. And you must go with your people."

Athène turned and began walking briskly across the dark grass, away from the voices. It was a moment before she realized Flora was keeping pace alongside her.

"What are you doing?"

Flora's answer was the same as ever—no words, only the unforgiving ice of those blue eyes, looking straight through her.

"They are calling for you." Nothing. "They are your family." Nothing. "So you are not wanting to go with them?"

A momentary twinge as she remembered not to say *chee* to signal the question; Gemma had taught her that.

Flora shook her head, so slightly it almost seemed a trick of the moonlight.

"Why not?"

The girl refused to answer, but Athène understood well enough. Flora was only doing what little sisters had done since time immemorial: following in the steps of their elder siblings. It was sweet, in its way, but also out of the question. It would be weeks of hard travel to the Villenaître, and waiting there were a ruined people who'd never been more mistrustful of Descendancy folk.

"You cannot come with me. You will not be safe with the Wesah. I am sorry."

"Flora! Where are you?"

The men would give up shouting and simply come after Flora soon. Athène had reached the limit of her patience.

"Do not follow me again," she said sharply, and began running.

And what did she expect? That this girl, blood relation to the woman who'd made herself Wesah by sheer force of will, who'd driven Athène crazy beneath the blankets night after night, who'd hunted like she was born on the plains, would simply obey? Flora skipped along next to her, lithe as a doe, silent as a spirit. Athène ran faster, and faster, and faster, until she reached the limit of her capability. It was just enough; Flora's short legs simply couldn't keep up. The girl slipped on the grass and crashed onto her belly.

That would teach her to challenge a Wesah warrior.

And that would teach Athène to dash the dreams of a little girl.

Flora's wail was piercing and pure: a siren's song, drawing Athène back against her will.

"I am sorry," she said, helping the girl to her feet. "Come. I'll bring you to your people."

Flora didn't look happy with that conclusion, but she allowed herself to be led back the way they'd come. Athène almost called out to Clive and Burns to announce her approach, yet the hunter's sense hadn't quite left her, and she stayed silent.

It was all that saved them.

Just in sight of Gemma's body (and had some part of her hoped it had all been some terrible mistake, and Gemma would be standing there with open arms?), Athène dropped to her stomach and wrenched Flora down beside her. A cadre of Protectorate soldiers was milling around the site of the murder. Likely they'd been sent to the pasture to seek out any Wesah who'd come to retrieve her horse. Clive and Burns had already been bound at ankle and wrist, and after a moment, they were marched back downhill toward the beach.

There was no hope of helping them, nor of retrieving Gemma's body.

"Come," Athène whispered to Flora. As quickly as they dared, the two of them began crawling away, their movements masked by the unceasing, uncaring rain.

The girl rode well enough, and in spite of the long days, never once complained. In fact, she never said anything at all; the closest she came to words were the tears that trickled down her cheeks for hours every day. Athène, on the other hand, hardly ever cried. She felt as if Flora were mourning for both of them, in a way. Still, she was glad when the fourth day had passed, and the time had come for the ritual.

It was early evening. They'd made camp by a shallow, sandy-bottomed stream. Flora was hunting for mushrooms in the woods nearby, just at the edge of sight. Athène took the opportunity to prepare what little she needed: a circle of river stones and some firewood, her blade, and the bone comb that she and Gemma had shared. The wood was wet, and it took a long time to catch. The kindling was still smoldering beneath the larger logs when Flora returned to the campsite. She frowned at the unfamiliar setup.

"For your sister," Athène said. "It is our way. Come. Sit."

Flora set her mushrooms down in a row—*little stumps*, as they were known in Wesah. Poisonous, unfortunately, but the girl would learn.

The two of them sat on opposite sides of the fire, which burned brightly now, sending out pungent clouds of smoke. Athène closed her eyes against the sting and began to sing. It was an old song—some said the first song. It told the story of Sparrow, Fox's wife, who took to the sky during the flame deluge and was struck down by a ball of fire. Fox followed her into the darkness, stole her from the very bed of Crow (who'd fallen in love with her), and began carrying her back up the great stairway to the land of the living. But Sparrow grew heavier with every step, and at the very threshold of escape, Fox's strength gave out. Sparrow slid back into the darkness, gone forever. At that moment, Crow appeared to Fox and chastised her.

"All must come to me someday, Fox. The morning that Mother Sun refuses to open her eye, you and Wolf will come to me as well, and then the world shall be born anew."

When the song was finished, Athène stood up. She drew her blade and raised it up to the level of her neck.

Flora gasped.

"Do not be afraid," Athène said. "I am no longer wanting to die."

She began sawing through the thick braid that hung halfway down her back: years to grow, seconds to cut short. Like a life. Gemma had been eighteen years old. So little time. Such a loss as could hardly be borne.

At first, it seemed as if the sound were coming from the very air, from the trees or the earth, from some place beyond human perception. But it was only Flora, her lips barely moving, her voice scarcely more than a whisper. The first words she'd spoken since they'd been traveling together, since Gemma had been taken from them. A Descendancy song, one that Athène recognized. The last strands of the braid came away. She dropped it into the fire, curl and crackle, a smell like the way she felt inside. But the gods, to say nothing of her grief, demanded more. She brought the blade to her scalp and cut as close to the skin as she could, gripping at the root, tearing where she had to.

When it was done, she knelt to pick up the bone comb. Not much there, only a few silky yellow hairs. She threw them into the fire to burn along with her braid. Flora was still singing, but she stopped when Athène began to speak.

"For four days, Gemma is walking beside us. Now she leaves us, to live forever in the land of the dead. The *otsapah* say that mourning must end here. Our grief ties Gemma to this world. She cannot go to be with Crow while we mourn. We may keep our sadness, but we will not wish her alive."

Flora stood up and kicked the burning logs, provoking a cloud of ephemeral fireflies. She was panting with anger.

"Spirits can be trapped here," Athène said. "They become ghosts. Nightmares. You want this for your sister?" Flora wouldn't meet her eye. "If you are to travel at my side, you must be a Wesah. You must be a woman. So let go this childishness. Let your sister rest."

Finally, Flora raised her gaze to meet Athène's. There was a new hardness in their unfathomable blue. A tug at her waist, the rasp of a knife being drawn from its sheath; suddenly Athène found herself facing down her own blade.

"Hurting me will not help anything," she said.

But that wasn't Flora's intention. She went to stand over the fire and flipped her loose, lank hair over her shoulder. The glass knife reflected the dancing flames. The locks fell like sheaves of grain, like leaves in autumn. Flora's tears sizzled on the ashy wood. When it was finished, she lay down between her blankets and fell asleep to the crackle of the dying fire. Athène watched the gentle rise and fall of the girl's chest as the darkness crept slowly over the forest glade. She closed her eyes for just a moment, and when she opened them again, a revenant was hovering behind the fire, gazing around at the world she'd never touch again. Her whole body was the color her eyes used to be, and her eyes were crimson.

"Where will you go?" the spirit said, in her perfectly imperfect Wesah.

"To my mother."

"Why?"

"To convince her to help me avenge you."

Gemma shook her head, disappointed. "You promised to let me go."

"This is anger, not grief. And what should I live for if not vengeance?"

"You may still live for vengeance. You must. But not for me." The presence floated over the smoldering embers of the fire, like a mist. "They killed our sisters. They slaughtered our people. Make them pay."

Athène nodded. "I will do my best."

"I know. And when it is done, you will come to me."

"And nothing will ever part us again."

Gemma glanced upward, and then it was as if something pulled her out of sight and space. Flora turned over and let out a slumberous sigh. Athène lay down next to her and quickly fell asleep. She dreamed an ocean of blood, and it was no nightmare.

RIVETED

BY *simon* teen ♥

BELIEVE IN YOUR SHELF

Visit RivetedLit.com & connect with us on social to:

DISCOVER NEW YA READS

READ BOOKS FOR FREE

DISCUSS YOUR FAVORITES

SHARE YOUR IDEAS

ENTER SWEEPSTAKES FOR THE CHANCE TO WIN BOOKS

Follow @SimonTeen on

to stay up to date with all things Riveted!

Jonathan Maberry returns to his critically acclaim world in this new series, with new characters and even more terrifying adventures.

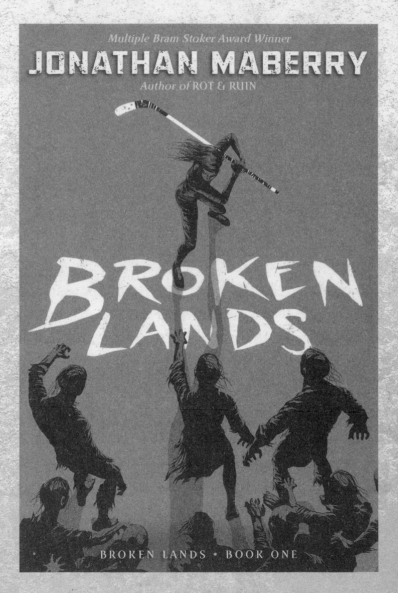

Praise for *Rabbit & Robot*

★"Those delving into Smith's zany dystopia will find much to laugh and gasp at, including comedic and serious musings upon sex and violence. But most of all, they will find many deep, essential questions worth pondering."

—*Booklist*, starred review

★"This provocative jaunt . . . dissects society, technology, othering, and what makes humanity human."

—*Publishers Weekly*, starred review

★"With nods to Vonnegut, Bradbury, and Burgess, Printz Honor winner Smith has woven an unpredictable, gross, and prescient rumination on modernity, media consumption, and machine-aided communication."

—*Booklist*, starred review

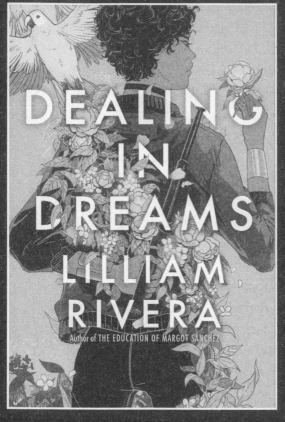